"I can't believe ~~you~~
cooked meal,
"Maggie's bisc
probably even b~~etter~~

"Please, Daddy. I'll go to bed right on time. I won't argue or anything."

Jace looked back at Lori. It was her first night here, and probably a rough one.

Lori smiled. "Now, that's a hard offer to turn down."

"You're no help," he told Lori.

"Sorry, us girls have to stick together."

That was what he was afraid of. He was losing more than just this round. He hated that he didn't mind one bit.

"Okay, but we can't stay long. We have a bedtime schedule."

"I promise I'll go to bed right on time," Cassie said again, and then took off toward the kitchen.

He looked at a smiling Lori. "Okay, I'm a pushover."

"Buck up, Dad. It's only going to get worse before it gets better."

Suddenly their eyes locked and the amused look disappeared. Lori was the first to speak. "Please, I want you to stay for dinner. I think we both agree that eating alone isn't fun."

"Yes, we can agree on that."

He followed Lori into the kitchen, knowing this woman could easily fill those lonely times. He just couldn't let it happen. No more women for a while—at least not over the age of seven.

Dear Reader,

I can't tell you how happy I am to be returning to Destiny for my next story. The small Colorado town has always been one of my favourite locations—so, for those of you who remember, I'll also be revisiting the Keenan family and their historical inn.

This time I move on to another famous family in town: the Hutchinsons. A hundred years ago Raymond Hutchinson built the mining town after he struck gold in the area. When great-grandson Lyle passes away suddenly his estranged daughter, Lorelei, returns to town for the first time in twenty years to learn she's the only heir to the family fortune. There's a catch. Lori must live in Destiny for a year and run the Hutchinson Corporation. That brings her face to face with angry contractor Jace Yeager.

Jace doesn't have time to deal with any more delays on his construction project—especially when his new partner could stop the project at any time. His first priority is his seven-year-old daughter and getting permanent custody. He doesn't want or need any other female in his life. So it's strictly business with Lorelei Hutchinson—until they're snowed in together…

Enjoy!

Patricia Thayer

SINGLE DAD'S HOLIDAY WEDDING

BY
PATRICIA THAYER

First published in Great Britain 2012
by Mills & Boon, an imprint of Harlequin (UK) Limited,
Eton House, 18-24 Paradise Road, Richmond, Surrey TW9 1SR

© Patricia Wright 2012

ISBN: 978 0 263 89477 6
ebook ISBN: 978 1 408 97150 5

23-1112

Harlequin (UK) policy is to use papers that are natural, renewable and recyclable products and made from wood grown in sustainable forests. The logging and manufacturing processes conform to the legal environmental regulations of the country of origin.

Printed and bound in Spain
by Blackprint CPI, Barcelona

Originally born and raised in Muncie, Indiana, **Patricia Thayer** is the second of eight children. She attended Ball State University, and soon afterwards headed West. Over the years she's made frequent visits back to the Midwest, trying to keep up with her growing family.

Patricia has called Orange County, California, home for many years. She not only enjoys the warm climate, but also the company and support of other published authors in the local writers' organisation. For the past eighteen years she has had the unwavering support and encouragement of her critique group. It's a sisterhood like no other.

When she's not working on a story, you might find her travelling the United States and Europe, taking in the scenery and doing story research while thoroughly enjoying herself, accompanied by Steve, her husband for over thirty-five years. Together, they have three grown sons and four grandsons. As she calls them: her own true-life heroes. On rare days off from writing you might catch her at Disneyland, spoiling those grandkids rotten! She also volunteers for the Grandparent Autism Network.

Patricia has written for over twenty years, and has authored more than forty-six books. She has been nominated for both a National Readers' Choice Award and the prestigious RITA® Award. Her book *Nothing Short of a Miracle* won an *RT Book Reviews* Reviewers' Choice award.

A longtime member of Romance Writers of America, she has served as President and held many other board positions for her local chapter in Orange County. She's a firm believer in giving back.

Check her website, www.patriciathayer.com for upcoming books.

To my Vine Street Sisters.
I've enjoyed our time together. Bless you all.

CHAPTER ONE

SHE still wasn't sure if coming here was a good idea.

Lorelei Hutchinson drove along First Street to the downtown area of the small community of Destiny, Colorado. She reached the historic square and parked her rental car in an angled spot by a huge three-tiered fountain. The centerpiece of the brick-lined plaza was trimmed with a hedge and benches for visitors. A pathway led to a park where children were playing.

She got out, wrapped her coat sweater tighter against the cold autumn temperature and walked closer to watch the water cascade over the marble structure. After nearly twenty years many of her memories had faded, but some were just as vivid as if they'd happened yesterday.

One Christmas she remembered the fountain water was red, the giant tree decorated with multicolored lights and ornaments and everyone singing carols. She had a family then.

A rush of emotions hit her when she recalled being in this exact spot, holding her father's hand as he took her to the park swings. One of the rare occasions she'd spent time with the man. He'd always been too busy building his empire. Too busy for his wife and daughter. So many times she had wanted just a little of his attention, his love. She never got it.

Now it was too late. Lyle Hutchinson was gone.

With a cleansing breath, she turned toward the rows of storefront buildings. She smiled. Not many towns had this step-back-into-the-nineteen-thirties look, but it seemed that Destiny was thriving.

The wind blew dried leaves as she crossed the two-lane street and strolled past Clark's Hardware Store and Save More Pharmacy, where her mother took her for candy and ice cream cones as a child. A good memory. She sure could use some of those right now.

There was a new addition to the block, a bridal shop called Rocky Mountain Bridal Shop. She kept walking, past an antiques store toward a law office with the name Paige Keenan Larkin, Attorney at Law, stenciled on the glass.

She paused at the door to the office. This was her father's town, not hers. Lyle Hutchinson had made sure of that. That was why she needed someone on her side. She pushed the door open and a bell tinkled as she walked into the reception area.

The light coming through the windows of the storefront office illuminated the high ceilings and hardwood floors that smelled of polish and age, but also gave off a homey feeling.

She heard the sound of high heels against the bare floors as a petite woman came down the long hall. She had dark brown hair worn in a blunt cut that brushed her shoulders. A white tailored blouse tucked into a black shirt gave her a professional look.

A bright smile appeared. "Lorelei Hutchinson? I'm Paige Larkin. Welcome home."

* * *

After exchanging pleasantries, Lori was ushered into a small conference room to find a middle-aged man seated at the head of the table, going through a folder. No doubt, her father's attorney.

He saw her and stood. "Lorelei Hutchinson, I'm Dennis Bradley."

She shook his offered hand. "Mr. Bradley."

When the lawyer phoned her last week, and told her of her father's sudden death and that she'd been mentioned in his will, she was shocked about both. She hadn't seen or talked with her father since she'd been seven years old.

All Lori was hoping for now was that she could come into town today, sign any papers for Lyle's will and leave tomorrow.

The middle-aged attorney began, "First of all, Lorelei, I want to express my condolences for your loss. Lyle wasn't only my business associate, but my friend, too." He glanced at Paige and back at her. "I agreed to see you today knowing your reluctance. Your father wanted the formal reading of his will at Hutchinson House tomorrow."

Great. Not the plans she had. "Mr. Bradley, as you know, I haven't seen my father in years. I'm not sure why you insisted I come here." He'd sent her the airline ticket and reserved a rental car. "If Lyle Hutchinson left me anything, couldn't you have sent it to me?"

The man frowned. "As I explained on the phone, Ms. Hutchinson, you're Lyle's sole heir." He shook his head. "And that's all I'm at liberty to say until tomorrow at the reading of the will. Please just stay until then. Believe me, it will benefit not only you, but this town."

Before she could comprehend or react to the news,

the door opened and another man walked into the room. He looked her over and said, "So the prodigal daughter finally made it to town."

The big man had a rough edge to him, his dark hair a little on the shaggy side. He was dressed in charcoal trousers and a collared shirt, minus the tie. His hooded blue-eyed gaze fringed by spiky black lashes didn't waver from her.

Paige stood. "Jace, you shouldn't be here. This is a private meeting between me and my client."

He didn't retreat. "I just wanted to make sure she doesn't take the money and run. Lyle had obligations he needed to fulfill before that happens."

Lori wasn't sure how to handle this—Jace's attack. But having heard of her father's shrewd business deals, she wasn't surprised by the man's anger.

"I'm Lorelei Hutchinson, Mr...."

He stepped closer. "Yeager. Jace Yeager. Your father and I were partners on a construction project until I realized Lyle pulled one over on me."

"Jace," Bradley warned. "Work stopped because of Lyle's death."

The man made a snorting sound. "It wouldn't have if Lyle had put his share of money into the business account in the first place." He glared at Lori. "Sorry if my impatience bothers you, but I've been waiting nearly three weeks and so have my men."

"Be patient a little while longer," Bradley told him. "Everything should be resolved tomorrow."

That didn't appease Mr. Yeager. "You don't understand. I can't keep the project site shut down indefinitely, or I go broke." He turned that heated look on her and she oddly felt a stirring. "It seems tomorrow you're coming into all the money. I want you to know that a chunk of that belongs to me."

Lori fought a gasp. "Look, Mr. Yeager, I don't know anything about your partnership with Lyle, but I'll have Paige look into it."

Jace Yeager had to work hard to keep himself under control. Okay, so he wasn't doing a very good job. When he'd heard that Lorelei Hutchinson was coming today, he only saw red. Was she going to stroll in here, grab her daddy's money and take off? He wasn't going to be on the losing end with a woman again.

Not when his business was on the chopping block, along with his and Cassie's future. Just about every dime he had was wrapped up in this project. And it was already coming to the end of October as it was, with only bad weather on the horizon. It needed to be completed without any more delays.

Jace looked over Lyle's daughter. The pretty blonde with big brown eyes stared back at him. She had a clean-scrubbed look with a dusting of freckles across her nose, and very little makeup.

Okay, she wasn't what he expected, but he'd been wrong about women before. And the last thing he wanted to do was work for her. After his ex-wife, he wasn't going to let another woman have all the control.

He looked at Bradley. "What does Lyle's will say?"

"It won't be read until tomorrow."

Lori saw Jace Yeager's frustration, and felt obligated to say, "Maybe then we'll have some news about the project."

He glared. "There's no doubt I will. I might not have your father's money, Ms. Hutchinson, but I'll fight to keep what's mine."

Jace Yeager turned and stormed out right past a tall redheaded woman who was rushing in. "Oh, dear," she said, "I was hoping I could get here in time." Her green eyes lit up when she saw Lori. "Hi, I'm Morgan Keenan Hilliard."

"Lori Hutchinson," Lori said as she went to shake Morgan's hand.

"It's nice to meet you. As mayor, I wanted to be here to welcome you back to town, and to try and slow down Jace. Not an easy job."

Since Paige and Bradley had their heads together going over papers, they walked out into the hall. "I'm not sure if you remember me."

"I remember a lot about Destiny. Like you and your sisters. You were a little older than I was in school, but everyone knew about the Keenan girls."

Morgan smiled. "And of course being Lyle's daughter, everyone knew of you, too. I hope you have good memories of our town."

Except for her parents' marriage falling apart, along with her childhood. "Mostly, especially the decorated Christmas tree in the square. Do you still do that?"

Morgan smiled. "Oh, yes and it's grown bigger and better every year." She paused. "Our mom said you have a reservation at the inn for tonight."

She nodded. "I don't feel right about staying at the house."

The redhead gripped her hand. "You don't have to explain. I only want your visit here to be as pleasant as possible. If there is anything else, any details about your father's funeral."

Lori quickly shook her head. "Not now."

Morgan quickly changed the subject. "Look, I know

Jace isn't giving you a very good impression at the moment, but he's having some trouble with the Mountain Heritage complex."

"I take it my father was involved in it, too."

Morgan waved her hand. "We can save that discussion for another time. You need to rest after your trip. Be warned, Mom will ask you to dinner…with the family."

Lori wasn't really up to it. She wanted a room and a bed, and to make a quick call back home to her sister.

Morgan must have sensed it. "It's only the family and no business, or probing questions. We'll probably bore you to death talking about kids."

Lori relaxed. She truly didn't want to think about what would happen tomorrow.

"You're right. That's what I need tonight."

That evening as Jace was driving to the Keenan Inn, he came to the conclusion that he'd blown his chance earlier today. He tapped his fist against the steering wheel, angry about the entire mess.

"Daaad, you're not listening."

Jace looked in the rearview mirror to the backseat. "What, sweetie?"

"Do I look all right?"

He glanced over his shoulder. His daughter, Cassandra Marie Yeager, was a pretty girl. She had on stretchy jean pants that covered coltish long legs and a pink sweater that had ruffles around the hem. Her long blond hair had curled around her face with a few tiny braids. Something she'd talked him into helping with.

"You look nice. But you always do."

"We're going to Ellie's grandmother's house. Ellie Larkin is my best friend."

"I think she'll like your outfit."

"What about my hair?"

"Honey, I've always loved your blond curls. The braids are a nice touch."

That brought a big smile to her face and a tightening in his throat. All he ever wanted was for her to be happy.

When they'd moved here six months ago, it hadn't been easy for her. He still only had temporary custody of his daughter. It was supposed to be only during the time when her mother remarried a guy from England. Jace had different plans. He wanted to make Cassie's life here with him permanent. Optimistic that could happen, he went out and bought a run-down house with horse property. Although it needed a lot of work, it felt like the perfect home for them. A couple horses helped coax his seven-year-old daughter into adjusting a little faster to their new life.

A life away from a mother who'd planned to take his Cassie off to Europe. He was so afraid that his little girl would end up in boarding school and he'd only get to see her on holidays.

No, he wouldn't let that happen. A product of the foster care system himself, he'd always longed for a home and family. It hadn't worked out with ex-wife Shelly, and that mistake cost him dearly—a big divorce settlement that had nearly wiped him out. Jace hadn't cared about the money, not if he got his daughter. He only hoped they weren't going to be homeless anytime soon.

His thoughts turned to Lorelei Hutchinson. He didn't like how he reacted to her. Why had she angered him so much? He knew why. She had nothing to do with Lyle's business dealings. But she was due to inherit a lot of money tomorrow, and he could be handed the shaft at the same time. It could cost him everything that mattered. His daughter. No, he wouldn't let that happen.

He pulled up in front of the beautiful three-story Victorian home painted dove-gray with white shutters and trim. The Keenan Inn was a historical landmark, a bed-and-breakfast that was also the home of Tim and Claire Keenan. Jace had heard the story about how three tiny girls had been left with them to raise as their own. That would be Morgan, Paige and Leah. After college all three returned to Destiny to marry and raise their own families.

Right now there was someone else staying in the inn—Lorelei Hutchinson. Somehow he had to convince her that this downtown project needed to move forward. Not only for him, but also for Destiny.

Just then Tim Keenan came out the front door, followed closely by some of their grandkids, Corey, Ellie and Kate.

His daughter grabbed her overnight bag and was out of the car before he could say anything. He climbed out, too.

Tim Keenan waved from the porch. "Hello, Jace."

"Hi, Tim." He walked toward him. "Thank you for inviting Cassie to the sleepover. I think she's getting tired of her father's bad company."

"You have a lot on your mind."

Tim was in his early sixties, but he looked a lot younger. His wife was also attractive, and one of the best cooks in town. He knew that because the Keenans had been the first to stop by when he and Cassie moved into their house. They'd brought enough food for a week.

"Hey, why don't you stay for supper, too?"

He wasn't surprised by the invitation. "Probably not a good idea. I don't think I made much of an impression on Ms. Hutchinson."

The big Irishman grinned. "Have faith, son, and use a little charm. Give Paige a chance to help resolve this." They started toward the door, as Tim continued, "I'm concerned about Lorelei. She wasn't very old, maybe seven, when her parents divorced. Lyle wrote them off, both his ex-wife and his daughter. As far as I know, he never visited her. Now, she has to deal with her estranged father's mess."

Jace felt his chest tighten because this woman's scenario hit too close to home. "That's the trouble with divorce, it's the kids who lose."

They stepped through a wide front door with an etched glass oval that read Keenan Inn and into the lobby. The walls were an ecru color that highlighted the heavy oak wainscoting. A staircase with a hand-carved banister was open all the way to the second floor. All the wood, including the hardwood floors, were polished to a high gloss. He suspected he wasn't the only one who was an expert at restoration.

"This house still amazes me," he said.

"Thanks," Tim acknowledged. "It's been a lot of work over the years, but so worth it. The bed-and-breakfast has allowed me to spend more time with Claire and my girls."

Jace shook his head. "I can't imagine having three daughters."

Keenan's smile brightened. "You have one who gives you joy. I'm a lucky man, I tripled that joy." Tim sobered. "Too bad Lyle didn't feel the same about his child. Maybe we wouldn't be having this conversation tonight."

The sound of laughter drifted in from the back of the house. "That sounds encouraging," Tim said. "Come on, son. Let's go enjoy the evening."

They walked through a large dining room with several small tables covered in white tablecloths for the inn's guests. They continued through a pantry and into a huge kitchen.

Okay, Jace was impressed. There was a large working area with an eight-burner cooktop and industrial-sized oven and refrigerator, and all stainless steel counters, including the prep station. On one side a bank of windows showed the vast lawn and wooded area out back and, of course, a view of the San Juan Mountains. A group of women were gathered at the large round table. He recognized all of them. Morgan because she was married to his good friend Justin Hilliard, another business owner in town. Paige he'd met briefly before today. The petite blonde was Leah Keenan Rawlins. She lived outside of town with her rancher husband, Holt.

And Lorelei.

Tonight, she seemed different, more approachable. She was dressed in nice-fitting jeans, a light blue sweater and a pair of sneakers on her feet. Her hair was pulled back into a ponytail and it brushed her shoulders when she turned her head. She looked about eighteen, which meant whatever he was feeling about her was totally inappropriate.

Those rich, chocolate-brown eyes turned toward him and her smile faded. "Mr. Yeager?"

He went to the group. "It's Jace."

"And I go by Lori," she told him.

He didn't want to like her. He couldn't afford to, not with his future in the balance. "Okay."

"Oh, Jace." Claire Keenan came up to them. "Good, you're able to stay for dinner. We don't get to see enough of you." She smiled. "I get to see your daughter when I volunteer at school."

He nodded. "And I'm happy Ellie and Cassie are friends. Thank you for including her in the kids' sleepovers." He glanced out the window to see his daughter running around with the other children. Happy. "Your granddaughter Ellie helped Cassie adjust to the move here."

Claire's smile was warm. "We all want to make sure you both got settled in and are happy."

That all depended on so many things, he thought. "You've certainly done that."

The older woman turned to Lori. "I wish I could talk you into staying longer. One day isn't much time." Claire looked back at Jace. "Lori is a second grade teacher in Colorado Springs."

Lori didn't want to correct Claire Keenan. She *had* been a second grade teacher before she'd been laid off last month. So she didn't mind that her dear father had decided to leave her a little something. It would be greatly appreciated.

But, no, she couldn't stay. Only long enough to finish up Lyle's unfinished business. She hoped that would be concluded by tomorrow.

Claire excused herself. Tim arrived, handed them both glasses of wine and wandered off, too, leaving them alone.

Lori took a sip of wine, trying not to be too obvious

as she glanced at the large-built man with the broad shoulders and narrow waist. No flab there. He definitely did physical work for a living.

"How long have you lived in Destiny, Mr.... Jace?"

"About six months, and I'm hoping to make it permanent."

She didn't look away. "I'm sure things will be straightened out tomorrow."

"I'm glad someone is optimistic."

She sighed. "Look, can't we put this away for the evening? I've had a long day."

He studied her with those deep blue eyes. "If you'd rather I leave, I will. I was only planning to drop my daughter off."

In the past few hours Lori had learned more about Jace Yeager. She knew that Lyle probably had the upper hand with the partnership. "As long as you don't try to pin me down on something I know nothing about. It isn't going to get us anywhere except frustrated."

He raised his glass in salute. "And I'm way beyond that."

CHAPTER TWO

Two hours later, after a delicious pot roast dinner, Lori stood on the back deck at the Keenan Inn. She'd said her goodbyes to everyone at the front door, but wasn't ready to go upstairs to bed yet.

She looked up at the full moon over the mountain peak and wondered what she was doing here. Couldn't she have had a lawyer back in Colorado Springs handle this? First of all, she didn't have the extra money to spend on an attorney when she didn't have a job and very little savings. She needed every penny.

So this was the last place she needed to be, especially with someone like Jace Yeager. She didn't want to deal with him. She only planned to come here, sign any papers to her father's estate and leave.

Now there was another complication, the Mountain Heritage complex. She had to make sure the project moved forward before she left town. She didn't need to be told again that the project would mean employment for several dozen people in Destiny.

"Why, Dad? Why are you doing this?" He hadn't wanted her all those years, now suddenly his daughter needed to return to his town. How many years had she ached for him to come and visit her, or to send for her.

Even a phone call would have been nice. The scars he'd caused made it hard for his daughter to trust. Anyone.

She felt a warm tear on her cold cheek and brushed it away. No. She refused to cry over a man who couldn't give her his time.

"Are you sad?"

Hearing the child's voice, Lori turned around to find Jace Yeager's daughter, Cassie.

Lori put on a smile. "A little. It's been a long time since I've been here. A lot of memories."

The young girl stood under the porch light. "I cried, too, when my daddy made me come here."

"It's hard to move to a new place."

"At first I didn't like it 'cause our house was ugly. When it rained, the ceiling had holes in it." She giggled. "Daddy had to put pans out to catch all the water. My bedroom needed the walls fixed, too. So I had to sleep downstairs by the fireplace while some men put on a new roof."

"So your dad fixed everything?"

She nodded. "He painted my room pink and made me a princess bed like he promised. And I have a horse named Dixie, and Ellie is my best friend."

Her opinion of Jace Yeager just went up several notches. "Sounds like you're a very lucky girl."

The smile disappeared. "But my mommy might come and make me go away."

Jace Yeager didn't have custody of his daughter? "Does your mom live close?"

The child shook her head. "No, she's gonna live in England, but I don't want to live there. I miss her, but I like it here with Daddy, too."

It sounded familiar. "I'm sure they'll work it out."

The girl studied her with the same piercing blue eyes as her father. "Are you going to live here and teach second grade? My school already has Mrs. Miller."

"And I bet you like her, too. No, I'm not going to teach in town, I'm only here for a visit. My dad died not too long ago, and I have to take care of some things."

"Is that why you were crying, because you're sad?"

"Cassie…"

They both turned around and saw Jace.

"Oh, Daddy," Cassie said.

Jace Yeager didn't look happy as he came up the steps. "Ellie's been looking for you." He studied Lori. "The rest of the girls took the party upstairs."

"Oh, I gotta go." She reached up as her father leaned over and kissed her. "'Bye, Daddy, 'bye, Miss Lori." The child took off.

Jace looked at Lori Hutchinson as his gaze locked on her dark eyes.

Finally Lori broke the connection. "I thought you'd left."

"I'd planned to, but I got caught up at the front porch with the Keenans."

He had wanted to speak to Paige, hoping she could give him some encouragement. She'd said she'd work to find a solution to help everyone. Then she rounded up her husband, Sheriff Reed Larkin, leaving her daughters Ellie and Rachel for Grandma Claire's sleepover.

The other sisters, Morgan and Leah, kissed their parents and thanked them for keeping the kids. He caught the look exchanged between the couples, knowing they had a rare night alone. The shared intimacy had him envious, and he turned away. He, too, planned to leave when he spotted his daughter on the back deck with Lori.

"And I was finishing my coffee." He'd had two glasses of wine at dinner. He had to be extra careful, not wanting to give his ex-wife any ammunition. "Well, I should head home."

She nodded. "Your daughter is adorable."

"Thank you. I think so." Jace had to cool it with Lori Hutchinson. "I just wanted to say something before tomorrow...."

She raised a hand. "I told you, I'll do everything I can to get your project operational again."

He just looked at her.

"Whether you believe it or not, I don't plan to cause any more delays than necessary."

"I wish I could believe that."

"After the meeting, how about I come by the building site and tell what happened?"

He shook his head. "The site's been shut down. Until this matter is settled, I can't afford to pay the subcontractors. So you see there's a lot at stake for me."

"And I understand that. But I still have no idea what's going to happen tomorrow, or what Lyle Hutchinson's plans are. It's not a secret that I haven't seen the man in years." She blinked several times, fighting tears. "He's dead now." Her voice was hoarse. "And I feel nothing."

Jace was learning quickly that Lyle Hutchinson was a piece of work. "Okay, we can both agree your father was a bastard."

She turned toward the railing. "The worst thing is, you probably knew the man better than I did." She glanced over her shoulder. "So you tell me, Jace Yeager, what is my father planning for me? For his town."

* * *

Tim Keenan stood at the big picture window at the inn as he waved at the last of dinner guests left.

He was a lucky man. He loved his wife and his family. He'd been blessed with a great life running the inn for the past thirty-plus years. Mostly he enjoyed people and prided himself on being able to read body language.

For example, Jace and Lori had been dancing around each other all night. Not too close, but never out of eye sight. And the looks shared between them...oh, my.

Claire came down the steps and toward him, slipping into his arms. "I got the girls settled down for now, but I have a feeling they're plotting against me."

He kissed her cheek. "Not those little angels."

She smiled. "Seems you thought the same about your daughters, too."

"They are angels." He thought about the years raising his girls. And the grandchildren. "And we're truly blessed." He glanced out to see the lonely-looking woman on the porch. Not everyone was as lucky.

Lori watched from the inn's porch as Jace walked to his truck. He was strong and a little cocky. She had to like that about him. She also liked the way he interacted with his daughter. Clearly they loved each other. What about his ex-wife? She seemed to have moved on, in Europe. Who broke it off? She couldn't help but wonder what woman in her right mind would leave a man like Jace Yeager. She straightened. There could be a lot of reasons. Reasons she didn't need to think about. Even though she'd seen his intensity over the project, she'd also seen the gentleness in those work-roughened hands when he touched his daughter.

She shivered. One thing was, he wasn't going to be

put off about the project. And she couldn't wait for this mess to be settled. Then she could put her past behind her and move on.

She walked inside and up to the second floor. Overhead she heard the muffled voices of the kids. Her room was at the front of the house. A large canopy bed had an overstuffed print comforter opposite a brick fireplace. She took out her cell phone and checked her messages. Two missed calls.

Fear hit her as she listened to the message from Gina. She could hear the panic in her half sister's voice, but it had been like that since childhood.

Lori's mother had remarried shortly after moving to Colorado Springs. Not her best idea, losing Lyle's alimony, but Jocelyn was the type of woman who needed a man. She just hadn't been good at picking the right ones. Her short union with Dave Williams had produced a daughter, Regina. Lori had been the one who raised her, until big sister had gone off to college.

Without Lori around, and given the neglect of their mother, Gina had run wild and ended up pregnant and married to her boyfriend, Eric Lowell, at barely eighteen. Except for Gina's son, Zack, her life had been a mess ever since. It became worse when her husband became abusive, though the marriage ended with the man going to jail. Now Lori was tangled up in this mess, too.

She punched in the number. "Gina, what happened?"

"Oh, Lori, I think Eric found us."

Over a year ago, Lori had moved her sister into her apartment while Eric served a jail sentence for drug possession and spousal abuse. This hadn't been the first time he'd smacked Gina around, but the first conviction. That was the reason they'd planned to move out of state when Lori had been notified about Lyle's death.

"No, Gina, he doesn't get out until the first of the month."

"Maybe he got an early release."

"Detective Rogers would have called you. You still have a few weeks."

"What about you? Are you flying home soon?"

She knew this delay would worry Gina more. "I can't yet. I still need to meet with the lawyer tomorrow."

She heard a sigh. "I'm sorry, Lori. You've done so much for us. You have a life of your own."

"No, Gina. You're my sister. Zack is my nephew. I told you, I won't let Eric hurt you again. But I still need a day or so to get things straightened out. Then hopefully we'll have some money to start over and get away from Eric." She prayed that her father had left her something. Since their mother had died a few years ago, there wasn't anything holding them in Colorado Springs. They could go anywhere. "Think about where you and Zack want to move to." Preferably somewhere they needed a second grade teacher.

"No, you decide, Lori. We'll go anywhere you want. We just can't stay here. I won't survive it."

Lori could hear the fear in her voice. "I promise I'll do whatever it takes to keep you safe. Now go get some sleep and give my special guy a kiss from me."

Lori hung up the phone and hoped everything she said was true. Unlike Lyle Hutchinson, she didn't walk away from family.

The next morning, Lori was up early. She was used to being at school ahead of her students to plan the day.

Not anymore. Not since she'd gotten her pink slip at the start of the school year. She'd been told it was because of cutbacks and low enrollment, but she wondered if it was due to the trouble Eric had caused her at the up-scale private school where she taught.

No, she couldn't think about that now. She needed to have a clear head for the meeting. Was Lyle Hutchinson as wealthy as people said? Normally she wouldn't care, but it could help both her and Gina relocate to another part of the country. Somewhere Gina could raise Zack without the fear of her ex-husband coming after her again. Enough money so Lori had time to find a job.

She drove her car to the end of First Street. A six-foot, wrought-iron fence circled the property that had belonged to the Hutchinsons for over the past hundred years. Her heart raced as she raised her eyes and saw the majestic, three-story white house perched on the hilltop surrounded by trees. Memories bombarded her as she eased past the stone pillars at the gate entrance. The gold plaque read Hutchinson House.

She drove along the hedge-lined circular drive toward the house. She looked over the vast manicured lawn and remembered running through the thick grass, and a swing hanging from a tree out back. She parked in front of the house behind a familiar truck of Jace Yeager. Oh, no. Was the man following her?

Then she saw him standing on the porch leaning against the ornate wrought-iron railing. He was dressed in jeans and a denim shirt and heavy work boots. Without any effort, this man managed to conjure up all sorts of fantasies that had nothing to do with business.

She pulled herself out of her daydream. What was he doing here?

He came down the steps to meet her.

She got out of her car. "Jace, is there a problem?"

He raised a hand in defense. "Mr. Bradley called me this morning. Said he needed me here for after the reading."

Lori was confused. "Why?"

"I hope it's to tell me it's a go-ahead on the Mountain Heritage project."

They started up the steps when she saw a man in a khaki work uniform come around the side porch. He looked to be in his late sixties, maybe seventies. When he got closer she saw something familiar.

"Uncle Charlie?"

The man's weathered face brightened as he smiled. "You remember me, Miss Lorelei?"

"Of course I do. You built me my tree swing." She felt tears sting her eyes. "You let me help plant flowers, too."

He nodded and gripped her hands in his. "That was a lot of years ago, missy. You were a tiny bit of a thing." His tired eyes locked on hers. "You've turned into a beautiful young lady." His grip tightened. "I'm so sorry about your father."

Before Lori could say anything more, another car pulled up. Paige Larkin stepped out of her SUV. Briefcase in hand, she walked up the steps toward them.

They shook hands and Paige spoke briefly to Charlie before the man walked off. Paige turned to Jace. "So you've been summoned, too."

"I got a call from Bradley first thing this morning."

Paige frowned. "Dennis must have a reason for wanting you here." She turned back to her client. "Let's not speculate until we hear what's in Lyle's will."

Lori nodded and together they walked up to the large porch, where greenery filled the pots on either side of the wide door with the leaded glass panels.

She knew that her great-great-grandfather had built this house during the height of the mining era. It was said that Raymond Hutchinson never trusted banks. That was why he didn't lose much during the Great Depression.

They went inside the huge entry with high-gloss hardwood floors. A crystal chandelier hung from the high ceiling and underneath was a round table adorned with a large vase of fresh-cut flowers. The winding staircase circled up to the second story, the banister of hand-carved oak. Cream and deep maroon brocade wallpaper added a formality to the space.

Lori released a breath. "Oh, my."

She was reminded of Jace's presence when he let out a low whistle. "Nice."

"Do you remember this house?" Paige asked.

"Not much. I spent most of my time in the sunroom off the kitchen."

Paige shook her head. "Well, I wouldn't be surprised if this becomes yours. And then you can go anywhere in it you want."

Lori started to tell her she didn't want any part of this house when a thin woman came rushing into the room. Her gray hair was pulled back into a bun. She looked familiar as she smiled and her hazel eyes sparkled. Lori suddenly recognized her.

"Maggie?" she managed to say.

The woman nodded with watery eyes. "Miss Lorelei."

"I can't believe it." Lori didn't hesitate, and went

and hugged the woman. It felt good to be wrapped in the housekeeper's arms again. Years ago, Maggie had been her nanny.

"It's good to have you home." The older woman stepped back and her gaze searched Lori's face. "How pretty you are."

Lori felt herself blush. She wasn't used to all this attention. "Thank you, Maggie."

The housekeeper turned sad. "I'm so sorry about your father." Then squeezed her hands tighter. "I want you to know he went in his sleep. They said a heart attack. Maybe if we would have been there…"

Lori could only nod. "No. He couldn't be helped." She had no idea this would be so hard.

Dennis Bradley walked down the hall. "Good. You made it." He turned and nodded toward Jace. "Mr. Yeager, would you mind waiting a few minutes until I've gone over the will with Ms. Hutchinson?"

"Not a problem." He looked at Maggie and smiled. "I wonder if you could find a cup of coffee for me."

"I'll bring some out."

Once she left, the lawyer said, "We should get started."

He motioned them down the hall and into an office. Lori paused at the doorway. The walls were a deep green with dark stained wainscoting. The plush carpet was slate-gray. Bradley sat down behind the huge desk that already had a folder open.

After they were seated, the lawyer began, "I'll read through Lyle's requests. His first was that the will be read here at the family home." He handed Paige and her copies. "We can go over any details later."

The lawyer slipped on his glasses. "I don't know if

you knew that Lyle had remarried for a short time about ten years ago."

Nothing about her father surprised her. She shook her head.

"There was a prenuptial agreement, then two years later a divorce." He glanced down at the paper. "Lyle did have one other relative, a distant cousin who lives back in Ohio." He read off the generous sum left to Adam Johnson. Also he read the amount given to the household staff, which included Maggie and Charlie.

"I'm glad my father remembered them," Lori said.

Bradley smiled. "They were loyal to him for a lot of years." He sighed. "Now, let's move on to the main part of the will.

"Lyle Hutchinson has bequeathed to his only living child, Lorelei Marie Hutchinson, all his holdings in Hutchinson Corp." He read off the businesses, including Destiny Community Bank, two silver mines, Sunny Hill and Lucky Day. There were six buildings on First Street, and this house at 100 North Street along with all its contents, the furnishings and artwork.

Lori was stunned. "Are you sure this is right?" She looked down at Paige's copy to see the monetary amount stated. "My father was worth this much?"

Bradley nodded. "Lyle was a shrewd businessman. Maybe it was because your grandfather Billy lost nearly everything with his bad investments and eccentric living. Lyle spent years rebuilding the family name and recouping the money. And he also invested a lot into this town."

Bradley looked at her, then at Paige. "Are there any questions?"

Lori gave a sideways glance to her lawyer.

"I probably will once we go over everything."

Bradley nodded. "Call me whenever you need to. Now, for the rest I think Mr. Yeager should hear this. Do you have any objections, Lorelei?" With her agreement, he went to the door and had Jace come in.

He sat down in the chair next to Lori.

Bradley looked at Jace. "Whatever you thought, Mr. Yeager, Lyle went into the Heritage project honestly. The business complex was to promote more jobs and revenue for the town. He wasn't trying to swindle you. As we all know, his death was sudden and unexpected."

Jace nodded. "Of course I understand, but you have to see my side, too. I need to finish this job, get tenants in and paying rent."

Bradley nodded and looked at Lori. "And that will happen if Lorelei will agree to the terms."

"Of course I'll agree to finish this project."

"There is a stipulation in the will." Bradley paused. "You are the last living heir in the Hutchinson line, Lorelei. And this town was founded by your great-great-grandfather, Raymond William Hutchinson, after he struck it rich mining gold and silver. But other business has been coming to Destiny and your father invested wisely. He wants you to continue the tradition."

"And I will," she promised. "I plan to release money right away so the work on Mountain Heritage complex can resume."

Bradley exchanged a look with Paige, then continued on to say, "Everything your father left you is only yours if you take over as CEO of Hutchinson Corporation... and stay in Destiny for the next year."

CHAPTER THREE

Lori had trouble catching her breath. Why? Why would her father want her to stay here to run his company?

"Are you all right?" Jace asked.

She nodded, but it was a lie. "Excuse me." She got up and hurried from the room. Instead of going out the front door, she headed in the other direction.

She ended up in the large kitchen with rows of white cabinets and marble countertops. Of course it was different than she remembered. The old stove was gone, replaced with a huge stainless steel one with black grates.

Suddenly the smell of coffee assaulted her nose and she nearly gagged.

"Miss Lorelei, are you all right?"

She turned around to see a concerned Maggie. She managed a nod. "I just need some air." She fought to walk slowly to the back door and stepped out onto the porch. She drew in a long breath of the brisk air and released it, trying to slow her rapidly beating heart.

Two weeks ago, she couldn't say she even remembered her life here, or the father who hadn't had any time for her. Then the call came about Lyle's death, and she'd been swept up into a whirlwind of emotions and confusion. She couldn't even get herself to visit his grave site.

"Are you sure you're okay?"

She turned around and found Jace standing in the doorway. A shiver ran through her and she pulled her sweater coat tighter around her. "You were there. Would you be okay?"

He came to the railing. "Hell, with that kind of money, I could solve a lot of problems."

She caught a hint of his familiar scent, soap and just his own clean manly smell. She shifted away. She didn't need him distracting her, or his opinion.

"Easy for you to say, your life is here, and you wouldn't have to pull up and move." Lori stole a glance at him. "Or have Lyle Hutchinson running that life."

Jace didn't know the exact amount of money Lyle had left his daughter, but knew it had to be sizable from the investigation Jace had done before he'd entered into the Mountain Heritage project. And he needed that project to move ahead, no matter what he had to do. "It's only a year out of your life."

She glared at him. "That I have no control of."

He studied her face. She was pretty with her small straight nose and big brown eyes. His attention went to her mouth and her perfectly formed lips. He glanced away from the distraction.

Yet, how could he not worry about Lorelei Hutchinson when her decision could put his own livelihood in jeopardy? His other concern was having any more delays, especially when the weather could be a problem. This was business. Only.

"Look, I get it that you and your father had problems,

but you can't change that now. He put you in charge of his company. Surely you can't walk away."

She sent him another piercing look. "My father didn't have a problem walking away from his daughter."

He tried to tell himself she wasn't his problem. Then he remembered if she didn't take over the company, then that was exactly what he'd have to do. Walk away from Cassie. "Then don't walk away like he did. This town needs Hutchinson Corporation to exist."

"Don't you think I know that?"

He sat on the porch railing facing her. "I know it's a three-hundred-mile move from Colorado Springs, but you'll have a great income and a place to live." He nodded toward the house. Then he remembered. "I know you'll have to give up your teaching job."

She glanced out at the lawn. "That I don't have to worry about. I was laid off when the school year started. I have my résumé out in several places."

Jace felt bad for her, but at the same time was hopeful. "It's a bad time for teachers. So maybe it's time for a change. Why can't you take over your father's company?"

"There's so many reasons I can't even count them. First of all, I'm not qualified. I have limited business experience. I could lose everything by managing things badly."

He felt a twinge of hope. "You can learn. Besides, Lyle has lawyers and accountants for a lot of it. I'll be the person at the construction site. You can check out my credentials. I'm damn good at what I do."

This time she studied him.

"I can give you references in Denver," he offered.

Lori couldn't help but be curious. Her life had been

exposed, yet she knew nothing about him. "Why did you leave there? Denver."

"Divorce. I had to sell the business to divide the joint assets. Moving here was my best chance to make a good home for my daughter. Best chance at getting full custody."

She might not like the man's bad attitude toward her, but wanting to be a good father gave him a lot of points.

"Once I finish Mountain Heritage and the spaces are leased, I'll have some revenue coming in. It'll allow me to control my work hours. I can pick and choose construction jobs so I can spend more time with Cassie." His gaze met hers. "Best of all, Destiny is a great place to raise children."

She smiled. "That I remember about this town, and how they decorated at Christmas."

She watched conflict play across his face. "That's what I want Cassie to experience, too. I don't want her in some boarding school in Europe because her mother doesn't have time for her." He stood, and quickly changed the subject. "I also have several men that are depending on this job."

"I need to talk to my lawyer before I can make any decision." And she needed to speak to Gina. Her sister weighed heavily in this decision. She turned toward Jace. "I know you were hoping for more."

He nodded. "Of course I was, but I can't wait much longer. Just so you know, I'll be contacting my own lawyer. I have to protect my investment."

Lori tried not to act surprised as she nodded. Jace Yeager finally said his goodbye as he stepped off the porch and walked around the house to the driveway.

She heard his truck start up. Just one more problem to deal with.

"Thanks, Dad." She glanced skyward. "You couldn't give me the time of day when you were alive, but now that you're gone, you turn my life upside down."

She walked back inside the house and back into her father's office. Paige and Mr. Bradley had their heads together. They spent the next twenty minutes going over all the details. She could contest the will, but if she lost, she'd lose everything and so would this town.

Mr. Bradley checked his watch, gathered up his papers and put them in his briefcase. "Lorelei, if you need anything else from me, just call." He handed her a business card. "There's one other thing I didn't get a chance to tell you. You only have seventy-two hours to make your decision," he said then walked out the door.

Lori looked at Paige. "How can I make a life-changing decision in three days?"

"I know it's difficult, Lori, but there isn't a choice. What can I say? Lyle liked being in control." The brunette smiled. "Sorry, I hate to speak ill of the dead."

"No need to apologize. Over the years, my mother never had anything nice to say about the man. It doesn't seem as if he ever changed."

She thought about what Lyle had done to Jace Yeager. The man would lose everything he'd invested in this project if he couldn't complete it. She closed her eyes. "What should I do?"

"Are you asking me as your lawyer or as a citizen of Destiny?"

"Both."

"As your lawyer, if you turn down Lyle's bequest, the corporation and the partnerships would be dissolved and all moneys would be given to charity. You'd get nothing, Lori." Paige went on to add, "As a citizen of a town I love, I hope you accept. Hutchinson Corporation employs many of the people in this community."

She groaned. "Lyle really did own this town."

Paige shrugged. "A fair share of it. But remember, the Hutchinsons built this town with the money they got from mining." She smiled. "Times are changing, though. My brother-in-law Justin is moving at a pretty good pace to take that status. He has an extreme skiing business. And don't count out Jace Yeager. He's got some other projects in the works."

"And now he's tied up in this mess," Lori said. "Dear Lord, you all must have hated my father."

"Like I said there's always been a Hutchinson here to deal with. Your grandfather Billy was a piece of work, too. He'd done a few shady deals in his time. The family has done a lot of good for Destiny." She tried not to smile. "Maybe Lyle was a little arrogant about it."

"And now it looks like you all have me to continue the tradition."

Paige raised an eyebrow. "Does that mean you're staying?"

"Do I have a choice?" She knew it was all about Lyle protecting the Hutchinsons' legacy. Not about his daughter's needs or wants. He had never cared about that.

Well, she had to think about what was best for her family. She and Gina had planned to move away from Colorado, and her sister's ex-husband. Most important they had to be safe. Could Eric find them here in Destiny? Would he try? Of course he would if he had any idea where to look.

If Lori decided to stay, at least she could afford to hire a bodyguard. "I need to talk to my sister. She would have to move here, too."

Paige nodded. "I understand. So when you make your decision give me a call anytime. I need to get back to the office." Her lawyer walked out, leaving her alone.

Lori went to the desk, sat down and opened the file. She stared once again at the exorbitant amount of money her father was worth. Although she was far from comfortable taking anything from Lyle, how could she walk away from this? The money would help her sister and nephew so much. Not to mention the other people in Destiny.

But she'd have to be able to work with Jace Yeager, too. The man had his own anger issues when it came to a Hutchinson. Could she handle that, or him? No, she doubted any woman could, but if she stayed out of his way, they might be able to be partners.

She took her cell phone from her purse and punched in the familiar number. When Gina answered, she said, "How would you feel about moving into a big house in Destiny?"

The next morning, Jace took his daughter to school then drove to the site. He needed to do everything he could to save this project. That meant convince Lori Hutchinson to stay. And that was what he planned to do.

He unlocked the chain-link fence that surrounded the deserted construction site. After opening the gate, he climbed back into his truck, pulled inside and parked in front of the two-story structure. The outside was nearly completed, except for some facade work.

Yet, inside was a different story. The loft apartments

upstairs were still only framed in and the same with the retail stores/office spaces on the bottom floor. He got out as the cool wind caused him to shove his cowboy hat down on his head. Checking the sky overhead, he could feel the moisture in the air. They were predicting rain for later today. How soon before it turned to snow? He'd seen it snow in October, in Colorado.

He heard a car and looked toward the dirt road to see Lori pull in next to his truck and get out. Though tall and slender, she still didn't reach his chin. He glanced down at her booted feet, then did a slow gaze over those long legs encased in a pair of worn jeans. Even in the cold air, his body took notice.

Calm down, boy. She was off-limits.

His gaze shot to her face. "Good morning. Welcome to Mountain Heritage."

"Morning," Lori returned as she burrowed deeper in her coat. "I hope this tour is going to be on the inside," she said. "It's really cold."

He nodded. "Come on."

He led her along the makeshift path through the maze of building materials to the entry. He'd been surprised when he'd gotten the call last night from her, saying she wanted to see Mountain Heritage.

"As you can see, the outside is nearly completed, just a little work left on the trim." He unlocked the door, and let her inside.

"We're ready to blow in insulation and hang Sheetrock. The electricians have completed the rough wiring." He glanced at her, but couldn't read anything from her expression. "This is going to be a green building, totally energy efficient, from the solar panels on the roof, to the tankless water heaters. Best of all, the outside of the structure blends in with the surrounding buildings. But this complex will offer so much more."

He pushed open the double doors and allowed her to go in first. He followed as she walked into the main lobby. This was where it all looked so different. The open concept was what he loved the most about the business complex. He'd done most of the design himself and was proud of how well it was turning out.

The framework of a winding staircase to the second-story balcony still needed the wooden banister. He motioned for her to follow him across the subfloor to the back hall, finding the elevators. He explained about the hardwood floors and the large stone fireplace.

"It's so large."

"We need the space to entice our clients. These back elevators lead to the ten loft apartments upstairs. Both Lyle and I figured they'd rent pretty well to the winter skiers. Of course our ideal renter would be long-term. We were hoping to make it a great place to live, shop and dine all without leaving the premises.

"We have a tentative agreement to lease office spaces for a ski rental company from Justin Hilliard. He's planning on doing a line of custom skis and snowboards."

"How soon were you supposed to have this all completed?"

Was she going to stay? "We'd been on schedule for the end of November." Now he was hoping he still had a full crew. Some of the subcontractors he'd been working with had come up from Durango.

Lori felt ignorant. She'd never been to a construction site. Doubts filled her again as she wondered for the hundredth time if she'd be any good taking over for

Lyle. So many people were depending on her. "How are you at teaching, Jace?"

He looked confused, then said, "I guess that depends on the student and how willing they are to learn."

"She's very serious." She released a sigh. "It looks like we're going to be partners."

Damn. Jace had a woman for his partner, a woman who didn't know squat about construction. And he was even taking her to lunch. He'd do whatever it took to provide for his daughter.

He escorted Lori into a booth at the local coffee shop, the Silver Spoon. He hadn't expected her to accept his lunch invitation, but they'd spent the past two hours at the site, going over everything that would need to happen in the next seven weeks to meet completion. She took notes, a lot of notes.

He'd made a call to his project manager, Toby Edwards, and had asked him to get together a crew. Within an hour, his foreman had called back to tell him they got most of the people on board to start first thing in the morning.

So it seemed natural that he would take her to lunch to celebrate. He glanced across the table. She still looked a little shell-shocked from all the information she'd consumed this morning, but she hadn't complained once.

"This place is nice, homey," she said. "Reminds me of the café I worked in during college."

Okay, that surprised him. "It's your typical family-run restaurant that serves good home cooking, a hearty breakfast in the morning and steak for supper. Outside of a steak house, there isn't any fine dining in Destiny, and Durango is forty-eight miles away. We're hoping a restaurant will be added to our complex. Not only more revenue for us, but more choice when you want to go out."

He smiled and Lori felt a sudden rush go through her. No. No. No. She didn't want to think about Jace Yeager being a man. Well, he was a man, just not the man she needed to be interested in. He was far too handsome, too distracting, and they would be working together. Correction, he was doing the work, she would be watching…and learning.

"I hear from your daughter that you've been remodeling your house."

"Restoration," he corrected. "And yes, it's a lot of work, but I enjoy it. So many people just want to tear out and put in new. There is so much you can save. I'm refinishing the hardwood floors, and stripping the crown moldings and the built-in cabinet in the dining room. What I've replaced is an outdated furnace and water heater."

She smiled. "And the roof?"

He raised an eyebrow.

She went on to say, "Cassie told me that you had to put out pans when it rained."

She caught a hint of his smile, making him even more handsome. "Yeah, we had a few adventurous nights. We stayed dry, though."

She couldn't help but be curious about him, but no more personal questions. Focus on his profession. "I bet my father's house could use some updating, too."

"I wouldn't know. Yesterday was the first time I'd been there. I conducted all my business with Lyle in his office at the bank."

She didn't get the chance to comment as the middle-aged waitress came to the table carrying two mugs and a coffeepot. With their nods, she filled the cups.

"Hi, Jace. How's that little one of yours?"

"She keeps me on my toes." He smiled. "Helen, this is Lorelei Hutchinson. Lori, this is Helen Turner. She and her husband, Alan, are the owners of the Silver Spoon."

The woman smiled. "It's nice to meet you, Ms. Hutchinson. I'm sorry about your father."

"Thank you. And please, call me Lori."

"Will you be staying in town long?" the woman asked.

Lori glanced at Jace. "It looks that way."

She couldn't tell if Helen was happy about that or not. They placed their order and the woman walked away.

"I guess she hasn't decided if she's happy about me staying."

Jace leaned forward. "Everyone is curious about what you're going to do. Whether you'll change things at Hutchinson Corp." He shrugged. "These days everyone worries about their jobs."

"I don't want that to happen. That's one of the main reasons I'm staying in town."

Jace leaned back in the booth. "Of course it has nothing to do with the millions your father left you."

Lori felt the shock. "Money doesn't solve every problem."

"My ex-wife thought it did."

Before she could react to Jace's bitter words, Helen brought their food to the table. Their focus turned to their meal until a middle-aged man approached their booth.

"Excuse me, ma'am, sir," he began hesitantly. "Helen told me that you're Mr. Hutchinson's daughter."

Lori smiled. "I am Lori Hutchinson and you are...?"

"Mac Burleson."

She had a feeling that he wasn't just here to be neighborly. Had her father done something to him? "It's nice to meet you, Mr. Burleson."

Mr. Burleson looked to be in his early thirties. Dressed in faded jeans, a denim shirt and warm winter jacket, he held his battered cowboy hat in his hands. "I hope you'll pardon the intrusion, ma'am, but your father and I had business before his death. First, I'm sorry for your loss."

She nodded. "Thank you."

"I was also wondering if you'll be taking over his position at the bank."

She was startled by the question. "To be honest with you, Mr. Burleson, I haven't had much chance to decide what my involvement would be. Is there a problem?"

The man was nervous. "It's just that, Mr. Neal, in the loan department, is going to foreclose on my house next week." The man glanced at Jace, then back at her.

"I know I've been late on my payments, but I haven't been able to find work in a while. No one is hiring...." He stopped and gathered his emotions. "I have three kids, Miss Hutchinson. If I can have a little more time, I swear I'll catch up. Just don't make my family leave their home."

Lori was caught off guard. Her father planned to evict a family?

"Mac," Jace said, drawing the man's attention, "do you have any experience working construction?"

Hope lit up the man's tired eyes. "I've worked on a

few crews. I can hang drywall and do rough framing. Heck, I'll even clean up trash." He swallowed hard. "I'm not too proud to do anything to feed my family."

Lori felt an ache building in her stomach as Jace talked. "If you can report to the Mountain Heritage site tomorrow morning at seven, I'll give you a chance to prove yourself."

"I'll be there," Mac promised. "Thank you."

Jace nodded. "Report to the foreman, Toby."

Mac shook Jace's hand. "I won't let you down, Mr. Yeager." He turned back to Lori. "Could you tell Mr. Neal that I have a job now? And maybe give me a few months to catch up on my payments."

Lori's heart ached. She didn't even know her loan officer, but it seemed she needed to meet him right away. "Mac, I can't make any promises, but give me a few days and I'll get back to you."

He shook her hand. "That's all I can ask. Thank you, Ms. Hutchinson." He walked away.

Lori released a sigh. "I guess I have a lot more to do now than worry about one building."

"Your job as Hutchinson CEO covers a lot of areas."

Helen came over to the table, this time wearing a grin.

"I hoped you've enjoyed your lunch."

"Great as usual," Jace said.

The waitress started to turn away, then stopped and said, "By the way, it's on the house." She picked up the bill from the table. "Thank you both for what you did for Mac."

"I haven't done anything yet," Lori clarified, now afraid she'd spoken too soon.

"You both gave him hope. He's had a rough time of

late." Helen blinked. "A few years ago, he left the army and came back home a decorated war hero. At the very least, he deserves our respect, and a chance. So thank you for taking the time to listen to him." The woman turned and walked back toward the kitchen.

She looked at Jace, remembering what he said about her inheritance. She also wasn't sure she liked being compared to his ex. "I better go and stop by the bank." She pushed her plate away. "Who knows, maybe all those 'millions' just might do some good."

CHAPTER FOUR

LORI couldn't decide if she was hurt or angry over Jace's assumption about the inheritance. She'd lost her appetite and excused herself immediately after lunch.

She was glad when he didn't try to stop her, because she had a lot of thinking to do without the opinion of a man she'd be working with. And who seemed to have a lot of issues about women.

Was he like her father? What she'd learned from her mother about Lyle over the years had been his need to control, whether in business or his personal life. When Jocelyn Hutchinson couldn't take any more she'd gotten out of the marriage, but their child had still been trapped in the middle of her parents' feud. The scars they'd caused made it hard for Lori to trust.

But was coming back to Destiny worth putting her smack-dab into dealing with the past? All the childhood hurt and pain? It also put her in charge of Lyle's domain, and his business dealings, including the Mountain Heritage complex. And a lot more time with the handsome but irritating Jace Yeager.

The man had been right about something. She had a lot of money and it could do a lot of good. She recalled the look of hope on Mac Burleson's face and knew she needed to find an answer for the man.

She crossed the street to Destiny Community Bank. The two-story brick structure was probably from her grandfather's era. With renewed confidence she walked inside to a large open space with four teller windows. Along the wall were portraits of generations of the Hutchinson men—Raymond, William, Billy and Lyle. They were all strangers to her. She studied her handsome father's picture. This man especially.

She turned around and found several of the bank customers watching her. She put on a smile and they greeted her the same way as if they knew who she was.

She went to the reception desk and spoke to the young brunette woman seated there. "Is it possible to see Mr. Neal? Tell him Lorelei Hutchinson is here."

"Yes, Miss Hutchinson." The woman picked up the phone, and when she hung up said, "Mr. Neal said to have a seat and he'll be out…shortly."

Lori wasn't in the mood to wait. "Is he in a meeting?"

The girl shook her head.

"Then I'll just head to his office. Where is it?"

The receptionist stood and together they went toward a row of offices. "Actually, he's in Mr. Hutchinson's office."

Lori smiled. "Oh, is he? Excuse me, I didn't get your name."

"It's Erin Peters."

"Well, Erin, it's very nice to meet you. I'm Lori." She stuck out her hand. "Have you worked at the bank for long?"

"Three years. I've been taking college classes for my business degree."

"That's nice to know. I'm sure my father appreciated his employees continuing their education."

Erin only nodded as they walked toward the office at the end of the hall. Lori knocked right under the nameplate on the last door that read Lyle W. Hutchinson. She paused as she gathered courage, then turned the knob and walked in.

There was a balding man of about fifty seated behind her father's desk. He seemed busy trying to stack folders. When he saw her he froze, then quickly put on a smile.

"Well, you must be Lorelei Hutchinson." He rounded the desk. "I'm Gary Neal. It's a pleasure to finally meet you. Lyle talked about you often."

She shook his hand, seriously doubting Lyle said much about her. Her father hadn't taken the time to know her. Now, did she have to prove herself worthy of being his daughter?

"Hello, Mr. Neal."

"First off, I want to express my deepest sympathies for your loss. Lyle and I were not only colleagues, but friends. So if there is anything you need…"

"Thank you, I'm fine." She nodded. "I've only been in town a few days, but I wanted to stop by the bank. I'm sure you've already heard that I'm going to be staying in Destiny."

He nodded. "Dennis Bradley explained as much."

She hesitated. "Good. Do you have a few minutes to talk with me?"

"Of course."

Still feeling brave, she walked behind the desk and took the seat in her father's chair as if she belonged.

She didn't miss the surprise on the loan officer's face. "Where's your office, Mr. Neal?"

He blinked, then finally said, "It's two doors down the hall. Since your father's death, I've had to access some files from here. Lyle was hands-on when it came to bank business. I'm his assistant manager."

"Good. Then you're who I need to speak with." She motioned for him to sit down, but she was feeling a little shaky trying to pull this off. This man could be perfectly wonderful at his job, but she needed to trust him. "I take it you handle the mortgage loans." With his nod, she asked, "What do you know about the Mac Burleson mortgage?"

The man frowned. "Funny you should ask, I was just working on the Burleson file."

"Could I have a look?"

He hesitated, then relented. "It's a shame we're going to have to start foreclosure proceedings in a few days."

Neal dug through the stack, located the file and handed it to her. She looked over pages of delinquent notices, the huge late fees. And an interest rate that was nearly three points higher than the norm. No wonder the man was six months behind. "Has Mr. Burleson paid anything during all this time?"

"Yes, but it could barely cover the interest."

"Why didn't you help him by dropping the interest rate and lowering the payments?"

"It's not the bank's policy. Your father—"

"Well, my father is gone now, and he wanted me to take over in his place."

"I'm *sure* he did, but with your limited experience…"

"That may be, but I feel that given the state of the economy we need to help people, too. It's a rough time."

She knew firsthand. "I want to stop the foreclosure, or at least delay it."

"But Mr. Burleson isn't even employed."

"As of an hour ago, he's gotten a job offer." She looked at the remaining eight files. "Are these other homes to be foreclosed on, too?"

The loan officer looked reluctant to answer, but nodded. "Would you please halt all proceedings until I have a look at each case? I want to try everything to keep these families in their homes." She stood. "Maybe if we can set up a meeting next week and see what we can come up with."

Mr. Neal stood. "This isn't bank policy. If people aren't held accountable for their debts, we'd be out of business. I'm sure your father wouldn't agree with this, either."

For the first time in days, Lori felt as if she were doing the right thing. "As I said before, my father left me in charge. Do you have a problem with that, Mr. Neal?"

With the shaking of his head, she tossed out one more request. "Good. I also need money transferred into the escrow account for the Mountain Heritage project as soon as possible. Mr. Yeager will have his crew back to work first thing in the morning. And if you have any questions about my position here, talk to Mr. Bradley."

She walked out to the reception desk and found Jace standing there, talking with Erin. He was smiling at the pretty brunette woman. Why not? He was handsome and single. And why did she even care?

He finally saw her and walked over. "Hi, Lori."

"What are you doing here? I told you that I'd get the money for the project."

"I know you did, but that's not why I'm here—"

"I'm really busy now, Jace. Could we do this later?" She cut him off and turned to the receptionist. "Erin, would you schedule a meeting for all employees for nine o'clock tomorrow in the conference room?"

With Erin's agreement, Lori walked out of the bank, feeling Jace's gaze on her. She couldn't deal with him. She had more pressing things to do, like moving out of the inn and into her father's house, where she had to face more ghosts.

Jace was angry that he let Lori get to him. He'd wasted his afternoon chasing after a woman who didn't want to be found. At least not by him.

He hadn't blamed Lori for walking out on him at lunch. Okay, maybe he had no right to say what he did to her. Damn. He'd let his past dictate his feelings about women. Like it or not, Lori Hutchinson was his partner. More importantly, she had the money to keep the project going. If he wanted any chance of keeping Cassie he had to complete his job.

An apology was due to Lori. And he needed to deliver it in person. If only she'd give him a minute to listen to him. He also needed her to sign some papers that needed her authorization.

Jace left the bank to meet up with his foreman to finalize the crew for tomorrow. Then the search for Lori continued as he'd gone around town and ended up at the inn, where he finally got an answer as to her whereabouts.

He had to pick up Cassie from school, but went straight to the Hutchinson house after. He drove through the gates, hoping he could come up with something to say to her. The last thing he wanted was to start off on the wrong foot.

"Wow! Daddy, this is pretty. Does Ms. Lori really live here?"

He parked in the driveway and saw the rental car there. "Yes, she does. It was her father's, now it's hers."

He climbed out and helped Cassie from the backseat. They went up the steps as the front door opened and Maggie appeared. "This is a wonderful day. First, Ms. Lorelei comes home and now, Mr. Yeager and this beautiful child come to visit."

"Hi, Maggie," Jace said. "This is my daughter, Cassie. Cassie, this is Maggie."

They exchanged greetings then the housekeeper opened the door wider.

"I'd like to see Lori if she isn't too busy."

"Of course." Maggie motioned them inside the entry. "She's in her father's upstairs office." The housekeeper looked at Cassie. "Why don't I take you into the kitchen and see if there are some fresh baked cookies on my cooling rack? They're so good along with some milk." The housekeeper looked concerned. "Coming back here is hard for her."

"I expect it is. Are you sure it's okay?"

Maggie smiled. "I think that would be good. The office is the first door on the left."

Still he hesitated.

"You should go up," the woman said. "She could use a friend right about now."

Jace glanced up the curved staircase and murmured, "I'm not sure she'd call me 'friend' right now."

* * *

Lori had trouble deciding where to put her things. There were six bedrooms and a master suite. One had been turned into an office, and the one next to it was nondescript, with only a queen-size bed covered by a soft floral comforter. It had a connecting bath, so that was where she put her one bag.

She unpacked the few items she had, but went into her father's office. She couldn't get into his computer because she didn't have access.

"Okay, need to make a call to Dennis Bradley first thing tomorrow."

What she knew for sure was she needed to have someone to work with. Someone she trusted. As far as she knew her father had worked out of his office at the bank and from home. Did Lyle handle everything himself? Had he not trusted anyone? She rubbed her hands over her face. She didn't know the man. She stood up and walked out.

In the hall curiosity got the best of her and she began to look around. She peeked into the next room, then the next until she came to the master suite. She opened the door but didn't go inside.

The dark room had a big four-poster bed that dominated the space. The windows were covered with heavy brocade drapes and the bedspread was the same fabric. The furniture was also stained dark. Bits and pieces of childhood memories hit her. She pushed them aside and journeyed on to the next room. She paused at the door, feeling a little shaky, then she turned the knob and pushed it open.

She gasped, seeing the familiar pale pink walls. The double bed with the sheer white canopy and matching sheer curtains. There was a miniature table with stuffed animals seated in the matching chairs as if waiting for a tea party.

Oh, my God.

Nothing had been changed since she'd lived here. Lori crossed the room to the bed where a brown teddy bear was propped against the pillow.

"Buddy?" She picked up the furry toy, feeling a rush of emotions, along with the memory of her father bringing the stuffed animal home one night.

She hugged the bear close and fought tears. No, she didn't want to feel like this. She didn't want to care about the man who didn't want her. Yet, she couldn't stop the flood of tears. A sob tore from her throat as she sank down onto the mattress and cried.

"Lori?"

She heard Jace's voice and stiffened. She quickly walked to the window, wiping her eyes. She fought to compose herself before she had to face him.

He followed her, refusing to be ignored.

"It's okay to be sad," he said, his voice husky and soft.

She finally swung around. "Don't talk about what you know nothing about."

Jace was taken aback by her anger. "It seems that everything I've said to you today has been wrong. I won't bother you again."

She stopped him. "No, please, don't go."

She wiped the last of the tears off her face. "It's me who should apologize for my rudeness. You caught me at a bad moment. Why are you here?"

"Maggie sent me up to Lyle's office. I have some papers for you to sign, but they can wait. Believe it or not, Lori, I came to apologize for what I said to you at lunch. I had no right to judge your motivation."

Jace glanced around the bedroom and hated what he was feeling. What Lyle must have felt when his daughter left. Would this happen to him if his ex got Cassie back? "I take it you were about six or seven when you left here?"

She nodded. "It was so long ago, I feel silly for letting it upset me now."

"You were old enough to have memories. Your childhood affects you all your life. It was your father who chose not to spend time with you." It seemed odd, he thought, because Lyle had kept her room like a shrine.

Lori suddenly brightened as if all the pain went away. "Well, as you can see, I'll need to do some painting. My sister, Gina, is coming soon along with my nephew, Zack." She put on a smile. "I don't think he'd like a pink bedroom."

Before Jace could say anything, he heard his daughter calling for him. "I'm in here, Cassie. I picked her up from school, and I wanted to see you before work tomorrow. To make sure everything is okay…between us."

The expression on his seven-year-old's face was priceless as she stopped at the door. "Oh, it's so pretty." She looked at Lori. "Do you have a little girl, too?"

An hour later, with Cassie busy doing homework at the kitchen table, Jace and Lori went to do their work in Lyle's office.

"I hate that you have to keep going over everything again and again," Lori told him.

"It's not a problem. Better now, when I'm around to answer your questions. There aren't too many decisions to make right now. If you'd like to put in some input on finishes, like tile and countertops, you're more than welcome. A woman's touch." He held up a hand. "I didn't mean anything about that. A second opinion would be nice."

"I'd like that."

She smiled and he felt a tightening in his gut. Damn. He looked back at the work sheet.

"Well, the crew is showing up tomorrow to start the finish work on the outside. If we're lucky the weather will hold and we can complete everything before the snow comes."

"Will it affect the work inside?"

"Only if we can't get the materials to the site because the roads aren't passable."

She nodded, chewing her bottom lip. He found it hard to look away.

"What about Mac Burleson? Do you really have a job for him?"

Jace nodded. "If he can do the work."

"I wonder if Mac can paint," Lori said.

Jace looked at her to see a mischievous grin on her pretty face. She wasn't beautiful as much as striking. Those sparkling brown eyes and full mouth... "That was probably going to be one of his jobs—priming the walls once they're up. What were you thinking?"

"I doubt my father has done much work on this house in years." She shrugged. "I don't mind so much for myself, but Gina and Zack. I want this place..." She glanced around the dark room. "A little more homey. I want to talk to Charlie and see what he has to say about repairs."

"How soon are you expecting your family?"

"Next week. Gina is packing and putting most of the furniture in storage." She sighed. "I should go back to help her, but I want to make sure there won't be any holdup on the project."

Jace needed to remember that her entire life had been turned upside down by Lyle's death. "It's a shame you have to leave everything behind, like your friends. A boyfriend…?"

She looked surprised at his question. Not as much as he was. He stood and went to the window. "I only meant, Lyle had you make a tough choice."

"No, I don't have a boyfriend at the moment, and my sister is my best friend. So sometimes a fresh start is good." She turned the tables on him. "Isn't that why you came to Destiny?"

He didn't look at her, but that didn't mean he couldn't catch her scent, or wasn't aware of her closeness. He took a step back. "I came here to make a life for my daughter. She's everything to me."

Lori smiled at him and again his body took notice. "From what I've seen, Cassie feels the same way about you. You're a good father."

"Thank you. I'm not perfect. But I do try and want to make the job permanent."

His gaze went back to her. Darn. What was it about her that drew him? Suddenly he thought about his ex-wife, and the caution flag came out. He needed to stay focused on two things—business and his daughter.

A happy Cassie skipped into the room and rushed to him. "Maggie said to tell you that dinner is ready."

"Oh, honey. We should head home." He glanced at his watch. "Maybe another time."

"No, Daddy. We can't go. I helped Maggie make the biscuits, so we have to stay and eat them."

He was caught as he looked down at his daughter, then at Lori.

"I can't believe you're passing up a home-cooked meal, Jace Yeager," Lori said. "Maggie's biscuits are the best around, and probably even better with Cassie helping."

"Please, Daddy. I'll go to bed right on time. I won't argue or anything."

Jace looked back at Lori. It was her first night here, and would probably be a rough one.

Lori smiled. "Now that's a hard offer to turn down."

"You're no help," he told Lori.

"Sorry, us girls have to stick together."

That was what he was afraid of. He was losing more than just this round. He hated that he didn't mind one bit.

"Okay, but we can't stay long. We have a bedtime schedule."

"I promise, I'll go to bed right on time," Cassie said, then took off toward the kitchen.

He looked at a smiling Lori. "Okay, I'm a pushover."

"Buck up, Dad. It's only going to get worse before it gets better."

Suddenly their eyes locked and the amused look disappeared. Lori was the first to speak. "Please, I want you to stay for dinner. I think we both agree that eating alone isn't fun."

"Yes, we can agree on that."

He followed Lori into the kitchen, knowing this

woman could easily fill those lonely times. He just couldn't let that happen. No more women for a while, at least not over the age of seven.

CHAPTER FIVE

AT EIGHT-THIRTY the next morning, Lori was up and dressed, and grabbed a travel mug of coffee from Maggie, then she was out the door to the construction site. Not that she didn't think Jace could do his job, but she wanted to meet the crew and assure them that there wouldn't be any more delays with the project.

When she pulled through the gate and saw the buzz of activity, she was suddenly concerned about disturbing everyone.

She had every right to be here, she thought as she climbed out of her car and watched the men working on the trim work of the two-story structure. Jace hadn't wasted any time.

She walked carefully on the soggy ground. Okay, she needed more protection than her loafers. A good pair of sturdy boots was on her list. She headed up the plywood-covered path when a young man dressed in jeans, a denim work shirt and lace-up steel-toed boots came toward her.

He gave her a big smile and tipped back his hard hat. "Can I help you, ma'am?"

"I'm looking for Jace Yeager."

The man's smile grew bigger. "Aren't they all? I'm Mike Parker, maybe I can help you."

All? Lori couldn't help but wonder what that meant. She started to speak when she heard a familiar voice call out. They both turned to see Jace. He was dressed pretty much like the others, but he had on a leather vest over a black Henley shirt even though the temperature was in the low fifties.

Lori froze as he gave her a once-over. He didn't look happy to see her as he made his way toward them.

Jace ignored her as he looked at Mike. "Don't you have anything to do?"

"I was headed to my truck for some tools." He nodded to her. "And I ran across this nice lady. Sorry, I didn't catch your name."

"Lori Hutchinson."

Mike let out a low whistle. "So you're the big boss? I can't tell you how good it is to meet you, Ms. Hutchinson."

She tried not to cringe at the description. "It's Lori. I'm not anyone's boss. Jace is in charge of this project."

That was when Jace spoke up. "Mike, they've finished spraying the insulation up in the lofts, so I need you to get started hanging drywall."

"Right, I'll get on it." He tipped his hat to Lori. "Nice to meet you, ma'am."

"Nice to meet you, too, Mike."

She watched him hurry off, then turned back to Jace. "Good morning. Seems you've been busy. What time did you start?"

"I had a partial crew in at five."

"What about Cassie?"

He seemed surprised at her question. "I wasn't here,

but my foreman was. My daughter comes first, Lori. She always will."

"I didn't mean… I apologize."

That didn't ease the scowl on his face. "Were we supposed to meet this morning?"

She shook her head. "No."

"Did you come to work?" He looked over her attire. "You're not exactly dressed for a construction site."

She glanced down at her dark trousers and soft blue sweater under her coat. "I have an appointment at the bank later this morning. I wanted to stop here first to see if everything got off okay. Do you need anything?"

"No, it's fine. I know it looks a little chaotic, but things are running pretty smoothly for the first day back to work. It's most of the same crew so they know what I expect from them."

Lori had no doubt that Jace Yeager was good at his job. "So everything is on schedule?"

"If the weather holds." The wind picked up and brushed her hair back. "Come inside where it's a little warmer," he said. "I'll introduce you to the foreman."

"I don't want to disturb him."

"As you can see, it's a little late for that." He nodded toward the men who were watching.

She could feel a blush rising over her face as she followed Jace inside the building to a worktable that had blueprints spread out on top. A middle-aged man was talking with another workman.

"Hey, Toby," Jace called as he reached into a bin and pulled out a hard hat. He came to her and placed it on her head. "You need to wear this if you come here. Safety rules."

Their eyes met. "Thank you."

Toby walked up to them. "What, Jace?"

"This is Lori Hutchinson. Lori, this is my foreman, Toby Edwards."

The man smiled at her and tiny lines crinkled around his eyes. "So you're the one who saved this guy's as... sets."

Lori felt Jace tense. "I'd say I was just lucky to inherit some money," she told Toby. "Speaking of money..." She turned to Jace. "Were the funds transferred into the Mountain Heritage account?"

He nodded. "Yes. We're expecting materials to be delivered later today."

"Good." She glanced around, feeling a little excited about being a part of this. "It's nice to see all the work going on." It was a little noisy with the saws and nail guns.

Jace watched Lori. He wasn't expecting her here. Not that she didn't have a right, but she was a big distraction. He caught the guys watching her, too. Okay, they were curious about their attractive new boss. He hoped that was all it was. There could be a problem if she stopped by every day. And not only for his men, either. He eyed her pretty face and those big brown eyes that a man could get lost in.

No way. One woman had already cost him his career and future, and maybe his daughter. He wasn't going to get involved with another, especially in his workplace. Or any other place. He thought about the cozy dinner last night in the Hutchinson kitchen.

It was a little too cozy.

Enough reminiscing, he thought, and stuck his fingers in his mouth, letting go with a piercing whistle. "Let's get this over with so we can all get on with our day." All work stopped and the men came to the center of the main room.

"Everyone, this is Lorelei Hutchinson. Since Lyle Hutchinson's death, Lori will be taking over in her father's place. It's thanks to her we're all back to work on this project." The men let go with cheers and whistles. Jace forced a smile, knowing this was a means to get this project completed. But damn, being beholden to a woman stuck in his craw. "Okay, now back to work."

"Thank you," Lori said. "So many people in town have been looking at me like I have two heads."

"Has someone said anything to you?" he asked.

"No, but they're wondering what I'm going to do." She shrugged. "Maybe I should just make a big announcement in the town square. 'Hey, everyone, I'm not here to cause trouble.'"

A strange protective feeling came over him. "Now that the project has started up again, maybe they'll stop worrying."

"I hope so. I'm bringing my sister and nephew here to live. I want to be part of this community."

"What you did for Mac Burleson yesterday was a pretty good start."

"Oh, Mac. Is he here?"

Jace nodded. "Yeah, he was here waiting when Toby opened the gates."

She glanced around the area. "How is he doing?"

"Good so far."

She looked up at Jace. "There he is. Would you mind if I talked to him for a moment?"

"No, not a problem."

She walked across the large entry to the wall. Jace watched her acknowledge a lot of the workers before she got to Mac. She smiled and the man returned it. In fact he was smiling the whole time Lori was talking. Then he shook her hand and Lori walked back. "I just hired Mac to paint a couple of bedrooms at the house."

"Hey, are you stealing my help?"

"No. He's agreed to come over this weekend with his brother and paint the upstairs. I don't think my nephew wants to sleep in a pink room."

Jace nodded, knowing she would be erasing the last of her own memories of her childhood. "There are other bedrooms for him to sleep in."

"I know, but it should have been changed years ago."

"Maybe there was a reason why it hadn't been."

She looked at him. He saw pain, but also hope. "Lyle Hutchinson knew where I was since I left here twenty-two years ago. My father could have invited me back anytime. He chose not to."

Lori turned to walk out and he hurried to catch up with her. "Look, Lori. I don't know the situation."

She stopped abruptly. "That's right, you don't." She closed her eyes. "Look, it was a long time ago. My father is gone, and I'll never know why he never came to see me. And now, why in heaven's name does he want me to run his company?"

"I can't answer that, either."

"I've dealt with it. So now I move on and start my new life with Gina and Zack. I want them to have a fresh start here, in a new place, a new house and especially a new bedroom for my seven-year-old nephew."

Jace frowned. "I take it Zack is without his father."

Lori straightened. "His parents are divorced." She glanced around. "I should be going."

"I need to get back, too."

They started walking toward the door. "If there's anything you need," she offered, "just give me a call. You have my cell phone number. I'll be at the bank most of today."

He walked her out. "I can handle things here." Then he felt bad. "Maybe in a few days if you're available we could go over some samples of tiles and flooring."

She looked surprised at his request. "I'd like that. I want to be a part of this project."

Her steps slowed as she made her way over the uneven boards. He took Lori's arm, helping her along the path.

"What about the bank?"

"I doubt Mr. Neal will enjoy having me around." She stopped suddenly and nearly lost her balance. "Oh," she gasped.

"I got you." He caught her in his arms. Suddenly her trim body was plastered up against him. Even with her coat he wasn't immune to her soft curves. And he liked it. Too much. He finally got her back on her feet. "You need practical boots if you come to a construction site. Go to Travers's Outfitters and get some that are waterproof. You don't want to be caught in bad weather without protection."

She stopped next to her compact car. "I need a lot of things since I'll be living here awhile."

"Like a car that will get through the snow. This thing will put you in a ditch on the first bad day. Get something with bulk to it. You'll be driving your family around."

She nodded. "I guess I need to head down to Durango and visit a dealership next week when my sister flies in."

Before he could stop himself, he offered, "If you need any help, let me know."

She gave him a surprised look, mirroring his own feelings.

Two hours later, Lori glanced across the conference table at the Destiny Community Bank's loan officers, Gary Neal, Harold Brownlee and Larry McClain. The gentlemen's club. "I disagree. In this day and age, we need to work with people and help adjust their loans."

"In my experience," Neal said, "if we start giving handouts, people will take advantage. And no one will pay us."

She tried to remain calm, but she was so far out of her element it wasn't funny.

"I never said this is a handout, more like a hand up. All I suggested is we lower the interest rates on these loans." She pointed to the eight mortgages. "Two points. Waive the late fees and penalties. Just give these families a fighting chance to keep their homes. We'll get the money we loaned back." She paused to see their stunned looks and wondered if she were crazy, too.

She hurried on to say, "Mac Burleson has a job now, but he can't catch up on his mortgage if we don't help him."

"We've always done things this way," Larry McClain said. "Your father would never—"

Lori stiffened. "Well, I'm not my father, but he did put me in charge. In fact, I'm going to become more involved in day-to-day working here at the bank. I can see that there aren't any women in management positions. That needs to change, too."

The threesome gave each other panicked looks. "That's not true. Mary O'Brien manages the tellers."

Were these men from the Dark Ages? "I mean women in decision-making positions. It's a changing world out there and we need to keep up. I've seen the profit sheet for this bank. Over the years, it's done very well."

Neal spoke up again. "You can't come in here and just change everything. You're a schoolteacher."

Lori held her temper. "I became an expert when my father put me in charge of his company. Just so you know, not only am I a good teacher, but I also minored in business. So, gentlemen, whether you like it or not, I'm here."

She was feeling a little shaky. What if she was making a mistake? She glanced at her watch. "I think we've said about everything that needs to be said for now. Good morning." She took her purse and walked out.

She needed someone here on her side. She walked to Erin's desk.

The girl smiled when she approached. "Hello, Ms. Hutchinson. How was your meeting?"

"Not as productive as I would have liked." She sat down in the chair next to the desk. "Erin, could you help me?"

The girl nodded. "If I can."

"I'm looking for someone, a woman who is qualified for a managerial position. Could you give me some candidates?"

The pretty brunette looked surprised, but then answered. "That would be Mary O'Brien and Lisa Kramer. They've both worked for the bank for over five years.

I know Lisa has a college degree. I'm not sure Mary does, but she practically runs this bank."

"That's good to know, because I need someone to help me." She was going to need a lot of help. Since her father had never promoted a woman that was one of the things she needed to change. Immediately.

"Could you call a meeting with all the employees?" She looked at her watch. "And call the Silver Spoon and have them send over sandwiches and drinks."

Erin smiled. "This is going to be fun."

"We're going to need our strength to get this bank into the twenty-first century."

Two mornings later, Lori had been awakened by a call from a sick Claire Keenan, asking her for a favor. Would Lori like to take her place as a volunteer in the second grade classroom this afternoon?

There might have been several other things to do, but Lori found she wanted to check out the school. After her trip to the paint store and picking her colors for the bedroom, she had her purchase sent to the house.

She grabbed a quick lunch at the Silver Spoon, and after a friendly chat with Helen, she arrived at Destiny Elementary with time to spare. She went through the office then was taken down the hall to the second grade classroom.

Outside, she was greeted by the teacher. "It's good to meet you, I'm Julie Miller."

"Lori Hutchinson. I'm substituting for Claire Keenan. She's sick."

The young strawberry blonde smiled eagerly. "I'm glad you could make it. I've heard a lot about you."

"Well, I guess Lyle's long-lost daughter would be news in a small town."

Julie smiled. "No, I heard it all from Cassie Yeager. Seems you live in a castle and have a princess bedroom like hers."

That brought a smile to Lori's lips, too. "If only."

"I also heard you teach second grade."

"I did. I was laid off this year."

"I'm sorry to hear that, but you're welcome to come and help out in my class anytime. But it sounds like you've been pretty busy with other projects around town."

Lori blinked. "You must have a good source."

"My sister, Erin, works at the bank. You've really impressed her."

"Oh, Erin. She's been a big help showing me around. There do need to be some changes."

Julie smiled brightly. "I can't tell you how happy I am that you came to Destiny and I hope you stay."

"I'll be here for this year anyway. In fact, my sister and her son will be coming in next week. Zack will be in second grade."

"That's wonderful. Then you'll want to see how I run my class."

Julie Miller opened the door to a room that was buzzing with about twenty-five seven-year-olds. The room was divided in sections, half with desks, the other half with tables and a circle of chairs for reading time.

Suddenly two little blonde girls came up to her—Ellie Larkin and Cassie Yeager.

"Miss Lori, what are you doing here?" Cassie asked.

"Hi, girls. Ellie, your grandmother isn't feeling well today."

Both girls looked worried. "Really?" Ellie said.

"It's nothing serious, don't worry. But she asked if I'd come in her place."

They got excited again. "We're going to try out for our Christmas program today."

"That's wonderful," Lori said. This was what she missed about teaching, the children's enthusiasm.

"It's called Destiny's First Christmas," Cassie said as she clasped her hands together. "And everyone gets to be in it."

"But we want to be the angels," Ellie added.

Just then Mrs. Miller got their attention. "Okay, class, you need to return to your desks. We have a special guest today and we need to show her how well-behaved we are so she'll want to come back." A bright smile. "Maybe Miss Hutchinson will help us with our Christmas play."

CHAPTER SIX

LATER that evening, Jace finally headed home. He was beat to say the least. A twelve-hour day was usually nothing for him, but he'd been off for three weeks. He needed to oversee everything today to make sure that the schedule for tomorrow went off without a hitch. The one thing he knew, he didn't like to be away from Cassie that long. Luckily, he had good childcare.

He came up the road and the welcoming two-story clapboard house came into view. Although the sun had set an hour ago, he had installed plenty of lighting to illuminate the grounds, including the small barn. He had a lot of work yet to do on the place, but a new roof and paint job made the house livable for now.

The barn had been redone, plus he'd added stalls for his two horses, Rocky and Dixie. Maybe it was a luxury he couldn't afford right now, but it was something that had helped Cassie adjust to her move. Luckily he'd been able to hire the neighbor's teenage son to do the feeding and cleaning.

Jace frowned at the sight of a new SUV parked by the back door. Had Heather, the babysitter, gotten a new car? Then dread washed over him. Was it his ex-wife?

Panic surged through him as he got out of his truck

and hurried up the back steps into the mudroom. After shucking his boots, he walked into the kitchen. He froze, then almost with relief, he sagged against the counter when he saw his daughter at the kitchen table with Lori Hutchinson.

He took a moment and watched the interaction of the two. Their blond heads together, working on the math paper. Then Lori reached out and stroked Cassie's hair and it looked as natural as if they were mother and daughter. His throat suddenly went dry. His business partner had a whole new side to her, a very appealing side.

Too appealing. Lorelei Hutchinson was beginning to be more than a business partner and a pretty face. She had him thinking about the things he'd always wanted in his life. In his daughter's life.

Cassie finally turned to him. "Daddy." She got up and rushed over to him. "You're home."

He hugged her, but his gaze was on Lori. "Yes, sorry I'm so late."

"It's okay," she said. "Miss Lori drove me home." His daughter gave him a bright smile. "She's helping me with my homework."

"I thought Mrs. Keenan was going to do that." He'd made the arrangements with her yesterday.

Lori stood. "Claire would have, but she got sick. I took over for her this afternoon in Cassie's classroom, and I offered to bring her home. I knew you would be busy at the site."

Jace tensed. "My daughter is a priority. I'm never too busy to be here for her. At the very least I should have been called." He glanced around for the teenager who he depended on. "Where's Heather?"

"She had a 'mergency at her house," Cassie told him.

He turned to the jean-clad Lori. She didn't look much older than the high school babysitter.

"We tried to call you but I got your voice mail," Lori said. "It wasn't a problem for me to stay with Cassie until you got home."

Jace felt the air go out of him, remembering he hadn't had his phone on him. He wasn't sure where it was at the site. He looked at Lori. "Thank you. I guess I got wrapped up in getting things back on target at the job site."

"It's okay, Daddy." His daughter looked up at him. "'Cause we made supper."

Great. All he needed was for this woman to get involved in his personal life. "You didn't need to do that."

Lori caught on pretty quickly that Jace didn't want her here. She'd gotten rejection before, so why had his bothered her so much?

"Look, it's just some potato soup and corn bread." She checked her watch. "Oh, my, it's late, I should go."

"No!" Cassie said. "You have to stay. You said you'd help me practice my part in the play." She turned back to her father. "Daddy, Miss Lori has to stay."

Lori hated to put Jace on the spot. Whatever the issues he had about women, she didn't want to know. She had enough to deal with. "It's okay, Cassie, we'll work on it another time."

"But Miss Lori, you wanted to show Daddy your new car, too."

Lori picked up her coat and was slipping it on when Jace came after her.

"Cassie's right, Lori. Please stay."

His husky voice stopped her, but those blue eyes convinced her to change her mind about leaving.

His voice lowered when he continued. "I was rude. I should thank you for spending time with my daughter." He smiled. "Please, stay for supper and let me make it up to you."

Lori glanced away, knowing this man was trouble. She wasn't his type. Men like Jace Yeager didn't give her much notice. *Keep it light.* "We're getting an early start on the Christmas pageant. How are you at playing the part of an angel?"

Cassie giggled.

He smiled, too. "Maybe I'd do better playing a devil."

She had no doubt. "I guess I could write in that part."

She knew coming here would be crossing the line. They worked together, but it needed to stay business. Instead she was in Jace Yeager's home. And even with all the unfinished projects he had going on, it already felt like a real home. It set off a different kind of yearning inside her. That elusive traditional family she'd always wanted. Something all the money from her inheritance couldn't buy her.

Two hours later, Jace finished up the supper dishes, recalling the laughter he heard from his daughter and their guest.

It let him know how much Cassie missed having another female around. A mother. He tensed. Shelly Yeager—soon-to-be Layfield—had never been the typical mother. She'd only cared about money and her social status and her daughter ranked a poor second. More than anything he wanted to give Cassie a home and a life where she'd grow up happy and well-adjusted. He could only do that if she was with him. He'd do whatever it took to keep it that way.

In the past, money, mostly his, had pacified Shelly. Now, she'd landed another prospective husband, a rich one. So she had even more power to keep turning the screws on him, threatening to take Cassie back.

He climbed the steps to his daughter's bedroom and found her already dressed in pajamas. Lori was sitting with her on the canopy bed reading her a story.

His chest tightened at the domestic scene. They looked so much alike they could be mother and daughter. He quickly shook away the thought and walked in.

"The end," Lori said as she closed the book and Cassie yawned.

"I see a very sleepy little girl."

"No, Daddy." She yawned again. "I want another story."

He shook his head and looked at Lori. "The rule is only one bedtime story on a school night." He checked his watch. "Besides, we've taken up enough of Lori's time tonight."

Cassie looked at her. "I'm sorry."

"No, don't be sorry, Cassie." She hugged the girl. "I enjoyed every minute. I told you I read to my nephew."

Cassie's eyes brightened. "Daddy, Lori's nephew, Zack, is coming here to live. He's going to be in my class."

"That'll be nice. How about we talk about it tomorrow? Now, you go to sleep."

Jace watched Lori and his daughter exchange another hug, then she got up and left the room. After he kissed his daughter, he turned off the light and headed downstairs. He found Lori putting on her coat and heading for the back door.

"Trying to make your escape?"

She turned around. "I'm sure you're tired, too."

He walked to her. "I think you might win that contest. Spending four hours with my daughter, not counting the time at school, had to be exhausting."

She smiled. "Remember, I'm a trained professional."

His gut tightened at the teasing glint in her incredible eyes. "And I know my daughter. She can try anyone's patience, but she's the love of my life."

He saw Lori's expression turn a little sad. "She's a lucky little girl." She turned away. "I should get home."

Something made him go after her. Before she could make it to the back door, he reached for her and turned her around. "I wish things could have been different for you, Lori. I'm sorry that you had to suffer as a child."

She shook her head. "It was a long time ago and I've dealt with it."

"Hey, you can't fool a foster kid. I was in the system most of my life. We're experts on rejection."

Her gaze went to his, those brown eyes compelling. "What happened to your family?"

"My parents were in a car accident when I was eight. What relatives I had didn't want me, so I went into foster care."

"Oh, Jace," she whispered.

Her little breathless gasp caused a different kind of reaction from him. Then he saw the tears in her eyes.

His chest tightened. "Hey, don't. I survived. Look at me. A success story."

Jace reached out and touched her cheek. The next thing he knew he pulled her toward him, then wrapped her in his arms. He silenced a groan as he felt her sweet body tucked against his. It had been so long since he'd held a woman. So long since he'd felt the warmth, the glorious softness.

He pulled back trying to put some space between them, but couldn't seem to let her go. His gaze went to her face; her dark eyes mirrored the same desire. He was in big trouble.

He lowered his head and whispered, "This is probably a really bad idea." His mouth brushed over hers, once, then again. Each time she made a little breathy sound that ripped at his gut until he couldn't resist any longer and he captured her tempting mouth.

She wrapped her arms around his neck and leaned into him as her fingers played with the hair at his nape. He pushed his tongue into her mouth and found heaven. She was the sweetest woman he'd ever tasted, and the last thing he ever wanted to do was stop. He wanted so much more, but also knew he couldn't have it.

He tore his mouth away and took a step back. "Damn, woman. You pack a punch. I just can't..."

"It's okay." She pulled her coat tighter. "It would be crazy to start something."

He couldn't believe how badly he wanted to. "Right. Bad idea. We're business partners. Besides, I have room for only one female in my life. Cassie."

Her gaze wouldn't meet his. "I should go."

"Let me walk you out."

"No, you don't need to do that. It's too cold."

He tried to make light of the situation. "Right now, I could use a blast of cold air." He followed her out. Grabbing his coat off the hook, he slipped it on as they went through the mudroom. The frigid air hit him hard as they hurried out to the well-lit driveway and around to her side of the car.

"Nice ride." He glanced over the four-wheel-drive SUV. "You're ready for the snow." He held on to the door so she couldn't rush off. "Are you coming by the site tomorrow?"

"No." She paused. "Unless you need me for something."

He found he wanted to see her again. "I guess not."

"Okay then, good night, Jace."

"Thank you, Lori. Thank you for being there for Cassie."

"You're welcome. Goodbye." She shut her door and started the engine and was backing out of the drive before Jace could stop her. That was the last thing he needed to do. He didn't need to be involved with this woman.

Any woman.

It would be a long time before he could trust again. But if he let her, Lori Hutchinson could come close to melting his cold, cold heart.

Lori had spent the past two days at the bank where she'd been trying to familiarize herself with her father's business dealings. How many people expected her to fail at this?

She'd stayed far away from Jace Yeager, although that didn't change the fact that she'd been thinking about him.

Had he been thinking about her? No. If he had been, wouldn't he have called? Or maybe he'd resisted, knowing getting involved could create more problems.

Lori looked up from the desk as Erin walked into

the office. The receptionist had been such a big help to her, going through files and being the liaison between Lori and Dennis Bradley's office.

Erin sat down in the chair across from the desk. "I found this in an old personnel file, and it's kind of interesting. Kaley Sims did used to work for Mr. Hutchinson. It states that she managed his properties up until two years ago."

Lori had found this woman's notes on several contracts. "Why isn't she working for him now?"

Erin gave her a funny look and glanced away.

"You know something?"

"It's just some bank gossip, but there might have been something between Kaley and Mr. Hutchinson, beyond professional."

So her father had someone after his divorce. "I take it they were discreet."

"They went to business and social functions together, but no one saw any signs of affection between them."

Lori shrugged. "Maybe that's the reason Kaley left here. She wanted more from Lyle."

"If you want to talk to her, I could call her mother and see if she's available to come back to work here."

Lori needed the help. "I guess it wouldn't hurt to call. I sure could use the help, especially someone who already knows the business. I don't want to put in twelve-hour days."

Had Lyle Hutchinson become that much of a recluse that all he did was work? She was curious. Had her father driven off Kaley?

"Okay, I'll make the call tomorrow," Erin said as she stood. "Is there anything more you need today?"

Lori checked her watch. It was after five o'clock. "I'm sorry. You need to get home."

"Normally I'd stay, but I have a date tonight."

Lori smiled, feeling a little twinge of envy, and immediately thought about Jace. Since the kiss she hadn't heard a word from him in two days. *Stop.* She couldn't let one kiss affect her. She wasn't a teenager. "Well, you're great, Erin. I'm grateful to have all your help." She paused. "How would you like to be my assistant?"

"Really?"

"Really. But you have to promise to stay in college. We can schedule hours around your classes, and you'll get a pay raise."

"Oh, wow. Thank you. I'd love to be your assistant." Erin reached out and shook her hand. "And everyone thought you coming to town would be a bad thing."

"Oh, they did, huh?"

This time, Erin hesitated. "I think they thought that a lot of jobs might be lost." The pretty brunette beamed. "Instead, you've come here and come up with ideas so people can save their homes, and you're helping women advance, too."

Lori was happy she could do something. "So it's a good thing?"

"Very good." The girl turned and left the office.

Lori sank back into her father's overstuffed leather chair. "Lyle Hutchinson, you must have really been some kind of tyrant. What made you so unhappy?"

She thought about the sizable amount of money Lyle had acquired over the years. When the waiting period was over next year, she'd never be able to spend it all. She could give the money away. Right now, she received a large income just from his properties.

Sadness hit her hard. Seeing how her father lived, she realized he'd died a lonely man. Outside his few male friends, he didn't go out with anyone. "I was always there, Dad. Just a call away. Your daughter. I would have loved to spend time with you."

It might be too late for a family with her father, but there was a second chance, because she had a sister and nephew. Gina and Zack would always be her family.

A few days had passed and Jace hadn't been able to get Lori, or the kiss, out of his head. Even working nonstop at the site couldn't keep his mind from wandering back to Lori Hutchinson. Until work came to a sudden halt when problems with the staircase came up and didn't meet code. They had to make some changes in the design.

He needed Lori's okay to move ahead with the architect's revisions. He went by the bank, but discovered she was at home. So that was where he was headed when he realized he was looking forward to seeing her. Glad for the excuse.

He pulled up out front, sat there a moment to pull it together. Then he jerked open the door and got out of his truck. The early November day was cold. He looked up at the gray sky, glad that they'd finished the outside of the building. At the very least they would get some rain.

He walked up to the porch, but slowed his steps at the door, feeling his heart rate accelerate.

He hadn't seen Lori since the night at his house. When she had been in his arms. He released a breath. Even time away didn't change the fact that he was eager to see her.

Maggie opened the door with her usual smile. "Mr. Yeager. It's nice to see you again."

He stepped inside. "Hi, Maggie. Is Lori here?" He held up his folder. "I have more papers for her to sign," he said, suddenly hearing the noises coming from upstairs.

"Oh, she's here." Maggie grinned. "Been working all day trying to get things finished before her sister and nephew's arrival tomorrow. Charlie's helping." There was a big thud and Maggie looked concerned. "But maybe you should have a look."

Jace nodded. He headed for the stairs and took them two at a time to shorten the trip. He walked down the hall and was surprised when he found the source of the noise. It was coming from the room across from Lori's childhood bedroom.

He looked in the slightly open door and found Charlie and Lori kneeling on the floor with sections of wood spread out. The two were engrossed in reading a sheet of directions.

Lori brushed back a strand of hair, revealing her pretty face. Then his heart went soaring and his body heated up as she reached for something and her jeans pulled taut over her cute, rounded bottom.

"It says right here that *A* goes into *B*. Okay we got that, but I can't find the next piece." She held up the sheet of paper. "Do you see this one?"

Hiding his amusement, Jace stepped into the room. "Could you two use some help?"

They both swung around. "Mr. Yeager," Charlie said and got to his feet. "Oh, yes, we could use your expertise. And since you're here to help, I'll go do my work." The older man left, looking relieved.

Jace turned back at Lori. "What are you building?"

"Bunk beds," she offered.

Jace pulled off his jacket as he glanced over the stacks of boxes. "Why not buy it assembled?"

Lori stood. "I didn't have time to go to Durango, so I got them online. I didn't realize it would come in boxes."

"You should have called me. I would have sent Mac over." He took the paper from her. Their hands brushed, and he quickly busied himself by looking over the directions. "Okay, let's lay out the rails and the end pieces."

Lori took one end and he took the other. He set the bolts, then went to her end. He was close and could breathe in her scent, which distracted the hell out of him. He finally got the bolt tightened. He got up and went to the other side, away from temptation, but she followed him.

Over the next hour, they'd become engrossed in building the elaborate bunk-bed set. They stood back and looked over their accomplishment.

"Not bad work." He glanced at the woman beside him and saw her blink. "What's wrong?"

She shook her head. "Zack is going to love it. He's had to share a room with his mother the past few months. Thank you for this."

"Not a problem," he told her. "You helped me out with Cassie. I know how much you want to make a home for your sister and your nephew."

"They've had a rough time of it lately." She put on a smile. "It's going to be great for them to be here."

Jace looked around the freshly painted blue room. "I thought you were going to put Zack in your old bedroom."

She shrugged. "I tried, but I couldn't bring myself

to touch it." She looked at him and he saw the pain in her eyes. "I guess I'm still trying to figure out why my father kept it the same all these years. Crazy, huh?"

Unable to help himself, he draped his arm across her shoulders. "It's okay, Lori. You have a lot to work through. You've pulled up your roots and come back here. There's a lot to deal with."

She looked up. "But I have the funds now to take care of my family."

That was the one thing that kind of bothered him. He'd been pretty well-off financially before his divorce, but to have a woman with so much money when he was trying to scrape by hit him in his pride. But he truly thought it bothered her more.

"So how does it feel to have that kind of money?"

She scrunched up her nose. "Oddly strange," she admitted. "It's far too much. I'm the kind of girl who's had to work all my life, and when I lost my job a few months ago, I was really worried about what was going to happen, especially for Gina and Zack."

"They have you now."

She looked up at him, her eyes bright and rich in color. "And I have them. I wouldn't stay here in Destiny, money or no money, if they couldn't be with me. Their safety and well-being is the most important thing to me."

He frowned. "Why wouldn't they be safe here?"

She glanced away. "It's just a worry I have."

He touched her chin to get her to look at him. "Lori, what aren't you telling me? Is someone threatening you or your family?"

She finally looked at him. "It's Gina's ex-husband. He'll be getting out of jail soon."

"Why did he go to jail?"

"Look, Jace, I'm not sure Gina wants anyone to know her private business."

"I'm not a gossip. If your family needs protection then I want to help."

Lori was surprised at his offer. She wasn't used to anyone helping them. "Eric is in for drug possession and spousal abuse. He swore when he got out he'd make Gina pay for having him arrested."

She felt Jace tense. "So that's why you were headed out of state?"

She nodded.

"Does this Eric guy know where Gina is moving to?"

"No one knows. We haven't even told Zack. I want so badly for Gina to make a life here. She has full custody of her son, but we're still afraid of what the man might do."

"This house has a security system. I hope you're using it."

She nodded.

"And I think you should have protection for yourself, also. You're worth a lot of money and you could be a target for threats from this guy. Maybe a security guard isn't out of the question."

"I can't let my life be dictated by a coward."

Jace clenched his fists. "I don't care for a creep who gets his jollies by beating women, either, but you still need to take precautions. Not an armed guard, but maybe a security man disguised as a gardener or handyman."

She hesitated. "If Gina will agree."

"What about you? I'm sure you've had some run-ins with your brother-in-law."

Lori shivered, recalling Eric's threats.

Jace's eyes narrowed. "Did he hurt you, too?"

"Just a few shoves here and there, but I couldn't let him hurt Gina."

He cursed and walked away, then came back to her. He reached out and cupped her face. "He put his hands on you, Lori. No man ever has the right to do that unless the woman wants it."

She stared into his eyes. That was the problem. She wanted Jace's hands on her. Badly.

CHAPTER SEVEN

JACE had trouble letting go of Lori. He knew the minute he touched her again this would happen.

He cursed under his breath. "This isn't a good idea." His gaze searched her pretty face, those bedroom eyes, then he stopped at her perfect rosy mouth. He suddenly felt like a man dying of thirst. Especially when her tongue darted out over her lips. With a groan, he leaned down and brushed his mouth across hers, hearing her quick intake of breath.

"I swore I'd stay away from you. We shouldn't start something...." His mouth brushed over hers again and then again. "My life doesn't need to get any more complicated."

"Mine, either," she whispered.

He fought the smile, but it didn't stop the hunger, or the anticipation of the kiss he so desperately wanted more than his next breath.

Then Lori took the decision out of his hands as she rose up on her toes and pressed her mouth against his. That was all it took. His arms circled her waist and he pulled her against him, unable to tolerate the space between them any longer. Their bodies meshed so easily it was as if they were meant to be together. All he knew was he didn't want to let her go anytime soon.

His mouth slanted over hers, wanting to taste her, but all too quickly they were getting carried away.

He tore his mouth from hers, and trailed kisses along her jaw to her ear. "I could get drunk on you." Then he let his tongue trace her earlobe, feeling her shiver. He found her mouth again for another hungry kiss.

Then suddenly the sound of his cell phone brought him back to reality. He stepped back, and his gaze was drawn to Lori's thoroughly kissed mouth. Desire shot through him and he had to turn away.

"Yeager," he growled into the phone.

"Hey, Jace," Toby said. "What happened? I thought you were coming right back."

He glanced over his shoulder at Lori. "Sorry, something came up. I'm heading back now." He shut his phone. "I'm needed at the site."

"Of course," Lori said, wrapping honey-blond strands behind her ear. "I can't thank you enough for your help. I couldn't have done this on my own."

Unable to resist, he went back to her and stole another kiss. They were both breathless by the time he released her. "Your sister and nephew arrive tomorrow, right?"

She nodded.

"Okay, I'll have a security guy in place here before you get back from the airport." When Lori started to disagree, he put his finger over those very inviting lips. "He'll work with Charlie so Gina doesn't have to know. I want you and your family safe."

Lori smiled. "I wasn't going to disagree. I think it's a good idea."

He blinked. "You're agreeing with me? That's a first."

"Don't get used to it, Yeager."

The next afternoon, Lori had agreed to let Charlie drive her father's town car the 47 miles to the Durango airport to pick up Gina and Zack.

She couldn't hide her excitement as she watched her sister and nephew come out of the terminal. She gave them a big hug, then herded them into the backseat of the car while Charlie stowed the few belongings in the trunk.

They talked all the way to Destiny. It was as if they'd been apart for months instead of only two weeks.

Lori kept hugging her seven-year-old nephew beside her in the backseat. She'd missed him. "Zack. I was able to work in the second grade classroom last week and met your teacher, Mrs. Miller. I think you're going to like her."

The little dark-haired child didn't look happy. "But I don't know any kids."

"The class knows you're coming. And there's Ellie and Cassie, who will help you learn your way around the school."

"Girls?"

That brought a smile as Lori looked at her sister. Although beautiful, with her rich, dark brown hair and wide green eyes, Regina Williams Lowell looked a little pale and far too thin. Lori hoped she could erase her sister's fear once she knew she was safe living in Destiny. And her son would blossom here, too.

"It might take a little time, Zack, but I know you'll make lots of friends."

They drove through town, past the square and fountain, then down the row of storefronts. "Just wait. Soon they'll be putting up a big Christmas tree with colorful lights. The whole town will be decorated."

"Can we have a Christmas tree at your house?"

Suddenly Lori got excited. This was going to be a special holiday. And a new year that meant a fresh beginning for all of them. "You bet we can. And you can pick out a really big one."

Zack grinned as they pulled through the gate. "Wow!" The boy's eyes lit up. "Mom, are we really going to live here?"

"We sure are." Gina looked like a kid herself. "Although, I can hardly believe it myself."

Lori glanced at her sister's face. "That was my first reaction, too. Welcome to Hutchinson House."

Charlie drove up the long drive and stopped in front of the house. He opened the back door and helped them out, then sent them up the porch steps.

Maggie swung open the front door and opened her arms. "Welcome, welcome," the older woman said as she swept them inside the warm house. First, the older woman embraced Zack, then Gina.

"We're so happy you're here. Oh, my, and to have a child in this big house again is wonderful."

"It's so big," Zack said. "What if I get lost?"

"Don't worry. Charlie will show you around. The important thing to remember is there are two sets of stairs. One leads down here." Maggie pointed to the circular staircase. "Most important, the other one leads to the kitchen and I'm usually there."

Zack looked a little more comfortable after the quick explanation.

Maggie turned to Gina and smiled. "Goodness, my, you look so much like Lorelei and your mother. Your coloring might be different, but there's no doubt you're sisters. And both beautiful."

Her sister seemed embarrassed. "Thank you."

"How was your flight?"

"Not too bad, especially sitting in first class." Gina glanced at Lori. "It was a big treat for Zack and me."

"Well, we're planning on a lot of treats for Master Zack." The older woman placed her hands on the boy's shoulders. "After you go and see your new bedroom, come down to the kitchen so you can tell me all your favorite foods. And if it's okay with your mother you can sample some of my cookies." Maggie raised a hand and glanced at Gina. "I promise not to spoil his appetite for our special dinner tonight."

"The way my son eats, I doubt anything can." Gina smiled, which made Lori hopeful that her sister would start relaxing.

"We're also having a couple of guests for dinner," Maggie announced. "Mr. Yeager and his daughter, Cassie. And before you frown, Zack, the girl has a horse. That's a good friend to have."

Lori was surprised by the news, and a little too happy, feeling a stir of excitement. Maybe he was bringing the security guard they'd talked about.

Maggie gave her the answer. "Jace has something to discuss with you. So I invited them both to dinner."

Her nephew called to her. "Can I go see my new bedroom, Aunt Lori?"

"Sure. How about we all head up and see it?"

The child ran ahead of them, following Charlie up the steps with the bags.

Lori hung back with Gina. "Lori, you never said the place was a—" she looked around the huge entry, her eyes wide "—mansion."

"Okay, so the Hutchinson family liked things on the large size. Now that you and Zack are here, it's already starting to feel more like a home." She hugged her sister again. "I want you and Zack to think of this place as home. More important, I want you to feel safe here."

Gina looked a little panicked. "Just so long as Eric never finds us."

Another precaution had been for Gina to take back her maiden name, Williams.

"If he shows up in Destiny, you can believe he'll be arrested." Jace had convinced her to let Sheriff Reed Larkin in on the situation.

"Does everyone in town know?"

Lori shook her head. "No, only the people who work here at the house. And Jace Yeager, my business partner. He suggested that I hire some security." Lori raised a hand. "Only just as a precaution."

"That has to cost a lot of money."

Lori smiled. "Look at this place, Gina. Lyle Hutchinson might have been a lousy father, but he knew how to make money. And taking care of you and Zack is worth whatever it costs."

Tears filled her sister's eyes. "Thank you."

Before Lori started crying, too, she said, "Come on, I hope you like your bedroom. It's got a connecting bath with Zack's room."

They started up the steps arm in arm. "I can't imagine I wouldn't love it."

"If you don't like it, you can redo it. You're the one

with experience. In fact, I'd be happy if you would redo the entire place."

Gina turned to Lori. "Decorating a boutique window doesn't make me a professional." She looked around. "It's so grand as it is."

Lori knew what her sister had been thinking. There had been a lot of times when their living quarters hadn't been that great, especially when Gina was married. Being a school dropout, Eric hadn't been able to do much, and he spent his paycheck on alcohol instead of diapers.

"This is our fresh start, Gina. You don't have to worry about Eric anymore. I'm not going to let anything happen to either you or Zack."

Lori prayed that was a promise she could keep.

Three hours later, Jace walked up the steps to the Hutchinson home, carrying a bottle of wine and flowers. He normally didn't take Cassie out on a school night, but this was a special occasion and he knew how it was to be the new kid in town.

Okay, the truth was he wanted to see Lori. He'd tried to keep focused on work, but she was messing with his head. Last night he couldn't sleep, recalling their kisses, but he knew from now on that he had to keep his hands to himself. If Shelly got wind of any of this, she would make his life miserable just for the hell of it.

He had to focus on Cassie and getting the project completed on time. That was all. Once he had custody settled, he could think about a life for himself.

The front door opened and a little boy stuck his head out. "Hi," he said shyly.

His daughter answered back. "Hi. You're Zack. I'm Cassie Yeager. You're going to be in my class at school."

The boy looked up at Jace as if asking for help. His daughter never had a problem with being shy.

"I'm Jace. I think your aunt is expecting us."

Zack nodded. "You want to come in?"

"Sounds good. It's a little cold out here."

The door opened wider as another woman appeared. She smiled, showing off the resemblance to Lori.

"Hello, you must be Gina. I'm Jace Yeager. I'm Lori's business partner."

She took his hand. "It's nice to meet you."

"This is my daughter, Cassie."

His daughter beamed as she came up to Gina. "Hi, Miss Gina. My dad brought you flowers and for Miss Lori, wine. And I bought Zack a school sweatshirt." She held up the burgundy-colored shirt with Destiny Elementary School printed on it.

"Hello, Cassie. That's very nice."

Cassie turned to Zack. "My dad said you have a new bedroom."

"Yeah, it's cool."

"Can I see it?"

Zack looked at his mother for permission. With Gina's nod the two seven-year-olds took off upstairs.

"My son's a little shy," Gina admitted.

"Well, that won't last long if Cassie has anything to say about it."

He finally got a smile out of the pretty dark-haired woman with green eyes. There was definitely a strong resemblance between the two sisters, except for their coloring. Both women were lovely.

"Here, these are for you. Welcome to Destiny."

He watched her blush as she took the bouquet. "Thank you."

"It's rough having to pick up and move everything. I had to do it about six months ago, but it was worth it. Destiny is a wonderful place to raise kids. Cassie loves it here."

"I'm glad." Gina hesitated. "Lori said she told you about my...situation."

He watched her hesitation, maybe more embarrassment. "I assure you, Gina, no one else will know about your past. It's no one's business. Your sister only wants you safe. I agreed to help her take some precautions."

"I appreciate it, really. I'm sure Eric wouldn't think to look for us here. He knows nothing about Lori's father." She sighed. "But I wouldn't put anything past him. So I thank you for the extra security."

Jace was about to speak when Lori came down the steps. She was wearing a black turtleneck sweater and gray slacks. He was caught up in her grace as she descended the winding stairs. She smiled at him, and his insides went all haywire.

Lori felt Jace's gaze on her and it made her nervous, also a little warm. She'd missed seeing him. The last time had only been a little over twenty-four hours ago when he'd helped her with the bed, and they almost fell into it. A warm shiver moved up her spine. How did he feel about it?

She walked across the tiled floor, seeing her sister holding flowers. That was so nice of him. "Hi, Jace."

"Lori."

She went to him. "Sorry, I wasn't here when you arrived. I just saw Cassie upstairs."

"Has she reorganized Zack's bedroom yet?"

Lori couldn't help but laugh. "I think he's safe for the moment."

Gina spoke up. "Excuse me. I'll go put these in water, then go up and have the kids wash up for dinner." She turned and walked to the kitchen.

Jace looked at Lori. "I don't want to barge in on your family dinner."

"You're not at all. You're always welcome here," she told him, knowing that was probably admitting too much. "Maggie loves to have company. She hasn't been able to cook this much in a long time."

"Anytime she wants company tell her I'll be here." He held up the bottle. "I brought wine."

Lori smiled. "Why don't we open it?"

"Lead the way," he said and they started toward the dining room. Lori watched as he stared at the dark burgundy wallpaper, dark-stained wainscoting and long, long table with the upholstered chairs, also dark.

"It's pretty bad. This room is like a mausoleum. It's going to be my first redecorating project. In fact, I'll put Gina in charge. I hope you don't mind eating in the kitchen."

"I prefer the kitchen." He glanced down at his jeans and sweater pulled over a collared shirt. He followed Lori to the sideboard. In actuality, he preferred her over it all, but he tried to stay focused on the conversation. "As you can see, I'm not dressed for anything fancy."

Lori thought he was dressed perfectly. The man would look good in...nothing. Oh, no. *Don't think about that.* She busied herself by opening a drawer and searching for a corkscrew. Once she found it, she handed it to him, then crossed to the glass-front hutch and took out two crystal wineglasses.

"Gina won't drink, so we'll have to toast my sister and nephew's arrival on our own."

"I think I can handle that." He managed to uncork the bottle and when she brought over the glasses, he filled them with the rosy liquid.

He held out the stemmed glass to her. She brushed his hand and tried to remain calm. It was only a drink, she told herself.

Jace picked up his. "To yours, Gina's and Zack's new home," he said.

Lori took a slow sip, allowing herself to enjoy the sweet taste. She took another, and soon the alcohol went to her head, making her feel a little more relaxed. Then her eyes connected with Jace, and suddenly her heart was racing once again.

"This tastes nice," she said, unable to get her mouth to work. "I mean, I'm not much of a drinker, but I like this."

His deep sapphire gaze never left hers as he set his glass down on the sideboard. "Let me see." Then he leaned forward and touched his mouth to hers.

She froze, unable to do anything but feel as his firm mouth caressed her lips, coaxing her to open for him with a stroke of his tongue.

She whimpered as her hand rested against his chest, feeling his pounding heart. She only ached for more.

He pulled back a little. "You're right. Sweet." He took her glass from her and set it down beside his. "But I need another taste to be sure."

He bent down and took her mouth again. She went willingly as her arms circled his neck, and she wanted to close out the rest of the world. Just the two of them. She refused to think about how stupid it was to let this happen with Jace. When his tongue stroked against hers, and he drew her against his body, she lost all common sense.

Then it quickly returned when the sound of footsteps overhead alerted them to the fact that the kids were coming.

He broke off, and pressed his head against hers. "Damn, Lorelei Hutchinson, if you don't make me forget my own name."

She could only manage a nod. Then he leaned forward again. "Not that you don't look beautiful thoroughly kissed, but you might have to answer too many questions."

She smoothed her hair. "Tell everyone I'll be in shortly." She took off, knowing she was a fool when it came to this man. It had to stop before someone got hurt.

Jace had trouble concentrating on his pot roast dinner. Why couldn't he keep his hands off Lori? She wasn't even his type. Not that he had a type. He'd sworn off women for the time being. So why had he been trying to play tonsil hockey with her just thirty minutes ago?

"Daddy?"

He turned to his daughter. "What, Cassie?"

"Can Zack go riding with me tomorrow?"

Jace glanced at Gina and saw her concerned look. "Maybe it's a little cold right now, sweetheart. Let Zack and his mother get settled in first. Besides, you both have school all day."

Those pretty blue eyes blinked up at him. "I know, Daddy," she said. "I'm gonna help Zack get used to the class."

Jace fought a smile and stole a glance at Lori, then at the poor boy who'd become his daughter's newest project. "I'm sure Zack appreciates all your help, sweetheart, but remember, Miss Lori is a teacher. She can help, too."

The child looked deflated. "Oh."

"I can sure use your help," Lori said. "And we're all going to be working on the Christmas play together. I'm sure Zack would like to do that."

"I guess," he said. "Are there other boys in the play?"

Cassie nodded. "Everyone is in the play. Cody Peters and Owen Hansen and Willie Burns." She smiled. "And now, you."

Jace wasn't sure he liked how his daughter was smiling at Zack. *Oh, no, not her first crush.*

Maggie came in with dessert and after everyone enjoyed the chocolate cake, the kids were excused and went up to Zack's bedroom.

"Seems like they've become fast friends," Gina said. "I thank you, Jace. Your daughter is helping my son a lot." She glanced at her sister. "I hated that Zack had to go through all the pain of the last few years."

"You need to put that in the past. This is a new start."

Lori reached over and covered her sister's hand. "It's a new beginning, Gina. We're going to keep you safe."

"Lori's right," Jace told her. "The security guard is on duty as we speak. Wyatt McCray will be touring the grounds during the night. He's moved into the room behind the garage. His cover will be he's working with Charlie. No one is going to hurt you or your son again."

Tears formed in Gina's eyes. "Thank you."

Lori spoke up. "Has Eric been released yet?"

"Detective Rogers said he is scheduled to get out this Friday."

"Good." Jace nodded. "You and Zack were gone before he had a chance to know what your plans were. The fewer people who know the better. So we three, Maggie, Charlie, Wyatt and Sheriff Larkin are the only people who know about your situation. You're divorced, and your past life is private."

"I'm grateful, Jace. Thank you." Gina stood. "I think I'll go check on the kids."

Lori watched her sister leave. "She's still scared to death."

"I know," Jace said, hating that he couldn't do more. "And I almost wish the creep would show up here so I could get my hands on him."

"No, I don't want that man anywhere near them ever again. Zack still has nightmares." She put on a smile. "Thank you for all your help."

His gaze held hers for longer than necessary. "Hey, we're partners."

Problem was, he wanted to be so much more.

CHAPTER EIGHT

BY THE end of the week Gina and Zack had settled in and were getting into a routine. Her nephew had started school and was making new friends. Of course, Cassie was still taking charge of Zack's social schedule.

Life was great, Lori thought, as she arrived at the bank that cold, gray November morning. Thank goodness her car had seat warmers to ward off the near-freezing temperatures. She thought about the upcoming holidays and couldn't help but smile. Her family would all be together.

She also thought of Jace. She wanted to invite him and Cassie to Thanksgiving at the house. Would he come? The memory of the kisses they'd shared caused a shiver down her spine. She was crazy to think about a future with the man, especially when he'd been telling her all along he didn't want to get involved.

As she entered her office, she decided not to go to the construction site unless absolutely necessary. Besides, she had plenty to do at the bank to keep her busy for a long time. She looked down at the several stacks of files and paperwork covering the desktop. The last thing she wanted to do was spend all her time managing the number of properties, and the rest of the time at the bank. If only she could hire someone to oversee it all. And she didn't trust the "three amigos" loan officers to handle things on their own. They'd already thought she was in over her head. Maybe she was, but she wasn't going to let them see it.

She'd been working nearly two hours when there was a knock on the door. "Come in," Lori called.

Erin walked in. She wore a simple black A-line skirt and a pin-striped red-and-white blouse. She was carrying a coffee mug and a white paper sack. "Break time?"

"Thank you, I could use it. Everything is getting a little blurry."

"You should have more than coffee. Helen sent over some scones from the Silver Spoon. A thank-you for putting a six-month moratorium on foreclosures."

Lori thought of her own childhood after her mother remarried. They'd had some rough times over the years. "I refuse to let this bank play Scrooge especially with Christmas coming soon. The first thing on the agenda for the first of next year is reworking these loans."

Erin smiled. "You know, the other bank officers aren't happy with your decision."

Lori took a sip of her drink. "Yes. Mr. Neal has already decided to retire." She thought about the generous retirement package her father had given him. He wouldn't be giving up his lifestyle.

"Oh, I almost forgot," Erin said. "I located Kaley Sims. She's working for a management company in Durango. I have the phone number."

"Good. Would you put in a call to her and see if she's willing to talk with me?"

"Of course. Anything else?"

Erin was so efficient at her job, Lori wasn't sure what she would have done without her.

"There is one thing. In looking over my father's properties, I found a place called—" she searched through the list "—Hidden Hills Lodge. I'm not sure if it's a rental property, or what. It doesn't show any reported income."

"Maybe it was a place Mr. Hutchinson had for his personal use. Do you want me to find out more about it?"

Lori shook her head. "No, you have more than enough to do now." Maybe she would look into this herself. She had a great GPS in her new car. Surely she could find her way. She stood. "I'm going to be gone the rest of the afternoon. If you need me, call me on my cell phone."

Maybe it was time she delved a little further into her father's past and the opportunity was right in front of her.

Later that afternoon, Jace got out of his truck as snow flurries floated in the air, clinging to his coat and hat. He took a breath as he walked to the bank. Okay, he'd been avoiding going anywhere he might see Lori Hutchinson. He couldn't seem to keep his hands off the woman, but since he needed her signature on some changes in the project, he didn't have a choice.

He walked through the doors and Erin greeted him. "Is Miss Hutchinson in?"

"No, she's not. She left about noon."

"She go home?"

"No, I've tried to reach her there. I also tried her cell

phone, but it goes to voice mail." Erin frowned. "I'm worried about her, especially with this weather."

Suddenly Jace was concerned, too. "And she didn't say where she was going? A property? Out to the site?"

"That's what I'm worried about. I think she might have gone to the Hidden Hills Lodge."

"Where is this place?"

Erin sat down at her desk and printed out directions from the computer. Jace looked them over. He wasn't sure about this area, only that it was pretty rural.

He wrote down his number and handed it to Erin. "Give me a call if Lori gets in touch with you."

He left as he pulled out his cell phone and gave Claire Keenan a call, asking if she'd watch Cassie a little later, then he hung up and glanced up at the sky. An odd feeling came over him, and not a good one. "Where are you, Lori?"

An hour later, Lori had turned off the highway to a private road, just as her GPS had instructed her to do. She shifted her car into four-wheel drive and began to move slowly along the narrowing path.

It wasn't long before she realized coming today wasn't a good idea. Deciding to go back, she shifted her SUV into Reverse and pushed on the gas pedal, and all that happened was the tires began to spin.

"Great. Please, I don't need this." She glanced out her windshield as her wipers pushed away the blowing snow, which didn't look like it was going to stop anytime soon.

She took out her cell phone. No signal. The one thing that was working was her GPS and it showed her destination was a quarter mile up the road. What should she do? Stay in the car, or walk to Hidden Hills Lodge?

She buttoned her coat, wrapped her scarf around her neck and grabbed a flashlight. She turned on her emergency blinkers and climbed out as the blowing snow hit her. She started her trek up the dirt road and her fear rose. What if she got lost and froze to death? Her thoughts turned to Gina and Zack. And Jace. She cared more about the man than she even wanted to admit. And she wanted to see him again. She quickened her pace, keeping to the center of the dirt road.

Ten minutes later, cold and tired, she finally saw the structure through the blowing snow. It was almost like a mirage in the middle of the trees. She hurried up the steps to the porch and tried the door. Locked.

"Key, where are you?" she murmured, hating to break a window. It took a few minutes, but she found a metal box behind the log bench. After unlocking the dead bolt with nearly frozen fingers, she hurried into the dark structure and closed the door. She reached for the switch on the wall and light illuminated the huge main room. With a gasp, she glanced around. The walls were made out of rough logs and the open-beam ceiling showed off the loft area overhead. Below the upstairs were two doorways leading to bedrooms. The floors were high-gloss pine with large area rugs and overstuffed furniture was arranged in front of a massive fireplace. She found a thermostat on the wall and flipped it, immediately hearing the heater come on.

Shivering, Lori walked to the fireplace and added some logs. With the aid of the gas starter, flames shot over the wood. She sat on the hearth, feeling warmth begin to seep through her chilled body.

Once warmed, she got up and looked around. The kitchen was tucked in the back side of the structure, revealing granite counters and dark cabinets.

She checked out the two bedrooms and a bath on the main floor. Then she climbed up to the loft and found another bedroom. One of the walls was all windows with a view of the forest. She walked into the connecting bathroom. This one had a soaker tub and a huge walk-in shower.

"I guess if you have to be stranded in a snowstorm, a mountain retreat isn't a bad place to be." At least she'd stay warm until someone found her. When? Next spring?

She came back downstairs trying to think of a plan to get her back to town, when a sudden noise drew her attention. She froze as the door opened and Jace Yeager walked in.

"Jace!" she cried and leaped into his arms.

He held her close and whispered, "I take it you're happy to see me."

Jace didn't want to let Lori go. Thank God, she was safe. When he found her deserted car, he wasn't sure if she would find cover.

He pulled back. "Are you crazy, woman? Why did you go out in this weather?"

She blinked back the obvious tears in her eyes. "It wasn't this bad when I started out. Besides, I didn't think it was that far. I tried to go back when the weather turned, but my car got stuck. How did you know where I went?"

"I stopped by the bank. Erin was worried because she couldn't get ahold of you."

"No cell service."

Jace pulled out his phone and examined it. "I have a few bars." He walked toward the front door, where the signal seemed to be a little stronger. "I'll call the Keenans." He punched in the number and prayed he could get a message out. Tim answered.

"Tim. It's Jace." He went on to explain what had happened and that Lori was with him. Most importantly they were safe. He asked Tim to keep Cassie, then to call Lori's sister and let her know they wouldn't be back tonight. "Tell Cassie I love her and not to worry."

He flipped the phone closed and looked around the large room, then he turned back to Lori. "Tim will call Gina and let her know you're okay."

Lori's eyes widened. "We're not going back now?"

He shook his head. "Can't risk it. The storm is too bad so we're safer staying put." That was only partly true. He glanced around, knowing being alone with Lori wasn't safe anywhere. "I'd say this isn't a bad place to be stranded in." He looked at her. "This is one of your properties?"

She nodded. "I think my father came here...to get away."

Jace grinned. "So this was Lyle's secret hideaway?"

Lori frowned. "Please, I don't want that picture in my mind."

Jace looked around at the structure. "Well, whatever he used it for, it's well built. And it seems to have all the modern conveniences."

He went on a search, and found two bedrooms, then a utility room off the kitchen. There was a large generator and tankless water system. "Bingo," he called to Lori. "All the conveniences of home. In fact, it's better than back home." He nodded to the fire. "Propane gas for the kitchen stove and most importantly there's heat."

Lori looked at him. "You really think my father used this place for his own personal use?"

Jace shrugged. "Or he let clients use it. Come on, Lori, did you think your father lived like a monk?"

She shrugged. "Truthfully, I hadn't thought much about my father's personal business in a long time. So what if he came here." She walked to the kitchen. "Maybe we should look for something to eat." Opening the cabinets, she found some canned goods, soup, beans and tuna.

Jace opened the refrigerator. Empty, but the freezer was filled with different cuts of meat, steaks, chicken. "I'll say one thing about Lyle. He believed in being prepared." He pulled out two steaks. "Hungry?"

She arched an eyebrow. "Are you cooking?"

"Hey, I can cook." He took the meat from the package, put it on a plate and into the microwave to defrost. "I've been on my own for a long time."

Lori had wondered about his childhood since he'd mentioned that he'd been in foster care. "How old were you?"

"At eighteen they release you. So you're on your own," he told her as he found a can of green beans in another cabinet. "I got a job working construction and signed up for college classes."

Jace didn't have it much better than she did, Lori thought. "That had to be hard for you."

"Not too bad," Jace said. "I found out later, I had a small inheritance from my parents. It was in trust until I turned twenty-five." He turned on the broiler in the oven then washed his hands. "I used it to start my company. Yeager Construction."

Lori found she liked listening to Jace talk. He was a confident man, in his words and movements. Okay, so she more than liked him.

The microwave dinged and he took out the meat. "How about a little seasoning for your steak?" He held up a small jar.

"Sure."

He added the rub to the meat. She watched as he worked efficiently to prepare the meal. She couldn't help but wonder about how those broad hands and tapered fingers would feel against her skin.

She suddenly heard her name and looked at him. "What?"

He gave her an odd look. "How do you like your steak?"

"Any way you fix it is fine," she said, not really caring at all. Then he smiled and she couldn't find enough air to draw into her lungs.

He winked. "Medium rare it is," he said and slid the tray into the broiler.

Pull it together, girl, she told herself then went to the cupboard. She got out two plates and some flatware from the drawer, then set the table by the fire. No need for candles. She glanced around the room. It looked so intimate.

She went and found a can of pineapple and opened it, then heated the green beans just as the steaks came off the broiler.

Jace added another log to the fire, then they sat down to dinner. "Man, this looks good. Too bad we can't do a salad and some garlic bread."

"I find it amazing that there's so much food here."

"Your father struck me as well prepared. Hold on a minute." He got up, went into the utility room and came out with a bottle of wine. "In every way."

He opened the bottle and poured two glasses. He took them to the table, sat in his chair and began to cut his steak. "If he used this place, he wanted all the comforts money could buy," Jace said, nodding to the wine.

"I'm wondering who he shared all this with."

Jace took a drink. "You might never know. One thing for sure, Lyle had good taste."

She took a sip from her glass, too, and had to agree. Then she began to eat, discovering she was hungry. "I guess I'm still the daughter who wonders why he was such a loner, not even finding time for his only child."

"We can spend hours on that subject." Jace continued to eat. "Some people aren't cut out for the job of parenting."

She hated that her father's rejection still bothered her after all these years. She wanted to think she'd moved on. Maybe not.

She turned her attention back to the conversation. "Shelly hated anything to do with being a mother," Jace said. "That's why I can't let her have Cassie."

"Does Cassie want to live with her mother?"

"Cassie wants to be *loved* by her mother, but my ex is too selfish. She's been jealous of her daughter since her birth. And I'll do anything to prevent Cassie from taking a backseat to that. I know how it feels."

"Cassie's lucky she has you."

He smiled. "It's easy to love that little girl. I know I spoil her, but she's been so happy since she moved here. I have to make it permanent."

Lori put on a smile. "You're a good father, Jace Yeager." She placed her hand on his arm. "I'll help you in any way I can."

He stopped eating. "What do you mean? Help. I can afford to handle this custody battle on my own."

She shook her head. "I know that. I only meant that I know what it's like to not have a father in my life. I was offering moral support, nothing else. But don't be too bullheaded to take any and everything you can to keep your daughter. She needs you in her life, more than you know." Lori stood and carried her plate to the sink. Her appetite was gone.

He came to her. "I'm sorry, Lori."

She could feel his heat behind her. Good Lord, the man made his presence known. She wanted desperately to lean back into him. "For years Lyle Hutchinson never even acknowledged that I existed. I can't tell you how much that hurt."

She hated feeling needy. When Jace turned her around and touched her cheek, she couldn't deny she wanted his comfort.

"I can't imagine doing that to my child. I don't want to think about Cassie not being in my life. I know from experience that adults do dumb things, and in the end it's the kids that get hurt the most."

Lori felt a tear drop and he wiped it away. "It's not fair."

Jace leaned forward. "I wish I could change it." He brushed his mouth across hers. "I wish I could make you feel better."

She released a shaky breath. "What you're doing is nice."

His blue-eyed gaze searched her face. "Damn, Lori.

What I'm thinking about doing with you isn't nice." Then he pulled her close and captured her mouth. Desire burst within her, if possible more intense than ever before, pooling deep in her center. She could feel his heat even through their clothes as she arched into his body. She whimpered her need as his tongue danced against hers.

"You make me want so many things," he breathed as his tongue tormented her skin. He found his way to her collarbone. "I want you, Lorelei Hutchinson." His mouth closed over hers once again, giving her a hint of the pleasure this man offered her.

She arched against him, her fingers threading through his hair, holding him close. Mouths slanted, their tongues mated as his hands moved over her back and down to her bottom, pulling her closer to feel his desire.

Jace was on the edge. On hearing her soft moan, he drew back with his last ounce of sanity. Then he made the mistake of looking into her eyes and all good intentions flew out the window. "Tell me to stop now, Lori."

She swallowed. "I can't, Jace. I don't want you to stop."

His heart skipped a beat as he swung her up into his arms. With a quick glance around, he headed to one of the rooms under the loft, only caring there was a bed past the door.

The daylight was fading, but there was enough light from the main room. He set her down next to a four-poster bed. He captured her mouth in a long kiss, then reached behind her and threw back the thick comforter.

He returned to her. "I've dreamed of being with you

like this." He drew her into his arms. "So be sure you want the same."

She nodded.

He let out a frustrated breath. "You have to do better than that, Lori."

"I'm very sure, Jace."

Those big brown eyes looked up at him. He inhaled her soft scent and was lost, so lost that he couldn't think about anything except sharing this intimacy with this special woman.

His mouth descended to hers and the rest of the snowstorm and the world disappeared. There was only the two of them caught up in their own storm.

CHAPTER NINE

SOMETIME around dawn, Jace woke suddenly, aware he wasn't alone in bed. And it wasn't his bed. He blinked and raised his head from the pillow to find Lori beside him. He bit back a groan as images of last night came flooding into his mind.

He'd come looking for her, afraid she'd been stranded in the freak storm. He found her all right, and had given in to temptation. They'd made love last night. Right now her sweet body pressed against his had him aching again.

He lay his head back on the pillow. Why did she have to come into his life now? He didn't have anything to offer her. Not a future anyway. He couldn't let anyone distract him from getting custody of Cassie.

Lori stirred, then rolled over and peered at him through the dim light. Her soft yellow hair was mussed, but definitely added to her sex appeal.

"Hi," she said in a husky voice that had him thinking about forgetting everything and getting lost in her once again.

"Hi, yourself."

She pulled the sheet up to cover her breasts. "I guess

this is what they call the awkward morning-after moment."

He knew Lori well enough to know that she wasn't the type to jump into bed with just any man. That wasn't the type he needed right now. "The last thing I want to do is make you feel uncomfortable," he said, and leaned toward her. "It's just us, Lori."

She glanced away shyly. "I haven't had a relationship since college."

He found that made him happy. "That's hard to believe." He touched her face. "You're a very beautiful woman, Lorelei Hutchinson."

"Thank you." She glanced away. "I didn't have time for a personal life. Gina and Zack needed me."

"I take it Gina's ex has caused her and you a lot of trouble."

She nodded. "Sober Eric had a mean streak, but when drunk he was really scary. Even with his obvious abuse, it took a lot to convince Gina that the man would never change. Then one day he went after Zack and she finally realized how dangerous he was. That's what it took for her to go to court and testify against him. After that Eric threatened to come after her." Lori's large eyes met his. "That's why it was so hard for me to come to Destiny. When my father made the stipulation in the will about staying a year, I wasn't sure if I could."

"I'm glad you did," he told her, unable to stop touching her. His hand moved over her bare arm, her skin so soft.

She looked surprised. "Is that because I rescued your project?"

"No, it's because you're beautiful and generous." He decided not to fight whatever was going on between them any longer. He leaned down and brushed his mouth over hers, enjoying that she eagerly opened for him. He drew back and added, "You've also taken time with Cassie. Before we moved here she didn't have much female attention."

Lori wasn't sure what she'd expected this morning, but not this. "It's easy to be nice to her. Cassie's a sweet girl."

"Hey, what about me?"

She wrinkled her nose. "I wouldn't call you sweet. Not your disposition anyway."

"Maybe I can change your mind." He caressed her mouth again. "Is that any better?"

"Fishing for a compliment?"

He shifted against her. "How about we continue this without conversation?"

Though Lori wanted the same thing, they needed to get home. "Shouldn't we think about heading back?"

"It's barely dawn." He started working his magic as his mouth moved upward along her jawline. "What's your hurry?" His tongue circled her ear. "Are you trying to get rid of me?"

She gasped, unable to fight the sensation. "No, it's just that it's…" She forgot what she wanted to say as his lips continued along her neck. "Don't we need to leave?"

He raised his head and she could see the desire in his eyes. "I want to do one thing right and it only involves the two of us." He arched an eyebrow. "But if you'd rather go out in that cold weather and start digging out, I'll do it. Your choice."

Lori knew what she wanted, all right. This man. But the fear was that she could never really have him. Last night and these few early hours might be all she would ever have. She wrapped her arms around his neck and pulled his mouth down to hers. "I choose you."

Two hours later, Jace stood at the railing on the cabin porch, drinking coffee. The sun was bright, reflecting off the ten inches of snow covering the ground. The highways would be plowed by now, but not the private road that led to the cabin. He had four-wheel drive on his truck, so they could probably get out and make it to the main road. It better be sooner than later before he got in any deeper.

He had no regrets being with Lori. Making love with her had been incredible. He'd never felt anything like it in his life. Even the best times during his marriage hadn't come close to what he'd shared with Lori.

In just the past three weeks, he'd come to care about this woman more than he had any business doing. But he had strong feelings for Lori and that scared the hell out of him.

Worse, there was no guarantee and he couldn't even offer her a future. He had no extra money. Hell, he needed to rebuild his business. He had to get things settled with the custody issue before he could have a personal life. The question was, would he be able to walk away from Lori? Did he want to?

The front door opened and she stepped out. "I wondered where you went."

"Sorry." He pulled up the collar on her coat and kissed her. "I was just figuring out if we can make it back to town."

"I wouldn't mind getting stuck here a few more days," she admitted. "It's beautiful."

He wouldn't mind pushing reality away for a little

time with this woman. "That would be nice, but we both have jobs to do. Family to take care of."

"Oh, gosh. Gina. I bet she's going crazy with worry."

"Tim called her last night."

"She'll still worry, and be afraid."

Jace wondered who worried about Lori. Seemed she took care of everyone else. "Gina and Zack have Wyatt McCray, Lori. He'll protect them."

"I know," she said with a smile.

His heart began pounding in his chest. The effect she had on him could be a big distraction.

"Thank you for giving us that peace of mind. You've been so kind."

He wondered if she'd always think that. "I didn't do that much."

Those dark eyes locked with his. "You seem to be there whenever I need you."

He found he might not mind being that man. He leaned down to kiss her when he heard something and looked toward the road. "Looks like we're getting rescued."

Jace pointed to a large truck with a plow attached to the front. It stopped a few yards from the door and Toby and Joe climbed out.

Smiling brightly, his foreman called, "I hear some-one here might need a ride back to town."

"Toby," Lori cried and hurried down the steps Jace had cleared earlier.

He watched as she ran through the snow to get to Toby. She hugged the big foreman. Jace felt a stab of jealousy stir inside him, but he didn't have any right to claim her. Not yet, maybe never.

* * *

After stopping to get Jace's truck, the ride back to town took about thirty minutes. He followed behind the plow truck until they reached the highway. After Lori gave Toby her car keys, she got into Jace's truck and drove to the Keenan Inn.

She knew she should probably go straight to the house but asked Toby to tow her car to the inn. Besides, she wasn't ready to leave Jace yet.

When they got to the porch, the door opened and they were immediately greeted by Claire and Tim.

"Well, you had yourself quite an adventure," Tim said.

Lori felt a blush rising up her neck as they crossed the threshold. "I guess I should pay better attention to the weather forecast before heading out into the countryside. I did discover my father has a lovely cabin. Thank goodness there was heat."

"Where's Cassie?" Jace asked, looking around.

Claire looked worried. "She's in the kitchen. She's with one of our new guests."

Lori caught Jace's frown. Then he took off and Lori followed him through the dining area and into the large kitchen.

She found Cassie at the counter with a tall, statuesque woman. Her hair was a glossy black in a blunt shoulder-length cut. Her face was flawless, her eyes an azure-blue. She was a beautiful woman until she flashed a hard look at Jace.

The child ran to him. "Daddy. Daddy, you're back."

"Yes, baby." He hugged his daughter. "I told you we got stuck in the snow."

Cassie looked at Lori. "Miss Lori, did you get stuck, too?"

"Yes, your daddy found me."

The child turned back to her father and whispered, "Daddy, don't let Mommy take me away."

Shelly Yeager stood and walked toward them. "Hello, Jace." She gave Lori a once-over. "It's nice to see that you could make it back to take care of our daughter."

"Shelly. What are you doing here?"

"I came to take my little girl home, of course."

An hour later, Lori's car had arrived and she got in and drove home to find a relieved Gina. She'd taken a long shower and gotten dressed in clean clothes, but couldn't push aside the memories from last night. The incredible night she'd shared with Jace, then reality hit them in the face with Shelly Yeager.

She couldn't stop thinking about Cassie and what her mother had said. Was she going to take the child back to Denver? No, Jace couldn't lose his daughter. She wished she could help him, like he'd helped her.

Lori came downstairs to find her sister in the dining room working with Wyatt. The security guard was a retired army man in his forties with buzz-cut hair. She smiled. He didn't look out of place pulling down twenty-year-old brocade drapes. No doubt this wasn't in the man's job description.

Standing back, Maggie was smiling at what was going on. "It's about time someone got rid of those awful things, don't you think?"

"The room does look brighter." Lori had put her sister in charge of making changes to the house. Gina had told her a few days ago about the plans for the dining room. This was good since it had taken her sister's mind off her ex-husband and any trouble he could cause.

Gina finally turned around. "Oh, yes, you look better now. Still a little tired, but better." She walked over as Maggie left the room. "You okay?"

Lori wasn't sure what she was. "I'm fine. We'll talk later." She sighed, not ready to share what had happened with Jace. "So what are you doing in here?"

Her sister smiled. "I hope you don't mind. I decided to take you up on your suggestion and redo the room. I'm going to order some sheer curtains and light-colored linen drapes. Then I'll plan to strip the wallpaper and paint." She went to the sideboard to find the paint chips. "I've narrowed it down to either shaker beige, or winter sunshine."

Lori tried to focus on her sister's selection and push Jace out of her head. It wasn't working. "You're the decorator, you decide."

"Well, since I'm going to keep the woodwork dark, I'm thinking shaker beige." She glanced at Wyatt. "What do you like?"

Lori found herself smiling. At least something was going well today.

"I can do anything I damn well please," Shelly told Jace as she paced her suite upstairs at the inn. Cassie stayed downstairs with the Keenans while her parents talked.

Jace knew better than to get into a fight with this woman. "I thought you wanted me to have Cassie until the first of next year. You were going to be on an extended honeymoon."

Shelly glanced away. "Plans change."

She was hiding something. "So you're going to just rip Cassie out of school and drag her back to Denver? Well, that's as far as you're going, Shelly. You can't take her out of state, and forget about out of the country." He glanced around the large room and into the connecting bedroom. "Where is your so-called duke?"

Shelly glared at him. "His name is Edmund. And he's not a duke." She raised her head as if she was better than everyone. That was always what Shelly wanted to be, but she had come from the same background he had. "He might not be a duke, but he's got money and a bloodline linked to the royal family. And he can take care of me."

That always got to him. He could never make enough money to satisfy her. "I'm happy for you, Shelly. So why are you here and not with…Edmund?"

"There's been a delay in our wedding plans. I might be having second thoughts. So I decided I'd come to see Cassie. And you. You were always good at calming me down."

Something was up with her, and Jace was going to find out what it was. First stop was to visit his lawyer, Paige Keenan Larkin. No one was taking Cassie away from him.

That afternoon, Lori went into her office at the bank. She had to do something to keep her mind off what had happened at the cabin. She also had to think realistically. She couldn't hold out hope about having a future with Jace. His ex-wife showing up in Destiny proved that.

The most important thing she had to remember was that a child was in the middle of this mess. That meant Cassie's welfare had to come first. She had to stay away from Jace Yeager.

A sudden knock brought her back to the present. "Come in."

Jace walked into her office and her breath caught in her throat. Would she ever stop reacting to this man? Her gaze roamed over Jace's six-foot-two frame, recalling how she'd clung to those broad shoulders.

"Lori."

"Jace. What are you doing here?"

"I needed to see you."

Once again she got caught up in his clean-shaven face. Suddenly the memory of his beard stubble moving against her skin caused her to shiver. The sensation had nearly driven her out of her mind.

He closed the door and went to her desk. "I thought we should talk."

She managed a smile, hoping she was covering her insecurities. "There's no need to. Cassie's mother is in town and you need to take care of them. I understand."

"There's nothing to understand except I don't want you caught up in this mess. I have no idea what Shelly is even doing in Destiny. She was supposed to be in England, married and heading off on her honeymoon."

Lori stood. "Did she give you any explanation?"

"Only that plans change," he told her as he crossed the room toward her.

Lori wanted to back away, to tell Jace to leave, that being together now could be dangerous. Instead, she rounded the desk and met him in the middle of the room.

It wasn't planned, but she didn't turn away when his head descended and his mouth captured hers. She surrendered to his eager assault and returned the kiss, hungry for this man. Finally she came to her senses and broke away. "We shouldn't be doing this."

"Are we breaking any laws?"

"But I don't think Shelly was happy when I walked into the inn with you today."

"It's none of her business."

"Jace, you need to get along with her. At least for Cassie's sake."

He pressed his head against hers. "It's funny. Shelly thinks I'm not worthy of her, but she has this need to interfere in my life."

Lori sighed. "I'm so sorry, Jace."

He drew back. "That's the reason I don't want you involved in this fight, Lori. Maybe it would be best if we cool it for a while. I have to think about Cassie."

Lori knew in her head this was the way it had to be, but her heart still ached. She was losing someone she truly cared about. She managed to nod. "Of course. Besides, we both have too much going on to think that far in the future, or at least to make any promises."

This time he looked surprised.

She moved away from him, or he might see how she truly felt. "Come on, Jace. We work together. Last night we gave in to an attraction. It might not have been the wisest thing to do, but it happened."

He studied her a moment. "Are you saying you regret it?"

"That's not the point."

Jace glared at her. The hell it wasn't. He wanted to reach for her, wanted her to admit more than she was. To tell him how incredible their night was. The worst of it was she couldn't do it any more than he could. "You're right."

She nodded. "Goodbye, Jace."

That was the last thing he wanted to hear, but he would only hurt her more if he stayed. He nodded and walked toward the door. It was a lot harder than he ever dreamed it would be, but he couldn't drag Lori into his fight.

CHAPTER TEN

OVER the next three days, Lori felt like she was walking around in a fog. After the incredible night with Jace, then his quick, easy dismissal of it, how could she not? It would be so easy to pull the covers over her head and just stay in bed. If she were living alone she might do just that. Instead she'd stayed home and gotten involved in Gina's redecorating projects. She tried to fill her time with other things, rather than thinking about a tall, dark and handsome contractor.

Then she'd gotten a call from Erin, telling her that Kaley Sims was in town and had agreed to see her. Anxious for the meeting, Lori arrived right at one o'clock and found an attractive woman with short, honey-blond hair and striking gray eyes waiting in her office.

"Ms. Sims. I'm Lori Hutchinson."

Kaley Sims stood up and they shook hands. "It's nice to meet you. And please call me Kaley." The woman studied her and smiled. "I see some resemblance. You have Lyle's eyes." The woman sobered. "I am sorry to hear of his passing."

"Thank you." Lori motioned for Kaley to sit in the chair across from the desk. "I can't tell you how happy

I am that you agreed to meet with me. I see in my files that you worked for my father a few years back."

Kaley nodded. "I was selling real estate in Destiny before he offered me a job as his property manager. I worked for Lyle about three years."

"You managed all his properties?

"I did."

"I'm impressed," Lori said with a smile. "He has a big operation. I can't handle it all, nor do I have the experience to deal with the properties."

Kaley seemed to relax. "I was a single mother, so I needed the money. And the market was different then. Now, property values are a lot lower. You'd lose a fortune selling in this market."

"See, that's something I don't know. You've probably heard that my father left me in charge of all this."

Kaley's eyes widened, then she smiled. "Lyle would be proud. He talked about you a few times."

Lori froze. "He did?" Why did she still want Lyle's approval?

Kaley looked thoughtful. "One day I came in and found him looking at pictures of you. I think you were about eight or nine in the photo. And of course, Destiny being a small town, everyone knew about your parents' divorce. I mentioned to Lyle how cute you were and he should have you come back for a visit. He said he blew his chance."

Lori felt her chest tighten as she fought tears. This wasn't the time to relive the past. She blinked rapidly at the flooding emotions.

Kaley looked panicked. "I'm sorry, I didn't mean to make you sad."

Lori put on a smile, finding she liked this woman.

"You didn't. I never heard anything from my father since the day I left Destiny."

Kaley sighed. "That was Lyle. The only family he had was his father. Poor Billy had lived to be ninety-two and ended up in the nursing home outside of town until his death a few years ago." Kaley studied her. "Do you remember your grandfather?"

Lori shook her head. "No, he wasn't around that I recall."

"You were probably lucky. Old Billy boy was what my mother called a hell-raiser. He was one of the last of the miners. Spent his gold as fast as he dug it out. Story has it that he loved gambling and women." Kaley raised an eyebrow. "His exploits were well-known around town. He was nearly broke when he suffered a stroke. It was Lyle who took over running what was left of the family fortune."

"Looks like he did a pretty good job," Lori said.

Kaley nodded in agreement. "I worked for the man, so I know how driven he was." She paused. "I also went with him to visit his father. Old Billy Hutchinson never had a good word to say to his son."

Lori didn't want to get her hopes up that there was something redeeming about Lyle Hutchinson.

Nor did she want to know about any personal relationship her father might have had with Kaley.

She quickly brought herself back to the present. "Well, I didn't ask you to come in to reminisce about my childhood. I was wondering if you'd be interested in coming back here and being my property manager." When Kaley started to speak, Lori stopped her. "I'll double whatever my father paid you."

The woman looked shocked to say the least. "You want me to work for you?"

Lori shook her head. "No, I want you to work *with* me. You have a good business sense, or my father wouldn't have trusted you. The one thing my father didn't offer, I will. There's a place in this company for advancement. Seems the women employees have been overlooked."

Kaley laughed. "I'm sure your father is somewhere cursing your words."

For the first time in two days, Lori laughed. It felt good. "So what do you say, Kaley?"

"I hear around town that you have to stay a year before you get your inheritance. Will you leave after that?"

Lori thought about her sister and nephew. How easily they had adapted to their new life. How Lori herself had, but could she be around Jace knowing she'd never have a life with the man?

She looked at Kaley. "News does travel fast, but no, I want to stay. I care about the residents of Destiny and I want to see the town prosper. Maybe it's my Hutchinson blood, but I can't let the town die away. That's why I need your help. I want to bring more businesses here and create more jobs."

The pretty woman studied her. "I'd like that, too, but there's one thing you need to know about your father and me—"

Lori raised her hand to stop her. "No, I don't need to know anything about your personal life. Makes no difference to me. I only care that you want to work for Hutchinson Corporation." Lori mentioned a yearly salary and benefits.

"Looks like you've got me on your team."

Lori smiled. "How soon can you start?"

"Give me a week to get moved back and get my daughter, Heather, settled in school."

"Let me know if there's anything I can do to help." The phone began to ring. She said goodbye to Kaley then answered.

"Lori Hutchinson."

"Hello, Lori. It's Claire Keenan. I hope I'm not interrupting you."

"Of course not, Claire. What can I do for you?"

"I need a big favor."

Tim Keenan eyed his wife of nearly forty years as she hung up the phone. He knew when she was planning something.

"Okay, what's going on, Claire?"

She turned those gorgeous green eyes toward him. She was also trying to distract him. "Whatever do you mean?"

"I thought you were looking forward to your afternoon volunteering in Ellie's class."

"I was," she admitted. "But I think Lori might need it more. She has to miss teaching. Besides, they're starting the Christmas pageant practice. She's volunteered to help."

Tim arched an eyebrow. "I'd say she has plenty to do taking over for Lyle. What's the real reason?"

"Did you happen to notice Lori and Jace when they were here the other day?"

"You mean after they'd been stranded at the cabin overnight? It was hard not to."

She nodded. "There were several looks exchanged between them." She sighed. "That only proves what

I've known from the moment I saw them together. They would be so perfect for each other, if only they got the chance."

He drew his wife into his arms. Besides her big emerald-green eyes, her loving heart was what drew him to her. The feel of her close still stirred him. "Playing matchmaker again?"

"It's just a little nudge. I'm hoping maybe they'll catch a glimpse of each other when Jace picks up Cassie."

"Sounds good in theory, but what about Shelly Yeager?" He raised his eyes toward the ceiling. The suite on the second floor was still occupied by the ex-wife. "She's been all but shadowing Jace's every move."

A mischievous smile appeared on his bride's lovely face. "I have plans for her."

About four-thirty that afternoon, Jace pulled up at the school and parked his truck. He was tired. More like exhausted ever since Shelly had arrived in town. And she showed no sign of leaving anytime soon. Something was up with her, but he couldn't figure out what it was.

He climbed out of his truck and started toward the auditorium. The last thing he wanted to do was anger his ex so much she'd walk away with Cassie. That was the only reason he'd put up with her dogging him everywhere, including several trips to the construction site. She even showed up at his house most evenings.

He hoped that Paige Larkin would get things in order, and fast, so he could finally go to the judge and stop Shelly's daily threats to take their daughter back to Denver. He liked the fact that Cassie got to spend time with her mother, but only if Shelly didn't end up hurting her.

No, he didn't trust Shelly one bit.

He opened the large door and walked into the theater-style room. Up on stage were several kids along with some teachers giving directions. That was when he caught sight of the petite blonde that haunted his dreams.

He froze as he took in Lori. She had on dark slacks and a gray sweater that revealed her curves and small waist. He closed his eyes and could see her lying naked on the big bed, her hair spread out on the pillow, her arms open wide to him.

He released a long breath. As much as he'd tried to forget Lori, she wouldn't leave his head, or his heart. All right, he'd come to care about her, but that didn't mean he could do anything about it.

The rehearsal ended and his daughter came running toward him. "Daddy! Daddy!" She ran into his arms and hugged him. "Did you see me practice?"

He loved seeing her enthusiasm. "I sure did."

Jace glanced up to see Lori coming toward them. His heart thudded in his chest as his gaze ate her up. Those dark eyes, her bright smile. His attention went to her mouth as he recalled how sweet she tasted. He quickly pulled himself back to the present, realizing the direction of his thoughts.

"Hello, Lori."

Her gaze avoided his. "Hi, Jace."

"Looks like you've got your hands full here."

"I don't mind at all. I love working with the kids. I gladly volunteered."

Why couldn't he have met this woman years ago?

Cassie drew his attention back to her. "Daddy, did you know that our play is called *Destiny's First Christmas?* It's about Lori's great-great grandfather Raymond Hutchinson. On Christmas Eve, he was working in his mine, 'The Lucky Strike,' and found gold. That night he made a promise to his wife to build a town."

Jace looked at Lori. "Not exactly the traditional Christmas story."

She shrugged. "Not my choice, but the kids voted to do this one. Probably because of my father's passing."

"No, I'd say because of you. You've made a lot of positive changes in the last month."

She shook her head. "Just trying to bring Lyle Hutchinson's business practices into the new century."

Jace found he didn't want to leave, but he couldn't keep staring at her and remembering how it was to hold her in his arms and make love to her.

Cassie tugged on his coat sleeve. "Daddy, I forgot to tell you, Miss Lori invited us to her house for Thanksgiving."

That surprised Jace.

"She's invited a whole bunch of people. It's going to be a big party. Can we go?"

The last thing he wanted to do was disappoint his daughter. "We'll talk about it. Why don't you go get your books." After he sent Cassie off, he turned back to Lori. "Please, don't feel you have to invite us."

"I don't. I wanted to invite you and Cassie, Jace. Besides, practically everyone else in town is coming. The Keenans and Erin and her family. A lot of the bank employees." She glanced away, not meeting his eyes. "And I plan to extend the invitation to Toby and the construction crew. There's going to be a lot of people at the house. I did it mainly for Gina and Zack so they could meet everyone. So you and Cassie are welcome."

Jace wanted so badly to reach out and touch her. He told himself that would be enough, but that was a lie. He wanted her like he'd never wanted a woman ever. "If you're sure."

She frowned. "Of course. We're business partners."

And that was all they could be, he thought. "Speaking of that, you need to come by the site. We're down to doing the finish trim work and adding fixtures. I'd like your opinion on how things are turning out."

She nodded. "How soon to completion?"

"Toby estimates two weeks."

"That's great. Then we can concentrate on getting the spaces rented. I can help with that since I've hired a property manager, Kaley Sims. If it's okay with you, I'd like her to come by and talk with you about listing the loft apartments."

Jace smiled. "So she's handling the rest of your properties?"

Lori nodded. "Yes, she worked for my father years ago, so she knows what she's doing. I convinced her to come back to work with me."

"Good, I'm ready to get this done."

She stiffened. "And you don't have to deal with a rookie partner."

He cursed. "Ah, Lori, I didn't mean it that way. It's just with all the delays we've had, I'm ready to be finished. You're a great partner. I'd work with you again."

She looked surprised. "You would?"

"In a heartbeat." He took a step toward her. There was so much he wanted to say, but he had no right to make promises when he wasn't sure what was in store for him and Cassie. He was in the middle of a messy custody battle. "Just come by the site tomorrow."

Lori started to speak when he heard his name called. He turned around to find Shelly coming toward him. Great. He didn't need this.

He turned back around but Lori had walked off. He wanted to go after her, but he couldn't, not until he got things settled. He'd better do it quickly, or he might lose one of the best things that ever happened to him.

The next week, Lori did what Jace asked and came by the site. She'd purposely stayed away from the project to avoid the man, so she was amazed at the difference.

The chain-link fence had been removed. They'd already started to do some stone landscape. Planters and retaining walls had been built, and a parking area.

"I'm impressed," Kaley said as she got out of the car and looked at the two-story wood-and-stone structure.

So was Lori. "Wait until you see the inside."

They headed up the path to the double-door entry. The door swung open and Toby greeted them with a big smile.

"Well, it's about time you showed up again."

Lori returned the smile. "Well, I knew you were in charge so I didn't worry about things getting done. Hello, Toby."

After a greeting, the foreman turned to Kaley and grinned. "Well, well, who's your friend, Lori?"

Lori made the introductions. "Kaley Sims, Hutchinson Corp's property manager, Toby Edwards."

"So you're not just a pretty face," Toby said.

"And you'd be wise to remember that, Mr. Edwards."

She took a step toward him, grinning. "Now, let's go see if this place looks as good as Lori says it does."

"Well, damn. You're making my day brighter and brighter."

Lori was surprised to see these two throw off sparks. "Go on ahead and don't mind me," she called as the two took off, not paying any attention to her.

She stepped through the entry and gasped as she looked around. The dark hardwood floors had been laid and the massive fireplace completed. She eyed the golden tones of the stacked stones that ran all the way from the hearth to the open-beam ceiling.

Then her attention went to the main attraction of the huge room. The arching staircase. The new design was an improvement from the old as the natural wood banister wrapped around the edge of the first floor, showing off the mezzanine. A front desk had been built for a receptionist for the tenants.

"So how do you like it so far?"

Lori swung around to see Jace. "It looks wonderful."

Then she took in the man. In his usual uniform of faded jeans and a dark Henley shirt, Jace also wore a carpenter's tool belt around his waist. Somehow that even looked sexy.

"Am I disturbing your work?"

He grinned. "Darlin', you've been disturbing a lot more than my work since the minute I met you."

Jace was in a good mood today. Although Shelly had no plans to leave town, he had talked to Paige first thing that morning. He now had a court date and also a preliminary injunction so Shelly couldn't run off with Cassie. At least not until after the custody hearing back in Denver.

"We butted heads a lot, too," she said.

He leaned forward and breathed, "And there were times when we couldn't keep our hands off each other." Before she could do more than gasp, he took her hand. "Come on, I want to show you around."

"I need to go with Toby and Kaley."

He led her up the staircase. "I think Toby can handle the job." He took her into the first loft apartment, showing off ebony-colored hardwood floors. The open kitchen had dark-colored cabinets, but the counters weren't installed yet. "Here are some granite samples for the countertops and tile for the backsplash."

He watched her study the light-colored granite, with the earth-toned contrasting tile. The other was a glossy black, with white subway tile. "I like the earth tone," she told him.

He smiled. "My choice, too. The next stop is the bathroom." He led her across the main living space, where the floor-to-ceiling windows stopped her.

"Oh, Jace. This is a wonderful view."

He stood behind her, careful not to touch her as they glanced out the window at the San Juan Mountains. He worked hard to concentrate on the snow-filled creases in the rock formations and evergreen trees dotting the landscape. "It's almost as beautiful as the view from the cabin."

She glanced up at him and he saw the longing in her dark eyes. "It was lovely there, wasn't it?"

"You were even more beautiful, Lori."

She shook her head. "Don't, Jace. We decided that we shouldn't be involved."

"What if I can't stay away from you?"

Lori closed her eyes. She didn't want to hope and be

hurt in the end. Then his mouth closed over hers and she lost all reasonable thoughts. With a whimper of need she moved her hands up his chest and around his neck and gave in to the feelings.

He broke off the kiss. "I've missed you, Lori. I missed holding you, touching you, kissing you."

"Jace…"

His mouth found hers again and again.

Finally the sound of voices broke them apart. His gaze searched her face. "Lucky for you we're not alone. I'm pretty close to losing control." He sighed. "And with you, Lorelei Hutchinson, that happens every time I get close." He pulled her against him so there was no doubt. "Please, say you'll come by the house tonight. There are so many things I want to tell you."

Lori wanted to hope that everything would work out with Jace. Yet, still Shelly Yeager lingered in town. The last thing Lori wanted was to jeopardize Jace getting custody of his daughter.

Yet, she wanted them both—Jace and Cassie—in her life. Question was, was she ready to fight for what she wanted? Yes. "What time?"

CHAPTER ELEVEN

AT THE site, Jace kept checking his watch, but it was only two o'clock. He had three more hours before he could call it a day and see Lori again.

He was crazy to add any more complications to his life, but he hadn't been able to get her out of his head. For weeks, he'd tried to deny his feelings, tried to convince himself that he didn't care about Lori, but he did care. A lot.

He hadn't been able to forget her or what happened between them. The night at the cabin, what they'd shared, made him think it was possible to have a relationship again. Tonight, when she came by the house, he planned to tell her. He only hoped she could be patient and hang in there a little while longer, until this custody mess was finally straightened out.

"Hey, are you listening?"

Jace turned toward his friend Justin Hilliard. "Sorry, what did you say?"

Justin smiled. "Seems you have something or someone else on your mind."

"Yeah, I do. But I can't do anything about it right now so I'd rather not talk about it."

"I understand. If you need a friend to talk later, I'm your guy. I'll even buy the beer."

Justin was the one who'd brought him to Destiny after Yeager Construction tanked following his divorce. He'd always be grateful. "I appreciate that."

His friend nodded. "Now, tell me when can I move in?" He motioned around the office space on the main floor at the Mountain Heritage complex.

"Is next week soon enough?"

"Great. I'll have Morgan go shopping for office furniture. And I'll need a loft apartment upstairs for out-of-town clients. Is there someone handling the loft rentals?"

Jace nodded. "Kaley Sims. I'll have her get in touch with you to negotiate the lease."

"Good. I'm available all this week." Justin studied Jace. "So what are your plans for your next project?"

"Not sure." That much was true. "I've been so wrapped up in getting this project completed, I haven't thought that far ahead." He had Lori on his mind. "I know I'd like to stay here, of course, but until I get this custody mess taken care of, I'm still in limbo."

"Like I said, let me know if I can help." Justin slapped him on the back. "Just don't let Shelly get away with anything."

"Believe me, I won't." She'd taken him to the cleaners once. No more. "Besides, Paige is handling it all for me."

Justin nodded. "Yeah, my sister-in-law is one of the best. She'll do everything she can to straighten this out."

God, he hoped so. Jace wanted nothing more than to end Shelly's threats.

They walked out of the office space and Justin said, "If you think you'd be ready to start another project by March, let me know."

Jace stopped. He was definitely interested. "What kind of project?"

"It's an idea I've had in the works awhile. I waited until I had the right partner in place, and now, it's in the designing stages."

Jace was more than intrigued. "So what is it?"

"A mountain bike racing school and trails. I bought several acres of land about five miles outside of town and plan to build a track. I'm bringing in a pro racer, Ryan Donnelly, to design it."

"I don't do landscaping."

Justin smiled. "I know. I want your company to handle the structures, cabins to house the students and instructors, including a main building to serve meals and a pro shop."

They walked through the main area of the building as Justin continued. "Eventually, I hope to work with Ryan to design bikes. I want the plant to be right here in Destiny." Justin arched an eyebrow. "I want you to handle it all, Jace."

This was a dream come true. "And I want the project, Justin. By early spring I could have the subs and crew in place to start." He worked to hold in his excitement. "But I'll need the plans by February."

Justin nodded. "Shouldn't be a problem."

Now if his personal life straightened out by then. With this new project he could move forward, make a fresh start. He thought about Lori. He couldn't wait to tell her. Tonight. This could be their new beginning.

* * *

By six o'clock, Lori had gathered her things and left the office. She went home, showered and changed into a nice pair of slacks and white angora sweater. Excited about spending the evening with Jace, she took extra time with her clothes and makeup.

Her pulse raced as she realized how badly she wanted to be with him. He was everything she'd ever dreamed the man she loved could be. Handsome, caring and a good father. What woman wouldn't dream about forever with him?

She walked back into the connecting bedroom to find Gina.

"Sorry, Lori, I didn't mean to disturb you. I know you plan to go out tonight."

"You never could disturb me," Lori assured her sister. "Is something wrong?"

Gina smiled. "No. For the first time in a very long time, everything is going right." She went to her sister. "Thanks to you. I never thought I could feel this happy again. And Zack…"

Lori hugged her, praying that continued. That Eric would leave them alone. "We're family, Gina. Besides, it's Lyle's money."

"No, you were there for us long before you inherited the Hutchinson money. You were always there for me."

"You're my sister and Zack is my nephew. Where else would I be?"

"Having a life?" Gina said. "And finding someone special."

Lori wanted to believe. "I think that has already happened."

Her sister smiled. "If Jace Yeager is as smart as I think he is, he'll snatch you up."

Of course, Lori hoped that tonight the man would make some kind of commitment, but she also knew he had to tread cautiously. They both did. "Let's just see what happens."

About eight o'clock that evening, Jace had put Cassie to bed, but she made him promise when Lori got there she would come up to say good-night. He was happy that his daughter got along with her.

He smiled, knowing he'd have Lori all to himself for the rest of the evening. There were so many things he wanted to tell Lori tonight. He wanted them to move ahead together.

He checked on the dinners he'd picked up from the Silver Spoon. Then he took the wine out of the refrigerator and got two glasses from the cupboard. He looked around his half-finished kitchen.

Okay, this place had been neglected too long. It was going to be his top priority. He could probably make some headway by Christmas. Thanksgiving at the Hutchinson house, and maybe, Christmas dinner at the Yeager house. That would be his goal.

He hoped to have the rest of his life in order by then, too. His daughter with him and Lori with them. He'd made a start with the custody hearing.

He saw the flash of headlights as a car pulled into the drive. His heart began to pound when he saw Lori climb out and walk up the steps to the back porch. He opened the door and greeted her with a smile.

"Hi, there."

She smiled. "Hi. Sorry I'm late."

Jace drew her into his arms because he couldn't go any longer without touching her, holding her. "Well, you're here now and that's all that matters. I missed you." He kissed her, a slow but intense meeting of their mouths, only making him hungry for more.

He didn't want to let go of her, but he promised himself he'd go slow. He tore his mouth away. "Maybe we should dial it down a little." He tugged at her heavy coat. "At least until I feed you."

She smiled. "I am a little hungry." She brushed her hair back and looked around. "Where's Cassie?"

"I'm losing out to the kid, huh? She's upstairs in bed." He led her into the kitchen. "I told her you'd come up and say good-night. I hope you don't mind."

"Of course not." Lori started off, but he brought her back to him for another intense kiss. "Just remember you're mine for the rest of the night."

"I'll be right back."

Jace's heart pounded as he watched the cute sway of her hips as she walked out of the kitchen and up the stairs.

He sighed and worked to get it together. "You got it bad, Yeager." He turned down the lights, and put on some music from the sound system, then lit the candles on the table. Back at the kitchen counter, he opened the chilled bottle of wine and filled the glasses at the two place settings.

It was impossible not to remember their dinner together at the cabin. He wanted nothing more than to have a repeat of that night. But that couldn't happen. Not with Cassie here. He blew out a breath. There was no doubt in his mind, they'd be together again. And soon.

Smiling, Lori walked down the steps and it turned into a grin when she saw Jace in the kitchen. "That's what I like about you, Yeager. You're just not a handsome face, you're domestic, too."

Jace turned around and tossed her a sexy smile. "I can be whatever you want."

Her heart shot off racing. *How about the man who loves me?* she asked silently as he came to her and drew her against him. She wanted nothing more than to stay wrapped in his arms, to close out the rest of the world.

She looked up at him. "Kiss me, Jace."

"My pleasure, ma'am." He lowered his head, brushing her mouth with his. She opened for him, but he was a little more playful and took nibbling bites out of her bottom lip.

With her whimper of need, he captured her mouth in a searing kiss. By the time he pulled back, her knees were weak and she had trouble catching her breath. "Wow."

He raised an eyebrow. "That was just an appetizer." He stepped back. "But before I go back to sampling you again, we better eat."

She was a little disappointed, but knew it was better to slow things down a little. She accepted the wine he offered her.

She sipped it and let the sweet taste linger in her mouth. She caught Jace watching her and smiled, then took another sip. "How was your day at the site?"

"Oh, I meant to tell you that Justin stopped by. Besides the office space, he wants to lease a loft apartment. I gave him Kaley's number."

"Good." She raised her glass. "The first of many, I hope."

"You and me both. Justin might want more than one apartment. I'm hoping Kaley can convince him of that.

Maybe give him a few incentives like a six-month re-
duction in the rent."

"That sounds good. Is that usually done in real estate?"

He nodded. "All the time." He walked her to the table
and sat her down, then began filling their plates with
roast chicken and mashed potatoes. "The Silver Spoon's
Thursday night special."

Lori took a bite. "It's very good."

"Come spring," he began, "I'll barbecue us some
steaks on the grill. That's my specialty."

She paused, her fork to her mouth. He was talking
about the future. "I'd like that."

He winked and took a bite of food as they continued
to talk about Mountain Heritage, then he told her about
Justin's offer for the racing bike school.

"Oh, Jace, you have to be excited about that."

Jace wanted to be, but there were still problems
looming overhead. Like getting permanent custody of
his daughter. He prayed that Paige could pull this off.
"There's still a lot to work out."

Lori nodded.

He didn't want to talk about it right now. This was
just for them. No troubles, no worries, just them. Yet,
he knew he couldn't make her any promises. He'd never
thought he'd find someone like Lori, someone he'd want
to dream about a future together.

The meal finished, they carried the dishes to the sink
and left them. He offered her coffee, but she refused it.

A soft ballad came on the radio. He drew her into his
arms and began slowly dancing her around the kitchen
and into the family room, where soft flames in the fireplace added to the mood. He placed his hands against

her back, pulling his swaying body against hers. "I want you, Lori," he whispered. "Never have I wanted a woman as much as you." His lips trailed along her jaw, feeling her shiver. He finally reached his destination. "Never." He closed his mouth over hers, and pushed his tongue inside tasting her, stroking her.

His hands were busy, too, reaching under her sweater, cupping her breasts.

"Jace," she moaned. "Please."

"I definitely want to please you." He kissed her again and was quickly getting to the point of no return.

"Well, well. Isn't this cozy?"

Jace jerked back and caught sight of Shelly standing in the doorway. He immediately turned Lori away from view. "What are you doing here?"

The tall brunette pushed away from the doorjamb and walked into the room as if she had every right to be there.

"Since no one was answering the phone, I came to see what the problem was." She gave Lori a once-over. "Now I know why. You're having a little party here while our daughter is asleep upstairs."

"That's my business, Shelly. And that doesn't give you the right to come into my house without an invitation. And you weren't invited."

"I don't need to be. I have custody of Cassie." She shot an angry look at Lori. "In fact I think I should remove her from here right now."

Lori gasped.

Jace got angry. "I wouldn't try it, Shelly."

"Try and stop me."

When she started to move past him, Jace stepped in

front of her. "You can't. I have an injunction that says she stays with me until the court hearing."

She glared. "I know. I got served today."

So that was why she showed up. "And this should be settled in court."

"I want my daughter. Now!"

"Stop it! Mommy, Daddy, don't fight!"

They all turned and saw Cassie standing at the bottom of the stairs.

Lori wanted to go to the child, but it wasn't her place.

Jace took over and went to his daughter's side. "Oh, baby. I'm sorry we woke you."

"You and Mommy were fighting again?"

"I'm sorry. We're trying to work something out and we got a little loud."

"Please, I don't want you to fight anymore."

Jace looked at Lori. "Will you take Cassie back to her room?" With her nod, he glanced down at his daughter. "I'll be up in a minute."

Shelly came over and kissed her daughter and sent her along.

Once they were alone, Jace took Shelly's arm and walked her out to the utility room. "I'm not going to let you come here and upset Cassie like that."

"You're just mad because I interrupted your rendezvous with little Miss Heiress."

"Leave Lori out of this. She's a respectable person in this town."

"And you're sleeping with her."

Jace had to hold his temper. "We've done nothing wrong. If you think so, then talk to the judge. I'll see you in court, Shelly."

Shelly's face reddened in anger. "Don't think you've

won, Jace Yeager. This is not going to end in your favor."

He held on to his temper. "Why, Shelly? Why are we arguing about this? You know Cassie is better off here. She's made friends and is doing great in school. I have a job that has me home every night." He stopped in front of the woman he once loved, but now he only felt sorry for. "When you get married, Shelly, I will let you see her anytime you want."

"That might not happen. So the game plan will change."

"Oh, Cassie."

Lori cradled the small form against her as they sat on the bed. She inhaled the soft powdery smell and realized how much Cassie had come to mean to her. She could easily become addicted to this nightly ritual.

She silently cursed Shelly Yeager. How could anyone drag a child into this mess? "I wish I could make it better, sweetheart."

The child's lip quivered as she looked up. "Nobody can. They always fight."

"I'm sorry. That doesn't mean they don't love you. They just have to work out what's best for you."

A tear ran down the girl's cheek. "I want to live here with Daddy, but if I do, Mommy will go away." Cassie's big blue eyes looked up at her, and Lori could feel her pain. "And she's gonna forget about me." She started to sob and Lori drew her into a tight embrace.

"Oh, sweetheart, have you told your father how you feel?"

The child pulled back, looking panicked. "No! I don't

want them to fight anymore." Her face crumpled again. "So please don't tell Daddy."

"Don't tell me what?"

They both looked toward the door to see Jace. "Nothing." Cassie wiped her eyes. "I'm just talking to Miss Lori."

Lori got up and Jace sat down to face his daughter. "Sweetheart, I'm sorry."

The little girl suddenly collapsed into her father's arms. Lori backed out of the room, not wanting to intrude. She realized right away how much this custody battle had affected the child.

And Cassie had to come first.

Lori couldn't help but wonder if they could get through this situation unscathed, or would Shelly follow through on her threats?

Lori's chest tightened. She'd never forget the heartache she'd felt when she had to leave her childhood home. Her father standing on the porch. That had been the last time she'd ever seen Lyle Hutchinson. Oh, God. She couldn't let that happen to this little girl. No matter what it cost her.

Cassie finally went to sleep and Jace walked out into the hall, but he didn't go downstairs yet. Heartsick over his daughter's distress, he needed some time to pull himself together. Cassie had been dealing with problems he and her mother had caused. No child should have to choose which parent to love, which parent to be loyal to.

He sighed, knowing he had to do something about it.

Jace made his way down the steps and found Lori standing in the kitchen. He went to her and pulled her into a tight embrace. "I guess we should talk." He released her and walked around the kitchen in a daze. "You want something to drink?"

"No," she said. "Is Cassie asleep?"

He nodded, feeling the rush of emotions as he went and poured himself a glass. "I'm so angry at Shelly for starting all this."

"Divorce isn't easy for anyone, kids especially." Lori closed her eyes momentarily. "Cassie needs constant reassurance that her daddy's going to be around."

Jace tried to draw a breath, but it was hard. "And I have been right here for her. I've been doing everything possible to keep her with me."

He immediately realized the harshness of his words. "I'm sorry, Lori, that you had to witness this." He pulled her close, grateful that she didn't resist. "I'm so frustrated." He held her tightly. "I've worked so hard to have a good relationship with my daughter."

Lori pulled back, knowing there wasn't any simple solution. "I know, but Cassie is still caught in the middle."

"This is all a game to Shelly."

It wasn't for the rest of the people involved. "Well, she is here and you have to deal with her. For Cassie's sake."

"I've been doing that," he told her. "Paige has gotten a court date for a custody hearing with a judge in Denver."

Lori was surprised by Jace's news. "That's good. When?"

"This coming Monday."

She told herself not to react, not to be hurt that he hadn't said anything before now. "So soon?"

He studied her with those intense blue eyes. "If we

don't do it now, the holidays are coming up. It could be delayed until January. By then Shelly might have taken Cassie to Europe." He paused. "I was going to tell you about it tonight."

That didn't take away the pain of his leaving. "How long will you be gone?"

"Probably just a few days. Don't worry, Toby has the project under control."

She shook her head. "You think I'm concerned about that when Cassie's future is in jeopardy?"

He shook his head. "Of course not, Lori. I know you care about her."

"I care about both of you. I want this to work, because she should be with you."

He looked at her, his blue eyes intense. "I'm going to see that happens no matter what the judge's decision is."

Lori felt her heart skip a beat. "Does that mean you'll move back to Denver?"

He nodded slowly. "I hope there's another way. I don't want to leave here, but if that's the end result of this hearing…there's no choice."

He might be going away, she thought, fighting tears. "Cassie's your daughter, so of course you have to go there. You have to fight for her."

"I care about you, Lori. A lot. I know you have a year commitment here, or I'd ask—"

"Then don't, Jace," she interrupted, forcing a smile. "Neither one of us is ready to jump into a relationship. Like you said, we both have other commitments."

His gaze locked on hers. "I want to say the hell with all of Shelly's games, but I can't. Bottom line is, I can't give you any promises."

And she couldn't beg him to. There was too much

at stake here. Most importantly, a little girl. Lori had once been that little girl whose father let her go. Cassie deserved better.

Lori couldn't meet his eyes. She fisted her hands so he wouldn't see her shaking. "It's too soon to make plans when we don't know the future."

"Is it? What about what happened between us at the cabin? Unless it didn't mean anything to you."

She swallowed hard. "Of course it did." She'd always have those incredible memories. "It was...special."

"Seems not as special for you as it was for me."

She had to get away from him. "I'm sorry, Jace. I need to go. I hope everything works out for you and Cassie." She headed toward the door and paused. She took one last look at the man she loved. "Goodbye, Jace."

When he didn't say anything to stop her, she hurried out the door and got into her car. Starting the engine, she headed for the highway. He hadn't even asked her to wait it out. Tears filled her eyes, blurring her vision, until she had to stop.

She cried for her loss, for letting this between her and Jace to get this far. She never should have let herself fall in love with this wonderful man. A man she couldn't have. She'd finally opened herself and let love in, only to be hurt again.

She brushed away more tears, praying that the pain would stop. That the loneliness would go away soon. This was what she got for starting to dream of that happy ending.

The only consolation was she wouldn't let another little girl go through the misery she had. She would never prevent Jace from having his daughter.

CHAPTER TWELVE

THAT night, sleep eluded Lori.

When she'd gotten home earlier she'd made up an excuse to go to her room. She hadn't been in the mood to talk about her evening with Jace. Not even with Gina. And what good would it do? Neither one of them had a choice in the matter. There was nothing to say except they couldn't be together.

But after several hours of tossing and turning, she got out of bed. Restless, she ended up wandering around the big house. She checked in on her sleeping nephew and pulled the covers around him, knowing Jace would do the same thing with Cassie. Smiling, she realized that had been one of the reasons she'd fallen in love with the man. His relationship with his daughter was part of that. She would miss them both so much if they couldn't come back here. What were Jace's chances of getting custody? Probably slim.

Lori walked down the hall, passing her childhood bedroom. She stopped, wanting nothing more than to shake the feeling of abandonment she'd had since her mother took her away from here.

She slipped inside, waiting as the moonlight coming through the window lit her path to the canopy bed.

Loneliness swept through her as more memories flooded back. Her absent father had been too busy for her. He'd been too busy making money and that meant he hadn't been home much.

Then long-forgotten images flashed though her mind. There had been some happy times. She remembered sitting at the dinner table, hearing her parents' laughter. Lyle wasn't very demonstrative, but she would always cherish the time he'd spent with her. Guess he'd been as loving as he was able to be.

She smiled, thinking of those good-night kisses she would treasure. She brushed away a tear as she turned on a bedside lamp and caught sight of the stuffed animals lined up on the windowsill.

Another memory hit her. "Oh, Daddy, you gave me all of these."

"Lorelei?"

Lori turned to find Maggie standing in the doorway. She was wearing her robe over a long gown. "Oh, Maggie, did I wake you?"

The housekeeper walked in. "No, I was up getting something to drink. This old house has a lot creaks and I know them all. When I heard someone walking around, I thought it might be the boy." The older woman eyed the stuffed animals. "Land sakes, child. You can't keep coming in here and getting all sad."

"No, Maggie. Really, I'm fine." She smiled as she wiped away the tears and held out one of her childhood animals. "Look. I remembered that Dad bought this for me." She reached for another. "He bought these, too." She gathered all them in her arms.

Maggie smiled. "I'm glad you remember those times."

And so much more. "Every time he went on a business trip, he came home with a toy for me." Another memory. "And when he was home he would come into my bedroom and kiss me good-night." Tears flooded her eyes. "He loved me, Maggie."

"Of course he loved you. You were his little girl, his pride and joy."

"Then why, Maggie? Why didn't he want me?"

The housekeeper shook her head. "It wasn't that." She hesitated, then said, "You never knew your grandfather Billy. If you had you might understand your father better."

"Kaley Sims mentioned him. She said he'd gone into a nursing home after a stroke."

Maggie made a huffing sound. "It was probably better than he deserved. That man was a terrible example as a parent. What Lyle went through as a child was... Let's just say, Billy wasn't much of a human being, so I won't go into his fathering skills."

"Wouldn't that make Lyle a better one?"

Maggie took hold of Lori's hands and they sank down to sit on the window seat. "I believe your dad did the best he could, honey. When Billy nearly lost all the family money, and that included the bank, this town almost didn't survive. Your father spent a lot of years rebuilding the family wealth, and trying to get Billy's approval."

Maggie continued, "Your mother didn't like being neglected, either. She wanted all of her husband's attention. I think she left hoping Lyle would come after both of you. Your father took it as another rejection and just shut down."

Lori had no doubt Jocelyn Hutchinson would do that to get attention. "But he had a daughter who loved him."

Maggie looked sad. "I know. I wish I had a better answer for you. I recall a few phone conversations between your mother and father. He asked Jocelyn to bring you here. She refused. When your mother remarried, he told me that you'd do better without him."

She felt a spark of hope. "He wanted me to come back here?"

Maggie nodded. "For Christmas that first year. He told me once how much you loved the tree lights in the town square."

A tear ran down Lori's cheek. She had no idea he would remember.

Maggie pulled her into a comforting embrace. "He kept this room the same, hoping to have you back here. So keep hanging on to the good memories, child. I know that was what your father did."

Lori pulled back. "How can I?"

The housekeeper brushed back Lori's hair. "Because your father knew he caused enough pain over the years." Maggie smiled through her own tears. "Think about it, Lorelei. Your father finally brought you home. No mistaking, he wanted you here."

Lori began to sob over the lost years that father and daughter would never get back. The tears were cleansing, and she had some answers.

"Lori?"

Lori looked at the open door to find her sister. "Oh, Gina. Sorry, did we wake you?"

"I was just checking on Zack."

Maggie hugged them both. "Share with your sister, Lorelei. It will get better each time." The older woman left.

"Should I be worried?" Gina asked once they were alone.

"Not any longer. I've learned a lot about my father. Lyle wasn't perfect, but he loved me in his way." Lori went on to explain about her discovery.

"I'm so glad," Gina agreed. "Every child needs those good memories." She hesitated. "That's what I hope for Zack."

"He'll have those good memories. I promise," Lori told her, thinking about Cassie, too.

Lori never wanted that child to go through what she had. So that meant she had to accept it. Accept she might not be able to have Jace Yeager.

Gina's voice broke into her thoughts.

Lori looked at her. "What?"

"Something else is bothering you. Would it have anything to do with Jace? Did you two have a fight?" Gina asked, frowning. "Oh, no, it's his ex-wife causing trouble, isn't it?"

Lori agreed. "Jace has to go back to Denver for the custody case. If he loses, he wants to live close by Cassie. That means he'll have to move back there."

"I wish I could hate the guy, but he's a great father." Gina suddenly grinned. "So move to Denver."

Lori would in a minute. "I can't until I fulfill Lyle's will. If I leave before the year is up, the town might not survive."

"That doesn't mean you can't go visit Jace for long weekends."

She could go for that. Would Jace want a long-distance relationship? "He hasn't asked me."

Gina jumped up. "Of course he hasn't. He doesn't know anything yet. Lori, I believe Jace Yeager loves you. And if he can, he'll do whatever it takes to get Cassie and come back here to you."

Lori was heartened with her sister's enthusiasm. "You sure seem to have a better outlook toward men these days."

Her sister shrugged. "Maybe they aren't all jerks like Eric. I've met a few here in town that seem really nice. Now, that doesn't mean I want to get involved with any of them. I'm happy concentrating on raising Zack."

If one good thing came out of returning to Destiny it was helping Gina and Zack have a chance at a new life. "And we have each other."

"Always." Gina nodded. "Now, we need something to do to keep you busy." She looked around what once had been a little girl's room. "This entire house, at the very least, needs a fresh coat of paint. We should re-decorate the master suite, so you can move in there."

Lori knew Gina was trying to distract her, and she loved her for it. "The place is a little big for us, don't you think?"

"Of course it is. It's a mansion."

Lori turned to her sister. "What about moving into a smaller place?"

Her sister blinked. "Are you going to sell this house?"

She shook her head. "We have to live here for now. I think maybe Hutchinson House can be rented out for weddings and parties and the proceeds could go to the town." She couldn't help but wonder if Jace and Cassie would be living here in Destiny, too. "What do you think of that?"

"Lori, I think that's a wonderful idea." She hesitated.

"And you've been generous to Zack and me. But I feel I need to contribute, too. I know this mess with Eric still has me frightened, but thanks to you, I've felt safer than I have for years."

"I'm glad." Lori had already checked on her ex-brother-in-law. She'd contacted the police detective on the case. Eric had been staying with his family in Colorado Springs.

"I need a job," Gina blurted out. "It's not that I'm not grateful to you for everything, but I want to be more independent. I have to set a good example for my son. I don't want him to think he has an easy ride in life."

Lori hugged her, knowing the hell she'd gone through for years. "So you want a job. I just happen to have one."

Her sister frowned. "Lori, you can't make up a job for me."

"I hate to tell you, sis, but most of the people in Destiny work for Hutchinson Corp. And honestly, I'm not making this job up. Kaley Sims is going to advertise the Mountain Heritage spaces to rent and she needs to stage them. You're the perfect decorator to do it. So what do you say?"

Gina gave her a big smile. "I say, when do I start?"

"I'll talk to Kaley in the morning." Lori smiled, but inside she was hurting. Everyone was moving forward, but she couldn't, not knowing what her future held. "Come on, we both need to get some sleep."

They walked back to their rooms. Lori climbed in bed just as her cell phone rang. She reached for it off her nightstand.

She glanced at the familiar caller ID. "Jace," she answered. "Is something wrong?"

"No, nothing's wrong. I'm sorry I called so late. I just wanted to let you know that Cassie and I are leaving."

She already knew that. "When?"

"First thing in the morning."

So soon.

Jace went on. "Toby has everything under control at the site. There are only a few finishing touches before the last walk through. Kaley Sims is now handling the Heritage project. I'll pass on the news to her."

"I appreciate that," she told him. "Is there anything else?"

Lori begged silently that he'd ask her to wait for him. At least tell her he cared.

"I hated the way we left things last night," he finally said. "God, Lori, I wish it could be different."

She swallowed back the lump in her throat. "You're doing what's right, Jace."

"I know. I just needed to hear your voice," he told her and there was a long pause. "Goodbye, Lori." Then he hung up.

The silence was deafening. She lay back in her bed, pulling up the covers to protect her from the loneliness. It didn't help. Nothing would help but Jace.

"Why are you dead set on making my life hell?" Jace demanded as he stepped through the door into his one-time Denver home the next day. Something else that Shelly had gotten from their divorce.

He glanced around the spacious entry of the re-furbished Victorian. The hardwood floors he'd refinished himself, along with the plaster on the walls. He stopped the search when unpleasant memories of his marriage hit him. He turned back to Shelly to see her stubborn look.

"You're the one who had me served with papers."

"Because you came to Destiny and disrupted Cassie's life. I'm done with your games, Shelly. It's time we settle this."

"Well, that's too bad." She strolled across the room to the three windows that overlooked the street. "I'm Cassie's mother, and after today, the judge will see that I should have our child permanently. Where is our daughter?"

"She's in good hands." Paige had offered to watch her back at the hotel while he tried to straighten out a few things. "She's with Paige Larkin."

Shelly frowned. "So what are you willing to give up to spend time with Cassie? Your little girlfriend?"

"I'm not willing to give up anything. Besides, my personal life is none of your business." He prayed he still had one. Not only couldn't he make any promises to Lori, but he also couldn't even tell her his feelings.

"It is if you're living with her with our child. Maybe the judge should know, too."

"Stop with the threats, Shelly." He walked toward the front door. He opened the door and glanced out at the man on the porch and motioned to him to come inside.

Shelly looked at Jace suspiciously. "What are you up to?"

"You're the one who plays games, Shelly. So if I can't talk any sense into you, maybe he can." He prayed that all his hard work would pay off and not backfire in his face.

"Don't push me, Jace. You'll only lose." She gasped as Edmund Layfield stepped through the front door.

The distinguished gentleman was in his early fifties. He was dressed in a business suit and had thick gray hair. Jace had spent only an hour with the man and realized that he truly loved Shelly. Edmund also liked Cassie, but didn't particularly want to raise another child full-time, since his kids were grown.

Shelly came out of her trance. "Edmund, what are you doing here?"

"I came to see you, love. And I'm not leaving here until I convince you that we're meant to be together." He reached out and pulled her into his arms. That was when Jace made his exit.

For the first time in days, he realized that maybe they could come to a compromise. They all might get what they wanted. His thoughts turned to Lori. And that included him.

Tim parked the small SUV next to several other cars at Hutchinson House. It was Thanksgiving and half the town had been invited to have dinner here.

"Are you okay with this?" he asked Claire.

She smiled. "Normally no, but I can share this special day with Lori and Gina. It's important they feel a part of Destiny." She sighed. "Besides, all the kids and grandkids will be here." She smiled. "It's all about family being together. If only we would hear from Jace. You'd think our own daughter could give us some information."

He reached across the car and took his wife's hand. "Come on, Claire, you know Paige is Jace's lawyer."

"I know, I know, client/lawyer confidentiality." She frowned. "But I've seen how sad Lori is. If two people should be together, it's them."

"And if it's meant to be it will work out."

"I've been praying so hard for that."

It had been a week, and not a word from Jace. Lori had tried to stay positive—after all, it was Thanksgiving.

She looked around the festive dining room. The long table could seat twenty. There were two other tables set up in the entry to seat another twenty. And with the kids' table in the sunroom off the kitchen, everyone would have a place.

Maggie had cooked three turkeys and with Claire's two baked hams and many side dishes from everyone, she couldn't imagine not having enough food.

"Miss Hutchinson."

Lori turned to see Mac Burleson. "Mac, I asked you to call me Lori."

"Doesn't seem right," he told her.

"It seems very right to me. Unless you don't consider me a friend."

His eyes rounded. "You're a very good friend. I'm so grateful—"

"You did it," she interrupted. "You proved yourself at every job you've taken on. You make us all proud."

"Thank you…Lori." He smiled. "Is there anything else you want me to do?"

Some laughing kids ran by, chasing each other. She smiled at their antics. Her father would probably hate this. "Enjoy today. We have a lot to be thankful for." She knew she was so lucky, but two important people weren't here to share it with her.

"Hurry, Daddy, we're gonna be late for Thanksgiving."

Jace smiled, but it didn't relax him as he drove his

truck down First Street toward Hutchinson House. "We'll get there, sweetheart."

He glanced toward the backseat where his daughter was strapped in. They'd been gone a week, having stayed in Denver longer than planned. With the lawyers' help, they'd worked out the custody issue without a judge having to make the decision.

And in the end, it had been Cassie who'd told her mother that she wanted to live in Destiny with her daddy and all her friends and her horse. Shelly finally agreed, but wanted visitation in the summers and holidays. So Jace became the custodial parent. There was only one other thing that could make him happier. Lori.

"I just can't wait to see Ellie and Mrs. K. and Miss Lori, to tell everybody that I get to live here and be in the Christmas pageant."

"I can't wait, either," he told his daughter, praying that a certain pretty blonde felt the same about the news.

"Daddy, are you gonna ask Miss Lori today?"

On the flight home, Jace had told her how he felt about Lori and about her being a part of their lives. That was crazy, considering he hadn't even talked with Lori yet.

"Not sure. There's going to be a lot of people there today. It might have to wait, so you have to keep it a secret, okay?"

"Okay, but could I tell Ellie about Mommy's wedding? And that I'm going to go visit a real castle this summer?"

He smiled. "Yes, about the wedding, but the castle is only going to happen if I can get time off work." He was definitely going with her. He hoped Lori could go, too.

His heart began to race as he pulled up and climbed

out of the truck. He grabbed the wine and hurried after his daughter to the front door.

When they rang the bell, the door opened and Zack poked his head out. "Hi, Cassie. Hi, Mr. Jace."

"Hi, Zack. We came for Thanksgiving."

The boy grinned and opened the door wider and allowed them into the entryway filled with a long table decorated with colorful flowers and a paper turkey centerpiece. Cassie took off before he could stop her.

Jace was soon greeted by Justin and Morgan, then Tim Keenan and Paige and Reed Larkin joined them. He wanted to join in the conversation, but his eyes kept searching for a glimpse of Lori.

"She's in the kitchen."

He glanced at Justin. "Who?"

"As if you two are fooling anyone," his friend said. "You need to go to Lori before she comes out here and sees you."

Jace nodded and took off toward the kitchen. He knew his way around this house, but there were so many people here it was hard to maneuver. How was he going to be able to get her alone?

He saw Maggie at the counter. Without asking anything, she nodded toward the sunroom. He walked there as kids ran past him. Okay, so they weren't going to have any privacy.

Then he saw her and everyone else seemed to disappear from view. She was seated on the floor with some of the little kids. She was holding a toddler who'd been crying, and she managed to turn the tears into a smile before the child wandered off. Jace fell in love with her all over again.

Lori stood. Dressed in black slacks and a soft blue

sweater he ached to pull her close and just hold her. Tell her how much he'd missed her. How much he wanted her...

She finally turned in his direction. Her hair was in an array of curls that danced around her pretty face. Her chocolate eyes locked on his. "You're back."

That was a dumb thing to say, Lori thought as she looked up at Jace. So much for cool and calm.

"Hello, Lori."

"Hi, Jace." She didn't take a step toward him. "Is Cassie with you? Please tell me that she's with you."

He beamed. "Yes, she is." He glanced around. "I need to talk to you. There are so many things I have to tell you."

Just then Maggie broke in. "Sorry to interrupt but dinner is on the table. And Tim Keenan is ready to say the blessing."

Lori glanced back at Jace. "I'm sorry. Can we talk later?" Without waiting for an answer, Lori took off and headed toward the front of the house. She felt Jace following behind her as they reached the dining room. Hopeful, she added an extra place at the table for him.

She smiled at all her family and the new friends she was sharing today with. That included Jace and Cassie.

It grew quiet and someone handed her a champagne glass. "First of all, Gina, Zack and I want to thank you all for coming today. I hope this is the first of many visits to Hutchinson House. I want you all to feel welcome, so you'll come back here." She raised her glass. "To friends, and to Destiny." After everyone took a drink, she had Tim Keenan say the blessing.

The group broke up, and mothers went off to fill

their children's plates and settle them in the sunroom. Maggie stood by, watching for any emergencies. Lori ended up back at the head table, while Gina was seated at the entry table. Somehow Jace was seated at her table, but at the opposite end. Every so often, he'd smile at her.

She kept telling herself in a few hours they could be alone. After dinner, she went into the kitchen to check on dessert and finally saw Cassie.

"Miss Lori." The girl came and hugged her. "I got to come back."

"I know. Your daddy told me."

"Did he tell you about the wedding?" Cassie's tiny hand slapped over her mouth. "Oh, no, I wasn't supposed to tell you about that."

"Whose wedding? Your mommy's?" When Cassie didn't answer, she asked, "Your daddy's?"

The child giggled. "Both of 'em. But don't tell Daddy I told you. It's a surprise."

Lori could barely take her next breath. Was that why Jace said he got Cassie? He had to remarry Shelly?

She couldn't do this. She turned and found Jace behind her, holding her coat. "Okay, we need to get out of here and talk." He grinned. "I know just the place."

She gasped. "There's no need to tell me. I already heard from Cassie about the wedding. I hope you and Shelly will be happy."

He frowned. "What? You think that Shelly and I..." He cursed.

Lori held up her hand to stop him, but he took it in his.

"We're definitely going to talk about this," he began. "We need to get a few things straightened out. Now."

"I can't leave now."

"So we should just talk here. I'm sure all your guests would love to hear what I have to say," he said, and held out her coat.

"Why are you doing this?" she asked, keeping her voice low.

"I hate the fact that you even have to ask. I hope I can change that." When she hesitated, he asked, "Can't you even give me a few minutes to hear me out? To listen to what I have to say."

Lori wasn't sure what to do, only that she didn't want a scene here. She slipped on her coat and told Maggie she was leaving for a little while.

The housekeeper smiled and waved them on saying, "It's about time."

CHAPTER THIRTEEN

Twenty minutes later, Jace was still furious as he pulled off the highway. The sun had already set, but he knew the way to the cabin.

"Why are you bringing me here?" Lori asked.

"So we can talk without anyone interrupting us." He glanced across the bench seat. "But if you want, I'll take you back home."

He watched her profile in the shadowed light. She closed her eyes then whispered, "No, it might be good if we talk. At least to clear the air."

"Oh, darlin', I plan to do more than clear the air."

Lori jerked her head around and even in the darkness he could see she was glaring. She opened her mouth but he stopped her words.

"Hold that thought. We're here." He pulled into the parking space and climbed out. No more snow had fallen since the last time he'd followed her here. It hadn't gotten any warmer, either.

He pulled his sheepskin coat together to ward off the cold as he went around to Lori's side. After helping her out, they hurried up to the lit porch. He took the key from his pocket and rushed on to explain, "I stopped by earlier." He unlocked the door, pushed it open and turned on the light inside the door.

"After you," he told her, watching surprise cross her pretty face. "Come on, let's get inside where it's warm."

Lori felt Jace's hand against her back, nudging her in. Once inside she stopped and looked around, trying not to think about the last time they'd been here. It didn't work. Memories flooded her head. How incredible it had been being in Jace's arms, making love with him.

"Just let me get a fire started." Jace went straight to the fireplace, where logs had been placed on the grate. He turned on the gas and the flames shot over the wood. He lit the candles that were lined up along the mantel, then turned to her. "You should be warm in a few minutes."

She recalled another time he hadn't waited for the fire to warm her. She pushed away the thought and walked to the table where she saw a vase of fresh flowers. Red roses. She faced him. "You bought these?"

He nodded.

"So you'd planned to bring me here?"

He pulled off his jacket and went to her. "I've been thinking about it since I left Denver. I want to be with you alone, to talk to you."

With her heart racing, she returned to the fire and held out her hands to warm them. Mostly, she wanted to gather her thoughts, but she was overwhelmed by this man. She wanted to be hopeful, but she also recalled what Jace had told her. He didn't want to get involved with another woman.

"Are you ready to listen to what I have to say?"

She stared into the fire. "So now you want to talk?

Why didn't you call me before? Let me know what was going on."

"Because I didn't know myself until recently. I was in mediation during the day with Shelly and her lawyers. At night, I was trying to ease my daughter's fears." His sapphire gaze met hers. "And I guess I've been so used to doing things on my own, I didn't know how to depend on someone else."

"You didn't have to be alone. I was here for you."

"I know that now. Yet, in the end, I had to make the decision based on my daughter's well-being. It was hard to know what was best for Cassie. Was I being selfish wanting her with me?"

Hearing his stress, she turned, but didn't go to him. "Oh, Jace. No, you weren't being selfish. You love Cassie enough to want to give her stability. I also believe that you love your daughter enough that if Shelly could give Cassie what she needed, you'd let her have custody."

He smiled. "It always amazes me how you seem to know me so well."

That wasn't true, she thought, praying he wanted the same thing she did. To be together. "Not so. I have no idea why you brought me here, especially since I haven't heard a word in the past week. And what about this wedding?"

This time he came to her. He stood so close, she could inhale his wonderful scent. The only sounds were the logs crackling in the fire as she waited for an explanation.

Then he took her hand. "I might have helped a little with a nudge to Edmund. He took it from there and went to see Shelly. They were married yesterday by the same judge who helped with the custody case. I escorted Cassie to her mother's wedding."

"Shelly got married?"

"Yes. I thought things would go smoother if I helped Shelly settle her problem with her now-husband. I contacted him the day I arrived, and got him to come with me to Shelly's place." He shrugged. "They took it from there, and now they're headed to England for their honeymoon and his family."

Jace met her dark eyes and nearly lost his concentration. "Before Shelly left we managed to sit down and decide what would be best for our daughter. In the end, Cassie told her mother she wanted to live with me in Destiny."

"That had to be hard on Shelly."

Jace nodded. "But she gets visitation, summers and holidays. She can't take Cassie out of the country until she's older." He studied Lori's pretty face and his stomach tightened. He wanted her desperately.

"It all finally got settled yesterday, and Cassie and I caught the first flight back here...and came to see you."

He reached for her hand and tugged her closer. "I want more, Lori. More than just having my daughter in my life. I also want you. No, not just want you, but need you."

Not giving her a chance to resist, his mouth came down on hers in an all-consuming kiss. He couldn't resist her, either. His hands moved over her back, going downward to her hips, drawing her against him.

With a gasp, she pulled back. "You're not playing fair," she accused.

"I want you, Lorelei Hutchinson. I'll use any means possible to have you."

"Wait." Lori pushed him away, not liking this. "What are you exactly talking about? Seduction?" She deserved more. "I won't be that secret woman in your life, Jace, that you pull out whenever it's convenient."

He frowned. "Whoa. Who said anything about that…" He stopped as if to regroup.

"First of all, I'm sorry that I ever made you feel that way. I asked a lot of you when I left here, and I know I should have called you. Believe me I wanted to, but I was so afraid that if I did, I'd confess how I felt about you. I didn't have a right yet. I needed all my concentration on Cassie. You and I both know what it's like to lose parents. I would do anything not to have that happen to my daughter." His gaze bore into hers. "No matter how much I care about you, Lori, I couldn't abandon my child and come to you." He swallowed. "No matter how much I wanted to. Not matter how much I love you."

She closed her eyes.

"No, look at me, Lori. I'm not your father. I'm never going to leave you, ever. How could I when I can't seem to be able to live without you. Even if I had to move back to Denver because of Cassie, I would have figured out a way to come and be with you, too."

"You love me?"

He drew her close and nodded. "From the top of your pretty blond hair, to your incredible brown eyes, down to your cute little ruby-red painted toes." He kissed her forehead, then brushed his lips against each eyelid. His mouth continued a journey to her cheek, then she shivered as he reached her ear. "I'll tell you about all your other delicious body parts later," he promised, then pulled back and looked down at her. "If you'll let me."

"Oh, Jace. I love you, too," she whispered.

"I was hoping you felt that way." He pulled her into his arms and kissed her deeply. By the time he released her they were both breathing hard.

"We better slow down a minute, or I'll forget what I was about to do." He went to his coat and pulled a small box out of his jacket pocket, then returned to Lori.

Her eyes grew round. "Jace?"

He felt a little shaky. "I want this to be perfect, but if I manage to mess up something, just remember how much I love you." He drew a breath. "Lorelei Hutchinson, I probably can't offer you a perfect life. I have a home that's still under construction. A business that isn't off the ground yet." His eyes met hers. "And a daughter that I'm going to ask you to be a mother to."

A tear ran down her cheek. "Oh, Jace, don't you know, those are assets. And I couldn't love Cassie any more than if she were my own."

"She loves you, too."

"So she's okay with me and you?"

He nodded. "She even approved of the ring." He opened the box and she gasped at the square-cut diamond solitaire with the platinum band.

"Oh, my. It's beautiful."

That was his cue. He got down on one knee. "Lorelei Hutchinson, you are my heart. Will you marry me?"

She touched his face with her hands and kissed him softly. "Yes, Jace, oh, yes."

With her mouth still against his, he rose and wrapped his arms around her as he deepened the kiss. He couldn't let her go. Ever.

He finally broke off the kiss, then slipped the ring on her finger. He kissed her softly, then pulled back. "Give me one second, then we'll have the rest of the night."

Lori nodded and looked down at her ring. She couldn't believe this was really happening. "Good, I'm going to need your full attention the rest of the night to convince me that this isn't a fairy tale."

He grinned, took out his cell phone and punched in a number. "You got it." He put it to his ear. "Hi, sweetheart," Jace said into the receiver. "She said yes." He looked at Lori and winked. "Yes, we'll celebrate tomorrow. I love you, too." He ended the call. "I hope you don't mind. Cassie wanted to know what your answer was."

"I don't mind at all. I think we have enough love that I can share it with your daughter." She wrapped her arms around his waist. "But maybe tonight, I'll let you show me."

"Not just tonight, Lori. Always. Forever."

EPILOGUE

It was nearly Christmas in Destiny.

This year, the town council had asked Lori to light the big tree in the town square. She was honored, to say the least. Of course, she didn't do it alone. She'd invited Zack and Cassie to help throw the switch that lit the fifty-foot ponderosa pine.

While enjoying the colorful light show and the children's choir singing carols, she recalled the first day she'd arrived in Destiny. She felt so alone, then she started meeting the people here. That included one stubborn contractor who made her heart race. Made her aware of what she'd been missing in life.

For Lori there were bittersweet memories, too. Her father was gone and she'd never had the chance to have a relationship with him. But with her new family, she wasn't going to be alone. Not only Gina and Zack, but also her future husband, Jace, and a stepdaughter, Cassie.

Suddenly she felt a pair of arms slip around her waist from behind. She smiled and leaned back against Jace's broad chest.

"So are you enjoying your big night?" he said against her ear.

"Oh, yes." She smiled, recalling the last time she'd been here with her father. She called them treasured memories now. "But I have to say, I'm glad the school play is over."

"Until next year," he reminded her.

"Very funny. I'm planning to be really busy."

"You do too much as it is," he said as they watched the children's choir singing beside the tree. He tightened his hold, his large body shielding her from the cold night. "Between the mortgage and college scholarship programs, you have no free time."

She and Jace had made the decision together about taking only a small part of the inheritance to put away for the kids; the rest would go back into the town. They both made an excellent income from Hutchinson Corp properties.

"I want to get the programs up and ready for when my father's money comes through next fall." She stole a glance over her shoulder at him. "You'd be proud of me. I've turned over my job on the mortgage committee to Erin. She'll go to all the meetings, and I'll work from her recommendations."

"However you get it done, you're a pretty special lady to be so generous to this town."

She turned in his arms. "I only want to be your special lady."

He grew serious. "You are, Lori, and will always be." He kissed her sweetly. "How about we ditch this place for something a little more private."

"Oh, I'd like that, but you know we can't. For one thing, Cassie and Zack are singing." They both looked at the children. "And we're all invited back to the Keenan Inn for a party and to finalize our wedding plans. It's going to be a big undertaking for Claire and Gina to pull this off, especially with the holidays."

"I know, the first wedding at Hutchinson House," he said.

"The first of many, I hope," she reminded him.

Jace had to smile. With the exception of Cassie's birth, he couldn't remember ever being this happy. Now he had it all, the woman he loved and his daughter permanently. "So I guess a wild night together is out of the question."

"Of course not. It's just postponed for a few weeks."

"Until New Year's Eve," he finished. The date they'd chosen for their wedding. "That's a long three weeks off." Even longer since they'd spent most of their time with Cassie trying to help her adjust to the new arrangement. He hated having to send Lori home every night.

"You sure we can't sneak off to the cabin tonight?"

She gave him a quick kiss. "Just hold that thought and I promise to make it worth your while after the wedding."

"You being here with me now has made my dreams come true."

Hutchinson House never looked so beautiful.

On New Year's Eve Lori stood at the window of the master suite. She could see over the wide yard toward the front of the property.

The ornate gates were covered with thousands of tiny silver lights and many more were strung along the hedges. It was only a prelude for what was to come as the wedding guests approached the end of the circular drive and the grand house on the hill.

The porch railings were draped in fresh garland, and

more lights were intermixed with the yards of greenery that smelled of Christmas. White poinsettias edged the steps leading to the wide front door trimmed with a huge fresh-cut wreath.

Lori smiled. The Hutchinson/Yeager wedding was going to be the first of many parties in this house.

Gina came in dressed in a long dark green grown. "Oh, Lori. You look so beautiful."

Lori glanced down at her wedding dress. She'd fallen in love with the floor-length ivory gown the second she'd seen it at Rocky Mountain Bridal Shop, from the top of the sweetheart neckline, to the fitted jeweled bodice with a drop waist and satin skirt. Her hair was pulled back, adorned with a floral headband attached to a long tulle veil.

"I hope Jace thinks so."

Gina handed her a deep red rose bouquet. "He will."

She felt tears forming. "I'm so lucky to have found him, and Cassie."

Gina blinked, too. "They're lucky to have you." She gripped Lori's hand. "I love you, sis. Thank you for always being there for us."

"Hey, you were there for me, too. And nothing will change. We're still family. I'm only going to be a few miles from your new place." Lori frowned, knowing they had arranged to live in their own house. "You feel okay about the move?"

Her sister nodded. "Zack and I are going to be fine."

Lori knew that. Her sister was working with Kaley, having hours that enabled her to be home when Zack got out of school. She still worried about Eric showing up someday, but they'd all keep an eye out.

Gina straightened. "Okay, let's get your special day started."

They walked into the hall toward the head of the stairs where Charlie was waiting. She couldn't lie, every girl dreamed of walking down the aisle escorted by her father. She wasn't any different. At least now she'd been able to make peace with it all.

She whispered, "I'll always miss you, Dad."

Smiling, Charlie had tears in his eyes when she arrived. "Oh, Miss Lorelei, you are a vision. I'm so honored to escort you today."

She gripped his hands. "Thank you, Charlie."

The older man offered her his arm. "I know there's an anxious young man waiting for his bride."

The music began and Cassie and Zack, the flower girl and ring bearer, started down the petal-covered stairs. The banister entwined with more garland that wound down to the large entry. Next Gina began her descent. Once her sister reached the bottom the music swelled.

Holding tight on to Charlie, Lori's heart raced when she made her way down. Once she touched the bottom steps, she took it all in.

The room was filled with flowers: roses, carnations and poinsettias, all white. Rows of wooden chairs, filled with family and friends, lined either side of the runner that led through the entry and into the dining room and ended at a white trellis covered in greenery. And underneath stood Jace. The man who was going to share her life.

Jace's breath caught when his gaze met Lori's. She was beautiful. His heart swelled. He never knew he could love someone so much.

She made her way to him and he had to stop himself from going to her. Finally she arrived and he took her hand. When he locked on her big brown eyes, everything else seemed to fade away. There was only her. It was just the two of them exchanging vows, making the life commitment.

The minister began the ceremony and the vows were exchanged. Jace listened to her speak and was humbled by her words.

Then came his turn. He somehow managed to get the emotional words past his tight throat. Then Justin passed him the ring, and he slipped the platinum band on her finger. He held out his hand so she could do the same.

He gripped both her hands and the minister finally pronounced them husband and wife. Jace leaned down, took her in his arms and kissed her.

There were cheers as the minister announced, "It's my pleasure to introduce to you, Mr. and Mrs. Jace Yeager."

Jace held his bride close, never wanting to let her go. She was his heart, his life, the mother of his future children.

It had been a long journey but they had found each other. He pulled back and looked at his bride. "Hello, Mrs. Yeager."

With tears in her eyes, she answered, "Hello, Mr. Yeager."

Together they walked down the aisle hand in hand past the well-wishers toward their future together. It was their Destiny.

* * * * *

She made her way toward and he had to stop himself from going to her. Finally, she arrived and he took her hand. When he looked on her big brown eyes, very long time she seemed to fade away. There was only her, it was like the two of them exchanging vows, making the ... the ceremony ...

The minister began the ceremony and the vows were exchanged. Jace listened to her speak and was humbled by her words ... an ... the appearance of ... ness that ...

Then came the ring. The ... a ... how managed to get the minister without much ... in his throat. Then he in passed him the ring, and he slipped the platinum band on her finger. He held out his hand so she could do the same.

He trapped both her hands and the minister finally pronounced them husband and wife. Jace leaned down, took her in his arms and kissed her.

There were cheers as the minister announced, "It's my pleasure to introduce to you, Mr. and Mrs. Jace Yeager."

Jace held his bride close, never wanting to let her go. She was his now, his future, the mother of his future children.

It had been a long journey, but they had found each other. He pulled back and looked at his bride. "Hello, Mrs. Yeager."

With tears in her eyes, she answered, "Hello, Mr. Yeager."

Together they walked down the aisle hand in hand, last the veil without looking their future together. It was their Dreams Come True.

∗∗∗

me inside the house, show
here I can eat and sleep, and get
ut of my life."

She'd meant to stay icy. She'd meant to stay dignified. So much for intentions.

Her last words were almost hysterical—a yell into the silence. No matter. Who cared what he thought? She flicked the trunk lever and stalked round to fetch her suitcase. Her foot hit a rain-filled pothole, she tripped and lurched—and the arrogant toe-rag caught her and held her.

It was like being held in a vice. His hands held her with no room for argument. She was steadied, held still, propelled out of the puddle and set back.

His hands held her arms a moment longer, making sure she was stable.

She looked up, straight into his face.

She saw power, strength and anger. But more. She saw pure, raw beauty.

It was as much as she could do not to gasp.

Lean, harsh, aquiline. Heathcliff, she thought, and Mr Darcy, and every smouldering cattleman she'd ever lusted after in the movies all rolled into one. The strength of him. The sheer, raw sexiness.

He released her and she thought maybe she should lean against the car for a bit.

It was just as well this place was a total disaster; this job was a total disaster. Staying anywhere near this guy would do her head in.

TAMING THE BROODING CATTLEMAN

BY
MARION LENNOX

First published in Great Britain 2012
by Mills & Boon, an imprint of Harlequin (UK) Limited,
Eton House, 18-24 Paradise Road, Richmond, Surrey TW9 1SR

© Harlequin Books S.A. 2012

Special thanks and acknowledgement are given to Marion Lennox for her contribution to THE LARKVILLE LEGACY series.

ISBN: 978 0 263 89477 6
ebook ISBN: 978 1 408 97151 2

23-1112

Harlequin (UK) policy is to use papers that are natural, renewable and recyclable products and made from wood grown in sustainable forests. The logging and manufacturing processes conform to the legal environmental regulations of the country of origin.

Printed and bound in Spain
by Blackprint CPI, Barcelona

Marion Lennox is a country girl, born on an Australian dairy farm. She moved on—mostly because the cows just weren't interested in her stories! Married to a 'very special doctor', Marion writes for Mills & Boon® Medical Romance™ and Mills & Boon® Cherish™. (She used a different name for each category for a while—readers looking for her past romance titles should search for author Trisha David, as well). She's now had more than seventy-five romance novels accepted for publication.

In her non-writing life Marion cares for kids, cats, dogs, chooks and goldfish. She travels, she fights her rampant garden (she's losing) and her house dust (she's lost). Having spun in circles for the first part of her life, she's now stepped back from her 'other' career, which was teaching statistics at her local university. Finally she's reprioritised her life, figured what's important and discovered the joys of deep baths, romance and chocolate.

Preferably all at the same time!

Marion Lennox is a country girl, born on an Australian dairy farm. She moved away to study but came back when... urged... in her spare time. Married to a very special doctor, Marion writes for Mills & Boon, Medical Romance™ and Mills & Boon Cherish™. She used a different name for each category for a while—until writing took over her non-Romance life. Now she writes for earlier Tilda David as well. She's now had more than seventy-five romance novels accepted for publication.

In her non-writing life, Marion cares for kids, cats, chooks and goldfish. She travels, she fights her rampant garden (she's losing) and her house dust (she's lost). Having spent much of her life in plaster from her roller-skating and reading sojourns at her local university, finally she organised her life, figured what's important and discovered the joys of deep baths, romance and chocolate.

Praise for all of the same time!

PROLOGUE

HE'D failed.

Jack Connor stood at his sister's graveside and accepted how badly he'd broken his promise to his mother.

'Take care of your sister.'

He'd been eight years old when his mother walked away. Sophie had been six.

What followed was a bleak, hard childhood, cramming schoolwork into his grandfather's demands for farm labour, and caring for his sister in the times between. Finally he'd escaped his grandfather's tyranny to the luxury of wages. From there he'd built a company from nothing. He'd had no choice. He'd been desperate for funds to provide the professional care Sophie so desperately needed.

It hadn't worked. Even though he'd made money, the care had come too late. For all that time he'd watched his sister self-destruct.

Sophie's social worker had come to the funeral. Nice of her. Her presence meant there'd been a whole three people in attendance. She'd looked into his grim face and she'd tried to ease his pain.

'This was not your fault, Jack. Your mother wounded your sister when she walked out, but the ultimate responsibility was Sophie's.'

But he stared down at the grave and knew she was

wrong. Sophie was dead and the ultimate responsibility was Jack's. He hadn't been enough.

What now?

Return to Sydney, to his IT company, to riches that had bought him nothing?

He stared down at the rain-soaked roses he'd laid on his sister's grave, and a memory wafted back. Sophie at his grandfather's farm, on one of the occasions his grandfather had been so blind drunk they weren't afraid of him. Sophie in what was left of his grandmother's rose garden. Sophie pressing roses into storybooks. *'We'll keep them for ever.'*

Suddenly he found himself thinking of horses he hadn't seen for years. His grandfather's horses, his friends from childhood. They'd asked for nothing but food, shelter and exercise. When he'd been with the horses, he'd almost been happy.

The farm was his now. His grandfather had died a year ago, but the demands of Sophie's increased illness meant he hadn't had time to go there. He guessed it'd be run-down. Even the brief legal contact he'd made had him sensing the manager his grandfather had employed was less than honest, but the bloodlines of his grandfather's stockhorses should still be intact. Remnants of the farm's awesome reputation remained.

Could he bring it back to its former glory?

Decision time.

He stared down at the rain-washed grave, his thoughts bleak as death.

If he was his grandfather, he thought, he'd hit something. Someone.

He wasn't his grandfather.

But he didn't want to return to Sydney, to a staff who treated him as he treated them, with remote courtesy.

The company would keep going without him.

He stood and he stared at his sister's grave for a long, long time.

What?

He could go back to the farm, he thought. He still knew about horses.

Did he know enough?

Did it matter? Maybe not.

Decision made.

Maybe he'd make a go of it. Maybe he wouldn't, but he'd do it alone and he wouldn't care.

Sophie was dead and he never had to care again.

CHAPTER ONE

Alex Patterson was having doubts. Serious doubts.

On paper the journey had sounded okay. Manhattan to
L.A. L.A. to Sydney. Sydney to Albury. Albury to Werarra.

Yeah, well, maybe it hadn't sounded okay, but she'd
read it fast and she hadn't thought about it. A few hours
before she'd reached Sydney she was tired. Now, after
three hours driving through pelting rain, she was just plain
wrecked. She wanted a long, hot bath, a long, deep sleep
and nothing more.

Surely Jack Connor wouldn't expect her to start work
until Monday, she thought. And where was this place?

The child she'd seen on the road a way back had told her
it was just around the bend. The boy had looked scrawny,
underfed, neglected, and she'd looked at him and her
doubts had magnified. She'd expected a wealthy neigh-
bourhood—horse studs making serious money. The child
looked destitute.

Werarra Stud must be better. Surely it was. Its stockhorses were known throughout the world. The website
showed a long, gracious homestead in the lush heart of
Australia's Snowy Mountains. She'd imagined huge bedrooms, gracious furnishings, a job her friends would envy.

'Werarra.' She saw the sign. She turned into the driveway—and she hit the brakes.

Uh-oh.

That was pretty much all she was capable of thinking. Uh-oh, uh-oh, uh-oh.

The website showed an historic photograph of a fabulous homestead built early last century. It might have been fabulous then, but it wasn't fabulous now.

No one had painted it for years. No one had fixed the roof, mended sagging veranda posts, done anything but board up windows as they broke.

It looked totally, absolutely derelict.

The cottage the child had come from had looked bad. This looked worse.

There was a light on somewhere round the back. A black SUV was parked to the side. There was no other sign of life.

It was pouring. She was so tired she wasn't seeing straight. It was thirty miles back to the nearest town and she wasn't all that sure Wombat Siding was big enough to provide a hotel.

She stared at the house in horror, and then she let her head droop onto the steering wheel.

She would not weep.

A thump on her driver's side window made her jump almost into the middle of next week.

Oh, my...

She needed to get a grip. Now.

You can cope with this, Alex Patterson, she told herself. You've told everyone back home you're tough, so prove it. You're not the spoilt baby everyone treats you as.

But this was...this was...

Another thump. She raised her head and looked out.

The figure outside the car was looming over the car window like a great black spectre. Rain-soaked and vast, it was blocking her entire door.

She squeaked. Maybe she even gibbered.

Then the figure moved back a bit from the car window, letting light in, and she came back to earth.

A man. A great, warrior-size guy. He was wearing a huge, black, waterproof coat, and vast boots.

The guy's face was dark, his thick black hair slicked to his forehead in the rain. He had weather-worn skin, stubble so thick it was close to a beard, and dark, brooding eyes spaced wide and deep.

He was waiting for her to open the car door.

If she opened it, she'd get wet.

If she opened it, she'd have to face what was outside.

He opened it for her, with a force that made her gasp. The rain lashed in and she cringed.

'You're lost?' The guy's voice was deep and growly, but not unfriendly. 'You need directions?'

If only she was, she thought. If only...

'Mr. Connor?' she managed, trying not to stutter. 'Jack Connor?'

'Yes?' There was sudden incredulity in his voice, as if he didn't believe what he was hearing.

'I'm Alex Patterson,' she told him. 'Your new vet.'

There were silences and silences in Alex's life. The silences as her mother disapproved—as she inevitably did—of what Alex was wearing, what she was doing. The silences after her father and brother's fights. Family conflicts meant Alex had been brought up with silences. It didn't mean she was used to them.

She'd come all the way to Australia to escape some of those silences, yet here she was, facing the daddy of them all.

This was like the silence between lightning and thunder—one look at this man's face and she knew the thunder was on its way.

When finally he spoke, though, his voice was icy calm. 'Alexander Patterson.'

'Yes.' Don't sound defensive, she thought. What was this guy's problem?

'Alex Patterson, son of Cedric Patterson, Cedric, the guy who went to school with my grandfather.'

She put a silence of her own in here.

Son of...

Okay, she saw the problem.

She'd trusted her father.

She thought of her mother's words. *'Alex, your father is ill. You need to double-check everything....'*

'Dad's okay. You're dramatising. There's nothing wrong with him.' She'd yelled it back at her mother, but even as she'd yelled it, she knew she was denying what was real. Alzheimer's was a vast, black hole, sucking her dad right in.

She hadn't wanted to believe it. She still didn't.

She'd trusted her father.

And anyway, what was the big deal? Man, woman, whatever. She was here as a vet. 'You thought I was male?' she managed, and watched the face before her grow even darker.

'I was told you were a guy. His son.'

'That's my dad for you,' she said, striving for lightness. 'A son is what he hoped for, but you'd think after twenty-five years he could figure the difference.' Deep breath. 'Do you think you could, I don't know, invite me in or something? I hate to mention it when the fact that I'm female seems to be such an issue, but an even bigger deal is that it's raining, I'm not wearing waterproofs and it's wet.'

'You can't stay here.'

This was bad, she thought, and it was getting worse.

But her dad's fault or not, this was a situation she had to face, and she might as well face it now.

'Well, maybe you should have told me that before I left New York,' she snapped, and she hauled herself out of the car. She was already wet. She might as well be soaked, and her temper, volatile at the best of times, was heading for the stratosphere. 'Maybe now I don't have a choice.'

Deep breath, she thought. Say it like it is.

'I,' she said, in tones that matched his for iciness and more, 'am at the end of a very long rope that stretches all the way back to New York. It's taken me three days to get here, give or take a day that seems to have disappeared in the process. I applied for a job here in good faith. I sent every piece of documentation you demanded. I accepted a work visa for six months on the strength of a job with a horse stud that looks—' she glanced witheringly at the house '—to be non-existent. And now you have the nerve to tell me you don't want me. I don't want you either, but I seem to be stuck with you, with this dump, with this place, at least until the rain stops and I've eaten and I've slept for twenty-four hours. Then, believe me, you won't see me for dust. Or mud. Now let me inside the house, show me where I can eat and sleep, and get out of my life.'

She'd meant to stay icy. She'd meant to stay dignified. So much for intentions.

Her last words were almost hysterical—a yell into the silence. No matter. Who cared what he thought? She flicked the trunk lever and stalked round to fetch her suitcase. Her foot hit a rain-filled pothole, she tripped and lurched—and the arrogant toerag caught her and held her.

It was like being held in a vice. His hands held her with no room for argument. She was steadied, held still, propelled out of the puddle and set back.

His hands held her arms a moment longer, making sure she was stable.

She looked up, straight into his face.

She saw power, strength and anger. But more.

She saw pure, raw beauty.

It was as much as she could do not to gasp.

Lean, harsh, aquiline. Heathcliff, she thought, and Mr Darcy, and every smouldering cattleman she'd ever lusted after in the movies, all rolled into one. The strength of him. The sheer, raw sexiness.

He released her and she thought maybe she should lean against the car for a bit.

It was just as well this place was a total disaster; this job was a total disaster. Staying anywhere near this guy would do her head in.

Her head was already done in. She was close to swaying.

Focus on your anger, she told herself. And practicalities. Get your gear out of the car. He's going to think you're a real New York princess if you expect him to do it for you.

But he was already doing it, grabbing her cute, pink suitcase (gift from her mother), glancing at it with loathing, slamming the trunk closed and turning to march toward the house.

'Park the car when it stops raining,' he snapped over his shoulder. 'It'll be fine where it is for the night.'

She was supposed to follow him? Into the Addams Family nightmare?

A flash of lightning lit the sky and she thought it needed only that.

Thunder boomed after it.

Jack had reached the rickety steps and was striding up to the veranda without looking back.

He had her suitcase.

She whimpered. There was no help for it, she whimpered.

Her family thought she was a helpless baby. If they could see her now, they'd be proven right. That's exactly how she felt. She wanted, more than anything, to be back in Manhattan, lying in her gorgeous peach bedroom, with Maria about to bring her hot chocolate.

Where was her maid when she needed her most? Half a world away.

More lightning. Oh, my...

Jack was disappearing round the side of the veranda. Her suitcase was disappearing with him.

She had no choice. She took a deep breath and scuttled after him.

He showed her to the bedroom and left her to it. Headed to his makeshift study and hauled open his computer. Grabbed the original letter.

Could he sack a worker just because she was female?

Surely he could if she'd taken the job under false pretences, he thought, reading the first letter he'd received.

My son, Alexander, is looking for experience on an Australian horse stud. Alex is a qualified veterinarian and is also willing to take on general farm work. The level of pay would not be a problem; what Alex mostly wants is experience.

My son.

He flicked through the emails, printing them out. After Cedric's first letter he'd corresponded directly with Alex. *Her.* There was no mention of what sex she was in her emails, he conceded. They'd been polite, businesslike, and they hadn't referred to her sex at all.

Yes, I understand the living conditions may be rougher than I'm accustomed to, but I'd appreciate even a tough job. My aim is to work on horse studs in the States, but getting that first job after vet school is difficult. If I do a decent job for you, it may well give me the edge over other graduates.

He'd expected a fresh-faced kid straight out of vet school, possibly not understanding just how tough it was out here, but ready to make a few sacrifices in order to get the job. Despite the conditions, Werarra produced horses with an international reputation. This would be a good career step.

He'd never have employed a woman.

He hadn't wanted to employ anyone, but sense had decreed he had no choice. This place had deteriorated to the point of being a ruin. The horses took all his attention. The house was derelict and the manager's cottage even more so. Brian, the guy who'd managed the place for his grandfather, preferred to live a half a mile down the road on the second of the farm's holdings. Jack had expected him to keep on working, but the moment Jack arrived he'd lit out, abandoning his wife and kids, disappearing without trace.

The letter from Cedric Patterson, addressed to Jack Connor, had come when he was overwhelmed. Despite his misgivings he'd thought, a vet...plus someone who could help with the heavy manual work like getting the fences back in order... The manager's house was unlivable, but maybe a kid could cope with sharing the big house with him.

He'd written back to Cedric explaining that the Jack he was writing to, the Jack he'd gone to school with, was dead. Cedric had visited Werarra, had stayed here, when he and his grandfather were young men, when his grandmother was alive and making the place a home. The house had deteriorated, he'd told him. There were no separate living quarters, but if Alex was happy to do it tough…

Alex himself…*herself*…had emailed back saying tough was fine.

What now? He didn't even have a working bathroom. Asking a guy to use the outhouse was a stretch, *but a woman*?

He could fix the bathroom. Maybe. But not tonight.

And he still didn't want a woman. The women in his life had caused him nothing but grief and anguish. To have another, sharing his house, sharing his life…

Stop it with the dramatisation, he told himself harshly. She wouldn't want to stay even if he wanted her to. She obviously had a romantic view of what an outback Australian horse stud would be. One look at the outside privy and she'd run.

He didn't blame her.

Meanwhile…

Meanwhile he needed to feed her. He hurled sausages into the pan, sliced onions as if he could get rid of his anger on the chopping board, tossed them on top of the sausages and fumed. At himself more than her. He shouldn't have tried to employ anyone until he had this place decent, *but a woman*?

She took one look at the outside privy and wanted to die.

There was an inside bathroom, but… 'Plumbing's blocked,' Jack had said curtly, as he showed her her bedroom. 'Tree roots. Use the outhouse. There's a torch.'

The outhouse was fifty yards from the back door. A massive, overgrown rose almost hid it from view, and she had to make her way through a tunnel of vine to reach it.

A couple of hefty beef cattle were hanging their heads

over the fence, dripping water in the rain, looking at her as if she was an alien.

That's how she felt. Alien.

She locked the outhouse door, and something scrabbled over the outhouse's tin roof. What?

She wanted to go home.

'You're a big girl,' she told herself, out loud so whatever it was on the roof would get the picture. 'You need to get in there, front Jack Sexist Connor, find something to eat, get some sleep and then find a way out of this mess.'

The rain had eased for a minute, which was why she'd taken the chance and run out here. It started again, sheeting in under the door.

'I want to go home,' she wailed, and the thing on the roof stilled and listened.

And didn't answer.

He was cooking sausages. Eight fat sausages, Wombat Siding butcher's finest. He cooked mashed potato and boiled up some frozen peas to go with them.

He set the table with two knives, two forks, a ketchup bottle and two mugs. What more could a man want?

A woman might want more, he conceded, but she wasn't getting more.

What did he know about what a woman would want? A woman who was supposed to be a man.

She pushed open the door, and his thoughts stopped dead.

She'd been wearing black pants and a tailored wool jacket when she arrived. Her hair had been twisted into a knot. She'd been wearing red ankle boots, with old-fashioned buttons. She'd looked straight out of New York.

Now...

He'd left a pitcher and basin in her bedroom and she'd

obviously made use of it. She'd washed—the tendrils of blond curls around her face were damp—and her face was shiny clean with no hint of make-up. She was wearing jeans and an oversize sweater. Her curls hung free to her shoulders.

She was wearing thick, pink socks.

The résumé she'd sent said she was twenty-five years old. Right now she looked about sixteen. Pretty. Really pretty. Also…scared?

Daniel in the lion's den.

Or woman in Werarra.

Same thing, only he wasn't a lion. But she couldn't stay here.

'Sit down and wrap yourself round something to eat,' he said roughly, trying to hold to anger.

'Thank you.' She sidled into a chair on the far side of the table to him, still looking scared.

'Three sausages?'

'One.'

'Suit yourself.' He put one sausage onto a chipped plate, added a pile of mash and a heap of peas and put it in front of her. He ladled himself more.

He sat and started eating.

She sat and stared at her plate.

'What?' he said.

'I didn't lie,' she said in a small voice.

'I have the documentation,' he said, pointing to the pile of papers he'd left on the end of the table. '*My son*. That would be a male.'

'Nothing in any of my emails to you said I was a guy.'

'They didn't have to. I already knew. Your father's letter. The visa application. My son, the letter said. Plus Alexander. It's a guy's name.'

'Yes,' she said, and shoved her plate back. 'It is.'

'So?'

'My father doesn't get on with my older brother.' She was speaking calmly, in a strangely dull voice, like she'd reached some point and gone past. 'I've never figured why, but there's nothing anyone can do to fix it. I have two older sisters, and by the time I arrived Dad was desperate for a male heir other than Matt. He was sure I'd be the longed-for son. He planned on calling me Alexander, after his dad, only of course I ended up being Alexandra. So Dad filled in the birth certificate. Maybe he'd had a few drinks. Maybe it was just a slip, or maybe it was anger that I wasn't what he wanted. I don't know, but officially I'm Alexander. My family calls me Alexandra but on official stuff, I need to use Dad's spelling.' She tilted her chin and tried to glare at him. 'So...does it matter?'

'Yes,' he said flatly. 'It does. Your father said you were his son. I want to know why he lied.'

'He made a mistake.'

'Fathers don't make that sort of mistake.'

'They do if they always wanted their daughter to be a boy,' she said dully. She closed her eyes and clenched her fists. 'They do if they have Alzheimer's.'

Silence.

Whatever he'd expected, it wasn't that. The word hung. She hadn't wanted to say it, he thought. Admitting your dad was ill... It hurt, he thought. It hurt a lot.

Anger faded. He felt...cruel. Like he'd damaged something.

'So why does it matter?' she demanded, hauling herself together with a visible effort. 'What have you got against women?'

'Nothing.'

'I applied for jobs after graduating,' she said. 'I want horse work. To work with horses, not ponies, not pets. You try and get a job on a horse ranch when you're twenty-five and blonde and cute.'

And she said the word *cute* with such loathing he almost smiled.

'I can imagine…'

'No, you can't,' she snapped. 'You're six feet tall, built like a tank and you're male. You know nothing at all about what it's like to want to handle yourself with horses. This job…six months at Werarra Stud…is supposed to give me credibility with the ranchers back home, but you're just the same as every redneck cowboy know-all who ever told me I can't do it because I'm a girl.'

'So you're prepared to put up with an outhouse for six months?' he demanded, bemused.

'Not if it comes with an arrogant, chauvinistic oaf of an employer. And not if I have to eat grease.' And she shoved her plate across the table at him with force.

He caught it. He piled the sausage and mash absently onto his plate. He thought *cute* was a really good description.

Don't go there. This was a mistake he had to get rid of. He did not want to think any woman was cute.

'So you'll go home tomorrow,' he said, and she looked around and he thought if she had another plateful she might just possibly throw it at him.

'Why should I? I didn't lie about this job. You did.'

'I didn't.'

'Liar.'

'I told you it'd be rough.'

'I assumed you meant no shops. Living in the outback. The house… On the website it looks gorgeous.'

'That picture was taken eighty years ago. Romantic old homestead.'

'It's false advertising.'

'I'm not advertising my house,' he said evenly. 'I'm advertising my horses. I wanted the website to show a sense of history, that Werarra workhorses are part of what this country is.'

'Show the picture of your outhouse, then,' she snapped. 'Very historic.'

'You'll starve if you don't eat.'

'I couldn't eat sausages if you paid me.'

'Don't tell me—you're vegan.'

'I'm not.'

'Then why...'

'Because I've travelled for three days straight,' she snapped. 'Because I'm jet-lagged and overtired and overwrought. Because if you must know, my stomach is tied in knots and I'd like a dainty cucumber sandwich and a cup of weak tea with honey. Not a half-ton of grease. But if I have to go to bed with nothing, I will.' She shoved back her chair and stood. 'Good night.'

'Alex...'

'What?' she snapped.

'Sit down.'

'I don't want—'

'You don't want sausages,' he said and sighed, and opened the oven door of the great, old-fashioned fire stove that took up half the kitchen wall. He shoved his plate in there. 'I'll keep mine hot while I make you something you can eat.'

'Cucumber sandwiches?'

He had to smile. She sounded almost hopeful.

'Nope,' he said. 'I clean forgot cucumber on my shopping list. But sit down, shut up, and we'll see if we can find an alternative.'

She sat.

She looked up at him, half distrustful, half hopeful, and he felt something inside him twist.

Sophie, bleak as death, stirring her food with disinterest. *'I can't eat, Jack....'*

Sophie.

Do not think this woman is cute. Do not think this woman is anything other than a mistake you need to get rid of.

But for tonight... Yeah, she was needy. The explanation for the mix-up...it had hurt her to tell him about her dad; he could see that it hurt. And she was right, it shouldn't matter that she was a woman.

It wasn't her fault that it did. That the thought of a woman sitting on the far side of the table, a woman who even looked a little like Sophie, stirred something inside him that hurt. A lot.

She wasn't saying anything. He poured boiling water over a tea bag, and ladled in honey. He handed her the mug and watched her cradle it as if she needed its comfort.

The stove was putting out gentle warmth. This room was the only place in the house that bore the least semblance to cosy.

She didn't look cosy. She looked way out of her depth.

He was being cruel. If she was leaving in the morning, it wouldn't hurt to look after her.

He eyed her silently for a moment while she cradled her mug and stared at the battered wood of the ancient kitchen table.

It wouldn't hurt.

She was so spaced, so disoriented, that if she'd crashed down on the surface of the table she wouldn't be surprised. She felt light-headed, weird. When had she last eaten? On the plane this morning? Last night? When was last night and this morning? They were one and the same thing.

She wasn't making sense, even to herself. She should make herself stand up, head back to her allotted bedroom and go to sleep. And then get out of here.

Instead she cradled her mug of hot tea and stared at the worn surface of the table and did nothing.

She wasn't all that sure her legs would let her do anything else.

Jack was at the stove. He had his back to her. She wasn't sure what he was doing and she didn't care.

She'd wanted this so badly....

Why?

Veterinary Science hadn't been a problem for her. She'd dreamed of taking care of horses since she was a child. She'd put her head down and worked, and she'd succeeded.

Getting a job, though, was a sight harder. Horse medicine was hard, physically tough. The guys in college who were good at it were those who came from farms, who were built tough and big, who knew how to handle themselves. But she'd done it. She'd trained in equestrian care, she'd proved she could do what the guys did; she used brains instead of brawn, got fast at avoiding flying hooves, learned a bit of horse whispering.

It worked until she hit the real world, the world of employment, when no rancher wanted a five-feet-four-inch, willow-thin, blonde, twenty-five-year-old girl vet.

Like this guy didn't want her.

Her dad had organised this job for her. She'd been humiliated that she'd had to sink to using family connections, and now it seemed even family connections weren't enough.

What now?

Go back to New York? Find herself a nice little job caring for Manhattan pets? Her mother would be delighted.

Her dad?

He loved that she was a vet. He loved it that she wanted to treat horses.

He'd have loved it better if she was a son.

'Let's see if this suits you better,' Jack said, and slid another plate in front of her.

She looked—and looked again.

No sausages. Instead she was facing a small, fine china plate, with a piece of thin, golden toast, cut into four neat triangles. On the side was one perfectly rounded, perfectly poached egg.

She stared down at the egg and it was as much as she could do not to burst into tears.

'You're beat,' he said gently. 'Eat that and get to bed. Things will look better in the morning.'

She looked up at him, stunned by this gesture. This plate…it was like invalid cooking, designed to appeal to someone with the most jaded appetite. Where had this man…?

'Don't mind me, but I'm going back to my sausages,' he said, and hauled them out of the oven and did just that.

She'd thought she was too upset to eat, that she'd gone past hunger. He stayed silent, concentrating on his own meal. Left to herself, she managed to clean her plate.

He made her a second mug of tea. She finished that, too. She wasn't feeling strong enough to speak, to argue, to think about the situation she was in. She'd sleep, she thought. Then…then…

'There's not a lot I can't do that a guy can do,' she said, not very coherently but it was the best she could manage at the end of the meal.

'No,' he said. 'But you wouldn't want to stay here.'

'Neither would any male vet I trained with.'

He nodded. 'I shouldn't have let anyone come.'

'You need me, why?'

'I don't need you.'

'Right,' she said, and rose. 'I guess that's it, then. Maybe I should say thank-you for the egg but I won't. I've just paid the airfare to come halfway round the world for a job that doesn't exist. Compared to that...well, it does seem an egg is pretty lousy wages.'

CHAPTER TWO

The bedroom was a faded approximation to her dreams. It had once been beautiful, large and gracious, with gorgeous flowered wallpaper, rich, tasselled drapes, a high ceiling, wide windows and a bed wide enough to fit three of her. It still was beautiful—sort of. She could ignore the faded wallpaper, the shredded drapes. For despite the air of neglect and decay, her bed was made up with clean, crisp linen. The mattress and pillows were surprisingly soft. Magically soft.

Soft enough that despite her emotional upheaval, despite the fact that it was barely seven o'clock, she was asleep as soon as her head touched the pillow.

But reality didn't go away. She woke up with a jolt in the small hours, and remembered where she was, and remembered her life was pretty much over.

Okay, maybe she was exaggerating, she decided, as she stared bleakly into the darkness. She had the money to have a holiday. She could go back to Sydney, do some sightseeing, head back to New York and tell everyone she'd been conned.

Her friends had been derisive when she'd told them what she was doing. 'You? On an outback station? Man-of-all-work as well as vet for stockhorses? Get real, Alex, you're too blonde.'

The teasing had been good-natured but she'd heard the serious incredulity behind it. No one would be surprised when she came home.

And then what? Her thoughts were growing bleaker. If this low-life cowboy kicked her off this farm...

He didn't have to kick her off. There was no way she'd stay here, with this ramshackle house, without a bathroom, with his chauvinistic attitudes.

Bleak-R-Us.

The silence was deafening. She was used to city sounds, city lights filtering through the drapes. Here, there was nothing.

If there was nothing, she had to leave.

Okay. She could do what her mother wanted, she thought. Concede defeat. Get a job caring for New York's pampered pooches. Her mother had all sorts of contacts who could get her such a job. Unlike her dad, who'd loved the idea of her working with horses, and who'd used the only contact he had. Which just happened to be forty years out of date.

And for a son, not for a daughter.

Her thoughts were all over the place, but suddenly she was back with her dad. Why did it make a difference? She'd never been able to figure why her dad wasn't happy with the son he had; why he'd been desperate to have another.

Like she couldn't figure why it was so important to Jack Connor that she was male.

He'd cooked her an egg.

It was a small thing. In the face of his boorish behaviour it was inconsequential, yet somehow it made a difference.

He was used to invalid cookery, she thought. Maria had made meals like that for her when she was ill. The fact that Jack had done it...

It meant nothing. One egg does not a silk purse make. He was still, very much, a sow's ear. A sow's ear she'd be seeing the last of tomorrow morning. Or this morning.

She checked her watch: 3:00 a.m. Four hours before she could stalk away from this place and never come back.

Admit defeat?

Yes, she told her pillow. Yes, because she had no choice.

She rolled over in bed and saw a flicker of light behind the curtains.

Jack, heading for the outhouse?

The outhouse was on the other side of the house.

Someone was out there.

So what? She shoved her pillow over her head and tried to sleep.

It was midday in Manhattan. She was wide awake.

The light.

Ignore it. Go to sleep.

Her legs were twitchy. She'd spent too long on too many planes.

So what? Go to sleep.

Or what?

Sancha was one of the stud's prize mares. This was her second foaling. He hadn't expected trouble.

At two-thirty he'd known things were happening but the signs were normal. He'd checked the foal had a nice healthy heartbeat. He'd brought in thick fresh straw, then sat back and waited. Foaling was normally explosively fast. Horses usually delivered within half an hour.

She didn't.

She was in trouble.

So was the foal. The presentation was all wrong. The heartbeat was becoming erratic.

He need a vet. Now.

He had one in the house. But…

He wasn't all that sure he trusted her credentials. Besides, he'd sacked her. He could hardly ask her to help.

But if he didn't…it'd take an hour to get the local vet here and that heartbeat meant he didn't have an hour.

He swallowed his pride and thought, Thank heaven he'd made the girl an egg.

She hauled on her fleecy bathrobe and headed out to the veranda. Just to see. Just because staying in bed was unbearable. She could see lightning in the distance but the storm was past. It had stopped raining. The air felt cool and crisp and clean. She needed cool air to clear her head.

She walked out the back door, and barrelled straight into Jack.

He caught her, steadied her, but it took a moment longer for her breath to steady. He was so big…. It was the middle of the night. This place was creepy.

He was big.

'Are you really a vet?' he demanded, and she stiffened and hauled away.

'Does it matter?'

'Yes,' he said curtly. 'I've a mare with dystocia. She's been labouring for at least an hour and nothing's happened. I can't get the presentation right—there are hooves everywhere. I'll lose her.'

'My vet bag's in the car,' she snapped. 'Get it and show me where she is.'

She was cute, blonde, female. She was wearing a pink, fuzzy bathrobe.

She was a veterinarian.

From the time she entered the stables, her entire attention was on the mare. He was there only to answer curt questions she snapped at him as she examined her.

'How long since you found her? Was she distressed then? Has she foaled before?'

'With no problem. I'm sure it's the presentation. I can't fix it.'

She hauled off her bathrobe, shoved her arm in the bucket of soapy water and performed a fast double-check. She didn't trust him.

Why should she?

The mare was deeply distressed. She'd been moving round, agitated, lying, rolling, standing again. Alex moved with her as she examined her, not putting herself at risk but doing what had to be done, fast.

Her examination was swift, and so was her conclusion.

'After an hour's labour, there's no way we'll get it out naturally from the position it's in and it's too risky to try and manoeuvre it. The alternative's a caesarean, but I'd need help and I'd need equipment.'

'I have equipment and I can help,' he said steadily, but he was thinking, Did he have enough? And...*to do a caesarean, here?* He knew the drill. What they needed was an equipped surgery, sterile environs, equipment and drugs to make this possible. Even the thought of moving the mare and holding her seemed impossible. If he had another strong guy...

He had a petite blonde, in a cute bathrobe.

But she hadn't seemed to notice that she was totally unsuited for the job at hand. She was checking the beams overhead.

'Are you squeamish?'

What, him? 'No,' he snapped, revolted.

'I'd need ropes and more water. I'd need decent lights.

I'd need warmed blankets—get a heater out here, anything. Just more of it. What sort of equipment are you talking?'

'I hope we have everything you need,' he told her, and led her swiftly out to the storeroom at the back of the stables.

The Wombat Siding vet had equipped the store. With over a hundred horses, the vet was out here often, so he'd set up a base here. Three hours back to fetch equipment wasn't possible so he'd built a base here.

And Alex's eyes lit at the sight of the stuff he had. She didn't hesitate. She started hauling out equipment and handing it to him.

'So far, so good,' she said curtly. 'With this gear it might just be possible. You realise I'm only aiming to save the mare. You know foal survival under these conditions is barely ten percent.'

'I know that.'

'You won't faint?'

'No.'

'I've seen tougher cowboys than you faint, but you faint and your mare dies. Simple as that. I can't do it alone.'

'I'm with you every step of the way.'

She stared at him long and hard, and then gave a brisk nod, as if he'd passed some unseen test.

'Right,' she snapped. 'Let's do it.'

It was hard, it was risky.

She was skilled.

She whispered to the mare. Administered the anaesthetic. Guided her down.

Together they rolled her into position, and he was stunned at the strength of her. She didn't appear to notice how much strength it took.

With the mare unconscious she set up a drip. She'd

teamed with Jack to rope the mare into position, using the beams above, but Jack still needed to support her. He was told to supervise the ventilator delivering oxygen plus the drip administering electrolytes and fluids.

She delivered curt instructions and he followed. This was her call.

There was no choice. If she wasn't here, he'd lose the mare. Simple as that.

She was a vet.

She was wearing a pink bathrobe. She'd tugged her hair back with a piece of hay twine. She shouldn't look professional.

She looked totally professional.

She was clipping the hair from the mare's abdomen, fast, sure, then doing a speedy sterile prep. Checking instruments. Looking to him for reassurance.

'Ready?'

'I'm ready,' he said, and wondered if he was.

He had to be.

He watched, awed, as she made a foot-long incision in the midline of the abdomen, then made an incision into the uterus giving access to the foal.

'Say your prayers,' she said, and hauled out a tiny hoof, and then another.

This was a big mare. The foal was small, but compared to this young woman... For her to lift it free...

He made a move to help her.

'Watch that oxygen,' she snapped. 'Leave this to me. It's mare first, foal second.'

He understood. Emergency caesareans in horses rarely meant a live foal. They were all about saving the life of the mare.

If the airway he was monitoring blocked, they'd lose the mare, so he could only watch as she lifted the foal free. She staggered a little under the weight, but he knew enough now not to offer to help. She steadied, checked, put her face against its nuzzle, then carried it across to the bed of straw where he'd laid blankets. He'd started a blow heater, directing it to the blankets, to make it warm.

Just in case...

Maybe there was a case.

He kept doing what he was doing, but he had space to watch as she swiftly cleared its nose, inserted the endotracheal tube he'd hardly noticed she'd set up, started oxygen, then returned briskly to the mare. All in the space of seconds. She couldn't leave the mare for any longer.

The foal was totally limp. But...

'There's a chance,' she said, returning fast to the job at hand. There was no time, no manpower, to care for the foal more than she'd done.

She had to stitch the wound closed. He had to stay where he was, supporting the mare, keeping the airway clear.

But he watched the foal out of the corner of his eye. Saw faint movement.

The mare shifted, an involuntary, unconscious shudder. 'Watch her,' Alex ordered. 'You want to risk both?'

No. He went back to what he was doing. Making sure she was steady. Making sure she lived.

Alex went back to stitching.

He watched her blond, bent head and he felt awed. He thought back to the sausages and outhouse and felt...stupid.

And cruel.

This woman had come halfway round the world so she could have a chance to do what she was doing brilliantly. And he'd begrudged her an egg.

There was no time for taking this further now, though. With the stitching closed, she removed the ropes. He helped her shove fresh straw under the mare's side, then manoeuvred her into lateral recumbency, on her side.

The foal...

'Watch her,' she said again, more mildly this time, and she left him to the mare and stooped back over the foal.

'We still have him,' she said, in a voice that said it mattered. Her voice held surprise and a little awe. She checked more thoroughly and he saw the foal stir and shift. *'Her,'* Alex corrected herself, and there was no concealing the emotion she felt. 'Let's get the birth certificate right on this one.'

A filly. Out of Sancha.

If he got a live mare and foal out of this night... He couldn't describe the feeling.

But it wasn't certain yet. She was setting up an IV line, then using more blankets to towel the foal. It...*she*...was still limp.

Everything had to go right with a foaling. Foals didn't survive premature delivery. They seldom survived caesareans. To get a good outcome...

Please...

Sancha stirred under his hands, whinnied, lifted her head.

'Hey.' He laid his head on her head, the way he used to do as a kid, the way his grandfather had taught him. His grandfather was a cruel drunk, mean to everything and everyone but his horses, but Jack had watched him and learned, and the skills were there when he needed them. 'There's no need to get up,' he whispered to her. 'Your baby's in good hands.'

She was.

They watched and waited. There seemed nothing of the Manhattan princess about Alex right now. She had all the time in the world, all the patience.

Jack whispered to his mare, watched his foal—and watched this woman who'd transformed before his eyes.

Finally the foal started to struggle, starting to search for her feet. Alex helped her up, a wobbly tangle of spindly legs and huge head, and Jack felt…felt…

Like a horseman shouldn't feel. He didn't get emotional. He didn't care?

The foal whinnied and the mare responded. She struggled, as well, and Alex was suddenly back with him. The mare rose, as unsteady as her daughter, but finally with their help she was upright.

She turned and nosed her daughter. The foal whinnied in response, and started magically to nose underneath her.

Alex smiled and smiled. She guided the foal to the teat and then stood back.

'I think we might just have won,' she whispered, and Jack might have been struggling to hide his emotions but Alex surely wasn't. Tears were tracking down her cheeks and he felt an almost irresistible urge to wipe them for her.

He watched her. He watched the foal and the sensations were indescribable. The urge to hug this woman, to lift her and spin her in triumph, to share this amazing feeling…

It had to be suppressed—of course it did—but nothing had ever been harder.

So she wiped her tears herself, swiping her bathrobe sleeve over her face, sniffing, smiling through tears, then started to clear away the stained straw. Moving on. Being sensible.

More sensible than him.

'She'll need to be kept quiet for weeks,' she said, trying to sound brusque rather than emotional—but not succeeding. 'This isn't like a human caesarean—all her innards are bearing down on those stitches. The foal will need exercise, though. It's imperative to allow her to run and frolic, so it'll be hand-walking the mare every day while her baby has her runs.'

She'd started loading her gear back into her bag. 'That's more work for you,' she said, still brusque. Not looking at him. 'A lot of extra work. You might need to think about finding extra help. Seeing as you've sacked me.'

She might not be looking at him, but he was looking at her. She was wearing a bloodstained and filthy bathrobe. Her hair was flying every which way.

He'd never seen anything more beautiful in his life.

Which was the sort of thing he needed to stop thinking if he was offering her a job.

He was offering her a job. He had no choice. He'd treated her appallingly and she'd replied by saving his mare and foal.

'The indoor bathroom drain only blocked last week,' he told her before he could let prudence, sense, anything, hold sway. 'I can pay priority rates and arrange a plumber to come this morning. We should have an operating bathroom by dusk. For now, though… The boiler in the outside laundry is full of hot water. I can cart water into the bath so you can get yourself clean.'

She stilled and stared at him. 'Hot water?' she whispered, as if he was offering the Holy Grail.

'Yes.'

'You're offering me a bath?'

'And a job.'

'Forget jobs, just give me a bath,' she said, breathing deeply. She straightened and looked at him full-on, as if reading his face for truth. 'A great big, hot, gorgeous bath? I'll cart the water myself if I must.'

'No more carting for you tonight,' he said gruffly. 'You've done enough. About this job…'

'Tomorrow,' she said. 'I'll think about anything you like, as long as the bath comes first.'

She headed for her bath. The ancient claw-foot tub was huge and it took a while to fill but she beamed the whole time he filled it. He made sure she had everything she needed, then headed back out to the stables.

He watched over his mare and foal and thought about what had just happened.

He'd arrived here after Sophie's death thinking he had a manager and a stablehand. The stablehand had been yet one more instance of his manager's fraudulent accounting. So had the costs he'd billed Jack for, for the upkeep of the buildings. Seemingly his grandfather hadn't worried about infrastructure for years and his crook of a manager had made things worse. The horses had been cared for, the cattle had kept the grass down, but nothing else had been done to the place at all. Jack was therefore faced with no help and no place fit to house anyone to help him.

When Cedric Patterson's letter came he'd been pushed to the limit. Cedric's offer had been for a farmhand and a vet, rolled into one.

The manager's residence was uninhabitable and he didn't have time to fix it. But could he put a young man into the main house? A wide-eyed student, who needed experience to get a job elsewhere? Who'd shrugged off his assurance that this place was rough as if it was nothing? Such a kid might well take the job. Such a kid might not intrude too much on his life.

He'd mulled over the letter for a couple of days before replying but it had been too tempting to resist. Now it was even more tempting. Alex was *some* vet.

So, he'd offered her the job. If she accepted, the decision was made.

Which meant living with her for six months.

He didn't want to live with anyone for six months, but he sat on a hay bale and watched mare and foal slowly recover from their ordeal, and he thought of Alex's skill and speed, and he knew this was a gift he couldn't knock back.

He thought of how he'd felt, watching her over the kitchen table. Remembering Sophie. Remembering pain. Those last few months as Sophie had spiralled into depression so great nothing could touch her were still raw and dreadful.

Alex had nothing to do with Sophie, he told himself harshly. All he had to do was stay aloof.

All he had to do was not to care. That was his promise to himself. Never to care again.

But she was lovely. And clever and skilled.

And gorgeous.

'Cut it out,' he growled, and his mare stirred in alarm. Her foal, however, kept right on drinking.

'See, that's what I need to be,' he told his beautiful mare. 'Single-minded, like your baby. I'm here to produce the best stockhorses in Australia and I'm interested in nothing else.'

Liar. He was very, very interested in the woman he'd just shown into the bathroom. He'd watched her face light when she'd seen the steaming bathtub of hot water and he'd wanted…he'd wanted…

It didn't matter what he wanted, he thought. He knew what he had to do.

He'd offered her a job. This stud needed her.

That was all it was. An employer/employee relationship, starting now.

If she stayed.

He shouldn't want her to stay—but he did.

* * *

Would she stay?

Did it matter?

She lay back in the vast, old-fashioned bathtub and let the hot water soothe her soul. Nothing mattered but this hot water.

And the fact that she'd saved a mare and foal. It was what she was trained to do and the outcome was deeply satisfying.

And the fact that Jack Connor had offered her a job?

She shouldn't take it. He was an arrogant, chauvinistic toad, she told herself. And this place was a dump.

Except…it wasn't. The stables were brilliant. The equipment Jack had, not just medical stuff but every single horse fitting, was first-class. He'd poured money into the stables, into the horses, rather than the house.

She could forgive a lot of a man who put his animals' needs before his own.

And he'd fix the bathroom. He'd promised. She could have a bath like this every night.

She wouldn't have to go home and do her mother's bidding.

She could stay…with Jack?

Maybe she needed a bit of cold water in this bath.

Whoa. That was exactly the sort of thing she didn't need to be thinking. Jack Connor was an arrogant man. The fact that he was drop-dead sexy, the fact that he'd smiled down at the foal and his smile made her toes curl…

Neither of those things could be allowed to matter.

Or both of those things should make her run a mile.

She shouldn't stay.

She poked one pink toe out of the water and surveyed it with care. She'd had her toenails painted before she left New York.

What was she thinking, getting her toenails painted to come here?

'Not to impress Jack Connor, that's for sure,' she told herself. 'If I stay here it'll be hobnail boots for the duration.'

Good. That was what she was here for. She was not here to impress Jack Connor.

She'd saved his mare and foal. She'd made that grim face break into a smile.

He'd made her an egg.

'You're a fool, Alex Patterson,' she told herself. 'Your father thinks of you as a boy. If you're going to stay here, you need to think of yourself as one, too. No interest in a very sexy guy.'

No?

No.

But her toe was still out of the water.

The toe was a symbol. Most of Alex Patterson was one very sensible vet. There was a tiny bit, though, that refused to be sensible.

There was a tiny bit remembering that smile.

CHAPTER THREE

SHE woke and it was eleven o'clock and someone was thumping outside her bedroom window.

Someones. Male voices.

She double-checked her clock—surely she hadn't slept so long. Her head didn't have a clue what time it was. Eleven in the morning—that'd make it...nine at night in Manhattan. She should be just going to bed.

She was wide awake. She crept over to the drapes and pushed one aside, a little bit. Expecting to see Jack.

A van was parked right by her bedroom window. Wombat Siding Plumbing, it said on this side. She could see three guys with shovels. Bathroom menders.

Jack might just be a man of his word, she thought, and grinned.

Where was he?

Did it matter? The sun was shining. The day was washed clean and delicious. Her bathroom was being prepared. How was her mare?

It took her all of two minutes to dress. She felt weirdly light-headed, tingling with the lighthearted feeling that this might work, that contrary to first impressions, here might be a veterinarian job she could get her teeth into.

And she'd be working beside a guy called Jack.

He wasn't in the kitchen. Instead she found a note.

Sorry, but you'll still need to use the outhouse this morning. Plumbing is promised by tonight. Help yourself to breakfast and go back to sleep. You deserve it. I'm working down the back paddock but am checking Sancha and her foal every couple of hours. They look great. Thank you.

There was nothing in that note to get excited about. Nothing to make this lighthearted frisson even more... tingly.

Except it did.

Go back to bed?

She'd thought she wanted to sleep until Monday. She was wrong.

Two pieces of toast and two mugs of strong coffee later—another plus, Jack obviously knew decent coffee—she headed out to the stables.

As promised, Sancha and her foal looked wonderful. The mare was a deep, dark bay, with white forelock and legs. Her foal was a mirror image. They looked supremely content. Sancha tolerated her checking her handiwork and she found no problem.

'I'll take you for a wee walk round the home paddock this afternoon,' she promised her. 'No exercise for you for a while but your baby needs it.'

Where was Jack?

She tuned out the sounds of the plumbers and listened. From below the house came the sounds of a chainsaw. Jack was working?

She should leave him to it.

Pigs might fly.

She headed towards the sound, following the creek just below the house. It really was the most stunning property, she thought. It had been cleared sympathetically, with massive river red gums still dotted across the landscape. A few hefty beef cattle grazed peacefully under the trees. They'd be used to keep the grass down, she thought, a necessity with such rich pasture. The country was gently undulating, with the high mountain peaks of the Snowies forming a magnificent backdrop. Last night's rain had washed the place clean, and every bird in the country seemed to be squawking its pleasure.

The Australian High Country. The internet had told her it'd be beautiful, and this time the web hadn't lied.

She rounded a bend in the creek—and saw something even more beautiful.

Jack. Stripped to his waist. Hauling logs clear from an ancient, long-dead tree, ready for cutting.

She stopped, stunned to breathlessness. She'd never seen a body so…ripped.

If she was a different sort of girl she might indulge in a maidenly swoon, she thought, and fought to recover.

He lifted his head and saw her—and he stilled.

'You're supposed to be sleeping.'

'I came here to work.'

'No more mares are foaling right now.'

'Thank heaven for that,' she said, and ventured a smile. Seeing if it'd work.

It didn't. He looked…disconcerted, she thought. As though he didn't know where to pigeonhole her.

As though he'd like her pigeonhole to be somewhere else.

She glanced around and saw a pile of chopped logs, neatly stacked on a trailer. There was an even bigger pile of non-stacked timber beside it.

She metaphorically spat on her hands, lifted a log and set it on the trailer.

'You can't do that.'

She heaved a second log onto the tractor and lifted another. 'Why not?'

'It's not your—'

'Job? Yes, it is. The agreement was I'd work as a vet and handyman.'

'Handy*man*,' he said, with something akin to loathing.

'Do we need to go there again?'

'No, but—'

'There you go, then,' she said, and smiled and kept on stacking.

How was a man supposed to work with a woman like this beside him?

He'd used the tractor to haul a dead tree out of the creek. Chopped, it'd provide a year's heating. The fire stove was nearly out. This needed doing.

Not with Alex.

She didn't know the rules. She was heaving timber as if she was his mate, rather than…

Rather than what? He was being a chauvinist. Hadn't he learned his lesson last night?

But the logs were far too heavy for a woman. Her hands…

She didn't want to be treated as a woman, he told himself. Her hands were her business.

No.

'If you were a guy, I'd still be saying put gloves on,' he growled. 'There's a heap up in the stables. Find your size and don't come back again until you have them on.'

'I don't need—'

'I'm your employer,' he snapped. 'I get to pay employee insurance. Gloves or you don't work.'

She straightened and stared at him. That stare might work on some, he thought, but it wasn't working on him.

'Your choice,' he said, and turned his chainsaw back on.

She glowered, then stomped up to the stables to fetch some gloves. And then came back and kept right on working.

They worked solidly for two hours, and Jack was totally disconcerted. He started chopping the logs a little smaller, to make it easier for her to stack, but he'd expected after half an hour she'd have long quitted.

She hadn't. She didn't.

He worked on. She piled the trailer high. He had to stop to take it up to the house and empty it. She followed the truck and trailer to the house and helped heave wood into the woodshed. Then, as he checked again on Sancha and the foal, without being asked, she took the tractor and headed back to the river to start on the next load.

Either she was stronger than she looked, or she was pig stubborn. He couldn't tell unless he could see her hands. He couldn't see her hands because she kept the gloves on. She worked with a steady rhythm he found disconcerting.

She was from New York. She shouldn't be able to heave wood almost as easily as he did.

She did.

Finally the second trailer was full.

Lunch.

He'd slapped a bit of beef into bread to make sandwiches to bring with him. He'd brought down beer.

There wasn't enough to go round, and it was time she stopped.

'There's heaps of food in the kitchen,' he told her. 'You've done a decent day's work. Head back up and get some rest.'

She shook her head. She'd been carrying a sweater when

she arrived. She'd laid it aside at the edge of the clearing. She went to it now, and retrieved a parcel from under it.

A water bottle and a packet of sandwiches. Neater than the ones he'd made.

'How did you know…?'

'You left the sandwich bread and the cutting board on the sink,' she said. 'It didn't take Einstein to figure sandwiches had been made. I figured if you were avoiding plumbers, I would, too.'

'I'm not avoiding plumbers.'

'Avoiding me, then? You want to tell me what you have against women?' She bit into her sandwich, making it a casual question. Like it didn't matter.

'I don't have anything against women. I just assumed you couldn't be up to the job.'

'And now you find I am,' she said, and looked at him and beamed—like he'd just given her the best of compliments

She was teasing him?

He smiled back. He had no choice in the face of that beam. 'More than up to the job,' he admitted. 'You made your full six months' wages last night. You can go home happy.'

'If I want to go home.'

'You want to stay?'

'Yes,' she said, and had a bit more sandwich. 'I have a reputation to make. Six months' hard work and a reference from Werarra at the end of it should see me set for a decent job back home. Mind, please don't update your website while I apply for jobs. This place is known internationally as a major stud. Seeing your outhouse would do your reputation no end of harm.'

'It's not the outhouse buyers are interested in. It's the horses.'

'Which is why you don't care for anything but?'

It was a question. She was waiting for an answer.

This was none of her business, he told himself. He didn't need to tell her anything.

But she was happily munching sandwiches she'd made herself. She'd worked hard all morning. She'd worked hard last night.

She'd come halfway round the world to take an appalling job.

'Werarra horses are some of the best stockhorses in the world,' he said, trying to keep emotion out of what he needed to tell her. 'Maybe they're the best. Since my grandmother died, my grandfather hasn't cared for anything but the horses, but he has cared for them.'

'My brother checked this place out for me on the internet,' she said conversationally. 'He says your grandpa died last year but the place has been run by a manager. You're the owner but you've not been near the place. You've been heading an IT company.'

'I've also been caring for my sister.'

Why had he said that? It had sounded like an explosion. It was an explosion.

She'd heard it for what it was. Her slight, teasing expression faded.

'She's dead,' she said, and it wasn't a question.

'She died,' he said, tight and hard. 'Black depression and its consequences. I couldn't care enough.'

'I'm sure you did,' she said softly. 'I can imagine just how much you cared, and I'm so sorry.'

She looked up toward the house. Three mares were standing on the hillside looking down at them. Their coats glistening in the midday sun. They looked perfectly groomed, perfectly cared for, perfect.

Sophie's death seemed a raised sword over their heads. He shouldn't have told her.

She shouldn't have instinctively understood, but he knew that she did.

'You learned to look after horses in your childhood?' she asked him, and he heard the slight softening in her tone, which, he thought, was all she was offering in the way of sympathy. He didn't even want that. Why had he told her? 'Here?'

'Here,' he snapped. He'd told her too much.

'Your grandfather taught you?'

'I watched him,' he said, and he knew by her expression that she'd heard the difference.

'And after his death you let the manager run the place until your sister died.'

'Yes,' he said, practically grinding his teeth. How did this woman know?

'So now, you've had time to get the horses up to scratch, but not the house,' she said briskly, and he needed to sound brisk, too. She was simply taking in information and moving on. Not getting emotional.

How rare was that in a woman? How rare was that in anyone?

'The house doesn't matter,' he told her.

'It does if it has tree roots in the sewer,' she said darkly. 'It does if I'm staying. I need new curtains for my bedroom. The plumbers nearly had a ringside seat this morning.'

He smiled. Emotion was done with. She was back to being bolshie again. Assertive.

Cute.

'I'll find you curtains,' he promised.

'Right,' she said. 'You want to get this wood done?'

For answer he leaned across and flicked off one of her gloves.

She tugged away but she couldn't tug fast enough. He took her hand and tugged open her fingers, exposing her palm.

Three blisters. Broken. Raw.

He knew it. She was a kid from Manhattan who'd just finished vet school. She played tough but she lied.

'Enough,' he said. 'Alex, enough.'

'I want this job.' It was a whisper, and suddenly emotion was out there, front and centre. 'You can't know how much I want this job.'

'Then toughen up,' he said, staring down at the raw, exposed skin. 'And you don't do that by hurling yourself into work like a bull at the gate. You do it by starting gradually and working up. By the end of six months you'll be hurling wood like the best of them. For now, take yourself back to the house, clean your hands up and rest.'

'I—'

'Just do it.'

She looked up at him.

Mistake.

She was too close. Too near. Her eyes were darkly shadowed—jet lag must be coming into play, as well as last night's drama. She looked too pale, too small. Her hand was in his.

She was looking at him like she was caught. Which was how he felt. Caught.

He did not want…

A rustle in the bushes caught his attention. Actually, anything would have caught his attention. He was desperate for his attention to be caught.

He dropped her hand and swivelled.

Oliver.

He knew this kid, the son of the previous manager. He was Brian's oldest, eleven years old. He was undersized for his age, freckled, his spiky, strawberry-red hair unbrushed and uncared for, too skinny, a bit bedraggled and as shy as the most nervous of his young horses.

He'd been his father's shadow when Jack first returned to the farm. His dad disappeared and so had Oliver, but for the past few weeks he'd seen him back here, on and off. He was a shadow in the undergrowth, silently watching him.

The last time he'd seen him, he'd managed to corner him and send him home. Kindly but firmly. He didn't want a kid around horses three times as big as he was. Jack couldn't be everywhere. To have the kid wandering the farm was dangerous.

He'd dropped in on Brenda—Brian's abandoned wife—and told her to keep an eye on her son. Told her to keep him away from the farm, away from the horses.

She'd told him the kid wasn't hers. He was the product of one of Brian's earlier relationships. She was stuck with him, caring for him as best she could, but with two small girls of her own she couldn't be expected to watch him all the time.

He'd been dismayed, but there was nothing he could do. 'Just keep him off my property,' he'd said. But regardless, the kid was in the bushes, watching them. He knew he shouldn't be here. As Jack saw him, he backed and looked like he'd run.

'Hey,' Alex said, before he could say a word. 'You're the kid who showed me where to come yesterday. Thank you. Would you like a sandwich?'

That was pretty much the opposite of what Jack had planned to say. He opened his mouth to tell him to leave, but Alex had already bounced up. 'Beef or jam,' she said. 'Nothing fancy. Jam's good.'

The kid was out of the bushes like he'd been grabbed and pulled. He had a sandwich in his hand, in his mouth, before Jack could say a word.

Alex grinned. 'I do like a guy who appreciates home cooking,' she said. 'What's your name?'

'Oliver.' Through sandwich.

'I'm pleased to meet you, Oliver.' She glanced to Jack. 'Is this a friend of yours?'

How to explain the connection? Son of an ex-manager who'd run off with another woman and a whole lot of money that rightfully belonged to the farm. Not possible.

'Oliver's mum owns the next-door property,' he said tightly.

That wasn't exactly true either. He owned the next-door property. Brenda was staying there free.

If he could kick Brenda out he might be able to fill it with a decent farm worker, but Brian had robbed Brenda, too. He didn't have the heart to evict her.

But he did not want this kid here. This kid whose neediness made him think of another child... Sophie's eyes, looking at him through Oliver.

'Your mum'll be worried,' he said to Oliver. Curtly.

'Brenda knows where I am.'

'She knows I don't like you here.'

'But I can help,' Oliver said, and grabbed another sandwich. 'With the horses. I want to.'

And once again, Alex beat him in responding. 'Maybe you can,' she said, watching him attack his sandwich like he hadn't eaten for days. 'We had a foal last night. You want to see? I'm about to take her mum out for a gentle walk in the home paddock. Would you like to help before you go home?'

'Yes,' Oliver said, but with a nervous look at Jack.

'Let's go, then,' Alex said. She glanced at Jack. 'I assume you have no objection if I take her out? It's what the vet recommends.'

'Oliver should be in school.'

'Saturday,' Oliver said, as if he was dumb.

Which pretty much summed up how he was feeling. Dumb. Or out of control.

He owned this stud. He did not want this woman here. He did not want this kid here.

'He'll be gone in a couple of hours,' Alex said, as if she could read his mind. 'You're stuck with me, though. Come on, Oliver, let's get our work done.'

'Your hands...' he said.

'I'll clean them first,' she said. 'Oliver can help me.'

'I'd rather help Jack,' Oliver said, and Jack thought that was exactly what the trouble was. Brenda was a mess; it was all she could do to cope with her four- and two-year-old. She was brusquely kind to Oliver but Oliver needed more.

There was no way Jack could go down that road. He helped Brenda financially. He let her stay in the house and that was an end to it.

'Help Alex if you like,' he growled. 'Do what you like as long as you let me be.'

Women... Children... He wanted nothing to do with either of them.

CHAPTER FOUR

SHE led Sancha out of the stalls. The gangly foal wobbled gamely behind her mother, with Oliver beaming by her side like a proud uncle. They walked at a snail's pace.

If Alex had her druthers she'd have kept Sancha confined for the next four weeks. The pressure on her stitches was enormous, but if the foal was to develop, she had to figure what grass was, what running was. Alex's job was to keep Sancha safe while the foal learned to be a foal.

Out in the paddock, Sancha raised her gorgeous velvety nose to the sun, as if she intended to soak up every ray.

'Will you let her go?' Oliver breathed.

'No. She has stitches across her tummy. She's not allowed to stretch them.' She hesitated, seeing the little boy's yearning face. She remembered, years ago, her father taking her to a friend's ranch. She'd been about the same age as Oliver. Her dad's friend had let her muck out the stables, and had taught her to groom.

Just touching horses…being with them…

She knew that longing, and she was seeing it now.

'Would you like to hold her?' she asked. 'You need to keep her very still.'

'Yes,' Oliver breathed, and took the bridle and held it like he was holding diamonds. 'He doesn't let me,' he said.

'He?'

'Jack. Dad used to let me help but now he's gone and Jack says I shouldn't come here any more.' He said it in the same tones as if announcing the end of the world. 'Brenda says it's no wonder. She says Dad robbed us blind and he robbed Jack, too. She says it's amazing he still lets us live here, and to leave him alone. But I used to ride Cracker. He's old and he's great but Jack's put him in the back paddock, and I really, really miss him.'

He sniffed, and Alex felt like sniffing, too. And she thought, What had this kid done to make Jack prevent him from being with the horse he so obviously loved?

'Can I have another sandwich before I go home?' the little boy asked.

'Yes,' she said, thinking she might just be heading for conflict here.

One needy kid.

Jack was her boss. She needed to be deferential.

Deferential wasn't in her nature. One sandwich? Jack was going to have to do better than that.

Jet lag was insidious. One minute she was wide awake, the next she was dead on her feet. Oliver left and she headed for bed. She woke and the sun was slipping behind the mountains. A weird bird was cackling in the gums outside her bedroom window. The breeze was making the faded drapes flutter, and she lay in bed and thought of the winter she'd left in Manhattan and she decided this could work.

Then she thought of Jack Connor and thought maybe not.

And not because he was arrogant. There was something about him....

Actually, there was a lot about him. She'd gone through vet school with testosterone-driven guys. Her college had organised her work experience on some decent ranches and she'd met some pretty hot men.

They hadn't pushed her buttons like Jack Connor did. She lay and sleepily thought of him, and her buttons were definitely pushed.

It was jet lag, she told herself. Lack of sleep and changing time zones would make any woman susceptible to the hunk that Jack Connor was.

He was arrogant. He was a chauvinist.

And he didn't let Oliver help with the horses.

On that idea she thrust back the covers. Hold the thought, she told herself. Arrogant, chauvinist and unkind. If she could hold on to that for six months, then she could do this job.

Please...

She headed for the kitchen. He was cooking. Sausages. Again. Terrific.

Be grateful he's cooking anything, she told herself. With this guy, it was a wonder he hadn't handed her an apron and a dishcloth the moment she walked in the door.

But sausages...

'I had chicken for a casserole,' he said before she could open her mouth. 'It seems to have disappeared. As does an entire piece of cold roast beef, the apple pie I bought yesterday and half our weekly fruit rations. That was some bedtime snack.'

'I gave it to Oliver,' she said, and watched him still.

'What gives you the right—'

'Take it out of my wages.' She tilted her chin and met his glare head-on.

'Don't encourage him.'

'He seems to be starving.'

'He's not starving. His mother's on the pension. I give her free rent. There's enough for food.'

'He's still starving.'

'He's not my business.' It was like an explosion, and she stilled.

She held his gaze and her heart hardened. Not my business. A starving kid.

'I'll check,' he said at last, sounding goaded. 'I'll talk to Brenda.'

'When?'

'This concerns you why?'

'Because he would have sold his soul for a jam sandwich,' she said evenly. 'But even then… Do you know what he said when I packed the food for him? He said, "I can't take it home if Jack'll be hungry." He's been watching you. He thinks you're great.'

She watched his face freeze. Watched something working behind that grim facade. 'I don't want it,' he said. 'I've given them free rent. What else do I have to do?'

'Care?'

'I don't care,' he said explosively. 'If you want to stay on this farm, you need to get used to that. I keep myself to myself, and I expect you to do the same.'

'For six months?'

'Yes.'

'I won't let a kid go hungry.'

He raked his hair. 'Neither will I. Thank you for giving him the chicken.'

'There's no need to be sarcastic.'

'Believe it or not, I wasn't,' he said wearily, and went back to his sausages. 'I was thinking it's better that you help him than me. If anyone needs to.'

'Anyone does.'

'Right, then,' he snapped. 'Two sausages?'

She looked at the sausages. She thought of the delicate meal she'd had the night before. She felt her tummy rumble.

She'd had a very long day. She'd have an even bigger one tomorrow, she thought. Hard physical work. Horses. Figuring what was happening to Oliver.

Figuring how to make Jack Connor care.

'Three,' she said, and plopped down to watch her chauvinistic, arrogant, overbearing boss cook her dinner.

He tried to focus on cooking. Sausages needed only so much focusing.

Behind him, Alex was watching. He could feel tension rising. She was here for six months?

She'd have to learn the ground rules. He might have got himself an employee but he would not allow her to mess with his life. He was a loner and he intended to stay that way.

She was messing with his head.

As was Oliver. He thought back to the kid, eating Alex's sandwiches like he hadn't been fed for a week, and he felt ill. He didn't care, but...

'I'll go over in the morning,' he said, and Alex beamed.

'Can I come, too?'

'Sancha needs watching. As do the pregnant mares.'

'None of the mares in the home paddock look near to dropping, and it'll take us how long to visit Oliver?'

Us. The word hung.

'I have work for you,' he said roughly.

'I'm having a sickie tomorrow,' she said. 'On full pay.' She held up her blistered palm. 'Work injury. The boss is responsible. I read up on Aussie work laws before I came. They cover me nicely.'

'You're planning to sue already?'

'Nope,' she said, happily tackling her sausages. 'Just

go with you to see Oliver. He's a great kid. And I've been thinking… You could pay him to exercise Sancha for the next month. Just a little bit, but enough to help with food. He could take her for a gentle walk around the yard while the colt frolics. It'll save you a lot of time and he'd love it.'

'That's why I'm employing you.'

'You can employ me better working with the horses,' she retorted. 'Or even working on this house. Your veranda rail's about to collapse. Your window frames are rotten. If you get me some decent timber I'll rebuild.'

'You?'

She raised one eyebrow. 'Yeah,' she said. 'Um, maybe personal observations about my boss are out of line, but you do seem to have a time warp problem with the sexes. You seem okay with the cooking side, but the rest… If you'd employed a guy and he'd offered to fix your veranda, would you have an issue?'

'You're twenty-five years old and you come from Manhattan,' he said. 'You expect me to believe you can build?'

'I can strip most car engines, too,' she said, mock modestly. 'And I also drink beer. My daddy taught me right. Speaking of which…' She held up her glass of water with dislike.

He eyed her with disbelief. She eyed him right back.

He took a beer bottle from the fridge and handed it to her.

She raised one eyebrow, knocked the top off on the corner of the battered table and drank a quarter of the bottle without stopping.

He couldn't help himself. He grinned.

So did she.

'You sure your daddy wasn't right and you're a guy, after all?' he demanded, and she chuckled. It was a great sound, he thought. An amazing sound. It filled the old kitchen with a warmth it hadn't known for years.

It had never known.

Insidious.

He was not about to be sucked in by a woman's laughter. She was drinking beer. She was smiling.

They ate on and he thought…insidious.

He finished. Started clearing. 'Go to bed,' he growled. 'You'll still be jet-lagged. I'll fix the dishes after I've checked the horses.'

'Nope,' she said, and cleared her own things. '*We'll* fix the dishes after *we've* checked the horses.'

'There's no need.'

'I'm a vet,' she said. 'Sancha's my patient.'

'Suit yourself,' he said, more brusquely than he intended, but she beamed as if he'd said he wanted her to go with him.

Why would she beam if he said that?

It was too hard. He was way out of his comfort zone. He grabbed his hat and headed out into the night, leaving Alex to follow if she wanted.

It was nothing to him if she did or if she didn't.

Liar.

But it had to be nothing.

The night was warm and still. The horses were in their stall, totally at peace. Sancha looked up as he approached and gave a gentle whinny of recognition but she didn't move. She had her foal. All was right in her world.

At least he still had his horses.

He thought back to his shock when he'd arrived back here. When he realised how much Brian had been stealing.

His grandfather had hated Jack. When he'd taken Sophie away he'd told him he wanted nothing more to do with him, ever. Yet for all Jack's time in the city, the thought of the horses had stayed with him, vaguely comforting. In the awful times with Sophie, he'd known the horses were still here and the knowledge helped.

But they were only just here. Brian had been siphoning funds every way he knew how. After his grandfather died, when he hadn't left a will so Jack had inherited by default and started asking for accounts, Brian had told him he was paying for farmhands—but not. He'd told him he was maintaining the place but not. The only thing he had maintained was horse care. He'd still bred and sold the great Werarra stockhorses.

Maybe he knew if the horses had been maltreated Jack would come after him with a gun.

Melodramatic? Maybe not.

He thought of Brian and felt again the surge of the anger he'd felt as he drove unexpectedly through the gates and seen what was left of the farm.

He thought of Brian's wife the day Brian had fled. Another woman. A trail of fraud.

Brenda had been gutted. He'd done what he could to help, but…

But the judgement in Alex's eyes said it wasn't enough.

Brian's wife and family were none of his business. He was letting her stay in the house rent free. What else could he do?

But he'd been shocked seeing Oliver today. Why was he hungry?

And Alex's judgement…

Yeah, he'd have to go over there. Throw some more money at it. Make the problem disappear.

'Oliver is all ready to idolise you,' Alex said from behind him, and he stilled. He'd hoped she wouldn't follow. What was she doing, acting as his conscience? He did not need a chirpy vet from Manhattan telling him what to do. 'He's been watching you with the horses. He thinks you're great.'

'Oliver is nothing to do with me,' he snapped.

'I've heard Australia has a decent welfare system,' she said as if she hadn't heard him. 'I wonder what the problem is?'

'I'll fix it,' he said, far more savagely than he meant to. 'They can't stay here if she can't manage. I'll organise their transport back to the city.'

'That'll help. Get the problem off your patch.'

'I'm paying their rent. What else do I have to do?'

'I don't know,' she said evenly. 'Talk to them for a start. Find out what's going on.'

'I'll do that in the morning.'

'In your current mood you'll be offering removal vans.'

'This is not your business.'

'The kid's starving,' she said evenly. 'Of course it's my business.'

He raked his hair. She was right.

Was she going to be right for six months? A chirpy little conscience, telling him to get involved.

And it was working. He should have been involved, anyway. He knew Brenda was isolated. He knew she was a single mum with a husband who'd robbed her blind.

He knew she was needy.

He felt his fists clench. He did not need this. He did not need anyone to depend on him.

'We'll just go see,' Alex said cheerfully. 'You never know, it might be simple, like a broken-down car and she can't get to the shops. I can fix the car while you go shopping.'

'Alex…'

'If you didn't want me to get involved you should never

have left me alone with Oliver,' she said evenly. 'He's a great kid. The best. And he's desperate for help. I'm out there on a limb for him, whatever you do or don't do. Will we go over in the morning?' She met his gaze and held. 'It's Sunday. Day of rest. I can work if you like but it's time and a half, and time off in lieu during the rest of the week. Plus if I work when I've been wounded while working—'

'You've been reading—'

'My employment contract,' she said happily. 'It was a very long plane ride.' She grinned at him. 'Boss,' she said. *Boss.*

He'd sent her the standard employment contract he used for his IT company. It was meant for city workers. He hadn't thought this through.

She was employed for forty hours a week. For forty hours a week he had control. The rest of the time she'd be living with him but she was free to do what she liked.

Like interfere with his life.

He was being melodramatic again. She was wanting to check on a kid she'd met. Fine. She could come along for the ride. She could watch while he did whatever had to be done.

She'd want what was best for the kid.

So did he, he thought, as long as it didn't involve him.

Oliver's all ready to idolise you. He knew it. He could see the need.

He didn't want it.

He'd done enough caring to last a lifetime and it had achieved nothing.

'I'm going to bed,' Alex said, still watching his face. 'What time are we going tomorrow?'

'Ten,' he said, because there was no choice.

'Great.' She stooped and fondled the little foal. 'Okay, then, everything's settled. Wake me if you need me.'

'I won't need you.'

'I thought that was why you employed me,' she said softly. 'But have it your way.' Then she rose and smiled at him. 'Don't be grumpy,' she said. 'It doesn't suit you. Good night.'

And she was gone, closing the stable door behind her.

CHAPTER FIVE

SHE was up at dawn. He was out in the stables when he saw
her leave the house. She was wearing jeans, T-shirt and
riding boots. Her curls were caught back in a simple tie.

She whistled as she headed down to the creek and he
felt an almost irresistible urge to join her. To walk along
the creek and show her the property. To introduce her to
the horses in the upper paddocks.

He didn't. He was cleaning out the stalls. Sancha was
the first of a dozen mares due to foal in the next few weeks.
He needed to get his nursery ready.

He'd have Alex here for the foaling.

The thought was both good and bad. To have a vet on
hand was great. To have a chirpy blonde conscience was
less than great.

He hoped she'd have a really long walk. He hoped she'd
give him some space in the morning—but he was unac-
countably peeved that she did.

She returned half an hour before they were due to leave
for Brenda's, strolling up from the creek, looking wind-
blown and flushed. She had grass seeds in her hair.

He came out of the stables and saw her crossing the
yard and something inside him stilled. She was here, in
his home.

She looked like she belonged.

She saw him. 'It's magic,' she called. 'It's utterly, wonderfully magic. I might even have stayed here if you hadn't fixed the plumbing.'

'Liar.'

She grinned. 'Yeah, okay, maybe not. Oh, but, Jack, it's fabulous. And the horses... I need you to introduce me. I said good-morning to everyone, but it was really hard when I didn't have names.'

'You'll learn soon enough,' he growled, thinking six months... Six months when she looked like this...

'Did you get out of bed on the wrong side again?' she demanded, and he winced. Was he so obvious?

'I'm always grumpy.' Why not say it like it is?

'Whoops,' she said cheerfully. 'But I'll ignore it. My dad says my whistling in the morning drives him crazy, but it's never stopped me. Can we ride over to Oliver's now?'

He'd like to see how she could ride. Her references said she could, but then... 'I've saddled Cracker for you,' he said, motioning to the two horses saddled and ready to go.

'Well, hi.' She approached both horses with just the right amount of quiet and confidence. In a minute they were her new best friends, with her rubbing just the right spots of both horses at once. 'Don't tell me,' she said cautiously. 'Your ride's the two-year-old with spirit and Cracker's the rocking horse.'

She was good. A minute and she had them both summed up. Maestro was his favourite mount, a spirited yearling just broken. Cracker was getting on for twenty. He'd been his grandfather's mount in his old age.

'No offence, Cracker,' she said, rubbing the old horse's ear just where he most loved to be scratched. 'But your owner's wanting to test my riding skill and he won't test anything if I'm sitting on you.' She swung herself up into Cracker's saddle with the skill of someone who'd spent years on horseback. 'What say we take you for a ride up the back paddock before we go, and swap you for someone who needs a good, hard ride. Which is what I'm aching for. Or alternatively, Jack could ride you.'

'I won't have you risking your neck,' Jack growled.

'If you wanted a girl, you should have advertised for one,' she said evenly. 'I applied for a job as hand on a horse stud. You think I'd have done that if I didn't love horses?'

'Stockhorses are different from horses you'll have ridden.'

'Which is why I want to ride them,' she said evenly. 'Don't patronise me, Jack. Let me ride.'

They rode together to the top paddock where he kept the best of his stockhorses, those who were almost ready to sell. For many of his horses the initial training was done here, and Brian had managed to at least maintain that. They couldn't be trained to perfection—a decent stockhorse took years—but by the time they left they knew the rudiments of working with stock.

His grandfather had prided himself on never having a horse returned. Thankfully Brian's skills with horses had not been compromised by his dubious accounting practices so Werarra's reputation had kept going, and Jack had no intention of letting it slip.

Training took time, though, and energy, which was why the house was looking pretty much as it had when he'd walked back in. His horses came first.

They did for Alex, too. She rode Cracker a little way ahead of him and he watched her hands, her seat, the way her eyes covered the ground in front, searching for traps like rabbit holes. She tossed a few comments over her shoulder as she rode, seemingly relaxed, but he knew her horse was her first priority.

By the time they reached the top paddock he was almost looking forward to seeing her on a decent ride.

A decent stockhorse might dent her confidence, he thought, and uncharitably he thought it mightn't hurt that confidence to be dented. She was too...perky. She thought the world was a great place, that nice things happen to nice people, that life was fair.

He knew who her father was. Her people had serious money. This woman would have had everything she wanted, from birth.

Maybe it wouldn't hurt to challenge her with one of his decent colts. A colt with a bit of spirit?

Not a rocking horse. He felt himself grin.

'You planning on teaching me a lesson?' she threw over her shoulder.

What? How the...? How did she know what he was thinking? She was in front of him, looking away. She hadn't even seen his face.

She could read him.

The thought was so disconcerting he didn't know how to handle it.

'You asked for a stockhorse, I'll give you a stockhorse,' he said through gritted teeth, and she waved without looking back at him.

'Hooray. Thank you. Cracker, old boy, I'm sorry I won't be riding you. Let's have a bit of a gallop now. Are you up for it?'

And Cracker flattened his ears and showed he was.

She only had to ask, Jack thought grimly as he watched her fly across the paddock ahead of him. A Manhattan princess, she only had to ask and the world gave her what she wanted.

* * *

These were young horses and spirited. They were roaming free in the huge top paddock where the boundaries were so far apart you could stand in the middle and not see a fence. The country was wild and undulating. It was a magic place for a young horse to be, but catching them, bringing them in, would be a skill in itself.

Alex sat on Cracker while Jack headed down the paddock, holding back, letting his horse do the approaching, letting the young horses sense Jack was simply an extension of the horse he was on.

That's what he looked like.

Ellie and Matt, always the protective older siblings, had done a bit of research on this man before she'd come. Jack had left the farm when he was seventeen. He'd moved to the city, into IT. He'd created a company her brother told her was competitive on the world stage. He'd stepped aside as working head only a few months ago.

She'd hardly expected him to be here, or if he was, it'd be in an owner/supervisor role. She hadn't expected…this.

Wherever he'd been for the past few years, he hadn't lost his skill with horses. He was approaching the cluster of yearlings now, and the young horses were starting to edge away.

He moved almost before she knew his intentions, his horse speeding, turning, cutting off a young horse before it realised what was happening. Catching its bridle and reassuring it. Settling.

He made it look easy, she thought, stunned. He was leading the young horse back to her already. If it was Alex doing the fetching she'd still be galloping after it.

Did she have the skills for this job?

She didn't have the skills of this man.

He led the young horse to her, slipped off his horse and raised an eyebrow.

'You want to swap the saddle with you still on it?'

She felt like an idiot. She slipped from the saddle, and reached for the buckles.

Jack was before her. The saddle was clear, the blanket lifted across, the saddle set on her new mount—and she was just in the way.

'This is Rocky,' he said. 'Grandson of Cracker. He's frisky. You sure you can handle him?'

'I'm sure.'

He linked his hands but she shook her head. Rocky was big by stockhorse standards but she had no trouble swinging herself into the saddle.

And all at once she felt...different. Rocky was a fabulous mount, gleaming black, young and eager. This was a fabulous place, a fabulous day, her horse was gorgeous... and Jack was looking at her and smiling.

'You think you have his measure?'

'We'll see,' she said, thinking she had.

'Remember he doesn't know how to curve. He stops and spins. And you're not wearing a seatbelt. Take him for a canter round the paddock. Nice and slow. Beware rabbit holes.'

'Teach your grandmother to suck eggs,' she said, and grinned, and gathered the reins and touched Rocky's gleaming flanks. 'Let's go.'

Okay, she wasn't quite a Manhattan princess. He'd been gobsmacked with her veterinarian skills. Now, he watched her ride and she was simply an extension of Rocky. Girl and horse moved seamlessly together, as if they'd worked and trained together for years.

Rocky was young and willful. He'd expected it'd take her a while to settle him, but she had his measure from the get-go.

She walked him a little way, and he saw her speaking to the horse, bending so he'd hear, and he thought, *Horse whisperer*. This skill to communicate, to settle fractious horses, to make them feel like she was in control but it was pure pleasure to submit...

His grandfather had had it and it was the only thing he'd loved about the brutal old man. He'd thought he had it himself, but the years away from the farm had dulled his skills, his instincts. He'd get there again, he thought, but meanwhile...

Meanwhile he had this woman who could do anything she wanted with a horse.

Except....

She'd allowed Rocky to move to a canter. She was heading along the long south boundary and he saw the moment she decided it was safe, she was in control, she could fly.

He hardly saw the moment she signalled to Rocky he could have his head, he could gallop as he'd been aching to gallop, but suddenly they were flying, girl and horse, and he didn't know which looked more wonderful.

Or maybe he did, but he wasn't going there.

They were nearing the eastern fence. Slow, he told her under his breath. Slow...

She didn't. Instead he saw her foot just touch Rocky's flank to guide him into the curve.

In most horses this signal was to curve, but to Rocky...

He didn't curve. He simply turned.

One moment Alex was as one with her horse. The next she was lying on the soft green pasture, staring up at the sky.

He'd warned her. He shouldn't have let her. He shouldn't...

He was with her in seconds, feeling ill. He'd known. If she was hurt...

She was lying flat on her back, looking straight up.

She looked awed and stunned. He slid from his horse and stooped—and she started to laugh.

Her laugh rang out over the valley, a low, gorgeous chuckle that turned his insides to water.

'Oh, my; you warned me,' she breathed. 'How stupid was that? Isn't he marvellous?' She held out a hand for him to pull her up, and she was still laughing.

He took her hand and tugged, feeling poleaxed. She came up fast, and she was right in front of him, her body touching his, her hand in his.

She looked up at him, and something caught within him, something he'd never felt. She was beautiful, pure and simple.

She was…

No. This wasn't just beauty. This was…

Danger. Step away.

But his hand still had hers and he couldn't let go.

'I'm guessing rein signal only for turns,' she said. 'Heels means stock work?'

'You got it.' He was having trouble getting his voice to work.

'Teach me.'

'Rocky will teach you.'

'His methods are painful.' She pulled back a little way then, but he saw something in her face, some acknowledgement that she was feeling the same sensations coursing through him. This tug…

He released her hand and it felt like a loss.

She glanced up at him, and then consciously turned away, watching Rocky rejoin his mates. She could have been hurt, he thought, but she was a horsewoman. The ground was soft after the rain. She knew how to fall.

'I need to double-check that contract,' she said. 'Am I

still covered for worker's insurance if I bust my butt on a Sunday?'

The tension eased. He grinned, and he thought, She's wonderful.

Do not go there.

To go down the path of caring...

What was he thinking? He wasn't thinking. It was a momentary aberration, a second's weakness and nothing more.

He swung himself up into the saddle and saw uncertainty, doubt, cross her face. Good. Only it shouldn't be uncertainty. It should be sureness that there would be no connection.

He was not interested in connection.

'I'll have to catch him all over again,' he said, more roughly than intended.

'Thank you,' she whispered, but he wasn't listening. He was turning to fetch her horse. He was moving on.

Oliver was sitting on the front step when they reached Brenda's. His bleached red hair was a bit too long, a bit too curly. His clothes were too small and his bare feet were filthy. His eyes lit up as he saw them, his beam almost splitting his freckled face, and Jack felt a surge of guilt.

Which was exactly what he didn't want to feel. He'd had enough guilt to last a lifetime. Sort this problem and move on.

'Is Brenda home?' he asked, and Alex shot him a look of surprise. Fair enough. It had been a curt question. Too curt.

'You want to hop up on Jack's horse while Jack talks to Brenda?' Alex asked, tossing him a look that might be interpreted as defiance. 'But only if you let me hold the reins.'

There was no hesitation. Oliver was down from the veranda before Jack was out of the saddle. Jack looked into his desperate little face, winced and lifted him high.

The kid swung into the saddle and beamed and beamed. 'I love Maestro,' he said simply.

How did the kid know Jack's horse?

'You're letting *her* ride Rocky?' Oliver demanded of him, and he could just as well have said: 'You're letting *a girl* ride a man's horse?'

'We've stuck some glue on her saddle,' Jack said, deciding it was impossible to be grumpy in the face of such pleasure. 'Do we need some on your saddle, too?'

'No,' Oliver said, mortally offended. 'I know how to ride. Don't I, Brenda?'

Jack turned and Brenda had emerged from the house. She was holding a toddler in her arms and a little girl clutched her leg.

She was wearing tattered jeans and a stained T-shirt. Her hair was long, in need of a wash. She looked almost emaciated. What the...

'I told Oliver not to go near your place,' she said in a dead voice. 'But thanks for the food. Oliver, get off.'

Something was seriously wrong.

He should have come here before this, he thought. He should have checked. Giving her a house rent free obviously wasn't enough. There was more going on.

And then, cutting into his thoughts came awareness of a car sliding into the clearing behind them. A large, black expensive saloon with tinted windows.

The horses startled back. He moved to check Maestro, but Alex had both horses firm and safe.

All the colour had washed from Oliver's face. Jack turned back to Brenda and found she looked the same.

Two guys emerged from the car. Cliché thugs, he thought. Like something out of the movies.

They should be wearing black suits and black ties and sunglasses. Instead they were in casual gear, jeans and T-shirts, but their clothes didn't disguise what they were. They looked like nightclub bouncers. Heavy, tattooed and menacing.

The driver looked from him to Alex. 'We're here on business,' he said almost pleasantly. 'You want to take the little lady for a ride while we talk to Brenda?' He smiled at the horses. 'Nice gee gees. Worth a quid, are they?'

'Two and six at the knackery,' Jack said, pseudo-pleasant, back. 'Brenda, would you like us to stay?'

'I…' Brenda looked from the men to Jack and back again, and her fear was obvious.

'We're staying,' Alex said. 'Brenda wants us here.'

'You going to sell a horse to help pay her debts?' The momentary niceness was slipping.

'What debts?' Jack asked.

'Brenda's hubby borrowed a whole lot of money,' the guy said, leaning back on the car and folding his arms. 'From my boss. My boss has been patient but the drips Brenda's been feeding us aren't enough. My boss loses money, he gets annoyed.'

'Brian stole money from me, too,' Jack said.

'Join the queue, then,' the guy said evenly. 'She pays us first.'

'Blood out of stone.' Jack's voice was carefully neutral. Impassive. Blunt. 'You think I'd have left anything if there was anything worth having? The bank's been in this week, declaring her bankrupt. They've gone through her assets like a dose of salts and now they've even put a garnish on her pension. She gets food for the kids at the local store and that's it. Every other service goes through the bank. Look at her… She's at rock bottom. No one's ever getting money here. Meanwhile Brian's sitting pretty on the Gold Coast. I can give you his address if you want.'

'Yeah?' The guy stared at Jack, alert. 'We can't find him.'

'His girlfriend's mother came whining to me last week,' Jack told him, watching Brenda, not him. 'The mum's just discovered her retirement savings have disappeared and there's not a lot of motherly love left. She thought a nice forwarding address might be useful to me. If you guys are interested...'

'We're interested,' the guy said.

'Excellent,' Jack said. He motioned to Brenda. 'I'm starting to feel sorry for her. Three kids... She's starving. I give you the address, you leave her be. Deal?'

'I dunno...'

'I'm not exactly without threats myself,' Jack said, and suddenly he wasn't Jack any more. He was, Alex thought, a guy who'd been raised as tough as these guys. 'I've half a dozen men employed on my place who know how to handle themselves.'

Whoa. He sounded mean and he looked mean. This was a don't-mess-with-me voice and the guys responded.

'No need to get your knickers in a twist, mate,' the guy said, suddenly placating. 'It seems reasonable. Though if it's a false address...'

'No promises but he was there last week.'

'Then we'd better get moving,' the guy said, and laboriously wrote the address on the back of his hand and signalled to his henchman to take off.

Leaving Brenda and Oliver and Alex, all staring at Jack.

'I hope you didn't want to protect the...' Jack started, and then looked at Oliver. 'The other party in the negotiations,' he corrected himself, and Brenda gave a sob that was simply heart-rending.

And Alex was off the horse in an instant, shoving the reins into Jack's hands, flying up the veranda steps and gathering the woman into her arms.

What was it with women? How did they do this?

Alex had never met Brenda in her life, and here she was hugging her. It made him feel...

He wasn't sure how it made him feel.

Yes, he did. It made him feel like an outsider, looking in.

That was what he wanted, wasn't it?

'Is Brenda crying because you made them go away?' Oliver asked, puzzled. 'She doesn't like them.'

'Have they been here often?'

'Every pension day,' he said. 'Only last pension the grocer said if we didn't give it all to him that was the last food we were getting and the men were really angry. They said they'd come back today. Only you made them go away.' He was high on Maestro, gazing down at him, and Jack could see hero worship, clear as day.

Uh-oh. He did not want this. A bereft kid who lived next door, who loved horses...

It was bad enough having Alex for six months. She'd been here for one day and already he could feel the outside world sucking him in.

Caring?

On the veranda Brenda was recovering. She turned to face him, within the safety of Alex's arms. Alex was holding her like a mother hen hovers over a chick.

This was not Alex's business. Had no one told her?

'You lied,' Brenda managed. 'You've never taken a cent from me. And you don't have half a dozen men on your farm.'

'If I'd come across as your defender, they would have been back. It seemed the best way.'

'But Brian's address?'

'That much is true. His girlfriend's mother was robbed, too, and she's vitriolic. She hoped I might do something with it. Today, seeing how he's left you, the least I could do was pass his address on to someone who cares.'

She gasped. 'Do you know how much he owes?' she demanded. 'And Brian's been living like royals.'

'I guess even royals have to face reality sometime,' he said. He glanced at Alex, who was watching him with a faint smile. She approved, he thought. She'd made him care? Yep, she'd sucked him right in, and she was pleased with herself.

'You guys need to go shopping,' she said happily. 'What if Jack and I take you tomorrow?'

Whoa.

He froze—and Brenda saw his expression and responded accordingly.

'I don't have money for shopping, and even if I did, I wouldn't trouble you further. You've done enough for us.'

'When's next pension day?' Alex demanded.

'Thursday week, but—'

'My family is wealthy,' Alex said, and she glanced at Jack and her glance told him exactly what she thought of him. She'd seen his expression. His lousiness was noted and she was moving on. 'It would be my real pleasure to take you shopping and buy you what you need to get you through to next pension day.'

'I won't take charity,' Brenda said in a strangled voice, and Jack knew that was all about his expression. She assumed he'd looked like that because he thought he was put-upon. When, in fact…

Yeah, okay, it was true; he did feel put-upon, but not financially.

He did not want to be sucked in.

'It's not charity, it's pleasure,' Alex was saying, stubbornly, glaring at him. 'And we don't need Jack. But he's my boss. If he'll give me time off...?'

It needed only that. He was the boss. She was asking permission to help someone he should have known was in trouble. She was asking permission to care for someone he should have cared for himself.

We don't need Jack.

He was being let off the hook. That was what he wanted. Wasn't it?

He glanced at Oliver. The boy's face was screwed in puzzlement as he tried to figure what was going on. He looked at Alex, who was carefully not looking at him.

He could sense her anger.

He'd protected Brenda from the debt collectors. He'd given her free rent.

Alex's expression said she'd expected more of him, and she was angry because he wasn't giving.

What right had she to be angry? No right at all.

They were all waiting for him to respond. To tell Alex she could have time off to give Brenda the help he should offer himself.

'No,' he said, and it was as if someone else was speaking, not the Jack he knew. 'Brenda has enough debts, she doesn't want more.'

'I'd never ask her to pay it back,' Alex said hotly, but Jack silenced her with a look.

'I'm offering Oliver a job,' he said, and he looked directly at Brenda. He was blocking Alex out, even though every nerve in his body was tuned to the judgement he saw there. 'One of my mare's just had a foal by caesarean section,' he told Brenda. 'She can't be allowed to run free, yet her foal needs freedom. Which means someone has to walk her gently for an hour at a time, for at least the next six weeks. Oliver, if you'll do that for me, twice a day at weekends and once a day on school days, I'll pay in advance by taking you all shopping tomorrow. I'll buy decent clothes. I'll cover your groceries until next pension day and I'll cover your fuel bills here. Is there anything else you need, Brenda?'

Brenda gasped—and so did Alex.

And from Maestro's back, Oliver's eyes grew enormous.

'I'm going to work to pay for our food?' he gasped.

'That's the one,' Jack said.

'By walking Sancha?'

'If you agree.'

'Yes,' Oliver said, so fast they all laughed.

Or the two women laughed. Jack watched them laugh and wondered just what he was letting himself in for.

Alex had been here for two days. Any longer...

Any longer, he didn't want to think about.

CHAPTER SIX

THEY returned to Werarra. Oliver arrived half an hour later, ready to take up his duties. Alex went with him to exercise the mare.

Jack headed back down the paddock to fix fences.

Sound carried a long way in the valley. He could hear them chatting like long-lost friends, and he thought, They're two kids.

Only they weren't. Alex was every inch a woman.

In years, he thought, but in truth she was still a child. She had no idea how much emotional entanglement hurt.

It didn't always. Other people had successful family lives.

Other people were lucky. Other people gambled because they didn't know the odds.

Like Alex didn't know the odds.

He wouldn't be the one to tell her.

He worked until dusk. When he finally reached the house he found a brief note on the kitchen table.

Jet lag. Head's still somewhere over Hawaii. Had an egg on toast and gone to bed.

He should have come up earlier, he thought, and then he thought no, this was good. This was back to normal.

Maybe they should have separate meals.

He ate alone. He always ate alone, but tonight it felt different.

Bleak.

He headed back out into the night to check the mares before he went to bed, and while he walked he thought he'd headed to this place for peace. He'd found it, but then along came one perky little vet from the U.S., pushing her nose into his business, messing with his equilibrium.

You've never had equilibrium, he thought.

It must be somewhere. He just had to find it.

Shopping with Brenda was fun—or it would be fun if Jack wasn't with them.

That wasn't exactly true, Alex thought, for from the time he'd loaded Brenda and the kids into his SUV, he'd set himself to be pleasant. He and Alex sat in the front. Brenda and the kids sat in the back. 'This feels like a family,' Oliver had said in deep satisfaction as they set off, and she'd seen Jack's mouth tighten and the mood for the day was set.

They arrived at the Wombat Siding shopping centre, a small plaza providing services for the surrounding farming community. Jack said something about farm tools and disappeared.

It was up to Alex to bully Brenda into trying clothes on the kids, steering her away from cheap and nasty, insisting she choose quality—and then Jack appeared at the end and settled the tab.

He did the same in the supermarket. Alex was having fun in the unfamiliar Australian environment—'What is this stuff called Vegemite?' and 'Do you really eat kangaroo?'—but she would have enjoyed herself more if Jack seemed more relaxed. It would have helped them all.

'Have you made him do this?' Brenda whispered at one stage, and that was the last straw. When Jack turned up at the checkout counter she turned on him.

'Brenda thinks this is charity,' she snapped at him. 'It's not. It's Oliver's wages. You know how much it'd cost you to have a trained vet nursemaid your horse every day, and you know Oliver's value. You need to get involved here, Jack Connor.'

'You can't speak to your boss like that,' Brenda whispered, appalled, and Alex grinned, unabashed.

'Why not? I just did. He's getting a good deal with me, too. I'm cheap for a vet and if he sacks me he'll be completely dependent on Oliver.' She was angry, but she tried to make this light. She managed a cheeky grin at her boss. 'Right. Brenda needs clothes for herself so this next bit is women's business. Jack, I need you to take care of the kids. There's a playground over there—'

'I don't do child care.' He looked horrified.

'Oliver will tell you what to do,' she said. She'd been carrying Brenda's rather grumpy two-year-old and she handed the baby over before he—or the toddler—could object. 'Here's Anna. Tracy, you go with Jack and Oliver and Anna. Jack will buy you all ice-creams. Your mum and I need some girls' time out.'

And she steered Brenda away before Jack knew what hit him.

He was sitting in the middle of a shopping plaza playground, surrounded by mums and kids. Oliver was whooping on the trapeze. Four-year-old Tracy was crawling through a worm-shaped tunnel. Two-year-old Anna was dripping ice-cream onto his knee.

He felt…he felt…

'Dadda,' Anna crowed, and it needed only that.

He looked at four-year-old Tracy and he saw Sophie. He looked at Oliver's gaunt young face and he saw Sophie.

He never wanted to feel like this.

One female vet who didn't know how to mind her own business...

'If I get on the swing, will you push me?' Tracy demanded.

'I need to hold Anna.'

'I will,' Oliver said, squaring his shoulders.

Oliver was having fun on the trapeze. There were a couple of boys his age, having a game with him.

He was climbing off the trapeze to do what Jack should do.

'I'll manage,' Jack said manfully, and heaved himself to his feet. Anna dropped her ice-cream and wailed.

'You need to multitask,' a broad grandma-type advised him kindly. 'You give me money and I'll buy the littly another ice-cream. The deal is that you keep an eye on my grandkid while I go.'

'Fine,' Jack said helplessly.

'Hey, it's fun if you just relax,' the grandma said. 'Lighten up and enjoy yourself.'

Alex and Brenda bought more in half an hour than Alex could believe. Clothes shopping in Manhattan was a serious business, but Brenda wanted it done fast. She was mortified that she needed help, but if she had to accept, then she was going to do it as quickly as possible.

Four pairs of jeans, T-shirts, windcheaters, a coat, smalls—Alex searched the shop, Brenda barely tolerated trying things on, Alex paid with the money Jack had left with her and they were done.

'I should never have agreed,' Brenda whispered as they

made their way back to the playground. 'I hate taking charity.'

'It's a lot harder to receive than to give,' Alex said, hugging her. 'Giving makes you feel great. So that's what you're doing. Making Jack feel great.'

'He isn't...'

But then they rounded the corner—and he was.

This was a different Jack. Both women stopped in their tracks and stared in amazement.

Jack was in the middle of a muddle of mums and kids and grandmas. An elderly grandma was sitting on the padded floor, holding Anna. Anna's face was practically buried in her ice-cream. The grandma was jiggling her and giggling, and the giggles were echoing around them.

There were two swings, side by side. Two little girls, Tracy and another who looked like she matched the Anna-holding grandma.

Jack was behind the swings. He was pushing, very carefully.

For out the front was Oliver, holding two ice-creams aloft. Ready for a lick a swing.

Jack's pushing had to be perfect.

If he pushed too little, the girls didn't reach their ice-creams. If he pushed too hard, the little girls' tongues would act as a bat and swipe the ice-cream out of Oliver's hands.

Oliver was holding the ice-creams for dear life. The little girls' concentration was absolute.

Half the population of the shopping centre seemed to have stopped, entranced.

Oliver was cheering, giggling, sneaking the odd lick of his sister's ice-cream, as well. He was turning into a kid again.

Alex found herself clutching Brenda and Brenda was clutching right back.

'See,' she said in a voice that wasn't quite steady. 'You've made Jack feel great.'

'You're great,' Brenda said, and her voice was just as wobbly. 'You've made this happen.'

'Nonsense,' Alex said, struggling to pull herself together. 'I didn't need to make anything happen. Some guys are a bit blind, but once they see... Jack's pretty great.'

'He is, isn't he,' Brenda breathed. 'And you're staying with him for six months?'

Her inference was obvious and Alex blushed.

''He's not that wonderful,' she retorted, and grinned. 'He hasn't bought us an ice-cream. You'd think a true hero would have all bases covered.'

Reluctant hero or not, he'd made Brenda happy. The little family sat in the back of the SUV and smiled and smiled all the way back to the farm.

But Jack looked rigidly ahead all the way, and Alex thought, Hmm, will he fire me the minute we leave Brenda's?

And then she remembered that two days ago she'd wanted to leave. Now the thought of leaving was appalling.

The parameters had changed.

Two days ago she'd been worried about leaving because she needed this job for her career. She didn't want her family thinking she'd failed. She didn't want to return to the States with her tail between her legs.

Now, she didn't want to leave because...

Of Brenda? Of Oliver?

Or because of Jack?

Because he'd looked wonderful pushing two kids on

swings. Because he'd made an entire shopping centre smile.

Because he'd made her smile.

That was a dumb thing to think. First rule for employment, don't fall for the boss.

She wasn't falling. How could she fall? But the transformation from a dark, shadowed enigma, to a guy who cared...

It was some transformation, and it was making something inside her twist.

'I don't like you staying out here by yourself,' he said to Brenda as they turned into Brenda's yard, and she thought, What? Is he about to offer to have them stay in the big house?

How many sausages would he need to cook, then?

'Would you like Alex to stay over tonight?' he asked, and she stilled.

She didn't say anything. She couldn't. He was her boss. He'd stipulated he'd provide accommodation. He hadn't specified where.

'I'm fine,' Brenda said. 'You need Alex at the farm in case the mares foal.'

Yes, you great lump, Alex thought, shooting Jack a private glare that could have frozen lesser men.

'Do you have parents?' Jack said, meeting her gaze fleetingly and moving on. Like this conversation wasn't about her.

'There's only my sister,' Brenda said.

'Would you like to go to her? Where is she?'

'I might,' Brenda said. 'But she's in Brisbane. It'd cost a fortune to move.'

'I might be able to help you.'

Here we go, Alex thought grimly. Pay to have the problem leave.

'No,' Oliver said, panicked. 'We can't leave the farm.'

'It was only your father who wanted the farm,' Brenda retorted. 'But you're right, we can't leave yet. Oliver has to pay back our debt.'

Oliver subsided but still looked anxious and Alex jumped right in. As was her wont.

'You can't move. We love having you here. And we love Oliver helping with the horses.' Alex was beaming back at Oliver, trying to make things better, but suddenly things had changed.

Jack's face grew grim.

'Don't we, Jack,' she prodded, knowing she was going too far but unable to help herself.

'Of course,' he said stiffly, and even managed a smile.

Oliver settled, happy again, but Alex knew, she just knew, she was in serious trouble.

They arrived at Brenda's, unloaded Brenda, the kids and their stuff, then headed back to Werarra.

With just her in the car Jack was back to looking grim.

She should ignore it, she thought. But then, when had Alex ever kept her peace? She'd spent her childhood in a conflicted family. She'd spent her childhood trying to make things right and she wasn't stopping now.

'What's wrong?' she said at last as the car drew to a halt.

'Leave it, Alex,' Jack snapped. 'You've had your way.'

'My way as in helping Brenda?'

'Yes.'

'So you'd have done nothing?' She took a deep breath, feeling a familiar surge of anger. It was the anger she felt when her father was unfair to his oldest two children, ignoring Matt, saying something cutting to Ellie. It was the helplessness she'd learned in a childhood when her father obviously didn't do what was just. But right now that anger, that helplessness, was directed straight at Jack.

'Oh, that's right. You *did* nothing,' she snapped. 'You did nothing until I poked you into reluctant action. How long has Brenda been coping on her own? She's your neighbour. I might live in Manhattan but even we know what's happening with the people in the next apartment.'

'Okay, so I should have checked,' he said, slamming the door of the SUV with a force that could have taken it off its hinges. 'I agree. Satisfied?'

'You'll keep checking?' she demanded, climbing out of the car after him, coming round to his side and keeping right on prodding.

'It seems I don't need to. My conscience will do it for me. I thought I was employing a farmhand with veterinarian qualifications. Not someone who's demanding I take the weight of the world—'

'Brenda's hardly the weight of the world.'

'She's not. And neither's Oliver or the two little girls, but as of today they're dependent.'

'So what?'

Enough, she thought, but she was still fuelled with anger. There was no way she was staying here for six months if Jack Connor was a boorish, uncaring oaf.

But the thing was, she knew he wasn't. He'd been wonderful today.

And now she was pushing him to stay being wonderful.

She could see conflict written all over his face. This wasn't coldness, the lack of passion of someone who truly didn't care. He looked…on the edge of a chasm, she thought, and the edge was crumbling.

'My big brother and sister did some research on you,' she said, softening a little, backing up a little. Her anger had flared but in the face of this man's confusion it ebbed to nothing. 'Matt was especially worried about me coming to the middle of nowhere to work for a guy he knew nothing about. So he had you checked. He says you built an incredibly successful IT company from nothing. He says your staff thinks the world of you, though you always hold yourself apart. Matt likes that—he said it's important not to blur employee/employer lines. But I'm wondering if it's just employer/employee lines. Is it everyone?'

He didn't answer. Well, why should he? He looked impassive, she thought, like what she was saying was nothing to do with him.

She should shut up now—but when had she ever?

'He also said your sister overdosed a few months ago,' she whispered. 'Rumour has it that Sophie had major problems all her life. Matt says talk within the company had you caring for her for ever. So I'm thinking, this was your grandfather's farm. There's been no talk of parents. Matt couldn't find anything out in the time he had, so I'm guessing, for all intents and purposes, there weren't any. I'm seeing one guy caring for his sister and losing, then deciding not to care again. Am I right, Jack?'

And the look on his face…

She'd gone far too far. She'd stepped right over the employer/employee boundary, and she'd kept right on going.

His face was like thunder. He was staring at her like she was something that had crawled out of a piece of cheese.

Apologise, she thought. But then she thought no, an apology would achieve nothing. She'd said it. Why not stand by it and face the consequences?

What did she have to lose?

Her job?

Maybe, but she thought of Oliver…

'If you cared, you could make Oliver's life good again,' she told him.

'No.'

'Because of your sister?'

'Alex, if you can't keep out of my personal affairs, then leave. Your choice.'

'I'm not good at minding my own business.'

'Learn.'

She glared but he gazed back, impervious.

What now? He'd been good to Brenda today, she reminded herself. He'd asked Oliver to work here. Maybe things would happen without her pushing.

But why did it seem that there was something wonderful right before her, something just out of reach…?

She was being fanciful and she was being dumb. She was putting her job on the line when Jack had already done what she'd asked.

Step back.

But she'd hurt him. She looked into his face and saw exposure.

She'd been right about his sister.

Before she could stop herself she reached out and took his hand.

'Jack, I'm sorry,' she whispered. 'Yes, I was out of line. Yes, your relationship with your sister is nothing to do with me, only I'm seeing someone who's trying to be a loner but not succeeding. You can't be a loner and react to those kids like you did today. You like people. You care.'

He stared down at her, looking baffled. He gazed at their linked hands like he didn't know what they were doing. Like this whole conversation was beyond him.

'I don't care,' he said roughly, as though it was a mantra. 'You come here, you come on my terms. You were supposed to be the guy who comes in and helps with the heavy work, helping me get the place back to where I can run it by myself again. If you can't accept the rules, then leave. I can cope on my own.'

'You'll always need a vet.'

'I can get one from town at need.'

'You'll lose horses.'

'It's the price I need to pay. When I get this place back to what it should be, I can set up accommodation, get decent staff, have it running like it should be running.'

'And step back again?'

'I won't need to step back. The place will run itself. I can stay living here—'

'In isolation?'

'So what's wrong with that?'

'Nothing,' she said stubbornly. 'If you were a different kind of person. But today I saw you with those kids and I know you're not built to be a hermit.'

'And you're not paid to be a psychoanalyst.'

He was still holding her hands.

And she was still holding his. There was a difference—but he hadn't pulled away.

Maybe he hadn't noticed, she thought, but there was no not noticing in her camp. She was noticing like anything.

'I'm not a shrink,' she managed. 'But I am a vet. I can recognise pain when I see it.'

'Then go and look at the horses. Do what you're paid for. Look for pain there.'

'I'll do that,' she said, but she still didn't let go his hands.

'Alex?'

'Mmm.'

'Don't do this.'

'What?' But she knew very well what he was talking about. She was gazing up at him, her eyes not leaving his, her hands still holding.

She could see him warring with himself.

He wanted her?

Was she crazy? If he did want her, she should run a mile.

She didn't run. She held him.

She waited.

It was four in the afternoon. There were horses to be fed and watered. He needed to ride up to the back paddocks and check the mares.

He shouldn't be standing beside his car, staring down at a pert, blonde American with a penchant for sticking her nose where it wasn't wanted.

He wanted nothing to do with this woman. She was a mistake. She was a woman when he'd wanted a man. She was smiles, laughter, caring, when he wanted none of those things.

He should pull away now. He should turn his back on her and go care for his horses, who asked nothing of him.

She was waiting for him to pull away.

The problem with pulling away was that he wouldn't get to kiss her.

Whoa.

Kiss her? Now there was a crazy thought. This woman was his employee. It was the middle of a Monday afternoon and there was work to be done. He needed a working relationship with this woman, boss to employee, formal, distant, workmanlike.

But she was looking up at him and she was worrying about him and it was doing his head in.

No one worried about him. No one had to.

'Jack...'

And the way she said his name... It twisted something inside him that had no right to be twisted. He hadn't been aware it was possible to feel like this.

Exposed? Fearful?

No. What he was feeling wasn't fear. It was something

far deeper, and far, far sweeter. It was as if life had thrown him a constant barrage of sour lemons, yet here was something sweet and wondrous, something he hadn't known existed.

She was gazing up at him with concern, and her concern was doing his head in. Or more. It was the fact that she smiled; she made Oliver smile. It was the way she drank beer like a guy and then grinned at him. It was her skill with horses, the way she heaved wood, her unexpected strength.

It was the way she was looking at him. It was the way the sun was glinting on her burnished curls.

Her eyes were wide, watchful, and her hands still held his.

'Jack...' she said again and what was a man to do?

That one word did his head in. That one word dispelled all caution.

Sensible or not, he did what he had to do.

He bent his head and he kissed her.

Alexander Patterson had been kissed before. Of course she had. She was cute and blonde and her family was part of Manhattan's Who's Who. She'd been regarded as a desirable girlfriend for as long as she could remember, and she'd enjoyed being a girlfriend.

She'd had some pretty cute boyfriends. None serious. She didn't do serious. But she did do kissing, or she'd thought she did.

But this wasn't kissing as it existed in the past world of Alexander Patterson. This was something else.

What was it with this guy? He had something...

Something indescribable.

From the moment his mouth touched hers, the warmth and the heat of him, the strength, the sheer masculinity of this man, seared straight into her body, and she felt herself begin to burn.

He hadn't wanted to kiss her. She'd known it. And okay, it hadn't actually been all his idea. She knew how to get a guy to kiss her and she'd looked up at him and held his hands and she'd wanted it.

If he was a terrible kisser she had only herself to blame, but nothing was further from the truth. She felt her lips fuse to his, she felt a weird buzzing sensation in her head, she felt her arms wrap round his broad, strong body and she felt… Or maybe she shouldn't feel. Maybe she should just be.

There didn't seem much choice. He was plundering her mouth, demanding response. He'd taken her face between his hands, tender yet firm, centring her, holding her, and the intense sensation was enough to make her weep.

She felt beautiful, desired, beloved?

Beloved? Stupid word.

Maybe she'd asked for this kiss. If it worked, it was a way to make the guy know he was human. Kissing was a game she was good at. It was nothing more.

But this…this was everything more. This was…

Jack.

Oh, the feel of him. The taste of him. The pure, raw strength of the man she held.

She clung and kissed and let herself be kissed and she felt herself change, transform, turn from a silly kid trying to make this guy human to a woman who wanted this man so much that if he swept her up right now she'd—

'No.' The word was wrung from him like it caused sheer physical pain to say it. Those same lovely, tender hands were putting her away from him with a strength she didn't believe possible, and she could have wept.

'N…no?'

But no it was. He was holding her at arm's length, and he was looking at her as if she was an alien from outer space. Like she was nothing he recognised.

'I don't want this.' The words seemed to be wrung out of him.

'I didn't think I did either,' she whispered, touching her mouth, which felt swollen and bruised. And hot. Really hot. 'Maybe, maybe I was wrong.'

'We have to live together for six months,' he growled. 'That's not going to happen if we can't keep our hands off each other.'

'I don't know,' she managed, trying to make her voice casual. Trying to find the strength to make a joke out of what was anything but humorous. 'That'd mean we only had to renovate the one bedroom.'

His breath hissed in. He stared at her like she'd grown two heads. He definitely thought she was alien, she thought. A scarlet alien.

'I do not want—'

'Of course you don't,' she said, and she was proud of the way she made her voice sound almost polite. Almost indifferent. 'And neither do I. But I'm a practical girl and did you know my bedroom roof leaks? But of course, a day on the roof and a bucket of nails is far less complicated than sharing your bedroom. So, shall we get on with our evening chores? You check the back paddocks, I'll see to Sancha. By the way, you need to decide whether you want to replace the red gum wood used to build your veranda posts or go for something cheaper like treated pine. So much to think about… Oh, and I bought Chinese takeaway for dinner. All we need to do is reheat it. Hooray, no sausages. Now, any other instructions…boss?'

How had she done that? A part of her was inordinately proud of herself. Somehow she'd made it sound like that kiss meant nothing. She'd made it sound like she kissed guys all the time, and this had been just one more kiss.

She'd made it sound like it didn't matter, but she looked into his face and she knew that it mattered a lot. And for her... She knew it mattered more than anything she'd ever felt in her life.

'Don't fall for the boss.' She heard her brother's advice ringing in her head and she thought, Too late, too late.

How could she have fallen in a matter of days?

She hadn't, she told herself savagely. This must be jet lag, loneliness, pure emotional nonsense. She was moving on and he was, too.

'Right,' he said in a voice she didn't recognise. 'Horses first.'

'Horses, it is,' she said, and she made herself sound cheerful. She made herself grin. 'Let's get on with it.'

'I shouldn't have—'

'And neither should I,' she said. 'It was the way you handled Anna. There is nothing sexier than a man with a baby. Remember it and stay clear in future. It's a wonder you weren't jumped by every woman in Wombat Siding. So enough of the kissing, and let's get on with what we need to do. Six months' work, coming up.'

CHAPTER SEVEN

FROM that moment on, Jack's new veterinarian and handyman threw herself into her work like it was the only thing in the world that mattered.

Alex worked with the speed of a guy, and the skill of two men.

She left him stunned.

The kiss was forgotten. Or maybe it wasn't completely forgotten. It was like the kiss had created new boundaries. They knew what would happen if they approached those boundaries and both of them were steering clear.

Alex had relaxed, though. The kiss seemed to have cleared the air, allowing her to be who she was. She worked with cheerfulness as well as skill. She whistled, she strolled the paddocks as if she belonged; she loved the horses, and she revelled in the beauty of his property.

She teased him, she laughed at him, she demanded he teach her how to handle a stockhorse…and every time he turned aloof she put her hands on her hips and glared.

'You want me to kiss you *again*?'

She was treating the kiss as a joke?

But it was the right thing to do, he conceded, as the days turned to weeks. The kiss had happened. If they skirted round it, it'd stand between them, a barrier to any normal relationship. By laughing about it, they could forge ahead.

And they were...forging.

When he'd employed Alex he'd hoped to get some decent farm help. That Alex was filling that function was doing his head in, but he had no choice but to accept it as fact.

He was almost totally occupied rebuilding neglected fencing. Maybe if she'd been a guy, maybe if the kiss hadn't happened, he'd have her helping, but he wasn't going there. He didn't intend spending every day working alongside her. He'd decided if she spent her time caring for the horses, making sure his pregnant mares were okay, she'd earn her money, but that was never going to be enough for this woman.

She made lists and demanded timber. She rebuilt the veranda rail and he couldn't believe the job she did. She repaired window frames.

She would have repaired the roof but he drew the line there. The ancient slates were slippery and brittle. He wasn't game to touch them himself, but in the face of Alex's determination to have a non-leaking roof he employed a roofing company.

'Wow,' Alex said two weeks after arrival. She was cooking her specialty—pasta—which seemed pretty much the only meal she knew how to cook. 'A working bathroom. A roof that doesn't drip. A veranda I can sit on—what luxury. If you're not careful you might have me for ever.'

'If you learned to cook I might want you,' he growled, and she grinned and passed over a loaded plate.

'Real men don't eat pasta?'

'Not every night.'

'Every second night,' she corrected him. 'Interspersed by your turn. And your sausages aren't so hot.'

'I do a neat poached egg. Aren't girls supposed to like cooking?'

'Only if they don't like hammering nails. My mom told me if I want to get on in life, I should never learn to cook and I should never learn to type.'

'Your dad and mom sound great.'

'They are,' she said. 'Mostly.'

'And sometimes not?' He hadn't meant to ask. They didn't cross personal boundaries. The question just seemed to have come out all by itself.

'Sometimes not,' she said, humour fading.

'Want to tell me about it?'

She gazed across the table, astonished. As if she'd never expected such a personal question. Fair enough. But it wouldn't hurt to relax a little, he thought. After two weeks, those boundaries were solidly in place.

'There are four kids in our family,' she told him. 'Ellie and Matt are twins—they're the oldest. Then there's Charlotte and finally me. We ought to be one big happy family but my dad's always played favourites. There's nothing he won't do for Charlotte and me, but for Ellie and Matt…it's like he always does what's fair. It's like he's pretending to love them and it doesn't work. He and Matt have been at each other's throats from the time I can first remember, and Ellie… Dad snaps at her and she stops eating. She's been struggling with anorexia all her life. It's made for a stressful home life—but not as stressful as yours. What were your parents like?'

He'd walked right into that. You tell me yours, I'll tell you mine. Could he now say, Mind your own business, and refuse to reply?

'My mum was single and flighty,' he told her, deciding to stick to facts. 'When Grandma was alive it was okay but after she died, things fell apart. Mum took off when I was eight and Sophie was six. Grandpa disappeared into grief and the bottle, and from then on we fended for ourselves.'

'You were left caring for Sophie?'

'Yes,' he snapped, and wished he hadn't.

'Ouch,' she whispered. 'And then she got sick. That makes our family fights pale into nothing.'

'We survived,' he said, but then he thought, No, *we* hadn't. Sophie had crumpled.

And she saw it. He looked across the table and he saw recognition of his pain.

He did not want this woman feeling sorry for him.

'So no one taught you to make anything but sausages,' she said thoughtfully, and he realised with relief that she wasn't following through. Maybe she realised how much he didn't want to go there.

'A bit of invalid cookery, too.' That was as far as he was prepared to go, and she saw the flicker of recognition for what lay behind those words.

'Maybe we could learn,' she said thoughtfully, and he thought, What?

'Sorry?'

'If I'm here for six months… At home we have a gorgeous maid who cooks like a gem. What if I write to her and ask to send us her favourite recipes. If I make one every second night, and you do the same, we could have fun.'

Fun. Fun was so far from where he was at, he felt flummoxed.

She was suggesting they use this big old kitchen for what it was meant for—cooking. Real cooking.

He thought back to the distant memories of when his grandmother was alive—a kitchen full of warmth and the smell of baking, and of kindness. It was a faint echo, insidious in its sweetness.

Don't go there.

But Alex was looking at him like an expectant puppy, big-eyed and eager.

'You do it,' he growled.

'Not if you don't, too,' she retorted. 'Don't cook or type. That's my mantra—unless I'm working for a guy who's prepared to cook and type, as well.'

'You reckon these fingers can still cope with a keyboard?' He held up a broad, work-worn hand and she grinned.

'Maybe not, so we both give typing a miss. But I'm thinking you don't need skinny fingers to make a peach pie.'

'Peach pie?'

'Maria's favourite.'

He gazed at her across the table and she gazed back, chin tilted, challenging.

Cook. In this kitchen. With this woman?

Nope. Not with this woman. He'd be cooking every second night while she did evening stables. And vice versa.

Fun?

Her challenging gaze said it could be fun. Eating Alex's peach pie.

Maybe he could hurry his turn at evening stables and watch her cook. A bit.

And in return?

Not peach pie. His gaze wandered to the shelf beside the stove, to a mass of cookery books. To one in particular, an ancient school exercise book, crammed with cutout recipes and handwritten notes.

His grandmother had died when he was seven, but before then that recipe book was out on this table every day.

Alex was following his gaze. 'Your grandma?' she asked, and he nodded.

'So Maria will be teaching me and your grandma can teach you.'

What was it about those simple words?

They made it feel like the kitchen could come alive again. Like it could breathe. He felt the echoes of the warmth he'd felt when his grandmother had lived, and he looked across the table at Alex and saw...

He wasn't sure what he saw. There was nothing of his grandmother in Alex. No shadows of the past.

But a promise of the future?

Ridiculous.

'Deal, then?' Alex asked, and he nodded, curtly.

'If you want.'

'You want, too,' she said.

Did he? No. He was doing it to humour her. She was right, sausages and poached eggs and pasta weren't a balanced diet. Her suggestion was sensible.

'I'll see if she has recipes for steak as well as sausages,' he said, and she grinned.

'You'll have to do better than that, boss,' she said. 'This is a competition. Every night we rate our dinner out of ten. At the end of six months, the winner gets to pay for a degustation meal in Sydney's best restaurant as a farewell dinner for me.'

'I can't leave the farm,' he said, startled. 'No.'

'You can't run the farm without help,' she said evenly. 'You know that. You need to get training solidly under way for the colts in the top paddock. You have a great breeding program going and that takes time, too. There'll always be disasters needing your attention. And how are you going to attend the sales, get to market, do what you have to do? I'm one of a long line of employees, Jack Connor.' She gave a cheeky smile. 'I may well be your best but I won't be your last. So my replacement will take care of the farm while you and I have a first and last date. Degustation meal in Sydney the night I leave. Deal?'

'Deal,' he said because he couldn't think of anything else to say.

They'd kissed, he thought, and then they'd moved on. Now she was proposing they could have one dinner together in Sydney, as she left. And that'd be the end of it.

'Excellent,' Alex said, and beamed. 'I'm off to email Maria. And you need to start reading. Winner gets to choose the restaurant. I'm starting research now.'

They'd achieved a deal with cooking. They hadn't achieved a deal with Oliver. Alex had taken him on as her personal project, and she was like a pesky battering ram with her demands for the child. Her demands weren't big enough to knock him over but they were bothersome all the same.

The kid came over after school, twice at weekends. He took Sancha out into the home paddock and gently led her round, let her graze and kept her controlled while her foal frolicked around her.

That was fine by Jack. It was what he'd agreed to. He even liked that it gave the kid pleasure. He was all for giving the kid some pleasure but what he didn't like was the way Oliver looked at him. Like he was some sort of superhero.

Sophie had looked at him like that. No matter how bad life got, she had an infallible belief that Jack could fix it.

There was no way he was going down that road again, no matter how hard Alex pushed. He knew, too well, that encouraging dependence did nothing, achieved nothing, and only meant future pain. When Oliver arrived he normally headed down to the creek, found fencing projects far away when the kid was here.

But Alex pestered him to stay, and finally, stuck in a stall waiting for a mare to foal, she fronted him directly.

'What is it with you and Oliver?' she demanded. 'He's aching to help more. You let him walk one horse. What he'd really like to do is ride. There are quiet mounts. He already loves Cracker. Why can't we let him?'

'I don't want him getting attached to this place.'

'He already is attached,' Alex retorted. 'You know he's had a rough deal. Brenda's not his mum—she's his step-mum. She's kind to him but it's not like he's her own and he knows it. His dad's disappeared. His mum's occupied with his two half-sisters. Thanks to you he has enough to eat and he's safe but he needs more.'

'If Brenda needs more help—'

'Brenda doesn't need more help,' she said, exasperated. 'But she's talking of moving back to the city to be with her sister. It's breaking Oliver's heart.'

'Kids are tough,' he said, thinking they have to be.

'When your mum walked out on you,' she said thoughtfully. 'Did the horses help?'

'This is not about me.'

'It's not,' she said evenly. 'It's about a little boy who needs your help. Are you afraid he'll depend on you like Sophie?'

Whoa. How had she got there? She was supposed to be a vet, not a shrink.

'This is nothing to do with you, and you need to be careful yourself. You'll return to the States. If you build a relationship, where will he be then?'

'With you.'

'You just said his mother's taking him to the city.'

'She's not his mother.'

'All the more reason not to get involved, then,' he

snapped. 'He needs to build a relationship with her. You're not suggesting I should adopt the kid, let him live here?'

'No, but—'

'Then it's kinder to put boundaries in place now.'

Silence.

They were sitting quietly at the rear of the stables, waiting for the mare to drop her foal. Maybe Alex had thought this was a good time to bring up Oliver, he thought grimly—when he was distracted enough to agree.

He wasn't agreeing to anything. Especially not to a freckle-faced, needy kid who could just as easily self-destruct.

He hadn't been able to make a blind bit of difference with Sophie. What did Alex think he could achieve with anyone else?

The mare gave one last, mighty contraction and the foal slithered out onto the hay. Unlike Sancha's, this was a fast, trouble-free birth. Alex checked the tiny muzzle, made sure there were no breathing problems and stepped back. The least human intervention while they bonded, the better.

Job done, they slipped out of the stall and stood looking down at mare and foal across the stable door. One tiny, gangly foal, learning his new act of balancing on legs that looked crazily inadequate, his mother, gently nuzzling, helping her baby find his feet.

It never ceased to feel amazing, Jack thought. He loved this part of the job, and having Alex here took the tension away, knowing he had a vet on hand.

He had her for another five months. After that he'd find decent help. Men who respected his boundaries.

Instead of one slip of a girl who worked like two men.

Who tried to shove one waif of a kid into his care.

'Is she okay?' The wavering voice came from behind

them. Oliver. Or course it was Oliver, here to take Sancha for her evening walk. But he was asking the question of Alex. He cast Jack just the one, nervous glance. Respectful. Hopeful.

Scared.

The thought made Jack feel a bit ill, but there was nothing he could do about it.

He knew he'd only make things worse.

'Alex can introduce you to our new foal,' he said brusquely. 'I have work to do.'

'A long way away,' Alex said dryly.

He didn't bother to answer. He left them to it, woman and child admiring one new foal.

He walked away, down to the area he was fencing, which just happened to be at the far boundary of the property.

She had no right to ask him for any more favours, he told himself. Oliver was fine.

But Brenda wasn't his mother. He'd seen the kid's expression when he'd gone to see her in the days after Brian left. The boy had seemed terrified as well as bereft.

Terrified he'd be alone?

He wasn't alone. He had Brenda. And he had Alex, who was putting her heart where it wasn't wanted.

Only it might be wanted. With Oliver?

She was going back to the States.

Steer clear, he told himself. Stick to your horses, and don't care.

He couldn't care. Caring was the way of nightmares.

Oliver walked Sancha and then Alex drove him home. He'd walk, but this way he could spend more time with Sancha, more time on the farm he so obviously loved.

He was always quiet on the way home, his small face growing stoic.

His stoicism was doing something to Alex's insides.

When she was a teenager her dad had taken her with him on a business trip to South-East Asia. She'd loved the experience, the food, the culture, but she'd been appalled at the poverty.

On her last day there she'd found a dog. It was half-grown, starved, pathetic. She'd fed it satay sticks from a hawker stall and demanded her father organise to take it home.

'We can't do that,' he'd said gently, citing disease, quarantine, so many problems for an animal that was half-dead. 'Don't feed it any more, Alex. You're prolonging the agony.'

She hadn't been able to walk away. She'd moved heaven and earth but she still hadn't been able to bring him home. Finally she'd insisted they find a veterinary clinic and have him put down.

And Oliver?

She couldn't take him home either. Oliver wasn't starving.

But he was starved of affection. She'd seen Brenda's sparse greeting as he returned home—'You're late, your dinner's in the oven'—and she'd thought, Push Jack some more?

He was already pushed to the limit. He was relaxing in her company. They were enjoying their cooking competitions. He was almost having fun.

'I have five more months,' she said out loud. 'Maybe by then I'll make him relax enough to fight for Oliver.'

But if Oliver reminded him of Sophie…?

'I should be a shrink,' she told herself. 'But then, I'm not so sure a shrink could get past those barriers either.'

She pulled to a halt in front of Werarra, taking a moment to admire her handiwork, the steady new veranda rails, the patched and painted window frames. Jack had cleared the weeds from along the front and remnants of an ancient garden were creeping through again. The place was beginning to look as it should.

Five more months... Too little time.

'You shouldn't be thinking that,' she told herself. 'You should be missing your family.'

She headed into the kitchen where Jack was attempting chicken cacciatore. It smelled fabulous.

He was wearing an apron. His grandmother's. A flowery apron over jeans and T-shirt.

It should look ridiculous.

It looked so sexy it made her toes curl.

He pointed to the mantelpiece. 'Mail,' he said.

That distracted her. Mail. Real mail? Not email. Who'd be sending her a real letter?

She picked it up and felt a weird sense of foreboding. It was a crisp, linen-weave envelope, old-fashioned. The kind of paper she knew her sister Ellie had a passion for.

Ellie's writing.

Ellie emailed her when she needed to communicate, so what was this letter about?

'This won't be done for fifteen minutes,' Jack said grimly. 'Or more. I seem to have a heap more cacciatore than chicken. Unless you want soup, you have time to read your letter in private.'

And then he glanced at her face, and his brows snapped down in concern. Maybe he saw her apprehension.

'I'll read it on the veranda,' she said.

'Take your time.' Jack met her gaze for a long moment and then returned deliberately to his casserole. Giving her space. 'It's thin soup at that.'

CHAPTER EIGHT

SHE didn't come in after a quarter of an hour. The casserole was less soupy—almost edible.

After half an hour the casserole was perfect but she still didn't appear.

He removed his apron, set the casserole to the side of the stove and went to find her.

She hadn't gone far. She was sitting on the edge of the veranda, holding her letter in her hand, staring sightlessly across the paddocks to the mountains beyond.

She looked shocked and defeated.

He sat down beside her without saying a word. Just sat.

'If it's really bad news people telephone,' he said gently. 'Usually. But this...what's so bad that it can only be told by snail mail?'

'My family,' she whispered, and he waited.

He knew so little about her, he thought as he waited. Her father had Alzheimer's. That was an appalling disease, but she'd known about it before she left. What was this?

'Your mum?' he asked.

She didn't say anything.

'You want me to bring your casserole out here?' he asked gently. He wouldn't push. Heaven knew he was the last to invade someone's privacy.

But he wanted to. The look on her face... He couldn't bear it.

'Or would you like to talk about it?' he heard himself say.

There was a long, long silence. The dusk was falling, the last hint of crimson sunset fading behind the distant mountains. The smell of his grandmother's roses, freed at last from their matt of weeds, pervaded the warm evening air. A flock of cockatoos was settling to roost in the massive gums behind the house, their squabbling for position making a weird evening symphony.

If this was bad news there were worse places to receive it, he thought. Worse places to come to terms with what was in her hand.

Would she tell him?

Did it matter?

But suddenly it did.

Maybe it was a Dear John letter. Did she have a boyfriend back home? He'd assumed not. The kiss...

She'd returned his kiss with a passion that said she was heart-whole. The look on her face now said she was anything but.

'It's ancient history,' she said into the stillness. 'It's nothing. But it's everything.'

She stopped and he thought, Don't push. She needed time.

He went inside and served two helpings of his casserole, carrying them outside. Maybe he should eat inside and let her be, but something about her face had him not wanting to leave her alone; had him believing his presence might even help.

If she'd had to receive bad news, he was suddenly absurdly glad that she was here, in this place. This night.

The stillness. The sound of the cockatoos. This farm had become his solace. It had its own form of healing.

She lay her letter aside and ate her casserole. The news can't have been too appalling, he thought. She was still hungry.

She cleared her plate and managed a smile. 'Eight,' she decreed.

'Eight?' he demanded, mock offended. 'That was a ten worth of effort.'

'The chicken's a bit stewed,' she said. 'It's shredded. Maria cooks cacciatore. I don't think it's supposed to be boiled for hours.'

'That was deliberate,' he said. 'You look upset and distracted. I was being considerate. I didn't want you choking while chewing.'

She smiled, but absently.

Ask.

Why?

He didn't seem to have a choice. The look on her face...

He was involved, like it or not.

'Would it help to tell me why you're looking upset and distracted?' he said gently, wondering at himself. He didn't get involved in employees' lives. He didn't care.

Right now, though, he found himself caring a lot.

But she didn't answer.

He carried the plates inside. Washed up. Thought about leaving her to it.

He couldn't. He walked back outside and sat and watched the moon rise over the valley.

He sat on the far side of the veranda steps to her. He was giving her space, but still he stayed.

A man and a woman...waiting?

'There was always something wrong in my family,' she said at last, and it was as if the words were a sigh. A long, drawn-out acceptance of sadness. 'There was always something. This...' She lifted the letter and waved it blindly towards him. 'It's from my sister. It explains so much.' She took a ragged breath and then corrected herself. 'But maybe...maybe she's not my sister,' she added. 'My...half-sister?'

'You want to explain?'

She stared down at the letter. It was too dark now to read it—he hadn't turned on the veranda lights and he didn't intend to. The moonlight created the illusion of privacy, a space where maybe she could talk. For a moment he thought she wouldn't, but then she sighed again and rose and stared out over the valley.

'My mother married twice,' she said. 'Fenella—my mom—had what she described as a disastrous first marriage and she found peace and security with my dad. My dad's great. He adores me. He adores my sister, Charlotte. But the twins... Ellie and Matt are older than us and he should love them to bits, but instead...he's kind, like Brenda's kind to Oliver. Like he does the best he can but it's not real. And now I know why.'

'You said half-sister.'

'It seems my mom was pregnant when she married.' She gave a half laugh. 'Actually we knew that—Ellie discovered birth and marriage certificates long ago. We've teased Mom about it, and she always laughed and said she and Dad were blindsided—couldn't keep their hands off each other. But now, what Ellie's found out... It seems Mom was pregnant from her first marriage. Mom lied. Matt and Ellie aren't Dad's kids at all.'

Silence.

'I guess...that happens,' he said at last, softly, cautiously, and she nodded.

'No big deal?'

'I can imagine it's a huge deal for your family, and especially for the twins.'

'I'm not sure how they'll react,' she said. 'Knowing there was a reason my dad didn't care.'

'But it sounds like he did care.'

'No,' she said strongly, almost violently. 'Caring's when you give your heart. Dad never did that for the twins. He did all the right things, like Brenda's doing for Oliver. Like you're doing for Oliver. You're doing what you need to do, what Oliver needs for survival, but you're not giving your heart. You know, when I think back to all those years, to Dad calling us Charlie and Alex rather than Charlotte and Alexandra, making it clear he was aching for a boy because he didn't want Matt to succeed him—being nice to Ellie but not playing with her, not hugging her like he did Charlie and me... It breaks my heart and now I know why. I want to go home and punch him. How could he have taken the twins in when he didn't have room in his heart for them? And now he has Alzheimer's and I still love him to bits, but the hurt he's given Matt and Ellie... What a lie for them to carry. And you know what? Their real father's dead. After all this time, they can't do anything. My mom and dad robbed them.'

He didn't move.

There were accusations against him in all this, he thought. The way he was treating Oliver...

That was hardly fair.

But this wasn't about him, though. It was about Alex.

'But you know what?' she asked, sniffing almost defiantly. 'In all this, Ellie's written to say she's fallen in love. She's met the man of her dreams and he sounds awesome. He's some sheriff in Larkville, Texas, where her real dad came from. So she's happy. That leaves only Matt...' She sniffed again.

'You love your brother.'

'Like you loved Sophie, I bet,' she said. 'Even if he's only my half-brother.'

'Use the house phone if you want to call him.'

'I will.' She sighed. 'In a while. Not now. I need to get my voice in order first.'

'You want to go for a walk along the creek?'

'It's too rough,' she said, sounding surprised.

'There's a track on the far side. I have a decent flashlight. We might even spot a platypus, and I promise to keep you safe from drop bears.'

'Drop bears?'

'Weird Australian marsupial,' he said. 'They cling high in the branches and drop at the first sign of life below. You're walking along and thump, there's a drop bear covering your head. Their claws are so long they usually need surgical removal. It's quite a business, carting drop bear victims to hospital with drop bear attached. It'd be easier to shoot the drop bear but they're heavily protected. If it's a choice between an American vet or an Aussie drop bear, the drop bear wins every time.'

She stared at him, her mouth open. And then slowly, the strain on her face disappeared and was replaced with a grin.

'You're joshing me.'

'Why, yes,' he said, grinning right back. 'Yes, I am.'

She giggled, and it felt good. More, it felt great. To take the strain from her eyes…

To someone with practically no family—okay, no family at all—it was hard for Jack to get his head around Alex being appalled to find two of her siblings had different fathers. He was pretty sure he and Sophie had different fathers, but he'd never bothered to ask or find out. It simply wasn't important.

With Alex, though, there was a goodly part of her that was a protected child of a wealthy American family. Up until now her world was black and white. Parents didn't lie. People were supposed to care. She couldn't see that caring had its own consequences, its own costs.

He thought about her family from her dad's point of view. The twins weren't his. Maybe he'd thought one day their real dad would make a claim. He may well have only been protecting himself.

Like Jack was doing with Oliver?

Like he was doing with Alex.

'I'm carrying the flashlight,' Alex said. 'Plus I'm wearing a hat. I might not believe in drop bears but I do believe you have pythons.'

'That'll hug you to death in seconds,' he said in a voice of dire warning.

'Just lucky I'm not huggable,' she retorted. 'And I know exactly what your nonvenomous pythons can and can't do. With hat and flashlight I'm fine. If you show me where to go I could go by myself.'

'Huggable or not, you need an escort,' Jack said, and then added, almost to himself, 'I care at least that much.'

They walked silently through the bushland, along the rippling creek, through country that looked weirdly different at night.

If Jack hadn't accompanied her she wouldn't have ventured far, she thought. Not that she was afraid of phantom drop bears and pythons, but it was dark and there were rustlings in the undergrowth and the moon wasn't bright enough to show the way.

But Jack had suggested it.

And Jack was with her.

She was shining her flashlight on the path ahead. Jack

was walking behind and close. Like a big cat, he didn't need a flashlight.

She was suddenly absurdly aware of an urge to drop back, to take his hand and let him lead her through the night.

Which was crazy. She didn't want him to.

Did she?

She shouldn't. This guy was her boss, a solitary farmer with so many shadows in his past he'd never get through them.

But tonight he'd cared. He'd fed her his casserole and he'd listened to her story.

He could have told her she was being dumb, that having two siblings who were now only half-siblings was no big deal. But he hadn't mocked her. Instead he'd stood back with eyes that were warm with sympathy and understanding, and he was here now, aware that she couldn't simply go to bed after news like this, that she needed to walk it out, to take time to come to terms with it, to take in the night.

The path was growing nearer to the creek. A line of rocks ran across as a mini-ford and suddenly Jack was grasping her hand, tugging her back.

'Wait,' he said softly, and he dug into his pocket and unfolded paper. Another pocket produced tape.

Cellophane. Red. 'What the…?'

'My grandma showed me this trick just before she died,' he told her. 'Grandpa was away at the horse sales and she brought Sophie and me down here.'

He fastened the cellophane over the flashlight. Instead of a piercing yellow beam, they now had a diffuse red glow.

'You need to be quiet,' he said softly. 'Look right into the middle of the creek, where the rocks form protection for the tiny night feeders.'

He held the flashlight and he took her hand in his again, leading her out onto the rocks.

The rocks were steady. There was no need for him to hold her but he wasn't letting her go.

And she didn't pull away. She couldn't. This night... the sound of the rippling creek...Jack—the combination was doing something to her insides.

The aching pain of an hour ago was fading to unimportant. There was only here, only now, only where Jack was taking her.

He led her right into the middle of the stream, then squatted on his haunches, tugging her down with him.

'Watch,' he whispered, and directed the flashlight into the water.

She looked and saw crystal-clear water running over smooth pebbles. The light was attracting insects, tiny moths and bugs.

There were traces of weed in the water. She watched on and saw the flash of silver, fish, no bigger than her thumbnail.

The more she looked, the more she saw. A whole universe was beneath the flashlight.

'Wait,' Jack breathed, and she waited, silent as the night, content to do what Jack told her, content to let this moment take however long Jack decreed it should take.

'This is the best place,' Jack whispered. 'If we're patient...'

And then he paused.

A platypus.

By the light of the flashlight she could see it clearly. It was little more than twelve inches long, covered with streamlined fur. What looked like a duck's bill was an elongated snout covered with soft, leathery skin. Its webbed feet looked weirdly incongruous.

It swam with its eyes closed, sensing its food rather than seeing, sweeping a yabby from the rocky bottom, snaffling a fish, almost surfacing to catch one of the moths that had fallen from the glow of Jack's light.

She'd seen one once, in a zoo, but here, seeing this wild, weird creature in its own habitat, the sensation was indescribable.

She couldn't believe she was here, in this place. With this man. Unconsciously—or almost unconsciously—her hand slipped back into Jack's and held.

She needed his hand to steady her. Or maybe…maybe she just needed his hand.

'He's a hungry little guy,' Jack said, seemingly unaware of her hand in his, but holding her with a warmth that was doing something to her insides. 'He needs to eat at least a third of his body weight every day.'

'I wonder if he likes chicken cacciatore?' she managed, and he grinned.

'Nicely stewed. Should I ask?'

'That's my breakfast you're offering,' she retorted, and went back to watching.

The little creature seemed oblivious to their presence. Maybe he thought the flashlight was the moon. Maybe he didn't see it at all. For whatever reason he grazed on, surfacing every now and then, heading to the bank to digest what he'd found, then returning to the hunt.

Her legs were beginning to cramp but she didn't want it to end.

'If we stay here much longer we'll need to call for a crane,' Jack said at last. 'My legs are going to sleep. Mind, yours are a lot younger than mine. You want to stand and tug me up?'

She grinned and did, and he stood too fast, and he was too close.

Or not close enough.

The night closed around them. The stillness turned to intimacy. The intimacy to need.

But yet…

'I don't want to hurt you,' Jack said into the silence, and her world stilled.

'How could you hurt me?'

'I don't do…close.'

'Then you'd better move away,' she managed. 'For we seem to be very close.'

'I should.'

'I guess…so should I.'

Neither moved.

She wanted, more than anything she'd ever wanted, to take his face in her hands, to draw him to her and to kiss him. But he was still and silent. His face was grim, and she thought, There's a war going on in here.

She'd taken one kiss. She'd been given one kiss. She'd made light of it, but if she went any further…

If she kissed him now, she'd end up in his bed. She knew that with the last shards of common sense that seemed left to her.

Was that what she wanted?

Maybe it was, she conceded—but she wanted more.

This was more than physical, but he didn't want it to be more. He had scars she had no hope of healing, hurts she had no hope of reaching.

If she let him take her to his bed, it'd make things worse. She was here for five months. This job was important to her.

If what was between her and her boss exploded, then she'd be gone and what hope then?

What hope of reaching him if she risked that?

Her thoughts were tumbling crazily through her head

as she looked up at him, as he gazed down at her in the moonlight, as the platypus continued grazing in the water at their feet.

He wanted her. She could see it in his eyes. His entire body was stiff with wanting.

But he was holding back. Knowing that to kiss her...

'Can I tell Oliver he can ride a horse tomorrow?' she said, and her voice came out crooked, desperate. Not how she wanted to sound at all.

Why had she asked that?

Because he needed to care, she thought. If he didn't care...

All or nothing? Start with Oliver.

'No.' He moved back from her, almost imperceptibly, but she noticed.

'Why not?'

'Because the boy needs a father,' he said, so harshly that she faltered and the creature in the water beneath their feet slipped silently into the darkness and disappeared. He glanced down and winced. 'See what you've done? It may not eat again tonight now that I've frightened it.'

'You've frightened me, too,' she retorted.

'You're not frightened. You're pushy.'

'Yes,' she conceded. 'You should be getting used to it.'

'Believe it or not, I am,' he said grimly. 'But I'm not about to let you talk me into something that'd be so disastrous.'

'What's disastrous about letting Oliver ride?'

'How could I not let him continue riding when you go home?'

'Would you need to?'

'Yes,' he said, and raked his hair. 'Yes, I would. Of course I would. Hell, Alex—'

'It's not,' she said, working on staying calm. 'It's not hell at all. It's giving one little boy pleasure by letting him ride.'

'You and I know it's more than that,' he snapped. 'You said yourself, Brenda's not his real mother and she's not acting like it. He's desperate for real parenting. When his father finally comes to his senses—'

'Is that likely to happen?'

'It has to happen.'

'He never talks about his dad. He talks about you.'

'And how's that supposed to make me feel?'

'Wanted.'

'I do not wish to be wanted.' It was almost an explosion. 'I wish to be left alone. I don't want a kid hanging on my heels. I don't want a kid worrying about me, missing me if I go to Sydney to the sales, always needing me. I don't want to be worrying about him.'

'And there's the crux of it,' Alex said shortly. 'That's what my dad never did with the twins. He never once let them close enough to worry about them. He did what he had to do.' She hesitated. 'Okay. The twins were short-changed but maybe something's better than nothing. Maybe you could let Oliver care for Cracker and take him home. He could ride at his place. You could pay Brenda for the feed and care. Hope Brenda does the worrying.'

'You don't leave a kid alone with a stockhorse, old or not,' he snapped.

'So buy him another.' She took a deep breath. 'A safe, kid mount. I'll buy him another, only it'll have to seem like it comes from you.'

'Why?'

'Because Oliver doesn't care about me,' she said, through gritted teeth. 'If you knew the pleasure it'd give Oliver to have you hand him a horse, keep an eye on him, teach him as he ought to be taught...'

'I do not want that kind of commitment.'

'Coward,' she said, and stepped from the rocks and slipped and ended up knee-deep in the stream.

She didn't swear. She simply stood with the clear creek water rippling around her legs, cooling her as she needed to be cooled.

Jack held out a hand to help her out. She ignored it. She glared at him and stepped back onto the rocks and squelched to the bank. 'I'm going home,' she said, grabbing the flashlight and ripping off the cellophane. Platypus watching was over. He could stay in the dark, alone. 'Don't come with me. I need to vent spleen.'

'Don't get lost.'

'What would you care if I did?' she snapped. 'What would you care if everyone got lost?'

He didn't follow her. Instead he stayed where he was, not moving, not thinking, simply trying to quiet his mind.

In a while the platypus came back. So much for his accusation that it'd stop feeding tonight. It wasn't afraid. Without the flashlight he couldn't see into the water but he could see it when it surfaced, to breathe, to digest the food it had gathered in its pouch.

A solitary creature.

Or not. This might be a female, desperate to eat to store fat and burrow to breed.

'Don't do it,' he told it—or her—and winced at his own stupidity. The world had to breed.

People had to care—just not him.

But he did care, he thought, growing angry. He'd sorted Brenda's problems. He'd allowed Oliver to help. The kid was now safe and fed, with a woman who'd do the right thing by him. Until his father came back.

And if his father didn't return?

The thought was bleak.

It was nothing to do with him.

Alex's fierce prodding made it everything to do with him.

Alex had to butt out. Alex was nothing to do with him either.

He must not care.

CHAPTER NINE

How to keep a working relationship after a night like that? He'd thought he couldn't, but Alex rose the next morning determinedly busy, demanding to see medical records of each individual horse, deciding they needed a more pro-active method of vaccinations, planning a database that would include every detail of every horse from planned conception on.

When it rained she worked on her database. When it was fine she worked outside, either hands-on with the horses or on her woodwork projects.

She was pleasant to him. She asked for orders and tried to sound deferential. She smiled when he smiled. They did the dumb scoring thing at each meal but the pleasure had gone out of it.

The boundaries had been set. It was for the best, but he didn't have to like it.

He wanted it to end, and yet he didn't.

Oliver still came over after school and walked Sancha.

Alex always chatted to the kid but Jack stayed clear. He heard them laughing, he called himself an idiot for not joining them, but years of training, years of solitude, couldn't and wouldn't be erased.

And then of course came the day Alex decreed Sancha was recovered enough to be let free.

'She'll stay in the home paddock for a couple more weeks,' she told Jack. 'But there's no need for Oliver to walk her any more.' She hesitated. 'It'll break his heart.'

'You don't break your heart after a month of walking a mare,' he snapped. A month of caring? It took far longer than that.

'The horses are important to him.'

'Let him keep on walking her, then,' he said roughly, and she shook her head.

'Sancha's restive now and Oliver's no fool. I'll tell him tonight. It's a shame we haven't any other recuperating mares to keep him on. Mind, he tells me he's ridden horses since he was a toddler. You could use him to exercise—'

'No!'

'Fine, then,' she said stiffly. 'I'll tell him. Did anyone ever tell you you're mean?'

'I tell myself,' he said grimly. 'And it doesn't change a thing.'

She told Oliver that night. He meant to stay away but he just sort of happened to be on the veranda. He watched the kid's shoulders slump. He watched Alex's shoulders slump.

The kid walked away, looking like the world had crashed down around him. He reached the home paddock gate and turned and yelled.

'I will get a horse. I will, I will. Someone will let me!'

He closed his eyes, Oliver's pain searing within, as tight in his chest as it must be in the child's.

Why not give in to it?

Maybe caring wasn't a choice. Maybe it was already there, like it or not.

Dear God, he didn't want it.

The choice staring at him was invidious. Have nothing

more to do with him. Trust Brenda to take care of her own kid, or trust Brian to come back and claim him.

That path seemed mean and small. It *was* mean and small.

The alternative?

You couldn't just give yourself a little bit, he thought savagely. He'd heard the despair. He'd seen the aching emptiness in Oliver's eyes.

But he'd tried to fill it for Sophie and he'd failed. To try again…

What cost if he failed again? Unthinkable.

Alex wandered back to the house and stared at him with judgement. 'Well?' she said. 'Satisfied?'

'Don't.'

And suddenly she softened.

'It's tearing you in two, isn't it?'

'Nothing's tearing me in two.'

'You want to help but you can't.'

'If I want psychological assessment, I won't go to a vet.'

'I'm a human first, Jack. Talking might help.'

'Nothing helps,' he said savagely. 'Things were fine before you came.'

'You want me to leave?'

'Yes!' And then he hauled himself together. This was irrational. All he had to do was get his emotions under control, get his head back together and put things back on an employer/employee basis.

'No,' he corrected himself. 'Of course I don't. You're a fine vet and a great worker. I can even lean on the veranda rail without falling off.'

'I aim to please,' she said, striving for lightness, but it didn't come out lightly at all.

'You aim to get your own way,' he growled, but he managed a smile at the end of it.

'I do,' she admitted. 'I worry myself sick over Oliver.'

'If it's any consolation so do I,' he told her. 'I'll keep an eye on the kid when you're gone.'

'From a distance. That's big of you.'

'Doing it any other way will make it worse. He needs to forge a bond with Brenda. If I step in, then she doesn't need to.'

'That's an excuse.'

He closed his eyes.

'Okay, I'm sorry,' she said hurriedly. 'I know there's more to this than what I'm seeing. I'll shut up.'

'Are you capable of shutting up?' he demanded, and she looked up at him and a glimmer of a twinkle started behind her eyes.

'Maybe not,' she admitted. 'Ask my family. They treat me as an annoying little buzz fly—no matter how they swat me, I'll always zoom right back into their faces. But they love me regardless. 'Cause I'm cute. And I get things done. Like now. One of the mares in the top paddock was looking a bit lame this morning. I couldn't see anything wrong—I suspect she stood on a stone and bruised herself but she needs checking again tonight. I'll walk up there now.'

'I'll walk with you,' he found himself saying, and she shot him a surprised look.

'I'll buzz,' she warned.

'I don't mind your buzzing.'

'Do you promise not to swat?'

'No.'

She grinned. 'Okay,' she said. 'I'm used to dodging. I'll buzz and you'll swat. An employee/employer relationship made in heaven. What's more, you can carry my gear in case I need to do anything. Perfect.'

* * *

They walked up through the paddocks. The sun was sinking in the west, the night was warm and still, and they stayed silent.

Contrary to her promise she didn't buzz at all.

She worried.

Letting things be was not Alex's style. All her life she'd tried to fix the conflict between Matt and Ellie and her father. She'd never succeeded.

She wasn't succeeding now. If anything Jack was growing more aloof.

It was his right, she thought, trying very hard to be fair. No matter how much Oliver needed a male figure in his life, she couldn't force it, and the look on Jack's face when she tried... She was starting to think she'd do more harm than good.

So now she shut up and walked beside him and tried to concentrate on the small sounds of the night, the birds coming in to roost, the frogs in the swamplands by the creek, the crickets complaining that their heat was fading. It didn't work. She was totally focused on this man beside her. On his pain.

For pain it was. For the first time tonight, she'd clearly seen his refusal to help Oliver for what it was. It wasn't selfishness but an aching certainty that help from him would achieve nothing.

She could badger him for ever about the moral imperative of helping, but to intrude on that pain?

She didn't know all the facts, like she hadn't known the facts about her father and Matt and Ellie. The world was a complicated place. It took figuring out.

Her sister's letter had thrown her, made her unsure of her foundations, and in the face of that uncertainty she knew she had to back off from pushing this guy beside her.

'You haven't talked for five minutes,' he said at last. 'Are you ill?'

She smiled, absurdly relieved at his note of teasing.

'Nope. Just enjoying this night. I grew up with a little-girl adulation of anything horsey. My parents sent me on summer camps—to ranches where I could ride my heart out. Matt—my brother—often came, too. I'm not sure that he liked horses as I did but he liked getting away from the friction between himself and Dad. But we used to ride. Because he was older the owners trusted him to take care of me. For a kid who lived in Manhattan it was the best of times, just my horse and my big brother. Only of course there were always other kids, always camp leaders watching. Out here, for the first time in my life I feel free and it feels fantastic. I wish I could bring Matt out here and let him feel it.'

'Invite him for a visit.'

'He's too busy now, growing his own company,' she said. 'I wish I knew how they're feeling—both the twins.'

'Phone them.'

'Be a buzz fly?'

'Maybe they like buzz flies,' he growled. 'They have their uses.'

She grinned and to her own astonishment she found herself slipping her hand into his. She felt him freeze—and then she felt him deliberately, consciously relax.

Had this guy ever walked in the moonlight holding a woman's hand?

He was her employer. She had no business asking.

No, she didn't, but his solitude caught her as nothing had caught her before. She held, not tightly, but still she held.

They walked on and the silence deepened.

'I'm not...good at this,' Jack said at last.

'Holding hands with a woman? Didn't you have movie theatres when you were thirteen?'

'There aren't a lot of movie theatres out here.'

'That's an awful lot of catching up you need to do, then,' she said lightly, and swung his hand and chuckled—and then stilled.

As did Jack.

The sound came from behind them, above. A horse, being ridden down the slopes from the upper paddocks, towards the creek.

Slow at first, and then faster...

A horse sounds different ridden to galloping free. The nuances are different—weight, the struggle between control and freedom.

Definitely ridden. Really fast.

Oliver's yell sounded through her head as clearly as if he was yelling it now. *I will get a horse...!*

'It's one of the colts,' Jack said in a voice that sounded strangled. 'Oliver? Oh, my God, if he tries to jump the creek...'

And he started to run.

They didn't see what happened. It took them what seemed half an hour but in probability it was only three or four minutes. Jack was well ahead by the time Alex burst through the clearing to the creek's banks.

When Alex reached the creek, the horse, a young, chestnut gelding, was pacing, wild-eyed and frantic, riderless, no saddle, reins hanging free.

Jack was in the water, fighting the current, waist-deep, eyes everywhere.

It didn't take skill to know what had happened. Oliver had simply decided to take the horse home. He'd set him at the creek, but the horse had balked and done a one-eighty turn these horses were famous for.

Oliver must be in the water.

There was debris everywhere. It had rained over the past few days and logs and leaf litter were being swept down.

Jack was searching with frenzy born of desperation, hauling logs aside, moving with a desperation that looked almost like madness.

She was in there with him, searching herself, not thinking of anything but one small boy, one tousled-headed kid who had to be here. Who must be.

The hills here were steep, and where Oliver had tried to jump was near a bend. There was always a mass of logs here, caught, gradually working their way free to where the creek widened as it turned.

Water was washing against a dam of logs.

Jack's flashlight was sweeping the water, searching, searching...

A flash of...something.

The flashlight was dropped as Jack dived.

In the light of the dropping flashlight—a glimpse of red-blond curls, tumbling under the water...

Alex dived forward but Jack was before her. Right under the water. Then rising, holding, dragging a limp child from under a matt of wood and leaf and water.

Totally limp.

No!

But then, as Jack lifted him higher than his chest, higher than the mass of litter-strewn water, he stirred and whimpered and coughed—and then was violently, distressingly and wonderfully ill.

Jack staggered to the bank. He knelt, turned Oliver sideways to clear his airway.

Alex staggered to reach them, hauled off her T-shirt,

using it to wipe his face clear, to make him safe, to let him breathe.

Jack simply knelt, holding the boy in his arms while she tended to him. Alex darted one glance at him and that was enough. His face was devoid of colour, ashen, grim as death.

He held and held, while she cleaned Oliver and whispered to him that he was safe and Jack had him and he was fine, and she noted that Jack's hold tightened rather than loosened, as if he was coming to terms with how close they'd come to tragedy.

'Drummer…' Oliver whispered, his first word, dragged out of him as if his throat was still half-choked, and Jack closed his eyes as if the word had physically stung.

'The horse is fine,' he said, sounding strangled. 'It wanted only that. You nearly kill yourself and your first thought is for your horse.'

'I didn't want to hurt him.' The little boy's voice was a sob. 'I wanted Cracker but he was too far away, and tonight I just wanted a horse. I just wanted…something.'

It was a cry from the heart, a piercing sob that shook the night. That shook Alex to the core.

There was a long, long silence where they all practiced breathing.

'Well, he's not the horse for you,' Jack said at last, and she knew he was striving desperately for control. 'Drummer's hardly broken. He needs solid training before he's a safe ride.'

'I can…I can ride!'

'If you got reins on Drummer and got him this far then I see that you can,' Jack said. 'But you and he both need work. If you need a horse that much, okay, in the morning we'll talk about you taking and caring for Cracker. You can help me train Drummer. You can improve your riding skills yourself and we'll go from there.'

'You mean...?' Oliver could hardly speak. He was still limp with shock and fear, and yet in the moonlight there was no disguising the look of blazing hope. 'You'll let me ride?'

'If the choice is between that and killing yourself, I have no choice,' Jack said grimly. 'Now let's get you home, young man. Your mother will be frantic.'

'She's not my mother,' Oliver said in a voice that came close to breaking Alex's heart. 'She's Brenda and she won't even know I'm gone.'

'She will soon,' Jack said grimly. 'Maybe after tonight both Brenda and I need to do a rethink about what one kid needs.'

Jack took Oliver home. Alex caught Drummer, led him to the home paddock and the stables beyond, calmed him, groomed him and checked him for damage.

She could see why Oliver had chosen him. He was, quite simply, magnificent.

'It wasn't your fault,' she told him as she rubbed him. 'You have the skills to be a great stockhorse and Oliver has the skills to be a great stockman. But you both need training. Jack's your intermediary. I'm thinking it'll work for you all.'

She rubbed him longer than she needed, waiting for the sound of the SUV returning. Finally it did. She waited longer, for Jack to appear in the stables. He came in looking grim-faced, stressed to the limit.

'Is he okay?' he demanded, tight and gruff.

The horse. Of course he'd be worried about Drummer.

'He's fine,' she said. 'And quiet. I'm thinking he's figured he had a hand in something ghastly.'

'Not that ghastly,' Jack said grimly. 'And it wasn't Drummer's fault. He's never been asked to jump water before, so of course he did a U-turn.' He looked grey, she thought. Grey and sick.

'I'm so glad it turned out okay,' she whispered.

'Thank God we were there,' he managed. 'It seems sometimes, that not caring—'

'Hey, it wasn't your fault,' she said, giving Drummer a final stroke and opening the stable door to let him into the safety of the home paddock. 'You did what you thought was right. You forbade him to ride.'

'His father taught him to love horses,' Jack said. 'I knew not letting him ride was cruel.'

'And now you've fixed it.'

'I've talked to Brenda,' he admitted. 'She's so taken up with her own two girls and her financial mess that she hasn't seen Oliver's needs.'

'And now she has?'

'I don't know if that's possible. But he's coming here tomorrow. He can take full care of Cracker, even help me train.'

'Wow,' Alex whispered. 'Oh, Jack, that's wonderful.'

'Yeah, and you'll go home and I'll still be doing it,' he said roughly. 'If it wasn't for you, Alex—'

'This is none of my doing,' she said roundly. 'It's your call.' But she looked into his face and saw such a depth of anguish there that her heart twisted in pain. He'd been railroaded. He had no choice now but to care about this little boy.

And if he could care about a child...

Don't go there, she told herself quickly. She had five more months of employment. That was all. Then she had to move on.

Which was what she wanted—wasn't it? To return to

the States with glowing references, get herself a job with one of the big horse ranchers, to prove to her family and her friends that she wasn't just a cute blonde bimbo who'd trained to treat kittens.

That *was* what she wanted. Wasn't it?

It had to be. But this gorgeous, wounded hero standing right in front of her was changing something inside of her.

She wanted to take two steps forward right now, wrap her hands around his waist and hold him. And hold him and hold him, until the armour he'd so carefully built around himself disintegrated to nothing.

She took one part of one step forward—and he backed out of the stall and turned away.

'I'm heading up the hill. I need to make sure Oliver didn't leave any gates open,' he said, more roughly than necessary.

'Do you want company?'

'No,' he snapped. 'Go to bed.'

'Is that an order, boss?'

'If that's what it takes,' he said grimly. 'Good night, Alex.'

'Good night,' she whispered, rebuffed.

'Oh, and, Alex?'

'Yes?'

'Thank you for today,' he said. 'We got him out and we kept him alive. I'm not sure if I could have managed alone.'

'Sure you could,' she said, and she couldn't keep her voice even. 'You've practiced alone for long enough to be really good at it. I know I'm messing with your head, so off you go and practice some more.'

He checked the upper paddock, and every gate. He spent a lot more time up there than he should.

Alex was messing with his head?

Yes, she was. She knew it, too. It was like she could

see right inside him and she knew how terrified he was to think a little boy could need him. And maybe she could sense how desperately he was trying not to care for her.

Don't care, he told himself savagely. *Don't care.*

Caring didn't help. He knew it. The mantra, the feeling of hopelessness, had been drummed into him since he was eight years old. Caring just tore apart both parties instead of one.

Sophie had died and a part of him had died with her. He never wanted to feel like that again.

But Alex was back in the house. Alex with her constant interfering, her prodding conscience, her laugher, her skill, her...

Her status as an employee.

She'd shoved Oliver on to him.

Or not.

Yes, she had. After Brian disappeared he'd caught Oliver up in the top paddock, trying to catch one of the wilder colts.

He'd sent him home with a flea in his ear—the original ogre growling at small children.

It was because Alex was here, Alex with her laughter and her open friendship, that Oliver had dared come back again.

It always came back to Alex.

He walked on. He should go home to sleep.

Sleep? What a laugh.

He walked.

She lay in bed and stared at the ceiling and thought. And thought and thought and thought.

She thought, weirdly, of her family. Of her father who'd pretended to care, had tried to care, but who hadn't pulled it off.

She thought of Jack, trying desperately not to care—and who wasn't succeeding either.

'So throw your hat in the ring,' she whispered into the dark, but she knew he already had, with his offer to teach Oliver, to let him come to the farm whenever he wanted. He couldn't be blind to the unadulterated hero worship in the little boy's eyes. By taking this step, he was exposed, all over again. He was hurting. He'd be hurting right now.

How could she sleep? She lay and stared at the ceiling and thought...and thought.

So many thoughts her head was likely to explode.

Give up.

What was a girl to do at two in the morning if she couldn't sleep?

She could think of nothing but Jack.

Ellie's letter... Surely she had to do something there. What she wanted was to get on a plane and go hug her—but to leave Jack?

No. Next best thing. She switched on her bed lamp and wrote long emails to Matt and to Charlotte. The letter Ellie had sent to Alex had been long and thoughtful and caring, an indication of how close they'd always been, but for some reason this night had her tuned to family nuances. Suddenly she was wondering whether Ellie could have maintained long, thoughtful and caring for two more handwritten letters? When Ellie was delirious about being in love? When relationships in the Patterson family had always been fraught?

So she wrote. Just to check they knew absolutely everything Ellie had told her. Just to tell them she loved them. It helped fill the void where she wanted Jack to be.

The emails were hard. She sent them and they did nothing to make her sleepy.

Family...

Jack.

Do not think of Jack.

Count stars? It had to be better than nothing. The night sky here was breathtaking but the veranda stopped her seeing the stars from her window.

Finally she tugged on the fleecy bathrobe that she'd thought was an indulgence until she'd seen this place. She'd nearly ruined it that first night and it had taken an age to clean but now her bathrobe was her best friend. She padded through the empty house, silent as a mouse, being even more silent past Jack's door.

She slipped out onto the veranda—and Jack was there before her.

He didn't hear her—and for a moment she stayed silent.

The sensible thing would be to retreat. *Now.*

But she wasn't being sensible. There was something about this night. There was something about this man.

A long time ago, sixteen years old, she'd broken her heart over a boy. She'd moped about the house for days and finally her mother had given her a solid talking-to.

'Alexandra, this is your time for having fun,' Fenella had scolded. 'It's time for making friends rather than committing for life. Don't break your heart now. There's no need. One day you'll meet someone so special that there'll be no chance he could ever leave you, or you him.'

'Is that how you feel about Dad?' Alex had whispered, and Fenella had smiled, a weird, tight smile that maybe Ellie's letter had explained. But…

'Of course I do, honey,' Fenella had told her. 'Your dad and I have something special and one day you'll find it, too.'

Had she found it? Here, with this man who was trying so hard not to care? She couldn't know, but what she did know was that she had five months to find out. Starting now?

He was staring out at the moon, staring at nothing, and her heart twisted. Somehow she knew this man. He was strong and silent and wise. He handled his horses with a skill and understanding that took her breath away. He was so good-looking he'd make any woman's heart do back-flips. He was hero material.

And yet it wasn't the hero she was seeing now. She was seeing a boy, desperately caring for his sister, facing a load far too heavy for even an adult to carry alone. She was seeing a man who'd learned that caring hurt.

And today his heart had been tugged right out of the protective shield he'd built for himself, and he was exposed.

In more ways than one.

He'd fallen for Oliver. He'd put the child on a horse—no big deal—but he'd promised to teach him, promised to let him come whenever he wanted. No one seeing Oliver's face could doubt what that promise meant.

It meant every night after school, every weekend, every holiday, Jack would have his personal shadow. Maybe she hadn't seen it as clearly as Jack had, that there were no half-measures in caring.

Up until now he'd held himself back, but today he'd promised to care for Oliver and he'd opened himself to whatever it was that he was most afraid of.

Jack's armour had been shattered.

Tomorrow he might have that armour back in place, she thought. Tomorrow he might have it figured that he could leave an Oliver-size hole but seal the rest.

So tonight…

She'd never had armour where this man was concerned. She'd fallen for him and she was still falling. He was her wonderful Jack, the guy who did things to her insides she couldn't imagine anyone else doing.

And as she watched him in the darkness, she thought this *could* be the man she could love with all her heart. Her mother had promised her she'd meet someone like this, and maybe she had.

So do something.

She sat down beside him on the veranda steps and she took his hand in hers.

'Jack, you were wonderful today,' she said simply. And then she said, 'We have five months together. There are no promises about the future, but for these five months, maybe they could be special for both of us. Maybe it wouldn't hurt if you let me hold you?'

CHAPTER TEN

THE world stilled.

Nothing moved. Nothing breathed. The words hung in the warm night air, waiting to explode.

All or nothing. She was an 'all' sort of girl, she thought ruefully. Her words got her into trouble but she thought it; why not say it?

'Why?' Jack asked at last, in a voice so ragged she wanted to gather him into her arms and hold him for ever.

'Because we both could do with holding?' she managed, trying to make it light but it didn't come out light. Her words came out deadly serious, and she knew she had to say more.

'Maybe…maybe it's more than just holding,' she said, weaving her fingers through his. Feeling the strength of them. 'I'm not sure, but what I'm feeling… I've had boy-friends,' she conceded. 'They've been fun, they've been friends. I thought that was all there was, but now… My mom told me one day wham might happen, and now maybe it has. One look at you and wham.'

'Wham?' he said, sounding astonished, but wonderfully there was a trace of a twinkle returning.

'Well, not completely at first look,' she admitted. 'First you scared me witless, standing in your great black water-proofs in the middle of a rainstorm, spouting all sorts of chauvinistic nonsense. But I saw straight through you. I thought, there and then, Here's a man who I want to hold and I want to hold me right back. This is a man who…'

And then she broke off. She'd been trying to keep it light but it wasn't working.

He was watching her intently, and suddenly there was room for nothing but the truth.

'I don't know,' she said simply. 'I don't know what makes me feel the way I'm feeling about you. How to explain? It's the way you look at me. It's the way you cared for Sancha that first night, and made me a poached egg. It's the way you showed me the platypus, and the way you left me to fix the veranda rail by myself and then didn't go overboard because a mere female had done it. It's the way you trusted me with your horses from the get-go— you respect my training. It's because you make me smile and I know you hurt and I know it almost broke something inside you today when we thought Oliver was dead and I know…I know if these five months are all I can have of you, then I'll take them and gladly. I'll hold you for as long as you want me to hold you.'

Enough. She could lay her heart on her sleeve no further.

She let his hand drop.

She thought about being asked to pack her bags right here, right now. Employee throws herself at her boss…

He was gazing at her in the moonlight, for what seemed like for ever, searching her face as if searching for what he knew was truth.

She met his gaze as calmly as she could, but inside she was anything but calm.

What had she done? Thrown her heart at him, when today he'd been stretched to the limit already? Asked him for yet more commitment?

Asked him to care.

'You feel that...' he said gently, but he didn't move '...about me?'

'Stupid, isn't it,' she said, and suddenly she was choking back a sob. 'I know you don't want it. I know you don't want anyone to care.'

'I didn't think I did,' he said, and finally, finally, he took her hands. He tugged her to her feet and she came, rising so she was hard against him. Her breasts were against the hardness of his chest. 'Alex, I can't....'

'Can't what?' she said, and pressed a little harder. Amazed at her own temerity. Amazed where her body was taking her. 'From where I'm standing if feels as if you definitely can.'

He stilled. Thought about it. Didn't pull away.

'You know, if I didn't care I'd take you to bed in a heartbeat,' he said at last, and she felt his heart beating and thought there was nowhere she wanted to be but right here, right now.

'I thought you didn't care.'

'That was the plan. One crazy vet later...'

'Who's crazy?'

'You,' he said softly into her hair. 'Alex, today, with Oliver... I'm not sure how much you realise how big a deal this is for me. And now, you say you want me.'

'I know,' she whispered. 'It's too much pressure. I should just give you the odd hint. Start by smiling coyly at you over the breakfast table. Maybe carve our linked initials in the stable doors. Send you a valentine—oh, wait, that's done for this year so it's another year away. Sorry, Jack, but I can't wait. You have me now.'

'So what am I supposed to do with you?'

She tugged back at that, looking up at him. Was he looking...trapped?

Trapped?

Whoa. A girl had some pride. Or a girl had to find some pride pretty fast.

She tugged right away and stood and glared at him. 'You needn't worry,' she managed. 'I'm no cavewoman with a club about to drag you off to my lair. I believe I may have said more than was wise. I believe I should retract. Should we go back to calling each other Mr Connor and Dr Patterson?'

She felt humiliated to her socks. She felt sick.

And Jack was still looking at her.

'Alex?'

'What?' It was a huffy sort of reply. Where was her dignity? Back in the States. Maybe that's where she had to go.

'Alex, all I meant to say is that I don't know how this can operate long-term,' he said, and he reached out and took her hands again. 'I made a vow about commitment and I meant it. I said I'd never care for anyone. It causes pain, it doesn't help. I've never seen it work. But yeah, all sorts of things happened today, or maybe they happened a month ago when you first came here but I was too dumb to see it. It seems, like it or not, I do care. Like it or not, I want you.' He took a deep breath. 'I want you in every sense of the word.'

'So...' she said, feeling like she was almost scared to breathe. 'Are you saying you're liking me against your better judgement. Have you read *Pride and Prejudice*?'

'At school but—'

'But you never thought about it again because you think of it as chick fiction,' she said cordially. 'So you didn't learn the Mr Darcy lesson. So here you are, liking me against your better judgement. But you need to think back. Think hard. Mr Darcy got his comeuppance and so might you.'

'I don't understand,' he said, and she believed him. He looked bewildered.

'Neither do dumb males everywhere,' she retorted, and she knew she needed to explain. She must. Because even though a girl had some pride, she wanted this man more than anything else in the world. 'Darcy took almost a whole book to realise he loved Elizabeth, and to know his judgement was just as dumb as his pride. So maybe we could do better. We could put them both aside right there, right now, and just...see. We could just take one woman and one man and put them together and see if we could make each other happy. I'm not saying it'll work. I'm saying we could just...see.'

'For five months.' His face was expressionless.

'That's the contract.'

'Alex...'

'No promises,' she said. 'I know that. But I also know that right now, right at this moment, I want you more than life itself, and I want you to want me right back. And I know for you life is heavy and everything has to be weighed but sometimes I truly believe you should go where your instincts tell you. Heart instead of head. Leap before you look if you like, and consequences be damned. Not that there would be consequences. Except maybe making us very happy for the next five months. So I'm thinking—'

'I'm thinking maybe you might want to stop thinking?'

And amazingly, wonderfully, he was laughing. Laughing!

'Has anyone ever accused you of being able to sell ice to Eskimos?' he demanded.

'Totally different,' she said, twinkling back at him. 'From where I'm standing you haven't seen ice for a very long time.'

He chuckled, a low delicious sound that sent the low simmer in her body into a fiery burn. She wanted...

And so, it seemed, did he. He caught her hands and held, not fiercely, not in the claim of a lover, but in the hold of someone who needed to make sure this was no mere whim.

'Alex, you know I can't make promises.'

'I'm not asking for promises.'

'And yet you're offering to come to my bed.'

'That's a very old-fashioned phrase,' she said. 'And it sounds wanton.' She hesitated. 'You know I'm not wanton.'

'I do know that,' he said gravely. 'And I know the gift you're offering. Alex, a man would need to be a lot stronger than me to resist.'

'I think,' she said softly, almost as a whisper but much more sure, 'that you need to do better than that. I'm not going to bed with a man against his better judgement, no matter how much I want him. I want you to want me. I want you to think we could have a wonderful, wonderful time if we managed to cut loose from our inhibitions for a few months. I'm thinking yes, I could give my heart, and in five months I may well cry all the way home but when I'm in my rocking chair in my nursing home I'll be thinking, Wow, that was mind-blowing, and I'll also be thinking that you'll have a grin on your toothless, ancient face, as well.'

'Toothless?' he said faintly.

'It's sooner than you think. You're really quite old.'

'Hey!'

'I say it as I see it,' she said, twinkling again. 'So I'm saying now, right now, I want you more than anything in the world and if you could just unzip that armour just a little bit...'

'And unzip anything else that came along?'

'That's the one,' she said approvingly. 'If you want me.'

'I do want you,' he said, and the smile died and the grip on her hands tightened. 'Right now, I want you so much it's like there's a black void that I don't know how to fill. Alex, I know nothing about love. I don't do caring. I'm on my own. But you... I just have to look at you and—'

'Your toes curl?' she said hopefully, and he laughed, a lovely, rich chuckle that sounded out over the valley. He tugged her to him and held, long, hard, folding her to his chest, simply holding. Resting his chin on her hair. Folding her to him.

And she didn't say a word. She was fighting with every weapon she had, she thought, but would it be enough? Could this man want her?

'It would be an honour and a privilege to take you to my bed,' he said at last.

'How about fun?' she managed, striving to be light, and he put her away from him, holding her at arm's length.

'Fun, too,' he said. 'But a gift without price for all that. No, I'm not taking you against my better judgement but it is selfish.'

'Two adults who want each other? What's selfish about that?'

'I guess...nothing at all.' He looked down at her gravely in the night. 'Alex Patterson,' he said, soft and low and sure. 'Would you do me the honour of coming to my bed?'

'Oh, for heaven's sake,' she whispered, and then she chuckled. 'I thought you'd never ask.'

He woke and she was spooned into the curve of his body. His face was in her hair. Skin against skin, she was moulded to him, held in his arms.

His.

For he was under no illusions. She'd given herself to him last night, with all the joy and generosity and wonder she possessed. She'd taken him to her as he'd taken her. Their bodies had merged and merged again, and it had felt like...coming home.

There was a peace about him this morning he'd never known, never thought he could know.

Maybe it was this place, he thought. He'd had relationships before—of course he had—but they'd been part of the tight, controlled life he'd built for himself in the city. Here, on this farm that he loved...

Did he love this farm?

There was a thought to let drift with all the others of this magic morning.

He'd loathed this place by the time he'd left it, but it had called him back. The memories of a grandmother who'd truly loved them. The time Sophie was happy. The garden... The horses...

He'd thought his mother's betrayal, Sophie's illness, his grandfather's brutality, had killed it. He'd come here because he'd loved the horses and he'd wanted to be alone, but now...

Now he had a little boy who was depending on him to be his friend and his defender.

Now he had a woman held warm against his body and her heat, her joy, was shattering defences he didn't know he had.

She stirred a little, moving slightly against him, and the feel of her skin on his was enough to take his breath away, to make him forget to think of anything but her, this woman, this warmth, this love.

Love?

He didn't do—

No. He didn't know what he didn't do. For now she was in his arms, twisting to kiss him good-morning, lac ing her arms around his neck, kissing him so deeply everything else slid away and there was only this moment, this woman, this joy.

He was hers.

She felt warm and sated and desired.

She felt loved.

For five months?

How could she feel like this about this man, how could she lie with him each night, and walk away after five months?

Don't care, she told herself. Don't think about it. Five months is an eternity. Five months is long enough for miracles to happen.

A miracle had happened. This big, brooding horse whisperer was making love to her with all the tenderness he knew how, with all the love she'd hoped for, with a passion she hadn't known existed.

He was loving her and she was loving him back—and everything else could take care of itself.

Everything else had to take care of itself. All she could think about right now, all she could feel, all she could taste, all she could want, was Jack.

Nothing had changed—yet everything had.

Employer/employee? Not so much. Jack paid her wages. Jack supposedly gave the orders but somewhere during that one night of passion, the dynamics changed.

Equal partners?

This farm needed massive work, but from the moment Alex slipped dreamily from Jack's bed and donned her work clothes, she no longer felt this was a job. She felt like this farm was part of her and she'd do everything in her power to make it wonderful.

Jack valued her as a vet. He'd been reluctant to let her share the heavy work but now she was insisting.

If he was heading down the paddock with the chainsaw, she was there, too. And somehow, this new thing that was between them gave her the power to insist.

'If you chop your leg off, you'll need a vet,' she growled, and he grinned.

'Do you know which way human feet get sewed back on?'

'I have instant surgery techniques on the internet on my phone,' she said with dignity. 'I'll manage.'

So she went with him and his time for being alone was over.

If he'd hated it she would have backed off. That first day as they worked side by side she caught him glancing at her, over and over, as if trying to work up strength to tell her to go. Head back to the house and find her own projects.

But every time she saw that look she'd bounce somehow, make him laugh, make him smile, demand he help her with what she was doing.

He'd relax again—sort of. She knew he wasn't totally relaxed about this new intimacy. She knew he expected it to shatter, but for now they'd work together, and at night they fell into bed again, together. Partners in every sense of the word.

Oliver was giving her joy, too. Jack put him back on Cracker, who was so quiet he'd almost forgotten what it was like to turn on a dime. Not completely, though. Oliver needed to be trained to manage him as a stockhorse, and Alex watched Jack help with wonder.

It was as if he'd shed a skin—or a suit of armour more like. This dark, solitary male was suddenly solitary no longer. She watched him care, she watched him smile and laugh. Occasionally she could see tension. She knew the shadows were there—the armour had been put aside but not thrown away—but she thought, between them, she and Oliver could fight any armour.

In five months?

No. She wasn't going there. Anything could happen in five months. For now, her life was wonderful.

Two weeks later they took delivery of the new windows that made the farm-worker's cottage watertight. Jack could now set it up as a cosy residence. Alex could move in. She could be the independent employee Jack had wanted.

She didn't. Instead, because Alex was in the main house, because the cottage was free, it meant the arrival of Cooper Barratt, an elderly, wiry horseman with hands of magic. This was the man Jack had sought to turn Wararra back into a training stable as well as a stud.

Cooper arrived with his two dogs and his lopsided grin and his lopsided deference. He called Jack 'Jack'—he might be an employee but he deemed himself an equal— but he called Alex 'Missus' and nothing Alex could say would budge him.

'I see the way Jack looks at you,' he said, and grinned. 'If he's the boss, you're the missus. You tell me it ain't true.'

He treated her with more respect than he did Jack and it made her squirm.

'It's me who should be sleeping in the worker's cottage,' she told Jack, and he grinned and hugged her.

'Then we'd have to put Cooper in the big house and the employer/employee relationship would be totally messed up.'

'It's messed up now.' She was lying in his arms, holding him tight, feeling like she had everything she wanted in the world.

'Nothing's messed up,' Jack told her, kissing her hair,

her nose, behind her ear—and then moving on to more intimate places. Places that made her gasp with pleasure. 'For now, things are perfect.'

'For now?' Hard to voice a doubt when he was doing... what he was doing.

'I can't think of tomorrow, my love,' he said huskily into the night. 'I can't think of anything past right now.'

Only he could think.

He woke in the small hours, as he often did, and it was then that the doubts crept in. Alex was curved against his body. She felt wonderful, magic, an extension of himself. She felt perfect.

But perfection didn't last. He cared for her so much, and that in itself was terrifying.

Where were they heading?

Marriage?

There was a thought to take his breath away.

Cooper called her 'Missus.' 'Missus' was the Australian vernacular for the boss's wife. It was a term of respect. It was a term of acknowledgement of what was happening—what had happened.

They were a couple.

If anything happened to her...

His mind closed hard against the thought, and as if she could sense it, she stirred and turned so she was sleepily facing him. Winding her arms around his neck. Kissing him softly.

'Problem?'

See, *that* was the problem. She had him figured. Every time he held back, she sensed it. Every time he worried she took his worry to her, shared it, forced him to say it out loud.

How could he tell her that the worry was that he cared too much?

How could he take this one last step—abandon fear and step forward with Alex in his arms?

How could he not?

'I'm worrying about resowing the top pasture before the end of autumn,' he managed, and she chuckled and held him closer.

'Liar. You've already ordered the seed. The forecast is for a gentle autumn. You've figured where we can keep the horses until it regenerates.'

'Mmm.'

'You're worried about *we*,' she said softly.

'Alex…'

'Don't,' she said soundly. 'You'll spoil things. For now, for right this moment, we're perfect. For now we have each other in our arms, and we fit like two halves of a whole. I'm not asking or expecting any more of you than that, Jack Connor. For now I'm loving you, and I'm wanting you, but I'm not holding you. My future's in the States, so stop worrying about it.'

'And if I asked that your future could be here?'

She stilled in his arms, but then she looked up at his troubled face and she shook her head.

'You don't want that,' she whispered. 'Not now, at least, and maybe not ever. I'm watching your face and I'm not seeing commitment. I'm seeing something akin to fear. Well, you can quit it with the fear. I come with no strings, Jack Connor, and I'm not letting you attach any. For now, we have now. That's all.'

Afterward he drifted back to sleep again and it was Alex who lay awake and stared into the night.

He'd almost asked her to stay.

Did she want him to?

Yes. Her head screamed that she was a fool for shushing him, for stopping him asking her to commit. For there was a part of Alex that wanted to commit more than anything in the world.

So what was stopping her taking and holding?

Strangely, it was the thought of her father. Of the letter Ellie had sent her, the letter that lay in the bottom of her suitcase explaining all.

Explaining that her parents' marriage had been built not on the mutual passion she'd always assumed but on reservations, where things weren't quite right, where honesty wasn't first and foremost.

She'd spent a lifetime trying to figure what was wrong with her family. Now she knew, and with that knowledge came the certainty that she didn't want that sort of relationship for herself.

Jack was starting to love her, she thought, but he was loving her despite his reservations. Despite his vows not to care.

As her father had loved her mother despite the fact that she was carrying another man's twins.

Despite...

It was a mean little word, and it stayed with her.

She wanted Jack. She knew that now; there was no *despite* in her language. She'd love him and hold him and care for him and she'd hope, with every ounce of her being.

But she would not let him commit to her *despite*... She wasn't going there. A cold, hard coil of common sense stayed with her.

Her plan had always been to work hard here and then return to the States and find the job of her dreams. Instead she'd found the man of her dreams right where she was.

So yes, if things worked out, if she was sure Jack could

love her, then she'd change her plans in a heartbeat—how could she not?—but she'd watched what *despite* had done to Matt, had done to Ellie.

She would not love this man *despite*.

CHAPTER ELEVEN

CHAPTER ELEVEN

WERARRA was blossoming. Autumn crept in, bringing lush pasture, a tinge of cool to the mountain breeze, an added energy to the horses in their care.

With three full-time workers the place was starting to look as it should. Tentatively Jack opened it to buyers. Until now he'd transported sale horses to Albury. Now, with Werarra's reputation growing, with good yards, a show-place that almost matched the website, horsemen from around the country and overseas were welcomed.

He could sell more horses than he could ever supply, Alex thought, but every horse leaving the property was perfect. He insisted on nothing less. So did Cooper, deeply approving of his boss's standards. And so did Alex. She cared for the horses in her charge with passion and she knew when she left this place it wouldn't just be Jack she missed with all her heart.

And so did Oliver.

Every moment he wasn't in school he was here, following Jack wherever he went.

Alex had expected him to adore Cracker, the horse Jack had decreed was his to care for, and he did, but a higher adoration was reserved for Jack.

He was mates with Alex, he respected Cooper and he liked Cooper's dogs. He loved Cracker, but he lived for Jack.

Cooper might be training a recently broken colt. Alex might be treating an older mare with problematic teeth—a procedure that took strength and skill. But if Jack was doing something as mundane as filling up potholes in the driveway, that was the most riveting thing Oliver could dream of to watch, and he did.

'I don't know what to do about it,' Jack said, the night of the pothole filling, and Alex grinned.

'Embrace it? He's doing no harm.'

'It can't last.'

'Why not? You're going nowhere. He'll grow out of hero worship.'

'Yeah,' Jack said roughly, and she knew it still worried him.

He cared, Alex thought. He cared, despite...

There was that word again.

'It's Saturday tomorrow,' she said into the stillness. 'How about we give ourselves a day off?'

'A day off.' He said it like it was another language.

'I've never been up to the far ridge,' she said. 'I was talking to Oliver about it. He says there's a waterfall. His dad took him there once. Do you know it?'

He did. She could see it in his face, but she could also see caution.

'It's five miles,' he said. 'You and me.'

'And Oliver,' she said hurriedly, because there was that *despite* thing again. She and Jack were working side by side, they were sleeping in each other's arms, yet to spend leisure time together seemed another thing entirely. Every night after dinner, Jack disappeared to his study. Alex read or watched television or wrote home. They came together when it was time to sleep, but she knew the thought of further intimacy was yet another step that left him feeling exposed.

She didn't want him exposed. She ached for him to feel that with her he was safe, that with her the terrible loneliness and responsibility he'd faced as a child and young man was over, but she'd do it one step at a time.

A picnic.

With Oliver to diffuse the strangeness of it.

'I know you have more potholes to fill,' she teased gently. 'And I know Oliver's aching to watch you fill them. But all my charges are in fine health, we have no buyers due, Cooper's more than able to hold the fort and I can make sandwiches.'

'Really?' His dark eyes suddenly flashed a twinkle. 'What score sandwiches?'

'Ten if I'd had some notice,' she said, and grinned. 'But because we're picnicking on a whim, they might only be about seven. But my brother tells me my bacon sandwiches are ten even if they look wobbly. What do you say, Jack? Can we take a day and have fun?'

'I should—'

'There are always "shoulds",' she said gently. 'But I really want to see the waterfall. Oliver's offered to take me himself but I don't trust him not to lose us both.'

That was a low blow. Five miles of bushland, they could well get lost and Jack knew it.

'You can't go on your own,' he growled.

'Well, then. Potholes or picnics, what's it to be, Jack Connor?'

And he agreed.

Despite...

Saturday morning. As usual, Oliver arrived before eight and from the moment she broke the news of the impending picnic and saw the glow of undiluted joy on his face, Alex knew it'd be a day to remember.

They rang Brenda to ask permission, but in truth Brenda didn't care. She was accustomed to Oliver spending most of his time on the farm, and Alex thought it was a relief to the woman.

Brenda was doing the 'right thing' by Oliver, but her heart wasn't in it. She'd been saddled with the boy, and she was caring for him *despite*...

Don't think of that word today.

They saddled the horses. They packed the saddlebags with Alex's sandwiches, with fruit, drinks and swimming gear, and they set off.

Cooper came out of the stables to wave them off.

'You look a beaut little family,' he said, and Alex saw Jack's expression change. He had his face under control in an instant, but she'd seen.

A family. He didn't do family.

Would four months be long enough to change something so intrinsic within him?

She refused to worry today.

She'd have a great time today...*despite* misgivings.

There was no way they would have found the waterfall without Jack. Indeed, she would have been lost within ten minutes of leaving the property boundary, she conceded. The bushland here was wild and mountainous. Werarra bordered a national park and there civilisation ended.

The horses nosed their way single file along vague tracks made by wombats or kangaroos. Amazingly they seemed to know where they were going—they needed to because Jack put Alex in front on Rocky, Oliver was in the middle on Cracker, and Jack and Maestro followed at the rear. Keeping watch.

Every now and then, Jack would call a direction, veer

left, slow here, ware low branches, but mostly they rode in silence.

Oliver seemed as awed as she was by the bushland, Alex thought, and knew his father hadn't brought him here often. Indeed, the more she learned of Oliver the more she wondered that his father had done anything for him at all.

He looked a bit small for the horse he was on. His freckled face was intent, his hands gripping the reins tight but not tugging on Cracker's mouth; he was consciously, fiercely, giving his horse his head.

He was a great little kid, Alex thought, and wondered at the deal that had given him a father who walked out on him, and only Brenda, who did her best.

Life wasn't fair. She glanced behind her once again to check him, and Jack was behind him, so she sort of checked on Jack at the same time.

Man and boy—and she knew instinctively that they'd shared harsh backgrounds.

If she was here with Matt right now, he wouldn't be talking either, she thought. Her big brother had been raised with a father who resented him. It had made him turn inward, become a loner.

She had two loners on her hands right now.

The cure?

'I spy,' she said, and got two groans for answer.

'Something beginning with *H*,' she said, doggedly determined, and Oliver gave an oversize, theatrical sigh.

'Horse.'

'Hey, you're a natural,' she said, and grinned. 'Your turn.'

'*M*,' Oliver ventured.

'Mountain,' Jack ventured, and Oliver beamed like Oliver himself had guessed and won.

'Cool. Your turn.'

'V,' Jack said, and Alex turned and met his gaze and he grinned at her and her heart did this crazy sort of back-flip with pike.

Oliver caught the look and stared at Alex, screwed up his nose and yelled, 'Vet!'

Cracker startled, but Jack was right there, grasping his reins, settling him, grinning at the small boy as if this was part of the game.

'Too good, mate. And here's the waterfall.'

Here it was. The creek had been widening as they rode—every time the 'track' neared it, it seemed wider and deeper. Now, one more bend in the track brought them to what the sound of rushing water had been announcing for some time.

It was the most magical place. It had Alex drawing in her reins and drawing in her breath.

'Take that, Manhattan Girl,' Jack said softly, riding up beside her. He must know there was nothing in New York that could possibly compare to this place.

The waterfall wasn't one steep drop, but rather half a dozen tumbles, from rocky plateau to rocky plateau. Vast boulders seemed scattered like marbles, with great mossy banks littered between. A cave beckoned mysteriously behind the water. 'Sophie and I camped in there once,' Jack said, and Alex glanced at him with wonder.

It was the first time she'd heard him talk of his sister with pleasure.

Maybe it was this place, she thought, for how could anyone be unhappy here? Here one could climb or swim or explore the cave or sleep—or simply stay on horseback and look, like she was doing now—but Rocky was already tugging downward to graze on the lush river grasses and Oliver was tumbling from Cracker to explore and Jack was looking at her quizzically as if she really might be comparing the streets of New York to here.

It was perfect.

The beds of moss…

If Oliver wasn't here…

'There is a downside to playing families,' Jack said dryly, and she blushed and he put his hands up and caught her as she slid from Rocky's back—and she knew he was thinking exactly what she was thinking.

'Swim,' he said, his dark eyes twinkling. 'Second best but it'll have to do.'

'It's a pretty poor second,' she retorted, and he hugged her and kissed her and Oliver turned round and saw them and sighed.

'Yuck. Aren't you two swimming?'

'Something beginning with *S*,' Alex managed, hugging Jack right back. Thinking surely this could work. Surely demons could be exorcised to make a happy ever after. 'Three things. Something beginning with *S*, then something with *P* and then something starting with *S*, as well.'

'Swim, picnic and sleep?' Jack demanded, still holding her.

'Sleep?' Oliver demanded, astounded. 'Who'd sleep here? Let's go.'

They swam their hearts out. Oliver adored the cave, declaring it his own secret hiding place, ducking in and out through the falls. Alex organised silly, active duck diving games and had them all playing. They clambered from plateau to plateau of the falls, following the course of the water. They explored every inch of this magic place.

Finally they ate their picnic. Alex curled up on the rug Jack had packed, snuggled Oliver to her—and to Jack's astonishment Oliver did snuggle—and they both closed their eyes.

Alex was sort of leaning against Jack.

Oliver was sort of leaning against Alex.

Family?

'I want to be like this for ever,' Oliver murmured, half asleep. 'Alex can be my mum and Jack will be my dad and I'll have a family.'

And with those few words, Alex felt things change. She could feel tension slam into Jack. The lovely, sensuous, sun-washed sleepiness was gone, just like that.

'Brenda's your mother.' Jack said it mildly but Alex knew it was far from mild. She could feel the stress.

'She doesn't want me,' Oliver said. He still sounded half asleep but he was matter-of-fact about it. He sounded as if he trusted them both, that they were simply an extension of him talking to himself. 'I hear her on the phone. She's got my dad's phone number now and she tells him he has to come and get me. She says, "He's a great kid. You're a louse for leaving us but for dumping him... He's not my kid, Brian, and if you think I'm taking him on so you can swan round playing the bachelor... End of the month or it's social services." And I don't know what social services are.'

The parroting of Brenda's voice was sickening. The whole statement was sickening.

How to respond?

'I guess it means your dad will come and get you by the end of the month,' Alex said, trying to sound sure.

'He doesn't want me,' Oliver said, snuggling further on her knee. She was stroking his hair, and he was soaking her warmth and touch like a puppy might. A lone puppy.

'He hasn't talked to me since he left,' he said, almost matter-of-factly. 'Last time Brenda talked to him she said

"Do you want to talk to him?" and he hung up. But this is so nice.'

And he closed his eyes, like he'd put the conversation away from him as something that no longer affected him—and he went to sleep.

They were left in the sleepy, sun-baked silence. The sound of the waterfall behind them was a gentle wash, a soothing message that all was right with a world that obviously wasn't. The horses were grazing lazily on the lush, grass-coated banks, and the sun-dappled shade gave them the perfect place to sleep themselves.

Alex was still leaning against Jack. She'd been feeling incredibly soporific.

Now all she could feel was his tension.

'I can't,' Jack said as the silence stretched out. As he became sure Oliver was asleep. As they both accepted the unanswered question that hung. He sounding stressed to breaking point. 'I could never—'

'I don't think I could myself,' Alex said cautiously. To take on the parenting of a child such as this one? She was twenty-six years old. She had no idea how to raise a child.

'It takes a village to raise a child,' she whispered. 'I read that somewhere.'

'And he has no one.'

'His dad...'

'I'll hunt the—' Jack stopped himself but she glanced at his face and she thought it was just as well Brian wasn't in range right now. 'I'll hunt him down and make him do what he has to do.'

'How do you force him to love his son?' Alex's fingers were still lightly stroking Oliver's hair. Jack was leaning against the smooth rock face and she was lying against his shoulder. She knew this man so well now, she thought. She'd been sleeping in his arms for almost a month. She knew his body, his smile, his laughter, his depth for loving—and yet she also knew his fear.

He'd failed his sister on his terms. To commit himself to that sort of caring again...

She knew he couldn't. She knew when her six months were up he'd let her go, and she knew he'd let Oliver go now.

Social services? Or the responsibility of Jack caring for another life?

But if Jack couldn't, then who?

The question drifted in her mind, demanding an answer. Who?

Maybe she could. She was starting to love this needful child, this kid who was brave and cheeky—and alone.

Was she crazy? How could she? She wasn't even a resident in this country. To take Oliver back to the US...?

There was surely no way a single American woman could adopt an eleven-year-old Australian. No way in the world.

And Oliver wouldn't want it.

It takes a village. Or two people.

She and Jack?

Jack couldn't commit, even to her.

'If I shift very gently, I can wiggle you back so you're leaning where I'm leaning,' Jack said, already starting to carefully shift. 'I need to go for a walk.'

'Without us?' she asked, and she knew she sounded desolate but there wasn't a thing she could do about it.

'Without you,' he said heavily. 'Alex, some things are just too hard.'

The ride home was made in heavy silence. Alex had hoped that Oliver's request had been a sleepy half dream, a vague, childish notion that he'd forget with the rest of a child's dreams. Instead he rode stolidly home between the two of them, he helped rub down the horses in unaccustomed silence and finally he backed away, preparatory to heading home. No. Heading back to Brenda's. They all knew he didn't think of Brenda's as his home.

'You're not going to, are you?' he asked in a tiny sulky voice that sounded nothing like him. He sounded scared and Alex's heart melted.

And she knew what the question meant. You're not going to care.

'Oliver, I'm going back to America,' she told him, glancing at Jack's grim face and then glancing away fast. 'I'm only here for a while. My family lives in the States.'

'We could be a family.' It was a desperate plea, but his face said he knew before he uttered the words what the answer would be.

'Mate, your dad's your family,' Jack said, and he walked forward and gripped Oliver's thin shoulders. It was meant to be a gesture of reassurance but Alex saw Oliver flinch. Like he knew what was coming. 'Alex has her mum and dad in New York. You have your dad in Brisbane—he's having an extended holiday now but he'll be back. And I have my horses. We don't fit together.'

We could, Alex thought, though the idea was terrifying. Taking on an eleven-year-old... But with Jack?

It takes a village... If she had Jack, she'd consider herself a village.

'It's all right,' Oliver said, but of course it wasn't.

He turned and raced into the dusk.

'Let me drive you home,' Jack called after him, but he was already gone.

That night they lay in each other's arms but things had changed. Things were different.

Things were finished.

It was as if the voicing of Oliver's dream had killed hers. She'd let herself dream.

She lay cradled in Jack's arms; she knew he wanted her, she wanted him with all her heart, but the damage to this man was heart-deep.

He was loving her now against his will.

He stirred a little and she realised he was awake, looking down at her, troubled as she was.

'Alex?'

'You'll let me go,' she whispered.

'I don't know what else to do.'

'You could let me stay,' she whispered back. 'I'd cling like a limpet. I'd care for your horses for ever, mend your verandas.' She took a deep breath. 'I'd love you. I think... I think I already do. The only thing is, you'd have to love me back.'

'I do,' he said softly, but she shook her head.

'Not all of me. Not the me who demands you care for whatever comes with me.'

And he knew what she meant.

The silence stretched on. On and on.

Decision time? Time for the truth. This wasn't just about Oliver. This was about...everything.

'You'd want kids,' he said at last, into the stillness. He was still holding her but there was nothing relaxed about this man. He sounded stretched to breaking. She held him close, skin against skin. She could feel his heart beating against her breast, but it wasn't in rhythm with hers. His heart was pounding.

This was such a big deal....

I should lie, she thought. I could make it just about us. If I can make him love me... Care for me... Commit to me... Then everything else could follow.

But the question was out there, a biggie. To have children…to not have children…

Her father hadn't wanted Matt and Ellie, and what damage had been done by that lack of care?

'Maybe,' she admitted. 'Not right away but yes, maybe I would. And I'd definitely want a dog. Why don't you have a dog, Jack Connor?'

'Dogs need you.'

'Like horses.'

'Not the same way.'

'Yeah, they look at you with great big soulful eyes, something like the way I'm looking at you,' she said.

'Don't look at me like that.'

'I have been for a month,' she whispered, trying hard to keep it light. 'In case you hadn't noticed, I'm smitten.'

'You'd ask me—'

'To care for me,' she said softly, knowing there was only room for truth. 'Yes, I would. And I'd also ask you to care for Oliver and any stray dog I brought home and also any kids we might or might not agree to have. But mostly, Jack, loving you means I want to be loved back. Despite nothing. I'll give you all of my heart, but it's unconditional and if you can't give that back…'

'I can't.' The words were wrenched out of him and she flinched.

'Your sister died,' she said, coldly now because that was the way she was feeling. Exposed and fragile and a little bit angry. Or maybe more than a little bit angry. What was he doing, taking her to his bed every night, loving her with his body, holding her with such tenderness, when it meant nothing? 'Does Sophie's death mean what's between us is dead, too?'

'It never really lived,' he said, and that was where she

drew her line in the sand. Something inside her died a little, right there.

She tugged away, out of his bed. She grabbed the top quilt and wrapped it round her in a gesture of pure defence.

'What was I thinking?' she whispered. He sat up and reached for her but she backed away. 'Don't.'

'Alex.'

'You can't have it both ways,' she managed. 'I didn't seduce you. We fell into each other's arms because we needed each other. Or I thought we needed each other. But if you can't...'

'Maybe I can,' Jack said, sounding desperate. 'If it's just you.'

'There isn't a just me.' Her anger got the better of her then, her history, the letter from Ellie, the sourness that underscored her family. 'That's what my father did. He married my mother—but he only married *her*. There's never been a doubt that he loved her to bits, but she came with strings. She was carrying another man's twins. I'm not carrying twins but I am carrying baggage. I've fallen for a kid called Oliver and if I lived here I'd want to be involved, right up to my neck. I'd want a dog or maybe three. I'd bring home injured wildlife and when and if they died, I'd cry my heart out. And yes, I'd want kids. All those things, Jack, all of them, I'd expect, want, know that you'd share, and you'd share not because you cared for me because that's what my father did and it didn't work, but because your heart was big enough to care for the whole crazy menagerie.'

'Alex...'

'Don't "Alex" me,' she said, backing into the doorway, and she was really yelling now. 'This is what I should have said a month ago. I didn't have it sorted in my head but today...today I wanted to care for Oliver so much, but

I wanted *us* to care. That's what we could be. Jack and Alex. Joined in the caring department. But it's not going to happen.'

'I don't know how.'

'And I don't know how to teach you,' Alex said, flatly now, passion spent and only desolation left. 'My mother couldn't teach my father in all their years of marriage, so what hope do I have? I think…I think we quit this now, Jack. Separate bedrooms. Separate lives. If we can't work together on these terms, then I leave.'

'You can't leave.'

'I should,' she whispered. 'But I don't want to. So…so I'll stay a little longer. But in my bedroom. In my work. If I didn't think Cooper would have kittens, I'd move into the worker's cottage with him, only—'

'There's no need to be ridiculous.'

'There's not, is there,' she said sadly. 'But there is a need to be sensible. That's what we have to be. Starting now.'

She turned and tried for a dignified exit. It didn't happen. She tripped on a corner of the trailing quilt. Jack was out of bed before she fell, catching her, steadying her. Holding her.

She let him hold her for a full minute, savouring the strength, the warmth, her sheer need of this man she'd come to know and love. And then, somehow, she managed to pull away.

She turned and walked down the passage with as much dignity as she could muster.

She hoped he'd call her back.

She hoped he'd follow.

He didn't.

He lay in the dark and missed her. He missed her warmth, the feel of her skin on his, her breath, her tiny movements, the knowledge that he'd let go a woman who could love him.

Who *would* love him, if she was to be believed.

Why wouldn't he believe Alex?

He wanted her. He was hungry for her with a depth he'd never known it was possible to feel.

It was too late to think he couldn't care for her—he knew that he did. When he held her he felt at peace, and the look on her face as she'd backed from the room was well nigh unbearable. That she'd break her heart over him...

She was young, he told himself savagely. Her family was from the other side of the world. She'd go home and she'd get over whatever she was thinking about him.

She'd get over loving him.

So why was that the desirable option? Why did he lie in his bed here and not lunge after her, take her in his arms, love her, promise himself to her, marry her...

It wasn't just Alex.

Loving Alex was commitment enough. To open himself to the vortex of caring, the great, sweet whirlpool that was love, where he cared and cared but could never care enough... Knowing the pain would come eventually, no matter what he did...

That was dumb. The logical part of him knew that what he'd felt for Sophie, what he'd tried to do, what had happened, was nothing to do with how he felt for Alex. But still, loving her, holding her, there was that same sense of standing on a ledge waiting for the world to tilt, so inevitably that falling must happen.

Coward.

He said it to himself out loud and it echoed around the big and empty room with a hollowness that echoed what he was feeling in his heart. You're condemning yourself to...nothing.

You're giving Alex the chance to find happiness with someone who deserves her.

Why was that a good option? He could try to hold her. He'd love her and protect her and care…

And she'd demand that he do the same for Oliver and more. Dogs?

Kids.

Children, dependent on him. Children, when he'd never been able to care for Sophie. He'd looked after her from the time she was six.

Children.

His mind simply blanked at the thought. To bring children into the world, to have someone so utterly dependent…

He thought of Oliver's set face. The pain…

Not Your Problem.

Selfish?

Yeah, maybe he was, but how much better to say at the beginning *I can't*, rather than stand at a graveside and say *I've failed*?

But the look on Alex's face…

No.

The moon outside slipped behind a cloud and the night grew darker. Alex was just down the passage. Distressed. Coming to terms with his cowardice.

She had to do it sometime, he thought grimly. There was no choice.

He should never have loved her.

He had to learn all over again what it was to be alone. He had to let her have a life with someone who cared.

CHAPTER TWELVE

WHAT followed was a week of silence. A week where Alex worked solidly on, intent on her tasks, doing what needed to be doing, seemingly enjoying the horses, seemingly enjoying her increasing friendship with Cooper and the dogs, being pleasant and distant to him.

If he didn't know her well he could almost think there was nothing wrong, but he knew this woman now. He saw the tension lines around her eyes, the flash of pain, quickly disguised, when he appeared. The strain in her voice whenever she spoke to him.

A lesser woman would quit, he thought, but this was Alex. She was here to earn her stripes as a vet on a horse stud, and a little thing like falling in love and being rejected by the owner wasn't about to stand in her way.

Heartbroken? Maybe, but she wasn't showing the world, and she wasn't showing him. She was making it possible for him to get on with his life without her.

Except he still had to watch her. He still had to see her.

He still had to see the way the horses responded to her and feel a searing, aching need deep in his gut.

That had to be put aside.

That was put aside.

Until the day Oliver disappeared.

* * *

The first they knew of it was a phone call just after dark.

They'd worked solidly all day—Alex working with Cooper with the yearlings, Jack working on the outbuildings, making a new roof secure. They were working fast. The weather was oppressively humid, dark clouds thickening through the day. The mother and father of all storms was in the offing and they knew it.

Cooper retired as he always did as soon as the work of the day was done to his solitude in the workman's cottage. Alex cooked but there were no points given any more. She retired to her bedroom but when the phone went in the hall she couldn't help but hear.

Jack's voice was curt and sounded concerned.

'No, he hasn't been here all day. We haven't seen him all week. Brenda, it's dark and with this storm, even if he had been here, I'd have sent him home long before this.'

There was a long silence while Jack listened, and then a terse demand.

'So you haven't seen him since seven this morning?'

She was suddenly out in the passage, pressing against the wall, listening. Watching Jack's face darken with anger. And worry.

'You could have told me… Okay, never mind. Does he have any money? Could he be trying to reach his dad?'

She could hear Brenda now, shrill in defensiveness. And, to give the woman her due, worry.

'Okay.' Jack was raking his hair, looking out through the porch window to the darkness of the storm beyond. 'If Cracker's missing… Does he have mates in town?'

Alex could hear Brenda's silence. It was like a great gaping void.

No mates. No family. Alex's heart seemed to freeze. One little boy and a night when no one should be out.

'I'll be there in ten minutes,' Jack said heavily, and replaced the receiver. He turned and at the look on his face had her reaching out in an automatic need for contact—and then, somehow, she drew back.

'Tell me.'

'Brenda's sister has decided they should buy a house they can share,' he said, his voice bleak as death. 'She's found one, in Brisbane. All of them are moving in. Brenda's sister and her four kids. Brenda and her two girls. But not Oliver. There's not room. Brenda's made an appointment with social welfare in Sydney next Monday. She told Oliver this morning—nicely, she said—that he couldn't keep living with her. She told him she'd find him some nice foster parents—and now he's gone.'

She drove with him—how could she not? The wind was strengthening by the minute, the rain a deluge. Somewhere out there was a child.

Brenda was standing on the veranda, looking distraught. She was staring out into the gathering storm as if she could find him simply by staring.

'It wasn't my fault,' she said before they could say a word. 'I can't keep him. The house has only got two kids' rooms and I can't make my girls share. It wouldn't be right. But we have to find him. The social services said they'll find a foster home.'

'What does he have with him?' Jack said, cutting across her defensiveness. 'We think he's on Cracker. Anything else?'

'I think he took his father's camping gear. I checked. Not the tent, but the sleeping bag. And there's stuff from the grocery cupboard missing. I'll kill him. Of all the stupid—'

'Let's find him first,' Jack snapped. 'Have you called the police?'

'Why would I call the police?'

Because a child's missing, Alex thought. A child, with this storm coming.

Jack stayed silent, his face rigid, staring at Brenda. Then...

'He'll be at the waterfall,' he said slowly. 'That's my guess. If he took camping equipment... He'll be intending to use the cave.'

Alex's heart seemed to still. She thought back to that last day together. Oliver, diving through the waterfall, exploring the cave. Figuring how he could get in without getting wet. Totally fascinated.

The day they were there, though, there'd been little recent rain. Now, the rain was one continuous sheet.

'If he tries to stay in there when the rain comes—' Jack broke off with an oath and headed back into the rain to the car. 'Stay with Brenda,' he growled over his shoulder. 'Tell the police.'

'Brenda can tell the police,' Alex snapped. 'I'm coming with you.'

They collected the horses and rode. There was no other way to get there.

The wind was rising and the horses edged together as though taking comfort from each other. They couldn't ride fast; they were picking their way, making sure each horse had the time to test the ground before setting its weight over a rabbit hole or wombat burrow.

No car could get up here. It was horses or nothing.

Somewhere up here was a child who no one wanted.

Jack was feeling gutted. The horses shouldn't be out in this. Alex shouldn't be out in this. How to make her go back?

He knew her well enough now to know he couldn't.

'I'm taking him back to the States when we find him,' Alex said into the night, and it was like a vow. 'Somehow... There's no way he's being left with foster parents.'

Her statement left him winded. Speechless.

She couldn't mean it.

'Foster parents can be great,' he managed, and she flashed him a look of pure anger.

'But they don't already love him. There's no guarantee they ever will. My family will help me. I can do it.'

'You came out here to get the qualifications to get a job on a ranch as an equine veterinarian. How will having an eleven-year-old child fit in with that?'

'It won't,' she said tightly, trying to control rage. 'But I've fallen in love. It's changed things.'

'With Oliver?'

'Who else do you think I mean?'

'Alex...'

'He'll be fine,' she said, even more tightly. 'If I have to get a job in the city here—get myself a resident's permit— then I will, but if I can get him home it'll be better. The Manhattan apartment's huge. Our maid, Maria, will love him to bits. I can do small-animal work and involve him. He'll like it. Somehow I'll get the right migration permissions. I *can* make it work.'

To say he was gobsmacked was an understatement. She was totally, absolutely serious. She'd change career, change direction, change her life, for a child she'd met less than two months before.

Whereas he...

He was too cowardly to take that first step.

He was afraid of doing harm.

He was afraid of not succeeding.

'That's some generous gesture,' he said at last, and he heard her breath draw in on a hiss.

'Gesture?'

'I only meant—'

'Gesture,' she spat, and Rocky lurched forward, startled. Jack had the reins in an instant.

'Let me go,' Alex said stiffly, collecting herself. 'I'm fine. But this is no gesture. You think I'd play with a child's life? I've thought about it a lot. I've even talked to my brother about it. Matt thinks the migration and custody issues might be prohibitive and while Oliver was safe with Brenda I accepted that, but now...'

'So this isn't an off-the-cuff decision?'

'Amazingly, it isn't,' she managed. 'I can care with my head as well as my heart, Jack Connor. So let's find him and get things moving.' She paused. 'The cave...the water—is it very dangerous?'

'Yes,' he said because there was nothing else to say. The rain had increased sometime during that extraordinary conversation, sheeting down as sleet as well as rain. 'If the river builds... But we can go no faster than we are now.'

'We can if we concentrate,' she muttered. 'We can if we only think of one hoof after another—and nothing else.'

It took them a long time to reach the waterfall, much longer than when they'd set off for the picnic, when there'd been bright sunshine and no rain. But they couldn't push too hard. A lame horse here meant stopping altogether. So Alex rode grimly on, every nerve straining for risk to her horse, for risk to the little boy ahead.

In the past few weeks she'd formed a bond with Oliver that had grown beyond explaining.

Or maybe she could explain it. He reminded her of Matt, her adored big brother. She remembered Matt at Oliver's age, standing before her father, condemned by some minor misdemeanour, stoic. She'd adored her big brother as she'd adored her father and their conflict tore her in two. Matt wrenched at her heartstrings before she even knew such things existed.

And now another little boy, even more needful, was doing the same.

She would help. In that appalling ride her mind settled. She'd already spoken to Matt, sounded him out about helping. He'd been negative—'The thing's crazy, Alex'—but she knew in the end that he'd help.

She could depend on Matt, whereas the man by her side...

She wanted, with all her heart, to depend on Jack.

He'd help tonight. He'd do what he had to do, but he'd go no further. To ask him to commit?

She couldn't. She'd pushed as hard as she could. From here on, she'd cope with this alone.

Something flew at them through the dark and sleet, a disoriented bat, something. Rocky shied and Jack's hands were on her reins, holding, settling.

He was with her, and yet not with her.

Jack...

Oliver. Think of Oliver.

Oliver had to be all that mattered. Jack couldn't love her, but Oliver...she'd love Oliver regardless.

And in the end they found him, quite easily, quite simply. Loneliness, desolation aside, Oliver was one sensible little boy. He'd left the cave when the water started sheeting, but he hadn't thought of going home. Home? Back to Brenda, who didn't want him. He had no options. They found him huddled on the bank of a river that was widening to a roaring torrent, soaked to the skin, holding Cracker's reins and simply waiting for what happened next.

Or expecting that nothing would.

The lightning was now almost one continuous sheet. They could see Oliver's silhouette against the riverbank. They could see his heaving shoulders, but as they approached there wasn't a sound. Even in despair, Oliver's sobs were silent.

Jack saw him, and Alex spotted him almost in the same instant. She was off her horse. Rocky's reins were thrust into Jack's hands and Alex was crouched beside him, tugging him to her, enfolding him to her in the age-old way a woman comforted a child she loved.

Loved.

Who could doubt it, the way she held him. Jack knew, looking at them both, that this was surely what he was seeing.

He had to see to the horses. When Alex reached him, Oliver had released Cracker's reins. All the horses were edgy with the thunder and lightning. He gathered them together, led them under the slight shelter of the cliff face so they were away from the frightening rush of water— thankfully at the foot of this waterfall there was little risk of lightning strike—and then he returned.

They were still entwined. Woman and child.

She cared with all her heart.

And so did he. He watched and things were twisting inside.

Or maybe not twisting. Maybe they were unravelling. A dark and bitter knot was being untied, let free.

His mother's words came back to him...

Take care of your sister.

He'd been eight years old.

It was like clearing mists. As he watched Oliver cling to Alex as if he'd been drowning, he thought, *I was three years younger than Oliver is now.*

And then he thought, *How can a child do anything but fail when given such a task?*

And the bitter sense of failure turned to something else. Something it should have been all along.

It turned to anger at a mother who could have made such a demand. It turned to anger at a grandfather who took it as read that Sophie was Jack's responsibility.

How could you have asked the impossible of me?

'I was eight years old,' he said to himself, and then he looked at what was before him and he said what had to be said.

'I couldn't do it then, but I can do it now.'

And then he walked across to the riverbank, to the crouched figures huddled in the driving rain. He hauled off his great sou'wester and he covered them all. And then, because his makeshift tent was tiny, because they had to be close and because he wanted to be close more than anything else in the world, he tugged them to him.

Both of them.

And they turned and melted into him, just like that. He held them against him. He felt their hearts beating against him. He felt Oliver's sobs subside and he felt Alex's breath against his face.

He felt her hold him as he was holding her, with Oliver sandwiched between them, and he felt a promise being made. The promise felt good. It felt right.

No matter the storm, here was home.

Here was caring.

Here was love.

Jack put Oliver before him, on Maestro, while Alex led Cracker. They didn't take him back to Brenda. They took him to Werarra. *Home.*

The little boy was past speech, past questions, past anything but clinging to Jack as he carried him into the house.

He was eleven years old but tonight he seemed so much younger.

The Wombat Siding cop was there, with Cooper. They'd been about to organise a wider search.

Jack watched Cooper's face break into a vast grin as he saw Oliver. He watched Cooper's dogs make a fuss of the little boy and he thought, Cooper was another he'd end up caring for.

For Cooper was already doing his share of caring.

And finally, finally, he was starting to get it. The load he'd been given as a child had been too great, but the concept was wonderful. You cared, and you were cared for right back.

Cooper disappeared to see to the horses, looking a bit embarrassed at the emotion. The cop left, relieved, and Jack thought there was another example of caring. Country cops... It was what they did.

Jack phoned Brenda, and heard her relief that Oliver was found, and heard even more relief that he'd like him to stay at Werarra for the night.

He had to stay at Werarra, for Jack knew a decision had been made.

Alex had Oliver in a hot bath before the phone call was ended. She washed him and teased him and made him smile a little, then towelled him dry, while Jack found a huge T-shirt for him to wear to bed.

In the end she even had the bedraggled little boy giggling at the sight of himself in the mirror. It wasn't a very loud giggle, but it sounded fine to Jack.

'He can sleep in my bed,' Alex said, and Jack shook his head.

'Let's put him in ours. Oliver, can you cope with sleeping between the pair of us?'

And Alex met his gaze over Oliver's head and something happened to her face.

Something wonderful.

So they tucked him into Jack's big bed and Jack sat on the end of the bed and watched as Alex cradled him and told him people loved him and nothing bad would happen and she thought she might buy him a puppy.

A puppy.

She'd take that on, too, he thought.

Nothing had been said. Nothing had been promised between them. What she was saying to Oliver now stood as a sole promise.

She'd keep that promise, he thought. She'd take a small boy back to Manhattan. She'd face down immigration and social services. She'd cope with quarantine and caring for a child and his puppy in New York. Alone.

It wasn't going to happen. Not if caring could help it.

Finally Oliver slept. Finally he could say what needed to be said.

But there were practicalities. They'd ridden together in the storm, and they looked and felt like it.

'Now it's our turn for a bath,' Jack decreed, and Alex looked at him and smiled, almost shyly.

'Together?'

'How can you doubt it,' he said, and smiled at her and held her and then washed every lovely inch of her. As she did him.

Finally they dried each other, and then they held each other for a long time after. They simply held. This night was too wonderful, too fragile, too precious, to take it any further.

Finally they slipped into bed, one on either side of a deeply sleeping child.

'We'll have to restore another bedroom, really fast,' Jack said softly into the night. 'He's going to be insecure for quite a while. What if we put a door through to next door—we can leave it open if he has nightmares. Then, when he gets older and feels more at home, we can give him the attic room. A teenager with his dog would like that. Maybe then...maybe then our adjoining room could be used for babies.' He hesitated again. 'That is, if you'd like babies.'

He heard her intake of breath. He heard a silence that went on and on. He couldn't reach for her—there was a child between them—but maybe that was just as well. He'd been less than perfect in his approach to this woman. Maybe she needed time to think.

'You'd take that leap of faith?' she whispered.

She knew. She understood. And he thought, She's always understood.

What makes a woman love a man? What makes a woman understand a man almost before he understands himself?

'I love you, Alex,' he said softly into the dark. 'I think I loved you from the moment I saw you, angry and wet and righteous. And now I love you more. You're brave and funny and clever, and you've beaten me seventeen times to my nine in the cooking stakes. And you lie here in my bed.'

'With a child between us...'

'See, that's what I've finally figured,' he said, figuring it still as he spoke. 'No matter the shadows, no matter what physically separates us, there's nothing between us. I'm not a man of pretty words, Alex. Maybe I never will be, but I'll try. Because I'm tired of being alone. Being alone was a survival technique before I knew you existed in the world, but my survival's changed. It's changed with loving you. Now my survival depends on one great-hearted vet. On one slip of a girl. It depends on you loving me. It depends on you letting me care, and on me caring right back.'

'Oh, Jack…' She sounded like she was almost afraid to speak. She sounded awed. 'But…babies even?'

'Caring comes in all forms,' he said, surely now, knowing this was right. 'I've figured it. If you're going to care, you might as well let in the whole human catastrophe. You, my love. Oliver. That puppy you just promised him. Cooper, maybe—he's a curmudgeonly old bachelor, but we both saw today how much he cares already and how can we not care back? His dogs. Our horses. All of this I'll care for—but mostly I care for you.'

She didn't answer. It seemed she couldn't.

He lay back in the dark and thought of all the ways a man should say what he wanted to say. After a romantic candlelight dinner? In a hot-air balloon? Via luxury cruises, roses, hearts and flowers?

But this was here, this was right, and this was real.

'Alexander Patterson,' he said simply into the dark. 'Would you do me the honour of becoming my wife?'

And from the darkness, from the other side of the sleeping child, came the answer he seemed to have been waiting all his life to hear.

'Why, yes, Conner,' she said simply. 'Yes, my love, I believe I will.'

* * * * *

MILLS & BOON® *Book Club* 2 Free Books!

Get your free books now at

www.millsandboon.co.uk/freebookoffer

Or fill in the form below and post it back to us

THE MILLS & BOON® BOOK CLUB™—HERE'S HOW IT WORKS: Accepting your free books places you under no obligation to buy anything. You may keep the books and return the despatch note marked 'Cancel'. If we do not hear from you, about a month later we'll send you 5 brand-new stories from the Cherish™ series, including two 2-in-1 books priced at £5.49 each, and a single book priced at £3.49*. There is no extra charge for post and packaging. You may cancel at any time, otherwise we will send you 5 stories a month which you may purchase or return to us—the choice is yours. *Terms and prices subject to change without notice. Offer valid in UK only. Applicants must be 18 or over. Offer expires 31st January 2013. **For full terms and conditions, please go to www.millsandboon.co.uk/freebookoffer**

Mrs/Miss/Ms/Mr (please circle)

First Name

Surname

Address

Postcode

E-mail

Send this completed page to: Mills & Boon Book Club, Free Book Offer, FREEPOST NAT 10298, Richmond, Surrey, TW9 1BR

Find out more at
www.millsandboon.co.uk/freebookoffer

Visit us Online

0712/S2YEA

Special Offers

Every month we put together collections and longer reads written by your favourite authors.

Here are some of next month's highlights— and don't miss our fabulous discount online!

On sale 16th November

On sale 16th November

On sale 7th December

Save 20%
on all Special Releases

Find out more at
www.millsandboon.co.uk/specialreleases

Visit us
Online

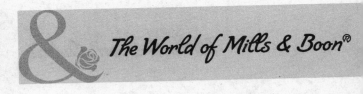

The World of Mills & Boon®

There's a Mills & Boon® series that's perfect for you. We publish ten series and, with new titles every month, you never have to wait long for your favourite to come along.

Blaze.
Scorching hot, sexy reads
4 new stories every month

By Request
Relive the romance with the best of the best
9 new stories every month

Cherish™
Romance to melt the heart every time
12 new stories every month

Desire™
Passionate and dramatic love stories
8 new stories every month